Herbert George Wells was born in Bromley, Kent in 1866, the third son of an unsuccessful shopkeeper. At eighteen he left his job as a draper's apprentice and became a pupil teacher at Midhurst Grammar School, from where he won a scholarship to the Normal School of Science, South Kensington, and studied biology under T. H. Huxley. Although distracted by politics, writing and teaching he obtained a B.Sc. in 1890 and then lectured for the University Tutorial College until the success of his short stories allowed him to become a full-time writer. Idealistic and impatient, he flung himself into contemporary issues – free love, Fabianism, progressive education, scientific theory, 'world government', human rights. His personal life was equally restless: after an early marriage to his cousin Isabel in 1890 ended in divorce, he married a pupil, Amy Catherine Robbins, in 1895, and was later involved with a series of remarkable women including Amber Reeves, Elizabeth von Arnim, Rebecca West and Moura Budberg. He died in London in 1946.

H. G. Wells wrote over a hundred books, achieving unparalleled international fame for a British writer. His work ranged from the famous scientific fantasies like *The Time Machine* (1895) and realistic comedies like *Kipps* (1905) to provocative topical novels such as *Marriage* (1912), *Mr Britling Sees It Through* (1916), *The Autocracy of Mr Parham* (1932) and controversial or encyclopedic works like *A Modern Utopia* (1905) or *The Outline of History* (1920). He describes his own life in the two-volume *Experiment in Autobiography* (1934) and *H. G. Wells in Love*, unpublished until 1984.

The Hogarth Press also publishes *Mr Britling Sees It Through*, *Christina Alberta's Father*, *In the Days of the Comet*, *The Passionate Friends* and *Marriage*.

THE WIFE OF
SIR ISAAC HARMAN

H. G. Wells

New Introduction by
Victoria Glendinning

THE HOGARTH PRESS
LONDON

Published in 1986 by
The Hogarth Press
Chatto & Windus Ltd
40 William IV Street, London WC2N 4DF

First published in Great Britain by Macmillan 1914
Hogarth edition offset from original British edition
Copyright the Executors of the Estate of H. G. Wells
New Introduction copyright © Victoria Glendinning 1986

ISBN 0 7012 0619 5

Printed in Finland by
Werner Söderström Oy

INTRODUCTION

The Wife of Sir Isaac Harman is, like so many of H. G. Wells's novels, a variation on a theme. It was published in 1914. The previous year, Wells had brought out another novel, *The Passionate Friends*, which centres, just as this one does, on the problem of jealousy and the position of women in marriage. Both these novels belong to a sequence of 'discussion' novels, in which the middle-aged Wells investigated sex and society, and which, as the series progressed, increasingly became vehicles for the communication of his own ideas about the future development of mankind, focusing chiefly but not solely on the relations between men and women.

Wells was investigating the unsatisfactory arrangements made between men and women for personal as well as propaganda reasons, and using, more often than many people thought proper, blatantly autobiographical material. He was married to his second wife Jane, and had two sons, but his sexual energies were not satisfied by his marriage, and he had a series of affairs, the most serious and scandalous of which was with Amber Reeves, half his age; he used this relationship in the novel *Ann Veronica*. She was followed by the novelist Elizabeth von Arnim. In late 1913 he broke with Elizabeth, and the twenty-year-old Rebecca West became his mistress; she had come to know him after she wrote an acerbic review of another novel in this sequence, *Marriage*. Rebecca was firmly established in his life, and had already given birth to their child, when *The Wife of Sir Isaac Harman* appeared; but in it Wells pays a pleasant tribute to his ex-mistress, when Lady Harman finds comfort and inspiration in reading Elizabeth von Arnim's *Elizabeth and the German Garden*, and its author is described as 'horticultural, bookish, whimsical, witty, defiant, happily careless' and is compared with Montaigne.

Lady Harman is, like most of Wells's heroines, the perfection of femininity – slender, charming, beautiful, as well as expensively dressed and obviously wealthy. She dazzles Mr Brumley, the benign and rather old-fashioned author whose country cottage she is thinking of taking. Walter Lippmann, reviewing this novel when it first came out, commented how Wells's heroines had gradually moved up in the world, 'so that of late a Wells heroine to have a soul and to suffer must also have a title'. The heroine of *The Passionate Friends* had been an earl's daughter who, just like Lady Harman, married a millionaire whom she did not love.

But Lady Harman is less frivolous, less worldly and less dependent on her physical attractiveness than Wells's earlier heroines, who all tended to serve his thesis that women, or the love of women, not only ruined men financially but prevented them from fulfilling their intellectual and spiritual potential. Lady Harman had more spiritual potential than her husband, and is, for all her exquisiteness, a serious person: she would like, she says, 'some work of my own', and has leanings towards religion and social responsibility. Her trouble is that she got married long before she was mature enough to know who she was or what her interests were. Another of Lippmann's criticisms of the novel was that Wells 'has written about the marriage as if the wife were all innocence and the husband all villainy', thus giving 'an absurdly simplified account of human motive'. The only complaint anyone could make about the faultless Lady Harman is that she shows a chilling lack of feeling for her children. To a modern feminist, her attitude may legitimately be seen as an acknowledgement that motherhood is not always a necessary or sufficient fulfilment for women, though it might be nearer to the truth to say that Wells did not want intelligent and desirable women to devote to children any of the time and attention that could be lavished on a lover – i.e., in real life, himself. In Lady Harman's case, her attitude is explained as a facet of her suppressed dislike of her husband.

Sir Isaac is a most satisfactorily unmitigated villain. His name and his entrepreneurial activity suggest that he is intended to be a Jew, and one critic at least, on this evidence and on the evidence of Jewish characters in the other 'discussion' novels, has accused Wells of anti-Semitism. It may be that Wells was not explicit about Sir Isaac's Jewishness in order to avoid just such a charge. It seems to me that Wells, here as elsewhere, is not so much anti-Jewish as Jew-conscious. Jews seem to have fascinated and impressed him, and Jewish businessmen had an energy and appetite for life that he admired. But in the stereotype of the close Jewish family, and the uxoriousness of the Jewish marriage, he found a successful working model for the sexual possessiveness which in these novels he set out to challenge. Sir Isaac's idea of marriage is a simple contract: 'He on his side had to keep her, dress her, to be kind to her, give her the appearance of pride and authority, and in return he had his rights and privileges and undefined powers of control.' This according to 'the existing rules' was the reality of nearly all marriages, as Wells points out, in those cases where the wife had no money of her own, as Lady Harman has not. Her pathetic subterfuges to find the money even for bus fares, when she begins to claim her independence, show what a prisoner the mistress of the mansion on Putney Hill really is.

Sir Isaac is possessive to the point of neurosis, or so it seems to us now. He acquired his wife as a commodity, having coveted her avidly. He 'insulted her utmost subjugations by an obtrusive suspicion and jealousy, he was jealous of her childish worship of her dead father, jealous of her disposition to go to church' or to read poetry, or listen to music. When she begins to exercise her rights as a grown adult to have her own friends and pursue her own interests, he longs only to reduce her to her earlier 'entirely hopeless submissiveness'.

In spite of his crusade for the freer expression of sexuality, Wells was never very good at writing love scenes; he skimped them with a scattering of lyrical phrases, and passed on. In this novel, however, his aim was to suggest – within the limits of what was possible in 1914 – the nastiness of bad sex, and he does this very effectively. Marriage with this 'clutching, hard-breathing little man' was *'unpleasant,* abounding indeed in crumpling indignities and horrible nervous stresses . . .'; and the scene in which Lady Harman plucks up courage to refuse him – 'the incredible incident' – has high drama and is strikingly graphic considering how little is made explicit. Unwanted sexual attention – or sexual harassment, in the modern phrase – is an important theme in the story, with echoes in every social class. Lady Harman learns what happens to young sewing-women in the big houses where they work, and to low-paid shop girls and waitresses without the proper means to support themselves.

In *The Passionate Friends*, Wells had already drawn a parallel between the servitude of sex and the servitude of labour, and there is a business enterprise at the centre of *The Wife of Sir Isaac Harman*. Sir Isaac's modern bakeries, with their mass-production methods, have made his fortune. In *The Passionate Friends*, Wells had argued how technology would break the antagonistic deadlock between labour and employers, bringing dignity and leisure to the working classes; in this novel he examines the less happy side of the picture, as Lady Harman gradually discovers how her husband's enterprises put small bakers out of work, changing the shapes of communities and bringing tragedy to individuals. In the tea-shops which are a profitable spin-off of his bakeries the girl-employees are exploited and discontented. In addition to all this, his advertisement hoardings deface the countryside, including the view from Mr Brumley's cottage. When the Harmans take over the cottage – set, like so many of Wells's fictional houses, in the pinewoods of Surrey, and with a garden that sounds as if it were designed by Gertrude Jekyll – Sir Isaac destroys its charm with his insensitive alterations and crude system-built additions. He represents everything that is destructive and damaging about capitalistic genius and modern ideas of 'progress'.

Lady Harman's liberation comes about from her growing involvement with these problems which, because of the plight of the shop girls, also draw her into suffragette and feminist circles. Wells, though he thought about the position of women seriously and called himself a feminist, had the traditional

Edwardian male's scorn and distaste for female militancy; it is expressed in all the 'discussion' novels. Here his target is chiefly Lady Harman's suffragist sister; the Votes for Women movement is 'the Great Insane Movement', and Agatha Alimony, the militant feminist who recurs like a running joke in all the discussion novels, has neither charisma, courage nor common sense. (Another recycled character is the secretary Miss Summersley Satchel, who 'had previously been in the service of the late Lady Mary Justin' – from *The Passionate Friends*; while Mrs Plessington and Mr Pope, who attend the opening of Lady Harman's residential hostel, come from *Marriage*, where they have larger parts to play.)

'I want ideas,' says Lady Harman, having progressed merely to 'a limited, ill-defined and quite unsecured freedom'. She begins to educate herself, with Mr Brumley as her companion and guide, and it is at this point that the novel becomes more didactic. Wells has made sure of our attention by the vividness and humour of the novel so far. The activities of Lady Beach-Mandarin, 'a great and audible tide of socially influential womanhood', the farcical moment when Sir Isaac hides in the garden shed, the revelations of lower-class life made by Susan the sewing-woman, are all social comedy of a lively and high order. Having hooked us, Wells begins, through his characters, to theorize.

'You see, if I may lecture a little . . .' begins Mr Brumley, regaling Lady Harman with an account of the evolution of social organisation. They discuss labour problems, the woman problem, the advisability of later marriages and easier divorce. But they are not, Wells suggests, the sort of people who change society. Lady Harman meets the novelist Edgar Wilkins (Wells himself), who tells her that 'the *really* inspiring people', the ones with vision, are disreputable and 'rotters', bad characters, 'disgraceful in love, *disgraceful*' – i.e., like Wilkins/Wells himself.

Lady Harman does not think about love very much. Wells wrote that he modelled her on two women – Mrs Pember Reeves (mother of Amber), and the wife of the writer W. W. Jacobs, both of whom sublimated their rebellion against marriage by throwing themselves into the suffragist cause. In his previous novels, women had only really existed in relation to men; here, he takes a step forward, as Mr Brumley has to: 'That a woman could not possibly rebel against one man without the sympathy and moral maintenance of another was still outside the range of Mr Brumley's understandings – and of a great many women's.' Mr Brumley assumes that Lady Harman must love him as he loves her, since he can only see her escape in terms of flight to some other man than her husband. He is amazed – as the reader will be – by the violent independence of action of which she shows herself capable, and realises that he is just as jealous and possessive about her as the kind of husband he deplores. 'Life was jealousy. It was all made up of fierce graspings, fierce suspicions, fierce resentments.' Humanity as a whole must be emancipated from jealousy before women can be emancipated. 'Our social order is built on jealousy, sustained by jealousy.' This is the message of *The Passionate Friends* restated – though Lady Harman retains her ability to surprise us to the very last page.

She is, in fact, the most independent-minded woman Wells had created so far, and to read all his discussion novels in their proper sequence is to see how he himself adapts and evolves in his thinking about women. But he does still tend to stress women's naturally subservient natures, against which they have to fight even as they have to fight against male power. There is sympathy, insight, and more than a touch of condescension in his attitude:

It is against instinct, it is with an enormous reluctance that women are bringing their quick emotions, their flashing unstable intelligences, their essential romanticism, their inevitable profound generosity into the world of politics and business . . . It is not in a day or a generation that we shall un-specialize women.

Yet when we remember that he was writing that in 1914 or earlier, and think how far some women have got in the ensuing decades, and how little, essentially, has changed for others, Wells's statements about this – as about sexual jealousy, material possessiveness and greed, and the devaluation of the 'little man' in a society of monopoly capitalism – must all be acknowledged as valid. He was justified when he wrote optimistically, shortly before he died, that 'as a fragment of social history' – not to mention entertainment – *The Wife of Sir Isaac Harman* would, he thought, survive.

Victoria Glendinning, London 1985

CONTENTS

THE WIFE OF
SIR ISAAC HARMAN

CHAPTER THE FIRST

INTRODUCES LADY HARMAN

§ 1

THE motor-car entered a little white gate, came to a
porch under a thick wig of jasmine, and stopped. The
chauffeur indicated by a movement of the head that
this at last was it. A tall young woman with a big
soft mouth, great masses of blue-black hair on either
side of a broad, low forehead, and eyes of so dark
a brown you might have thought them black, drooped
forward and surveyed the house with a mixture of
keen appreciation and that gentle apprehension which
is the shadow of desire in unassuming natures. . . .

The little house with the white-framed windows
looked at her with a sleepy wakefulness from under
its blinds, and made no sign. Beyond the corner was
a glimpse of lawn, a rank of delphiniums, and the
sound of a wheel-barrow.

"Clarence!" the lady called again.

Clarence, with an air of exceeding his duties,

decided to hear, descended slowly, and came to the
door.

"Very likely—if you were to look for a bell,
Clarence. . . ."

Clarence regarded the porch with a hostile air,
made no secret that he thought it a fool of a porch,
seemed on the point of disobedience, and submitted.
His gestures suggested a belief that he would next be
asked to boil eggs or do the boots. He found a bell
and rang it with the needless violence of a man who
has no special knowledge of ringing bells. How was
he to know? He was a chauffeur. The bell did not so
much ring as explode and swamp the place. Sounds of
ringing came from all the windows, and even out of
the chimneys. It seemed as if once set ringing that
bell would never cease. . . .

Clarence went to the bonnet of his machine, and
presented his stooping back in a defensive manner
against any one who might come out. He wasn't a
footman, anyhow. He'd rung that bell all right, and
now he must see to his engine.

"He's rung so *loud!*" said the lady weakly—
apparently to God.

The door behind the neat white pillars opened, and
a little red-nosed woman, in a cap she had evidently
put on without a proper glass, appeared. She surveyed
the car and its occupant with disfavour over her also
very oblique spectacles.

The lady waved a pink paper to her, a house-
agent's order to view. "Is this Black Strands?" she
shouted.

The little woman advanced slowly with her eyes
fixed malevolently on the pink paper. She seemed to
be stalking it.

"This *is* Black Strands?" repeated the tall lady. "I should be so sorry if I disturbed you—if it isn't; ringing the bell like that—and all. You can't think——"

"This is Black *Strand*," said the little old woman with a note of deep reproach, and suddenly ceased to look over her glasses and looked through them. She looked no kindlier through them, and her eye seemed much larger. She was now regarding the lady in the car, though with a sustained alertness towards the pink paper. "I suppose," she said, "you've come to see over the place?"

"If it doesn't disturb any one; if it is quite convenient——"

"Mr. Brumley is *hout*," said the little old woman. "And if you got an order to view, you got an order to view."

"If you think I might."

The lady stood up in the car, a tall and graceful figure of doubt and desire and glossy black fur. "I'm sure it looks a very charming house."

"It's *clean*," said the little old woman, "from top to toe. Look as you may."

"I'm sure it is," said the tall lady, and put aside her great fur coat from her lithe, slender, red-clad body. (She was permitted by a sudden civility of Clarence's to descend.) "Why! the windows," she said, pausing on the step, "are like crystal."

"These very 'ands," said the little old woman, and glanced up at the windows the lady had praised. The little old woman's initial sternness wrinkled and softened as the skin of a windfall does after a day or so upon the ground. She half turned in the doorway and made a sudden vergerlike gesture. "We

enter," she said, " by the 'all. . . . Them's Mr.
Brumley's 'ats and sticks. Every 'at or cap 'as a
stick, and every stick 'as a 'at *or* cap, and on the 'all
table is the gloves corresponding. On the right is the
door leading to the kitching, on the left is the large
droring-room which Mr. Brumley 'as took as 'is study."
Her voice fell to lowlier things. " The other door
beyond is a small lavatory 'aving a basing for washing
'ands."

" It's a perfectly delightful hall," said the lady.
" So low and wide-looking. And everything so bright
—and lovely. Those long, Italian pictures ! And how
charming that broad outlook upon the garden
beyond ! "

" You'll think it charminger when you see the
garding," said the little old woman. " It was Mrs.
Brumley's especial delight. Much of it—with 'er own
'ands."

" We now enter the droring-room," she proceeded,
and flinging open the door to the right was received
with an indistinct cry suggestive of the words, " Oh,
damn it ! " The stout medium-sized gentleman in an
artistic green-grey Norfolk suit, from whom the cry
proceeded, was kneeling on the floor close to the wide-
open window, and he was engaged in lacing up a boot.
He had a round, ruddy, rather handsome, amiable face,
with a sort of bang of brown hair coming over one
temple, and a large silk bow under his chin and a little
towards one ear, such as artists and artistic men of
letters affect. His profile was regular and fine, his
eyes expressive, his mouth, a very passable mouth. His
features expressed at first only the naïve horror of a
shy man unveiled.

Intelligent appreciation supervened.

There was a crowded moment of rapid mutual inspection. The lady's attitude was that of the enthusiastic house-explorer arrested in full flight, falling swiftly towards apology and retreat. (It was a frightfully attractive room, too, full of the brightest colour, and with a big white cast of a statue—a Venus! —in the window.) She backed over the threshold again.

" I thought you was out by that window, sir," said the little old woman intimately, and was nearly shutting the door between them and all the beginnings of this story.

But the voice of the gentleman arrested and wedged open the closing door.

" I—— Are you looking at the house ? " he said. " I say ! Just a moment, Mrs. Rabbit."

He came down the length of the room with a slight flicking noise due to the scandalized excitement of his abandoned laces. The lady was reminded of her not so very distant schooldays, when it would have been considered a suitable answer to such a question as his to reply, " No, I am walking down Piccadilly on my hands." But instead she waved that pink paper again. " The agents," she said. " Recommended— specially. So sorry if I intrude. I ought, I know, to have written first ; but I came on an impulse."

By this time the gentleman in the artistic tie, who had also the artistic eye for such matters, had discovered that the lady was young, delightfully slender, either pretty or beautiful, he could scarcely tell which, and very, very well dressed. " I am glad," he said, with remarkable decision, " that I was not out. *I* will show you the house."

" 'Ow *can* you, sir ? " intervened the little old woman.

" Oh ! show a house ! Why not ? "

" The kitchings—you don't understand the range, sir—it's beyond you. And upstairs. You can't show a lady upstairs."

The gentleman reflected upon these difficulties.

" Well, I'm going to show her all I can show her anyhow. And after that, Mrs. Rabbit, you shall come in. You needn't wait."

" I'm thinking," said Mrs. Rabbit, folding stiff little arms and regarding him sternly. " You won't be much good after tea, you know, if you don't get your after-noon's exercise."

" Rendez-vous in the kitchen, Mrs. Rabbit," said Mr. Brumley, firmly, and Mrs. Rabbit after a moment of mute struggle disappeared discontentedly.

" I do not want to be the least bit a bother," said the lady. " I'm intruding, I know, without the least bit of notice. I *do* hope I'm not disturbing you—— " she seemed to make an effort to stop at that, and failed and added—" the least bit. Do please tell me if I am."

" Not at all," said Mr. Brumley. " I hate my afternoon's walk as a prisoner hates the treadmill."

" She's such a nice old creature."

" She's been a mother—and several aunts—to us ever since my wife died. She was the first servant we ever had."

" All this house," he explained to his visitor's questioning eyes, " was my wife's creation. It was a little featureless agent's house on the edge of these pinewoods. She saw something in the shape of the rooms—and that central hall. We've enlarged it of course. Twice. This was two rooms, that is why there is a step down in the centre."

" That window and window-seat—— "

" That was her addition," said Mr. Brumley. " All this room is—replete—with her personality." He hesitated, and explained further. " When we prepared this house—we expected to be better off—than we subsequently became—and she could let herself go. Much is from Holland and Italy."

" And that beautiful old writing-desk with the little single rose in a glass ! "

" She put it there. She even in a sense put the flower there. It is renewed of course. By Mrs. Rabbit. She trained Mrs. Rabbit."

He sighed slightly, apparently at some thought of Mrs. Rabbit.

" You—you write—— " the lady stopped, and then diverted a question that she perhaps considered too blunt, " there ? "

" Largely. I am—a sort of author. Perhaps you know my books. Not very important books—but people sometimes read them."

The rose-pink of the lady's cheek deepened by a shade. Within her pretty head, her mind rushed to and fro saying " Brumley ? Brumley ? " Then she had a saving gleam. " Are you *George* Brumley ? " she asked,—" *the* George Brumley ? "

" My name *is* George Brumley," he said, with a proud modesty. " Perhaps you know my little Euphemia books ? They are still the most read."

The lady made a faint, dishonest assent-like noise ; and her rose-pink deepened another shade. But her interlocutor was not watching her very closely just then.

" Euphemia was my wife," he said, " at least, my wife gave her to me—a kind of exhalation. *This* "— his voice fell with a genuine respect for literary associations—" was Euphemia's home."

" I still," he continued, " go on. I go on writing about Euphemia. I have to. In this house. With my tradition. . . . But it is becoming painful—painful. Curiously more painful now than at the beginning. And I want to go. I want at last to make a break. That is why I am letting or selling the house. . . . There will be no more Euphemia."

His voice fell to silence.

The lady surveyed the long low clear room so cleverly prepared for life, with its white wall, its Dutch clock, its Dutch dresser, its pretty seats about the open fireplace, its cleverly placed bureau, its suntrap at the garden end; she could feel the rich intention of living in its every arrangement and a sense of uncertainty in things struck home to her. She seemed to see a woman, a woman like herself—only very, very much cleverer —flitting about the room and making it. And then this woman had vanished—nowhither. Leaving this gentleman—sadly left—in the care of Mrs. Rabbit.

" And she is dead?" she said with a softness in her dark eyes and a fall in her voice that was quite natural and very pretty.

" She died," said Mr. Brumley, " three years and a half ago." He reflected. " Almost exactly."

He paused and she filled the pause with feeling.

He became suddenly very brave and brisk and businesslike. He led the way back into the hall and made explanations. " It is not so much a hall as a hall living-room. We use that end, except when we go out upon the verandah beyond, as our dining-room. The door to the right is the kitchen."

The lady's attention was caught again by the bright long eventful pictures that had already pleased her. "They are copies of two of Carpaccio's St. George

series in Venice," he said. " We bought them together
there. But no doubt you've seen the originals. In a
little old place with a custodian and rather dark. One
of those corners—so full of that delightful out-of-the-
wayishness which is so characteristic, I think, of Venice.
I don't know if you found that in Venice ? "

" I've never been abroad," said the lady. " Never.
I should love to go. I suppose you and your wife
went—ever so much."

He had a transitory wonder that so fine a lady
should be untravelled, but his eagerness to display his
backgrounds prevented him thinking that out at the
time. "Two or three times," he said, "before our
little boy came to us. And always returning with
something for this place. Look ! " he went on, stepped
across an exquisite little brick court to a lawn of soft
emerald and turning back upon the house. " That
Dellia Robbia placque we lugged all the way back from
Florence with us, and that stone bird-bath is from
Siena."

" How bright it is ! " murmured the lady after a
brief still appreciation. " Delightfully bright. As
though it would shine even if the sun didn't." And
she abandoned herself to the rapture of seeing a house
and garden that were for once better even than the
agent's superlatives. And within her grasp if she chose
—within her grasp.

She made the garden melodious with soft appreciative sounds. She had a small voice for her size
but quite a charming one, a little live bird of a
voice, bright and sweet. It was a clear unruffled
afternoon ; even the unseen wheel-barrow had very
sensibly ceased to creak and seemed to be somewhere
listening. . . .

Only one trivial matter marred their easy explorations;—his boots remained unlaced. No propitious moment came when he could stoop and lace them. He was not a dexterous man with eyelets, and stooping made him grunt and his head swim. He hoped these trailing imperfections went unmarked. He tried subtly to lead this charming lady about and at the same time walk a little behind her. She on her part could not determine whether he would be displeased or not if she noticed this slight embarrassment and asked him to set it right. They were quite long leather laces and they flew about with a sturdy negligence of anything but their own offensive contentment, like a gross man who whistles a vulgar tune as he goes round some ancient church; flick, flock, they went, and flip, flap, enjoying themselves, and sometimes he trod on one and halted in his steps, and sometimes for a moment she felt her foot tether him. But man is the adaptable animal and presently they both became more used to these inconveniences and more mechanical in their efforts to avoid them. They treated those laces then exactly as nice people would treat that gross man; a minimum of polite attention and all the rest pointedly directed away from him. . . .

The garden was full of things that people dream about doing in their gardens and mostly never do. There was a rose garden all blooming in chorus, and with pillar-roses and arches that were not so much growths as overflowing cornucopias of roses, and a neat orchard with shapely trees white-painted to their exact middles, a stone wall bearing clematis and a clothes-line so gay with Mr. Brumley's blue and white flannel shirts that it seemed an essential part of the design. And then there was a great border of herbaceous perennials backed by delphiniums and monkshood already in flower and budding hollyhocks rising to their duty ; a border that reared its blaze of colour against a hill-slope dark with pines. There was no hedge whatever to this delightful garden. It seemed to go straight into the pinewoods ; only an invisible netting marked its limits and fended off the industrious curiosity of the rabbits.

"This strip of wood is ours right up to the crest," he said, "and from the crest one has a view. One has two views. If you would care—— ? "

The lady made it clear that she was there to see all she could. She radiated her appetite to see. He carried a fur stole for her over his arm and flicked the way up the hill. Flip, flap, flop. She followed demurely.

"This is the only view I care to show you now," he said at the crest. "There was a better one beyond there. But—it has been defiled. . . . Those hills ! . . . I knew you would like them. The space of it ! And yet——. This view—lacks the shining ponds. There are wonderful distant ponds. After all I must show you the other ! But you see there is the high-road, and the high-road has produced an abomination. Along here we go. Now. Don't look down please." His gesture covered the foreground. "Look right over the nearer things into the distance. There ! "

The lady regarded the wide view with serene appreciation. "I don't see," she said, "that it's in any way ruined. It's perfect."

"You don't see ! Ah ! you look right over. You look high. I wish I could too. But that screaming board ! I wish the man's crusts would choke him."

And indeed quite close at hand, where the road

curved about below them, the statement that Staminal Bread, the True Staff of Life, was sold only by the International Bread Shops, was flung out with a vigour of yellow and Prussian blue that made the landscape tame.

His finger directed her questioning eye.

" *Oh !* " said the lady suddenly, as one who is convicted of a stupidity and coloured slightly.

" In the morning of course it is worse. The sun comes directly on to it. Then really and truly it blots out everything."

The lady stood quite silent for a little time, with her eyes on the distant ponds. Then he perceived that she was blushing. She turned to her interlocutor as a puzzled pupil might turn to a teacher.

" It really is very good bread," she said. " They make it—— Oh ! most carefully. With the germ in. And one has to tell people."

Her point of view surprised him. He had expected nothing but a docile sympathy. " But to tell people *here !* " he said.

" Yes, I suppose one oughtn't to tell them here."

" Man does not live by bread alone."

She gave the faintest assent.

" This is the work of one pushful, shoving creature, a man named Harman. Imagine him ! Imagine what he must be ! Don't you feel his soul defiling us ?—this summit of a stupendous pile of—dough, thinking of nothing but his miserable monstrous profits, seeing nothing in the delight of life, the beauty of the world but something that attracts attention, draws eyes, something that gives him his horrible opportunity of getting ahead of all his poor little competitors and inserting—*this !* It's the quintessence of all that is

wrong with the world;—squalid, shameless huckster-
ing!" He flew off at a tangent. "Four or five years
ago they made this landscape disease,—a knight!"

He looked at her for a sympathetic indignation, and
then suddenly something snapped in his brain and he
understood. There wasn't an instant between absolute
innocence and absolute knowledge.

"You see," she said as responsive as though he had
cried out sharply at the horror in his mind, "Sir Isaac
is my husband. Naturally . . . I ought to have given
you my name to begin with. It was silly . . ."

Mr. Brumley gave one wild glance at the board, but
indeed there was not a word to be said in its mitigation.
It was the crude advertisement of a crude pretentious
thing crudely sold. "My dear lady!" he said in his
largest style, "I am desolated! But I have said it! It
isn't a pretty board."

A memory of epithets pricked him. "You must
forgive—a certain touch of—rhetoric."

He turned about as if to dismiss the board altogether, but she remained with her brows very faintly
knit, surveying the cause of his offence.

"It isn't a *pretty* board," she said. "I've wondered
at times. . . . It isn't."

"I implore you to forget that outbreak—mere
petulance—because, I suppose, of a peculiar liking for
that particular view. There are—associations——"

"I've wondered lately," she continued, holding on
to her own thoughts, "what people *did* think of them.
And it's curious—to hear——"

For a moment neither spoke, she surveyed the board
and he the tall ease of her pose. And he was thinking
she must surely be the most beautiful woman he had
ever encountered. The whole country might be covered

with boards if it gave us such women as this.   He felt
the urgent need of some phrase, to pull the situation
out of this pit into which it had fallen.   He was a little
unready, his faculties all as it were neglecting his needs
and crowding to the windows to stare, and meanwhile
she spoke again, with something of the frankness of one
who thinks aloud.

"You see," she said, "one *doesn't* hear.   One thinks
perhaps——   And there it is.   When one marries
very young one is apt to take so much for granted.
And afterwards——"

She was wonderfully expressive in her inexpressiveness, he thought, but found as yet no saving phrase.
Her thought continued to drop from her.   "One sees
them so much that at last one doesn't see them."

She turned away to survey the little house again ; it
was visible in bright strips between the red-scarred pine
stems.   She looked at it chin up, with a still approval
—but she was the slenderest loveliness, and with such a
dignity !—and she spoke at length as though the board
had never existed.   "It's like a little piece of another
world ; so bright and so—perfect."

There was the phantom of a sigh in her voice.

"I think you'll be charmed by our rockery," he said.
"It was one of our particular efforts.   Every time we
two went abroad we came back with something, Saxifrage
or House-leek or some little bulb from the wayside."

"How can you leave it ! "

He was leaving it because it bored him to death.
But so intricate is the human mind that it was with
perfect sincerity he answered : "It will be a tremendous
wrench. . . . I have to go."

"And you've written most of your books here and
lived here ! "

The note of sympathy in her voice gave him a sudden suspicion that she imagined his departure due to poverty. Now to be poor as an author is to be unpopular, and he valued his popularity—with the better sort of people. He hastened to explain. " I have to go, because here, you see, here, neither for me nor my little son, is it Life. It's a place of memories, a place of accomplished beauty. My son already breaks away,—a preparatory school at Margate. Healthier, better, for us to break altogether I feel, wrench though it may. It's full for us at least—a new tenant would be different of course—but for *us* it's full of associations we can't alter, can't for the life of us change. Nothing you see goes on. And life you know *is* change—change and going on."

He paused impressively on his generalization.

" But you will want—— You will want to hand it over to—to sympathetic people of course. People," she faltered, " who will understand."

Mr. Brumley took an immense stride—conversationally. " I am certain there is no one I would more readily see in that house than yourself," he said.

" But—— " she protested. " And besides, you don't know me ! "

" One knows some things at once, and I am as sure you would—understand—as if I had known you twenty years. It may seem absurd to you, but when I looked up just now and saw you for the first time, I thought—this, this is the tenant. This is her house. . . . Not a doubt. That is why I did not go for my walk—came round with you."

" You really think you would like us to have that house ? " she said. " *Still ?* "

" No one better," said Mr. Brumley.

" After the board ? "

" After a hundred boards, I let the house to you. . . ."

" My husband of course will be the tenant," reflected Lady Harman.

She seemed to brighten again by an effort: " I have always wanted something like this, that wasn't gorgeous, that wasn't mean. I can't *make* things. It isn't every one—can *make* a place. . . ."

§ 2

Mr. Brumley found their subsequent conversation the fullest realization of his extremest hopes. Behind his amiable speeches, which soon grew altogether easy and confident again, a hundred imps of vanity were patting his back for the intuition, the swift decision that had abandoned his walk so promptly. In some extraordinary way the incident of the board became impossible ; it hadn't happened, he felt, or it had happened differently. Anyhow there was no time to think that over now. He guided the lady to the two little greenhouses, made her note the opening glow of the great autumnal border and brought her to the rock garden. She stooped and loved and almost kissed the soft healthy cushions of pampered Saxifrage ; she appreciated the cleverness of the moss-bed—where there were droseras ; she knelt to the gentians ; she had a kindly word for that bank-holiday corner where London Pride still belatedly rejoiced ; she cried out at the delicate Alpine poppies that thrust up between the stones of the rough pavement ; and so in the most amiable accord they came to the raised seat in the heart of it all, and sat down and took in the whole effect of the place, and backing of woods, the lush borders, the neat lawn, the still neater orchard, the pergola, the nearer delicacies among the stones, and the gable, the shining white rough-cast of the walls, the casement windows, the projecting upper story, the carefully sought-out old tiles of the roof. And everything bathed in that caressing sunshine which does not scorch nor burn but gilds and warms deliciously, that summer sunshine which only northward islands know.

Recovering from his first astonishment and his first misadventure, Mr. Brumley was soon himself again, talkative, interesting, subtly and gently aggressive. For once one may use a hackneyed phrase without the slightest exaggeration; he was charmed. . . .

He was one of those very natural-minded men with active imaginations who find women the most interesting things in a full and interesting universe. He was an entirely good man and almost professionally on the side of goodness, his pen was a pillar of the home and he was hostile and even actively hostile to all those influences that would undermine and change— anything; but he did find women attractive. He watched them and thought about them, he loved to be with them, he would take great pains to please and interest them, and his mind was frequently dreaming quite actively of them, of championing them, saying wonderful and impressive things to them, having great friendships with them, adoring them and being adored by them. At times he had to ride this interest on the curb. At times the vigour of its urgencies made him inconsistent and secretive. . . . Comparatively his own sex was a matter of indifference to him. Indeed he

c

was a very normal man. Even such abstractions as Goodness and Justice had rich feminine figures in his mind, and when he sat down to write criticism at his desk, that pretty little slut of a Delphic Sibyl presided over his activities.

So that it was a cultivated as well as an attentive eye that studied the movements of Lady Harman and an experienced ear that weighed the words and cadences of her entirely inadequate and extremely expressive share in their conversation. He had enjoyed the social advantages of a popular and presentable man of letters, and he had met a variety of ladies; but he had never yet met anyone at all like Lady Harman. She was pretty and quite young and fresh; he doubted if she was as much as four-and-twenty; she was as simple-mannered as though she was ever so much younger than that, and dignified as though she was ever so much older; and she had a sort of lustre of wealth about her——. One met it sometimes in young richly married Jewesses, but though she was very dark she wasn't at all of that type; he was inclined to think she must be Welsh. This manifest spending of great lots of money on the richest, finest and fluffiest things was the only aspect of her that sustained the parvenu idea; and it wasn't in any way carried out by her manners, which were as modest and silent and inaggressive as the very best can be. Personally he liked opulence, he responded to countless-guinea furs. . . .

Soon there was a neat little history in his mind that was reasonably near the truth, of a hard-up professional family, fatherless perhaps, of a mercenary marriage at seventeen or so—and this. . . .

And while Mr. Brumley's observant and speculative faculties were thus active, his voice was busily engaged.

With the accumulated artistry of years he was developing his pose. He did it almost sub-consciously. He flung out hint and impulsive confidence and casual statement with the careless assurance of the accustomed performer, until by nearly imperceptible degrees that finished picture of the two young lovers, happy, artistic, a little Bohemian and one of them doomed to die, making their home together in an atmosphere of sunny gaiety, came into being in her mind. . . .

"It must have been beautiful to have begun life like that," she said in a voice that was a sigh, and it flashed joyfully across Mr. Brumley's mind that this wonderful person could envy his Euphemia.

"Yes," he said, "at least we had our Spring."

"To be together," said the lady, "and—so beautifully poor. . . ."

There is a phase in every relationship when one must generalize if one is to go further. A certain practice in this kind of talk with ladies blunted the finer sensibilities of Mr. Brumley. At any rate he was able to produce this sentence without a qualm. "Life," he said, "is sometimes a very extraordinary thing."

Lady Harman reflected upon this statement and then responded with an air of remembered moments : "Isn't it."

"One loses the most precious things," said Mr. Brumley, "and one loses them and it seems as though one couldn't go on. And one goes on."

"And one finds oneself," said Lady Harman, "without all sorts of precious things——" And she stopped, transparently realizing that she was saying too much.

"There is a sort of vitality about life," said Mr. Brumley, and stopped as if on the verge of profundities.

"I suppose one hopes," said Lady Harman. "And one doesn't think. And things happen."

"Things happen," assented Mr. Brumley.

For a little while their minds rested upon this thought, as chasing butterflies might rest together on a flower.

"And so I am going to leave this," Mr. Brumley resumed. "I am going up there to London for a time with my boy. Then perhaps we may travel—Germany, Italy, perhaps—in his holidays. It is beginning again, I feel, with him. But then even we two must drift apart. I can't deny him a public school sooner or later. His own road. . . ."

"It will be lonely for you," sympathized the lady.

"I have my work," said Mr. Brumley with a sort of valiant sadness.

"Yes, I suppose your work——"

She left an eloquent gap.

"There, of course, one's fortunate," said Mr. Brumley.

"I wish," said Lady Harman, with a sudden frankness and a little quickening of her colour, "that I had some work. Something—that was my own."

"But you have—— There are social duties. There must be all sorts of things."

"There are—all sorts of things. I suppose I'm ungrateful. I have my children."

"You have children, Lady Harman!"

"I've *four*."

He was really astonished, "Your *own*?"

She turned her fawn's eyes on his with a sudden wonder at his meaning. "My own!" she said with the faintest tinge of astonished laughter in her voice. "What else could they be?"

" I thought—— I thought you might have step-children. "

"Oh ! of course ! No ! I'm their mother ;—all four of them. They're mine as far as that goes. Anyhow."

And her eye questioned him again for his intentions.

But his thought ran along its own path. " You see," he said, " there is something about you—so freshly beginning life. So like—Spring."

" You thought I was too young ! I'm nearly six-and-twenty ! But all the same,—though they're mine, —*still*—— Why shouldn't a woman have work in the world, Mr. Brumley ? In spite of all that."

" But surely—that's the most beautiful work in the world that anyone could possibly have."

Lady Harman reflected. She seemed to hesitate on the verge of some answer and not to say it.

" You see," she said, " it may have been different with you. . . . When one has a lot of nurses, and not very much authority."

She coloured deeply and broke back from the impending revelations.

" No," she said, " I would like some work of my own."

§ 3

At this point their conversation was interrupted by the lady's chauffeur in a manner that struck Mr. Brumley as extraordinary, but which the tall lady evidently regarded as the most natural thing in the world.

Mr. Clarence appeared walking across the lawn towards them, surveying the charms of as obviously a charming garden as one could have, with the disdain and hostility natural to a chauffeur. He did not so much touch his cap as indicate that it was within reach, and that he could if he pleased touch it. "It's time you were going, my lady," he said. "Sir Isaac will be coming back by the five-twelve, and there'll be a nice to-do if you ain't at home and me at the station and everything in order again."

Manifestly an abnormal expedition.

."Must we start at once, Clarence?" asked the lady consulting a bracelet watch. "You surely won't take two hours—— "

"I can give you fifteen minutes more, my lady," said Clarence, "provided I may let her out and take my corners just exactly in my own way."

"And I must give you tea," said Mr. Brumley, rising to his feet. "And there is the kitchen."

"And upstairs! I'm afraid, Clarence, for this occasion only you must—what is it?—let her out."

"And no 'Oh Clarence!' my lady?"

She ignored that.

"I'll tell Mrs. Rabbit at once," said Mr. Brumley, and started to run and trod in some complicated way on one of his loose laces and was precipitated down the rockery steps. "Oh!" cried the lady. "Mind!" and clasped her hands.

He made a sound exactly like the word "damnation" as he fell, but he didn't so much get up as bounce up, apparently in the brightest of tempers, and laughed, held out two earthy hands for sympathy with a mock rueful grimace, and went on, earthy-green at the knees and a little more carefully towards the house. Clarence, having halted to drink deep satisfaction from this disaster, made his way along a nearly parallel path towards the kitchen, leaving his lady to follow as she chose to the house.

"*You'll* take a cup of tea?" called Mr. Brumley.

"Oh! *I'll* take a cup all right," said Clarence in the kindly voice of one who addresses an amusing inferior. . . .

Mrs. Rabbit had already got the tea-things out upon the cane table in the pretty verandah, and took it ill that she should be supposed not to have thought of these preparations.

Mr. Brumley disappeared for a few minutes into the house.

He returned with a conscious relief on his face, clean hands, brushed knees, and his boots securely laced. He found Lady Harman already pouring out tea.

"You see," she said, to excuse this pleasant enterprise on her part, "my husband has to be met at the station with the car. . . . And of course he has no idea——"

She left what it was of which Sir Isaac had no idea to the groping speculations of Mr. Brumley.

§ 4

That evening Mr. Brumley was quite unable to work. His mind was full of this beautiful dark lady who had come so unexpectedly into his world.

Perhaps there are such things as premonitions. At any rate he had an altogether disproportionate sense of the significance of the afternoon's adventure,—which after all was a very small adventure indeed. A mere talk. His mind refused to leave her, her black furry slenderness, her dark trustful eyes, the sweet firmness of her perfect lips, her appealing simplicity that was yet somehow compatible with the completest self-possession. He went over the incident of the board again and again,

scraping his memory for any lurking crumb of detail as
a starving man might scrape an insufficient plate. Her
dignity, her gracious frank forgiveness ; no queen alive
in these days could have touched her. . . . But it wasn't
a mere elaborate admiration. There was something about
her, about the quality of their meeting.

Most people know that sort of intimation. This
person, it says, so fine, so brave, so distant still in so
many splendid and impressive qualities, is yet in ways
as yet undefined and unexplored, subtly and abundantly
—for *you*. It was that made all her novelty and distinction and high quality and beauty so dominating
among Mr. Brumley's thoughts. Without that his
interest might have been almost entirely—academic.
But there was woven all through her the hints of an
imaginable alliance, with *us*, with the things that are
Brumley, with all that makes beautiful little cottages
and resents advertisements in lovely places, with us as
against something over there lurking behind that board,
something else, something out of which she came. He
vaguely adumbrated what it was out of which she came.
A closed narrow life—with horrid vast enviable quan-
tities of money. A life, could one use the word *vulgar?*
—so that Carpaccio, Della Robbia, old furniture, a
garden unostentatiously perfect, and the atmosphere of
belles-lettres, seemed things of another more desirable
world. (She had never been abroad.) A world, too,
that would be so willing, so happy to enfold her, furs,
funds, freshness—everything.

And all this was somehow animated by the stirring
warmth in the June weather, for spring raised the sap
in Mr. Brumley as well as in his trees, had been a restless time for him all his life. This spring particularly
had sensitized him, and now a light had shone.

He was so unable to work that for twenty minutes he sat over a pleasant little essay on Shakespear's garden that by means of a concordance and his natural aptitude he was writing for the book of the National Shakespear Theatre, without adding a single fancy to its elegant playfulness. Then he decided he needed his afternoon's walk after all, and he took cap and stick and went out, and presently found himself surveying that yellow and blue board and seeing it from an entirely new point of view. . . .

It seemed to him that he hadn't made the best use of his conversational opportunities, and for a time this troubled him. . . .

Toward the twilight he was walking along the path that runs through the heather along the edge of the rusty dark ironstone lake opposite the pinewoods. He spoke his thoughts aloud to the discreet bat that flitted about him. "I wonder," he said, "whether I shall ever set eyes on her again. . . ."

In the small hours when he ought to have been fast asleep he decided she would certainly take the house, and that he would see her again quite a number of times. A long tangle of unavoidable detail for discussion might be improvised by an ingenious man. And the rest of that waking interval passed in such inventions, which became more and more vague and magnificent and familiar as Mr. Brumley lapsed into slumber again. . . .

Next day the garden essay was still neglected, and he wrote a pretty vague little song about an earthly mourner and a fresh presence that set him thinking of the story of Persephone and how she passed in the spring-time up from the shadows again, blessing as she passed. . . .

He pulled himself together about midday, cycled over to Gorshott for lunch at the clubhouse and a round with Horace Toomer in the afternoon, re-read the poem after tea, decided it was poor, tore it up and got himself down to his little fantasy about Shakespear's Garden for a good two hours before supper. It was a sketch of that fortunate poet (whose definitive immortality is now being assured by an influential committee) walking round his Stratford garden with his daughter, quoting himself copiously with an accuracy and inappropriateness that reflected more credit upon his heart than upon his head, and saying in addition many distinctively Brumley things. When Mrs. Rabbit, with a solicitude acquired from the late Mrs. Brumley, asked him how he had got on with his work —the sight of verse on his paper had made her anxious —he could answer quite truthfully, " Like a house afire."

CHAPTER THE SECOND

THE PERSONALITY OF SIR ISAAC

§ 1

IT is to be remarked that two facts, usually esteemed as supremely important in the life of a woman, do not seem to have affected Mr. Brumley's state of mind nearly so much as quite trivial personal details about Lady Harman. The first of these facts was the existence of the lady's four children, and the second, Sir Isaac.

Mr. Brumley did not think very much of either of these two facts; if he had they would have spoilt the portrait in his mind; and when he did think of them it was chiefly to think how remarkably little they were necessary to that picture's completeness.

He spent some little time however trying to recall exactly what it was she had said about her children. He couldn't now succeed in reproducing her words, if indeed it had been by anything so explicit as words that she had conveyed to him that she didn't feel her children were altogether hers. " Incidental results of the collapse of her girlhood," tried Mr. Brumley, " when she married Harman."

Expensive nurses, governesses—the best that money without prestige or training could buy. And then probably a mother-in-law.

27

And as for Harman——?

There Mr. Brumley's mind desisted for sheer lack of material.   Given this lady and that board and his general impression of Harman's refreshment and confectionery activity—the data were insufficient.   A commonplace man no doubt, a tradesman, energetic perhaps and certainly a little brassy, successful by the chances of that economic revolution which everywhere replaces the isolated shop by the syndicated enterprise, irrationally conceited about it; a man perhaps ultimately to be pitied—with this young goddess finding herself. . . . Mr. Brumley's mind sat down comfortably to the more congenial theme of a young goddess finding herself, and it was only very gradually in the course of several days that the personality of Sir Isaac began to assume its proper importance in the scheme of his imaginings.

§ 2

In the afternoon as he went round the links with Horace Toomer he got some definite lights upon Sir Isaac.

His mind was so full of Lady Harman that he couldn't but talk of her visit.   " I've a possible tenant for my cottage," he said as he and Toomer, full of the sunny contentment of English gentlemen who had played a proper game in a proper manner, strolled back towards the clubhouse.   " That man Harman."

" Not the International Stores and Staminal Bread man."

" Yes.   Odd.   Considering my hatred of his board."

" He ought to pay—anyhow," said Toomer.   " They say he has a pretty wife and keeps her shut up."

" She came," said Brumley, neglecting to add the trifling fact that she had come alone.

" Pretty ? "

" Charming, I thought."

" He's jealous of her. Someone was saying that the chauffeur has orders not to take her into London— only for trips in the country. They live in a big ugly house I'm told on Putney Hill. Did she in any way *look*—as though—— ? "

" Not in the least. If she isn't an absolutely straight young woman I've never set eyes on one."

" *He*," said Toomer, " is a disgusting creature."

" Morally ? "

" No, but—generally. Spends his life ruining little tradesmen, for the fun of the thing. He's three parts an invalid with some obscure kidney disease. Sometimes he spends whole days in bed, drinking Contrexéville Water and planning the bankruptcy of decent men. . . . So the party made a knight of him."

" A party must have funds, Toomer."

" He didn't pay nearly enough. Blapton is an idiot with the honours. When it isn't Mrs. Blapton. What can you expect when ▮▮▮▮ ▮▮▮▮ "

(But here Toomer became libellous.)

Toomer was an interesting type. He had a disagreeable disposition profoundly modified by a public school and university training. Two antagonistic forces made him. He was the spirit of scurrility incarnate, that was, as people say, innate ; and by virtue of those moulding forces he was doing his best to be an English gentleman. That mysterious impulse which compels the young male to make objectionable imputations against seemly lives and to write rare inelegant words upon clean and decent things burnt

almost intolerably within him, and equally powerful
now was the gross craving he had acquired for personal
association with all that is prominent, all that is
successful, all that is of good report. He had found
his resultant in the censorious defence of established
things. He conducted the *British Critic*, attacking
with a merciless energy all that was new, all that was
critical, all those fresh and noble tentatives that admit
of unsavoury interpretations, and when the urgent
Yahoo in him carried him below the pretentious
dignity of his accustomed organ he would squirt out
his bitterness in a little sham facetious bookstall
volume with a bright cover and quaint woodcuts, in
which just as many prominent people as possible were
mentioned by name and a sauce of general absurdity
could be employed to cover and, if need be, excuse
particular libels. So he managed to relieve himself and
get along. Harman was just on the border-line of the
class he considered himself free to revile. Harman was
an outsider and aggressive and new, one of Mrs.
Blapton's knights, and of no particular weight in
society; so far he was fair game; but he was not so
new as he had been, he was almost through with the
running of the Toomer gauntlet, he had a tremendous
lot of money and it was with a modified vehemence
that the distinguished journalist and humourist ex-
patiated on his offensiveness to Mr. Brumley. He
talked in a gentle, rather weary voice, that came
through a moustache like a fringe of light tobacco.

"Personally I've little against the man. A wife too
young for him and jealously guarded, but that's all to
his credit. Nowadays. If it wasn't for his blatancy in
his business. . . . And the knighthood. . . . I suppose
he can't resist taking anything he can get. Bread

made by wholesale and distributed like a newspaper can't, I feel, be the same thing as the loaf of your honest old-fashioned baker—each loaf made with individual attention—out of wholesome English flour—hand-ground—with a personal touch for each customer. Still, everything drifts on to these hugger-mugger large enterprises; Chicago spreads over the world. One thing goes after another, tobacco, tea, bacon, drugs, bookselling. Decent homes destroyed right and left. Not Harman's affair, I suppose. The girls in his London tea-shops have of course to supplement their wages by prostitution—probably don't object to that nowadays considering the novels we have. And his effect on the landscape—— Until they stopped him he was trying very hard to get Shakespear's Cliff at Dover. He did for a time have the Toad Rock at Tunbridge. Still "—something like a sigh escaped from Toomer,—" his private life appears to be almost as blameless as anybody's can be. . . . Thanks no doubt to his defective health. I made the most careful enquiries when his knighthood was first discussed. Someone has to. Before his marriage he seems to have lived at home with his mother. At Highbury. Very quietly and inexpensively."

" Then he's not the conventional vulgarian ? "

" Much more of the Rockefeller type. Bad health, great concentration, organizing power. . . . Applied of course to a narrower range of business. . . . I'm glad I'm not a small confectioner in a town he wants to take up."

" He's—hard ? "

" Merciless. Hasn't the beginnings of an idea of fair play. . . . None at all. . . . No human give or take. . . . Are you going to have tea here, or are you walking back now ? "

§ 3

It was fully a week before Mr. Brumley heard anything more of Lady Harman. He began to fear that this shining furry presence would glorify Black Strand no more. Then came a telegram that filled him with the liveliest anticipations. It was worded: "Coming see cottage Saturday afternoon Harman. . . ."

On Saturday morning Mr. Brumley dressed with an apparent ease and unusual care. . . .

He worked rather discursively before lunch. His mind was busy picking up the ends of their previous conversation and going on with them to all sorts of bright knots, bows and elegant cats' cradling. He planned openings that might give her tempting opportunities of confidences if she wished to confide, and artless remarks and questions that would make for self-betrayal if she didn't. And he thought of her, he thought of her imaginatively, this secluded rare thing so happily come to him, who was so young, so frank and fresh and so unhappily married (he was sure) to a husband at least happily mortal. Yes, dear Reader, even on that opening morning Mr. Brumley's imagination, trained very largely upon Victorian literature and *belles-lettres*, leapt forward to the very ending of this story. . . . We, of course, do nothing of the sort, our lot is to follow a more pedestrian route. . . . He lapsed into a vague series of meditations, slower perhaps but essentially similar, after his temperate palatable lunch.

He was apprised of the arrival of his visitor by the sudden indignant yaup followed by the general subdued uproar of a motor-car outside the front door, even before Clarence, this time amazingly prompt, assaulted

the bell. Then the whole house was like that poem by
Edgar Allan Poe, one magnificent texture of clangour.

At the first toot of the horn Mr. Brumley had
moved swiftly into the bay, and screened partly by the
life-size Venus of Milo that stood in the bay window,
and partly by the artistic curtains, surveyed the glittering vehicle. He was first aware of a vast fur coat en-
closing a lean grey-headed obstinate-looking man with
a diabetic complexion who was fumbling with the door
of the car and preventing Clarence's assistance. Mr.
Brumley was able to remark that the gentleman's nose
projected to a sharpened point, and that his thin-lipped
mouth was all awry and had a kind of habitual com-
pression, the while that his eyes sought eagerly for the
other occupant of the car. She was unaccountably
invisible. Could it be that that hood really concealed
her? Could it be . . . ?

The white-faced gentleman descended, relieved himself tediously of the vast fur coat, handed it to Clarence
and turned to the house. Reverentially Clarence placed
the coat within the automobile and closed the door.
Still the protesting mind of Mr. Brumley refused to
believe! . . .

He heard the house-door open and Mrs. Rabbit in
colloquy with a flat masculine voice. He heard his
own name demanded and conceded. Then a silence,
not the faintest suggestion of a feminine rustle, and
then the sound of Mrs. Rabbit at the door-handle.
Conviction stormed the last fastness of the disappointed
author's mind.

" Oh *damn !* " he shouted with extreme fervour.

He had never imagined it was possible that Sir
Isaac could come alone.

§ 4

But the house had to be let, and it had to be let to Sir Isaac Harman. In another moment an amiable though distinguished man of letters was in the hall interviewing the great *entrepreneur*.

The latter gentleman was perhaps three inches shorter than Mr. Brumley, his hair was grey-shot brown, his face clean-shaven, his features had a thin irregularity, and he was dressed in a neat brown suit with a necktie very exactly matching it. "Sir Isaac Harman?" said Mr. Brumley with a note of gratification.

"That's it," said Sir Isaac. He appeared to be nervous and a little out of breath. "Come," he said, "just to look over it. Just to see it. Probably too small, but if it doesn't put you out—— "

He blew out the skin of his face about his mouth a little.

"Delighted to see you anyhow," said Mr. Brumley, filling the world of unspoken things with singularly lurid curses.

"This. Nice little hall,—very," said Sir Isaac. "Pretty, that bit at the end. Many rooms are there?"

Mr. Brumley answered inexactly and meditated a desperate resignation of the whole job to Mrs. Rabbit. Then he made an effort and began to explain.

"That clock," said Sir Isaac interrupting in the dining-room, "is a fake."

Mr. Brumley made silent interrogations.

"Been there myself," said Sir Isaac. "They sell those brass fittings in Ho'bun."

They went upstairs together. When Mr. Brumley

wasn't explaining or pointing out, Sir Isaac made a kind of whistling between his clenched teeth. "This bathroom wants refitting anyhow," he said abruptly. "I daresay Lady Harman would like that room with the bay—but it's all—small. It's really quite pretty; you've done it cleverly, but—the size of it!. I'd have to throw out a wing. And that you know might spoil the style. That roof,—a gardener's cottage? . . . I thought it might be. What's this other thing here? Old barn. Empty? That might expand a bit. Couldn't do only just this anyhow."

He walked in front of Mr. Brumley downstairs and still emitting that faint whistle led the way into the garden. He seemed to regard Mr. Brumley merely as a source of answers to his questions, and a seller in process of preparation for an offer. It was clear he meant to make an offer. "It's not the house I should buy if I was alone in this," he said, "but Lady Harman's taken a fancy somehow. And it might be adapted. . . ."

From first to last Mr. Brumley never said a single word about Euphemia and the young matrimony and all the other memories this house enshrined. He felt instinctively that it would not affect Sir Isaac one way or the other. He tried simply to seem indifferent to whether Sir Isaac bought the place or not. He tried to make it appear almost as if houses like this often happened to him, and interested him only in the most incidental manner. They had their proper price, he tried to convey, which of course no gentleman would underbid.

In the exquisite garden Sir Isaac said : "One might make a very pretty little garden of this—if one opened it out a bit."

And of the sunken rock-garden : " That might be dangerous of a dark night."

" I suppose," he said, indicating the hill of pines behind, " one could buy or lease some of that. If one wanted to throw it into the place and open out more.

" From my point of view," he said, " it isn't a house. It's—— " He sought in his mind for an expression—" a Cottage Ornay."

This history declines to record either what Mr. Brumley said or what he did not say.

Sir Isaac surveyed the house thoughtfully for some moments from the turf edging of the great herbaceous border.

" How far," he asked, " is it from the nearest railway station ? . . ."

Mr. Brumley gave details.

" Four miles. And an infrequent service ? Nothing in any way suburban ? Better to motor into Guildford and get the Express. H'm . . . And what sort of people do we get about here ? "

Mr. Brumley sketched.

" Mildly horsey. That's not bad. No officers about ? . . . Nothing nearer than Aldershot . . . That's eleven miles, is it ? H'm. I suppose there aren't any *literary* people about here, musicians or that kind of thing, no advanced people of that sort ? "

" Not when I've gone," said Mr. Brumley, with the faintest flavour of humour.

Sir Isaac stared at him for a moment with eyes vacantly thoughtful.

" It mightn't be so bad," said Sir Isaac, and whistled a little between his teeth.

Mr. Brumley was suddenly minded to take his visitor to see the view and the effect of his board upon it. But he spoke merely of the view and left Sir Isaac to discover the board or not as he thought fit. As they ascended among the trees, the visitor was manifestly seized by some strange emotion, his face became very white, he gasped and blew for breath, he felt for his face with a nervous hand.

"Four thousand," he said suddenly. "An outside price."

"A minimum," said Mr. Brumley, with a slight quickening of the pulse.

"You won't get three eight," gasped Sir Isaac.

"Not a business man, but my agent tells me—— " panted Mr. Brumley.

"Three eight," said Sir Isaac.

"We're just coming to the view," said Mr. Brumley. "Just coming to the view."

"Practically got to rebuild the house," said Sir Isaac.

"There!" said Mr. Brumley, and waved an arm widely.

Sir Isaac regarded the prospect with a dissatisfied face. His pallor had given place to a shiny, flushed appearance, his nose, his ears, and his cheeks were pink. He blew his face out, and seemed to be studying the landscape for defects. "This might be built over at any time," he complained.

Mr. Brumley was reassuring.

For a brief interval Sir Isaac's eyes explored the countryside vaguely, then his expression seemed to concentrate and run together to a point. "H'm," he said.

"That board," he remarked, "quite wrong there."

"*Well!*" said Mr. Brumley, too surprised for coherent speech.

"Quite," said Sir Isaac Harman. "Don't you see what's the matter ?"

Mr. Brumley refrained from an eloquent response.

"They ought to be," Sir Isaac went on, " white and a sort of green. Like the County Council notices on Hampstead Heath. So as to blend. . . . You see, an ad. that hits too hard is worse than no ad. at all. It leaves a dislike. . . . Advertisements ought to blend. It ought to seem as though all this view were saying it. Not just that board. Now suppose we had a shade of very light brown, a kind of light khaki—— "

He turned a speculative eye on Mr. Brumley as if he sought for the effect of this latter suggestion on him.

"If the whole board was invisible—— " said Mr. Brumley.

Sir Isaac considered it. "Just the letters showing," he said. "No,—that would be going too far in the other direction."

He made a faint sucking noise with his lips and teeth as he surveyed the landscape and weighed this important matter. . . .

"Queer how one gets ideas," he said at last, turning away. "It was my wife told me about that board."

He stopped to survey the house from the exact point of view his wife had taken nine days before. " I wouldn't give this place a second thought," said Sir Isaac, " if it wasn't for Lady Harman."

He confided. "*She* wants a week-end cottage. But *I* don't see why it *should* be a week-end cottage. I don't see why it shouldn't be made into a nice little country house. Compact, of course. By using up that barn."

He inhaled three bars of a tune. "London," he explained, " doesn't suit Lady Harman."

"Health?" asked Mr. Brumley, all alert.

"It isn't her health exactly," Sir Isaac dropped out. "You see—she's a young woman. She gets ideas."

"You know," he continued, "I'd like to have a look at that barn again. If we develop that—and a sort of corridor across where the shrubs are—and ran out offices. . . ."

§ 5

Mr. Brumley's mind was still vigorously struggling with the flaming implications of Sir Isaac's remark that Lady Harman "got ideas," and Sir Isaac was gently whistling his way towards an offer of three thousand nine hundred when they came down out of the pines into the path along the edge of the herbaceous border. And then Mr. Brumley became aware of an effect away between the white-stemmed trees towards the house as if the Cambridge boat-race crew was indulging in a vigorous scrimmage. Drawing nearer this resolved itself into the fluent contours of Lady Beach-Mandarin, dressed in sky-blue and with a black summer straw hat larger than ever and trimmed effusively with marguerites.

"Here," said Sir Isaac, "can't I get off? You've got a friend."

"You must have some tea," said Mr. Brumley, who wanted to suggest that they should agree to Sir Isaac's figure of three thousand eight hundred, but not as pounds but guineas. It seemed to him a suggestion that might prove insidiously attractive. "It's a charming lady, my friend Lady Beach-Mandarin. She'll be delighted—— "

"I don't think I can," said Sir Isaac. "Not in the habit—social occasions."

His face expressed a panic terror of this gallant full-rigged lady ahead of them.

"But you see now," said Mr. Brumley, with a detaining grip, "it's unavoidable."

And the next moment Sir Isaac was mumbling his appreciations of the introduction.

I must admit that Lady Beach-Mandarin was almost as much to meet as one can meet in a single human being, a broad abundant billowing personality with a taste for brims, streamers, pennants, panniers, loose sleeves, sweeping gestures, top notes and the like that made her altogether less like a woman than an occasion of public rejoicing. Even her large blue eyes projected, her chin and brows and nose all seemed racing up to the front of her as if excited by the clarion notes of her abundant voice, and the pinkness of her complexion was as exuberant as her manners. Exuberance—it was her word. She had evidently been a big, bouncing, bright gaminesque girl at fifteen, and very amusing and very much admired ; she had liked the rôle and she had not so much grown older as suffered enlargement—a very considerable enlargement.

"Ah !" she cried, "and so I've caught you at home, Mr. Brumley ! And, poor dear, you're at my mercy." And she shook both his hands with both of hers.

That was before Mr. Brumley introduced Sir Isaac, a thing he did so soon as he could get one of his hands loose and wave a surviving digit or so at that gentleman.

"You see, Sir Isaac," she said, taking him in, in the most generous way; "I and Mr. Brumley are old friends. We knew each other of yore. We have our jokes."

Sir Isaac seemed to feel the need of speech but got no further than a useful all-round noise.

" And one of them is that when I want him to do the least little thing for me he hides away ! Always. By a sort of instinct. It's such a Small thing, Sir Isaac."

Sir Isaac was understood to say vaguely that they always did. But he had become very indistinct.

" Aren't I always at your service ? " protested Mr. Brumley with a responsive playfulness. " And I don't even know what it is you want."

Lady Beach-Mandarin, addressing herself exclusively to Sir Isaac, began a tale of a Shakespear Bazaar she was holding in an adjacent village, and how she knew Mr. Brumley (naughty man) meant to refuse to give her autographed copies of his littlest book for the Book Stall she was organizing. Mr. Brumley confuted her gaily and generously. So discoursing they made their way to the verandah where Lady Harman had so lately " poured."

Sir Isaac was borne along upon the lady's stream of words in a state of mulish reluctance, nodding, saying " Of course " and similar phrases, and wishing he was out of it all with an extreme manifestness. He drank his tea with unmistakable discomfort, and twice inserted into the conversation an entirely irrelevant remark that he had to be going. But Lady Beach-Mandarin had her purposes with him and crushed these quivering tentatives.

Lady Beach-Mandarin had of course like everybody else at that time her own independent movement in the great national effort to create an official British Theatre upon the basis of William Shakespear, and she saw in the as yet unenlisted resources of Sir Isaac strong

possibilities of reinforcement of her own particular contribution to the great Work. He was manifestly shy
and sulky and disposed to bolt at the earliest possible
moment, and so she set herself now with a swift and
concentrated combination of fascination and urgency to
commit him to participations. She flattered and cajoled
and bribed. She was convinced that even to be called
upon by Lady Beach-Mandarin is no light privilege for
these new commercial people, and so she made no secret
of her intention of decorating the hall of his large but
undistinguished house in Putney, with her redeeming
pasteboard. She appealed to the instances of Venice and
Florence to show that " such men as you, Sir Isaac,"
who control commerce and industry, have always been
the guardians and patrons of art. And who more worthy
of patronage than William Shakespear ? Also she said
that men of such enormous wealth as his owed something
to their national tradition. " You have to pay your
footing, Sir Isaac," she said with impressive vagueness.

" Putting it in round figures," said Sir Isaac,
suddenly and with a white gleam of animosity in his
face, the animosity of a trapped animal at the sight of
its captors, " what does coming on your Committee
mean, Lady Beach-Mandarin ? "

" It's your name we want," said the lady, " but I'm
sure you'd not be ungenerous. The tribute success owes
the arts."

" A hundred ? " he threw out,—his ears red.

" Guineas," breathed Lady Beach-Mandarin with
a lofty sweetness of consent.

He stood up hastily as if to escape further exaction,
and the lady rose too.

" And you'll let me call on Lady Harman," she said,
honestly doing her part in the bargain.

"Can't keep the car waiting," was what Brumley could distinguish in his reply.

"I expect you have a perfectly splendid car, Sir Isaac," said Lady Beach-Mandarin, drawing him out. "Quite the modernest thing."

Sir Isaac replied with the reluctance of an Income Tax Return that it was a forty-five Rolls Royce, good of course but nothing amazing.

"We must see it," she said, and turned his retreat into a procession.

She admired the car, she admired the colour of the car, she admired the lamps of the car and the door of the car and the little fittings of the car. She admired the horn. She admired the twist of the horn. She admired Clarence and the uniform of Clarence and she admired and coveted the great fur coat that he held ready for his employer. (But if she had it, she said, she would wear the splendid fur outside to show every little bit of it.) And when the car at last moved forward and tooted—she admired the note—and vanished softly and swiftly through the gates, she was left in the porch with Mr. Brumley still by sheer inertia admiring and envying. She admired Sir Isaac's car number Z 900. (Such an easy one to remember!) Then she stopped abruptly, as one might discover that the water in the bathroom was running to waste and turn it off.

She had a cynicism as exuberant as the rest of her.

"Well," she said, with a contented sigh and an entire flattening of her tone, "I laid it on pretty thick that time. . . . I wonder if he'll send me that hundred guineas or whether I shall have to remind him of it. . . ." Her manner changed again to that of a gigantic gamin. "I mean to have that money," she said with bright determination and round eyes. . . .

She reflected and other thoughts came to her. " Plutocracy, " she said, " *is* perfectly detestable, don't you think so, Mr. Brumley?" . . . And then, " I can't *imagine* how a man who deals in bread and confectionery can manage to go about so completely half-baked."

" He's a very remarkable type," said Mr. Brumley.

He became urgent : " I do hope, dear Lady Beach-Mandarin, you will contrive to call on Lady Harman. She is—in relation to *that*—quite the most interesting woman I have seen."

§ 6

Presently as they paced the croquet lawn together, the preoccupation of Mr. Brumley's mind drew their conversation back to Lady Harman.

" I wish," he repeated, " you would go and see these people. She's not at all what you might infer from him."

" What could one infer about a wife from a man like that? Except that she'd have a lot to put up with."

" You know,—she's a beautiful person, tall, slender, dark. . . ."

Lady Beach-Mandarin turned her full blue eye upon him.

" *Now!* " she said archly.

" I'm interested in the incongruity."

Lady Beach-Mandarin's reply was silent and singular. She compressed her lips very tightly, fixed her eye firmly on Mr. Brumley's, lifted her finger to the level of her left eyelash, and then shook it at him very deliberately five times. Then with a little sigh and a sudden and complete restoration of manner she remarked that never in any year before had she seen peonies quite so splendid. " I've a peculiar sympathy with peonies," she said. " They're so exactly my style."

CHAPTER THE THIRD

Lady Harman at Home

§ 1

EXACTLY three weeks after that first encounter between Lady Beach-Mandarin and Sir Isaac Harman, Mr. Brumley found himself one of a luncheon party at that lady's house in Temperley Square and talking very freely and indiscreetly about the Harmans.

Lady Beach-Mandarin always had her luncheons in a family way at a large round table so that nobody could get out of her range, and she insisted upon conversation being general, except for her mother who was impenetrably deaf and the Swiss governess of her only daughter Phyllis who was incomprehensible in any European tongue. The mother was incalculably old and had been a friend of Victor Hugo and Alfred de Musset; she maintained an intermittent monologue about the private lives of those great figures; nobody paid the slightest attention to her but one felt she enriched the table with an undertow of literary associations. A small dark stealthy butler and a convulsive boy with hair (apparently) taking the place of eyes waited. On this occasion Lady Beach-Mandarin had gathered together two cousins, maiden ladies from Perth, wearing valiant hats, Toomer the wit and

46

censor, and Miss Sharsper the novelist (whom Toomer detested), a gentleman named Roper whom she had invited under a misapprehension that he was the Arctic Roper, and Mr. Brumley. She had tried Mr. Roper with questions about penguins, seals, cold and darkness, icebergs and glaciers, Captain Scott, Doctor Cook and the shape of the earth, and all in vain, and feeling at last that something was wrong, she demanded abruptly whether Mr. Brumley had sold his house.

"I'm selling it," said Mr. Brumley, "by almost imperceptible degrees."

" He haggles ? "

"Haggles and higgles. He higgles passionately. He goes white and breaks into a cold perspiration. He wants me now to include the gardener's tools—in whatever price we agree upon."

" A rich man like that ought to be easy and generous," said Lady Beach-Mandarin.

"Then he wouldn't be a rich man like that," said Mr. Toomer.

" But doesn't it distress you highly, Mr. Brumley," one of the Perth ladies asked, " to be leaving Euphemia's Home to strangers? The man may go altering it."

" That—that weighs with me very much," said Mr. Brumley, recalled to his professions. " There I put my trust in Lady Harman."

" You've seen her again ? " asked Lady Beach-Mandarin.

" Yes. She came with him—a few days ago. That couple interests me more and more. So little akin."

" There's eighteen years between them," said Toomer.

"It's one of those cases," began Mr. Brumley with a note of scientific detachment, "where one is really tempted to be ultra-feminist. It's clear, he uses every advantage. He's her owner, her keeper, her obstinate insensitive little tyrant. . . . And yet there's a sort of effect, as though nothing was decided. . . . As if she was only just growing up."

"They've been married six or seven years," said Toomer. "She was just eighteen."

"They went over the house together and whenever she spoke he contradicted her with a sort of vicious playfulness. Tried to poke clumsy fun at her. Called her 'Lady Harman.' Only it was quite evident that what she said stuck in his mind. . . . Very queer—interesting people."

"I wouldn't have anyone allowed to marry until they were five-and-twenty," said Lady Beach-Mandarin.

"Sweet seventeen sometimes contrives to be very marriageable," said the gentleman named Roper.

"Sweet seventeen must contrive to wait," said Lady Beach-Mandarin. "Sweet fourteen has to—and when I was fourteen—I was Ardent! There's no earthly objection to a little harmless flirtation of course. It's the marrying."

"You'd conduce to romance," said Miss Sharsper, "anyhow. Eighteen won't bear restriction and everyone would begin by eloping—illegally."

"I'd put them back," said Lady Beach-Mandarin. "Oh! remorselessly."

Mr. Roper, who was more and more manifestly not the Arctic one, remarked that she would "give the girls no end of an adolescence. . . ."

Mr. Brumley did not attend very closely to the subsequent conversation. His mind had gone back to

Black Strand and the second visit that Lady Harman, this time under her natural and proper protection, had paid him. A little thread from the old lady's discourse drifted by him. She had scented marriage in the air and she was saying, " of course they ought to have let Victor Hugo marry over and over again. He would have made it all so beautiful. He could throw a Splendour over—over almost anything." Mr. Brumley sank out of attention altogether. It was so difficult to express his sense of Lady Harman as a captive, enclosed but unsubdued. She had been as open and shining as a celandine flower in the sunshine on that first invasion, but on the second it had been like overcast weather and her starry petals had been shut and still. She hadn't been in the least subdued or effaced, but closed, inaccessible to conversational bees, that astonishing honey of trust and easy friendship had been hidden in a dignified impenetrable reserve. She had had the effect of being not so much specially shut against Mr. Brumley as habitually shut against her husband, as a protection against his continual clumsy mental interferences. And once when Sir Isaac had made a sudden allusion to price Mr. Brumley had glanced at her and met her eyes. . . .

" Of course," he said, coming up to the conversational surface again, " a woman like that is bound to fight her way out."

" Queen Mary !" cried Miss Sharsper. " Fight her way out !"

" Queen Mary !" said Mr. Brumley, " No !—Lady Harman."

" *I* was talking of Queen Mary," said Miss Sharsper.

" And Mr. Brumley was thinking of Lady Harman !" cried Lady Beach-Mandarin.

"Well," said Mr. Brumley, "I confess I do think about her. She seems to me to be so typical in many ways of—of everything that is weak in the feminine position. As a type—yes, she's perfect."

"I've never seen this lady," said Miss Sharsper. "Is she beautiful?"

"I've not seen her myself yet," said Lady Beach-Mandarin. "She's Mr. Brumley's particular discovery."

"You haven't called?" he asked with a faint reproach.

"But I've been going to—oh! tremendously. And you revive all my curiosity. Why shouldn't some of us this very afternoon—— ?"

She caught at her own passing idea and held it. "Let's Go," she cried. "Let's visit the wife of this Ogre, the last of the women in captivity. We'll take the big car and make a party and call *en masse*."

Mr. Toomer protested he had no morbid curiosities.

"But you, Susan?"

Miss Sharsper declared she would *love* to come. Wasn't it her business to study out-of-the-way types? Mr. Roper produced a knowing sort of engagement— "I'm provided for already, Lady Beach-Mandarin," he said, and the cousins from Perth had to do some shopping.

"Then we three will be the expedition," said the hostess. "And afterwards if we survive we'll tell you our adventures. It's a house on Putney Hill, isn't it, where this Christian maiden, so to speak, is held captive? I've had her in my mind, but I've always intended to call with Agatha Alimony; she's so inspiring to down-trodden women."

"Not exactly down-trodden," said Mr. Brumley, "not down-trodden. That's what's so curious about it."

"And what shall we do when we get there?" cried Lady Beach-Mandarin. "I feel we ought to do something more than call. Can't we carry her off right away, Mr. Brumley? I want to go right in to her and say 'Look here! I'm on your side. Your husband's a tyrant. I'm help and rescue. I'm all that a woman ought to be—fine and large. Come out from under that unworthy man's heel!'"

"Suppose she isn't at all the sort of person you seem to think she is," said Miss Sharsper. "And suppose she came!"

"Suppose she didn't," reflected Mr. Roper.

"I seem to see your flight," said Mr. Toomer. "And the newspaper placards and head-lines. 'Lady Beach-Mandarin elopes with the wife of an eminent confectioner. She is stopped at the landing stage by the staff of the Dover Branch establishment. Recapture of the fugitive after a hot struggle. Brumley, the eminent *littérateur*, stunned by a spent bun. . . .'"

"We're all talking great nonsense," said Lady Beach-Mandarin. "But anyhow we'll make our call. And *I* know!—I'll make her accept an invitation to lunch without him."

"If she won't?" threw out Mr. Roper.

"I *will*," said Lady Beach-Mandarin with roguish determination. "And if I can't——"

"Not ask him too!" protested Mr. Brumley.

"Why not get her to come to your Social Friends meeting," said Miss Sharsper. . .

§ 2

When Mr. Brumley found himself fairly launched upon this expedition he had the grace to feel compunction. The Harmans, he perceived, had inadvertently made him the confidant of their domestic discords and to betray them to these others savoured after all of treachery. And besides much as he had craved to see Lady Harman again, he now realized he didn't in the least want to see her in association with the exuberant volubility of Lady Beach-Mandarin and the hard professional observation, so remarkably like the ferrule of an umbrella being poked with a noiseless persistence into one's eye, of Miss Sharsper. And as he thought these afterthoughts Lady Beach-Mandarin's chauffeur darted and dodged and threaded his way with an alacrity that was almost distressing to Putney.

They ran over the ghost of Swinburne, at the foot of Putney Hill,—or perhaps it was only the rhythm of the engine changed for a moment, and in a couple of minutes more they were outside the Harman residence. "Here we are!" said Lady Beach-Mandarin, more capaciously gaminesque than ever. "We've done it now."

Mr. Brumley had an impression of a big house in the distended stately-homes-of-England style and very necessarily and abundantly covered by creepers and then he was assisting the ladies to descend and the three of them were waiting clustered in the ample Victorian doorway. For some little interval there came no answer to the bell Mr. Brumley had rung, but all three of them had a sense of hurried, furtive and noiseless readjustments in progress behind the big and bossy oak door. Then it opened and a very large egg-shaped butler with sandy whiskers appeared and looked down himself at them. There was something paternal about this man, his professional deference was touched by the sense of ultimate responsibility. He seemed to consider

for a moment whether he should permit Lady Harman
to be in, before he conceded that she was.

They were ushered through a hall that resembled
most of the halls in the world, it was dominated by a
handsome oak staircase and scarcely gave Miss Sharsper
a point, and then across a creation of the Victorian
architect, a massive kind of conservatory with classical
touches—there was an impluvium in the centre and
there were arches hung with manifestly costly Syrian
rugs, into a large apartment looking through four
French windows upon a verandah and a large floriferous
garden. At a sideways glance it seemed a very pleasant
garden indeed. The room itself was like the rooms of
so many prosperous people nowadays; it had an effect
of being sedulously and yet irrelevantly over-furnished.
It had none of the large vulgarity that Mr. Brumley
would have considered proper to a wealthy caterer, but
it confessed a compilation of " pieces," very carefully
authenticated. Some of them were rather splendid
" pieces "; three big bureaus burly and brassy dominated
it; there was a Queen Anne cabinet, some exquisite
coloured engravings, an ormolu mirror and a couple of
large French vases that set Miss Sharsper, who had a
keen eye for this traffic, confusedly cataloguing. And
a little incongruously in the midst of this exhibit,
stood Lady Harman, as if she was trying to conceal the
fact that she too was a visitor, in a creamy white dress
and dark and defensive and yet entirely unabashed.

The great butler gave his large vague impression of
Lady Beach-Mandarin's name, and stood aside and
withdrew.

"I've heard so much of you," said Lady Beach-
Mandarin advancing with hand upraised. "I had to
call. Mr. Brumley—— "

"Lady Beach-Mandarin met Sir Isaac at Black Strand," Mr. Brumley intervened to explain.

Miss Sharsper was as it were introduced by default.

"My vividest anticipations outdone," said Lady Beach-Mandarin, squeezing Lady Harman's fingers with enthusiasm. "And what a charming garden you have, and what a delightful situation! Such air! And on the very verge of London, high, on this delightful *literary* hill, and ready at any moment to swoop in that enviable great car of yours. I suppose you come a great deal into London, Lady Harman?"

"No," reflected Lady Harman, "not very much." She seemed to weigh the accuracy of this very carefully. "No," she added in confirmation.

"But you should, you ought to; it's your duty. You've no right to hide away from us. I was telling Sir Isaac. We look to him, we look to you. You've no right to bury your talents away from us; you who are rich and young and brilliant and beautiful——"

"But if I go on I shall begin to flatter you," said Lady Beach-Mandarin with a delicious smile. "I've begun upon Sir Isaac already. I've made him promise a hundred guineas and his name to the Shakespear Dinners Society,—nothing he didn't mention eaten (*you* know) and all the profits to the National movement —and I want your name too. I know you'll let us have your name too. Grant me that, and I'll subside into the ordinariest of callers."

"But surely; isn't his name enough?" asked Lady Harman.

"Without yours, it's only half a name!" cried Lady Beach-Mandarin. "If it were a *business* thing——! Different of course. But on my list, I'm like dear old Queen Victoria you know, the wives must come too."

" In that case," hesitated Lady Harman. . . . " But really I think Sir Isaac—— "

She stopped. And then Mr. Brumley had a psychic experience. It seemed to him as he stood observing Lady Harman with an entirely unnecessary and unpremeditated intentness, that for the briefest interval her attention flashed over Lady Beach-Mandarin's shoulder to the end verandah window; and following her glance, he saw—and then he did not see—the arrested figure, the white face of Sir Isaac, bearing an expression in which anger and horror were extraordinarily intermingled. If it was Sir Isaac he dodged back with amazing dexterity; if it was a phantom of the living it vanished with an air of doing that. Without came the sound of a flower-pot upset and a faint expletive. Mr. Brumley looked very quickly at Lady Beach-Mandarin, who was entirely unconscious of anything but her own uncoiling and enveloping eloquence, and as quickly at Miss Sharsper. But Miss Sharsper was examining a blackish bureau through her glasses as though she were looking for birth-marks and meant if she could find one to claim the piece as her own long-lost connection. With a mild but gratifying sense of exclusive complicity Mr. Brumley reverted to Lady Harman's entire self-possession.

" But, dear Lady Harman, it's entirely unnecessary you should consult him,—entirely," Lady Beach-Mandarin was saying.

" I'm sure," said Mr. Brumley with a sense that somehow he had to intervene, " that Sir Isaac would not possibly object. I'm sure that if Lady Harman consults him—— "

The sandy-whiskered butler appeared hovering.

" Shall I place the tea-things in the garden, me

lady," he asked, in the tone of one who knows the answer.

"Oh *please* in the garden!" cried Lady Beach-Mandarin. "Please! And how delightful to *have* a garden, a London garden, in which one *can* have tea. Without being smothered in blacks. The south-west wind. The dear *English* wind. All your blacks come to *us*, you know."

She led the way upon the verandah. "Such a wonderful garden! The space, the breadth! Why! you must have Acres!"

She surveyed the garden—comprehensively; her eye rested for a moment on a distant patch of black that ducked suddenly into a group of lilacs. "Is dear Sir Isaac at home?" she asked.

"He's very uncertain," said Lady Harman with a quiet readiness that pleased Mr. Brumley. "Yes, Snagsby, please, under the big cypress. And tell my mother and sister."

Lady Beach-Mandarin having paused a moment or so upon the verandah admiring the garden as a whole, now prepared to go into details. She gathered her ample skirts together and advanced into the midst of the large lawn, with very much of the effect of a fleet of captive balloons dragging their anchors. Mr. Brumley followed, as it were in attendance upon her and Lady Harman. Miss Sharsper, after one last hasty glance at the room, rather like the last hasty glance of a still unprepared schoolboy at his book, came behind with her powers of observation strainingly alert.

Mr. Brumley was aware of a brief mute struggle between the two ladies of title. It was clear that Lady Harman would have had them go to the left, to where down a vista of pillar roses a single large specimen

cypress sounded a faint but recognizable Italian note,
and he did his loyal best to support her, but Lady
Beach-Mandarin's attraction to that distant clump of
lilac on the right was equally great and much more
powerful. She flowed, a great and audible tide of
socially influential womanhood across the green spaces
of the garden, and drew the others with her. And it
seemed to Mr. Brumley—not that he believed his eyes
—that beyond those lilacs something ran out, something
black that crouched close to the ground and went very
swiftly. It flashed like an arrow across a further space
of flower-bed, dropped to the ground, became two
agitatedly receding boot soles and was gone. Had it
ever been? He glanced at Lady Harman, but she was
looking back with the naïve anxiety of a hostess to her
cypress,—at Lady Beach-Mandarin, but she was proliferating compliments and decorative scrolls and
flourishes like the engraved frontispiece to a seventeenth-
century book.

"I know I'm inordinately curious," said Lady
Beach-Mandarin, " but gardens are my Joy. I want to
go into every corner of this. Peep into everything.
And I feel somehow "—and here she urged a smile on
Lady Harman's attention—"that I shan't begin to
know *you*, until I know all your environment."

She turned the flank of the lilacs as she said these
words and advanced in echelon with a stately swiftness
upon the laurels beyond.

Lady Harman said there was nothing beyond but
sycamores and the fence, but Lady Beach-Mandarin
would press on through a narrow path that pierced the
laurel hedge, in order, she said, that she might turn
back and get the whole effect of the grounds.

And so it was they discovered the mushroom shed.

" A mushroom shed ! " cried Lady Beach-Mandarin. " And if we look in—shall we see hosts and regiments of mushrooms ? I must—I must."

" I *think* it is locked," said Lady Harman.

Mr. Brumley darted forward ; tried the door and turned quickly. " It's locked," he said and barred Lady Beach-Mandarin's advance.

" And besides," said Lady Harman, " there's no mushrooms there. They won't come up. It's one of my husband's—annoyances."

Lady Beach-Mandarin had turned round and now surveyed the house. " What a splendid idea," she cried, " that wistaria ! All mixed with the laburnum ! I don't think I have ever seen such a charming combination of blossoms ! "

The whole movement of the party swept about and faced cypress-ward. Away there the sandy-whiskered butler and a footman and basket chairs and a tea-table, with a shining white cloth, and two ladies were now grouping themselves. . . .

But the mind of Mr. Brumley gave little heed to these things. His mind was full of a wonder, and the wonder was this, that the mushroom shed had behaved like a living thing. The door of the mushroom shed was not locked and in that matter he had told a lie. The door of the mushroom shed had been unlocked quite recently and the key and padlock had been dropped upon the ground. And when he had tried to open the mushroom shed it had first of all yielded to his hand and then it had closed again with great strength—exactly as a living mussel will behave if one takes it unawares. But in addition to this passionate contraction the mushroom shed had sworn in a hoarse whisper and breathed hard, which is more than your mussel can do. . . .

§ 3

Mr. Brumley's interest in Lady Harman was to be almost too crowded by detail before that impulsive call was over. Superposed upon the mystery of the mushroom shed was the vivid illumination of Lady Harman by her mother and sister. They had an effect of having reluctantly become her social inferiors for her own good ; the mother—her name he learnt was Mrs. Sawbridge—had all Lady Harman's tall slenderness, but otherwise resembled her only in the poise of her neck and an occasional gesture ; she was fair and with a kind of ignoble and premeditated refinement in her speech and manner. She was dressed with the restraint of a prolonged and attenuated widowhood, in a rich and complicatedly quiet dress of mauve and grey. She was obviously a transitory visitor and not so much taking the opulence about her and particularly the great butler for granted as pointedly and persistently ignoring it in an effort to seem to take it for granted. The sister, on the other hand, had Lady Harman's pale darkness but none of her fineness of line. She missed altogether that quality of fineness. Her darkness was done with a quite perceptible heaviness, her dignity passed into solidity and her profile was, with an entire want of hesitation, handsome. She was evidently the elder by a space of some years and she was dressed with severity in grey.

These two ladies seemed to Mr. Brumley to offer a certain resistance of spirit to the effusion of Lady Beach-Mandarin, rather as two small anchored vessels might resist the onset of a great and foaming tide, but after a time it was clear they admired her greatly. His attention was, however, a little distracted from them by the fact that he was the sole representative of the more serviceable sex among five women and so in duty bound to stand by Lady Harman and assist with various handings and offerings. The tea equipage was silver and not only magnificent but, as certain quick movements of Miss Sharsper's eyes and nose at its appearance betrayed, very genuine and old.

Lady Beach-Mandarin having praised the house and garden all over again to Mrs. Sawbridge, and having praised the cypress and envied the tea things, resumed her efforts to secure the immediate establishment of permanent social relations with Lady Harman. She reverted to the question of the Shakespear Dinners Society and now with a kind of large skilfulness involved Mrs. Sawbridge in her appeal. "Won't *you* come on our Committee ?" said Lady Beach-Mandarin.

Mrs. Sawbridge gave a pinched smile and said she was only staying in London for quite a little time, and when pressed admitted that there seemed no need whatever for consulting Sir Isaac upon so obviously foregone a conclusion as Lady Harman's public adhesion to the great movement.

" I shall put his hundred guineas down to Sir Isaac and Lady Harman," said Lady Beach-Mandarin with an air of conclusion, " and now I want to know, dear Lady Harman, whether we can't have *you* on our Committee of administration. We want—just one other woman to complete us."

Lady Harman could only parry with doubts of her ability.

" You ought to go on, Ella," said Miss Sawbridge suddenly, speaking for the first time and in a manner richly suggestive of great principles at stake.

"Ella," thought the curious mind of Mr. Brumley. "And is that Eleanor now or Ellen or—is there any other name that gives one Ella? Simply Ella?"

"But what should I have to do?" fenced Lady Harman, resisting but obviously attracted.

Lady Beach-Mandarin invented a lengthy paraphrase for prompt acquiescences.

"I shall be chairwoman," she crowned it with. "I can so easily *see you through* as they say."

"Ella doesn't go out half enough," said Miss Sawbridge suddenly to Miss Sharsper, who was regarding her with furtive intensity—as if she was surreptitiously counting her features.

Miss Sharsper caught in mid observation started and collected her mind. "One ought to go out," she said. "Certainly."

"And independently," said Miss Sawbridge, with meaning.

"Oh independently!" assented Miss Sharsper. It was evident she would now have to watch her chance and begin counting all over again from the beginning.

Mr. Brumley had an impression that Mrs. Sawbridge had said something quite confidential in his ear. He turned perplexed.

"Such charming weather," the lady repeated in the tone of one who doesn't wish so pleasant a little secret to be too generally discussed.

"Never known a better summer," agreed Mr. Brumley.

And then all these minor eddies were submerged in Lady Beach-Mandarin's advance towards her next step, an invitation to lunch. "There," said she, "I'm not Victorian. I always separate husbands and wives—by at least a week. You must come alone."

It was clear to Mr. Brumley that Lady Harman wanted to come alone—and was going to accept, and equally clear that she and her mother and sister regarded this as a very daring thing to do. And when that was settled Lady Beach-Mandarin went on to the altogether easier topic of her Social Friends, a society of smart and influential women; who devoted a certain fragment of time every week to befriending respectable girls employed in London, in a briskly amiable manner, having them to special teas, having them to special evenings with special light refreshments, knowing their names as far as possible and asking about their relations, and generally making them feel that Society was being very frank and amiable to them and had an eye on them and meant them well, and was better for them than socialism and radicalism and revolutionary ideas. To this also Lady Harman it seemed was to come. It had an effect to Mr. Brumley's imagination as if the painted scene of that lady's life was suddenly bursting out into open doors—everywhere.

"Many of them are *quite* ladylike," echoed Mrs. Sawbridge suddenly, picking up the whole thing instantly and speaking over her tea cup in that quasi-confidential tone of hers to Mr. Brumley.

"Of course they are mostly quite dreadfully Sweated," said Lady Beach-Mandarin. Especially in the confectionery——" She thought of her position in time. "In the inferior class of confectioners' establishments," she said and then hurried on to: "Of course when you come to lunch,—Agatha Alimony. I'm most anxious for you and her to meet."

"Is that *the* Agatha Alimony?" asked Miss Sawbridge abruptly.

"The one and only," said Lady Beach-Mandarin

flashing a smile at her. " And what a marvel she is !
I do so want you to know her, Lady Harman. She'd
be a Revelation to you. . . ."

Everything had gone wonderfully so far. " And
now," said Lady Beach-Mandarin, thrusting forward a
face of almost exaggerated motherliness and with an
unwonted tenderness suffusing her voice, " show me the
Chicks."

There was a brief interrogative pause.

" Your Chicks," expanded Lady Beach-Mandarin,
on the verge of crooning. " Your *little* Chicks."

" *Oh !* " cried Lady Harman understanding. " The
children."

" Lucky woman ! " cried Lady Beach-Mandarin.
" Yes."

" One hasn't begun to be friends," she added,
" until one has seen—them. . . ."

" So *true*," Mrs. Sawbridge confided to Mr. Brumley
with a look that almost languished. . . .

" Certainly," said Mr. Brumley, " rather."

He was a little distraught because he had just seen
Sir Isaac step forward in a crouching attitude from
beyond the edge of the lilacs, peer at the tea-table
with a serpent-like intentness and then dart back
convulsively into cover. . . .

If Lady Beach-Mandarin saw him Mr. Brumley felt
that anything might happen. . . .

§ 4

Lady Beach-Mandarin always let herself go about
children.

It would be unjust to the general richness of Lady
Beach-Mandarin to say that she excelled herself on this

occasion. On all occasions Lady Beach-Mandarin
excelled herself. But never had Mr. Brumley noted
quite so vividly Lady Beach-Mandarin's habitual self-
surpassingness. She helped him, he felt, to understand
better those stories of great waves that sweep in from
the ocean and swamp islands and devastate whole
littorals. She poured into the Harman nursery and
filled every corner of it. She rose to unprecedented
heights therein. It seemed to him at moments that
they ought to make marks on the walls, like the marks
one sees on the houses in the lower valley of the Main to
record the more memorable floods. " The dears ! " she
cried ; " the *little* things ! " before the nursery door was
fairly opened.

(There should have been a line for that at once on
the jamb just below the lintel.)

The nursery revealed itself as a large airy white
and green apartment entirely free from old furniture
and done rather in the style of an aesthetically
designed hospital, with a tremendously humorous
decorative frieze of cocks and puppies and very
bright-coloured prints on the walls. The dwarfish
furniture was specially designed in green-stained wood
and the floor was of cork carpet diversified by white
furry rugs. The hospital quality was enhanced by the
uniformed and disciplined appearance of the middle-
aged and reliable head nurse and her subdued but
intelligent subordinate.

Three sturdy little girls, with a year step between
each of them, stood up to receive Lady Beach-
Mandarin's invasion ; an indeterminate baby sprawled
regardless of its dignity on a rug. " Aah ! " cried
Lady Beach-Mandarin, advancing in open order.
" Come and be hugged, you dears ! Come and be

hugged!" Before she knelt down and enveloped their shrinking little persons Mr. Brumley was able to observe that they were pretty little things, but not the beautiful children he could have imagined from Lady Harman. Peeping through their infantile delicacy, hints all too manifest of Sir Isaac's characteristically pointed nose gave Mr. Brumley a peculiar—a eugenic, qualm.

He glanced at Lady Harman and she was standing over the ecstasies of her tremendous visitor, polite, attentive—with an entirely unemotional speculation in her eyes. Miss Sawbridge, stirred by the great waves of violent philoprogenitive enthusiasm that circled out from Lady Beach-Mandarin, had caught up the baby and was hugging it and addressing it in terms of humorous rapture, and the nurse and her assistant were keeping respectful but wary eyes upon the handling of their four charges. Miss Sharsper was taking in the children's characteristics with a quick expertness. Mrs. Sawbridge stood a little in the background and caught Mr. Brumley's eye and proffered a smile of sympathetic tolerance. . . .

Mr. Brumley was moved by a ridiculous impulse, which he just succeeded in suppressing, to say to Mrs. Sawbridge, "Yes, I admit it looks very well. But the essential point, you know, is that it isn't so. . . ."

That it wasn't so, indeed, entirely dominated his impression of that nursery. There was Lady Beach-Mandarin winning Lady Harman's heart by every rule of the game, rejoicing effusively in those crowning triumphs of a woman's being, there was Miss Sawbridge vociferous in support and Mrs. Sawbridge almost offering to join hands in rapturous benediction, and there was Lady Harman wearing her laurels, not indeed with indifference but with a curious detachment. One might imagine her genuinely anxious to understand why Lady Beach-Mandarin was in such a stupendous ebullition. One might have supposed her a mere cold-hearted intellectual if it wasn't that something in her warm beauty absolutely forbade any such interpretation. There came to Mr. Brumley again a thought that had occurred to him first when Sir Isaac and Lady Harman had come together to Black Strand, which was that life had happened to this woman before she was ready for it, that her mind some years after her body was now coming to womanhood, was teeming with curiosity about all she had hitherto accepted, about Sir Isaac, about her children and all her circumstances. . . .

There was a recapitulation of the invitations, a renewed offering of outlooks and vistas and Agatha Alimony. "You'll not forget," insisted Lady Beach-Mandarin. "You'll not afterwards throw us over."

"No," said Lady Harman, with that soft determination of hers. "I'll certainly come."

"I'm so sorry, so very sorry, not to have seen Sir Isaac," Lady Beach-Mandarin insisted.

The raid had accomplished its every object and was drifting doorward. For a moment Lady Beach-Mandarin desisted from Lady Harman and threw her whole being into an eddying effort to submerge the already subjugated Mrs. Sawbridge. Miss Sawbridge was behind up the oak staircase explaining Sir Isaac's interest in furniture-buying to Miss Sharsper. Mr. Brumley had his one moment with Lady Harman.

"I gather," he said, and abandoned that sentence.

"I hope," he said, "that you will have my little house down there. I like to think of *you*—walking in my garden."

" I shall love that garden," she said. " But I shall feel unworthy."

" There are a hundred little things I want to tell you—about it."

Then all the others seemed to come into focus again, and with a quick mutual understanding—Mr. Brumley was certain of its mutuality—they said no more to one another. He was entirely satisfied he had said enough. He had conveyed just everything that was needed to excuse and explain and justify his presence in that company. . . . Upon a big table in the hall he noticed that a silk hat and an umbrella had appeared since their arrival. He glanced at Miss Sharsper but she was keenly occupied with the table legs. He began to breathe freely again when the partings were over and he could get back into the automobile. " Toot," said the horn and he made a last grave salutation to the slender white figure on the steps. The great butler stood at the side of the entrance and a step or so below her, with the air of a man who has completed a difficult task. A small attentive valet hovered out of the shadows behind.

§ 5

(A fragment of the conversation in Lady Beach-Mandarin's returning automobile may be recorded in a parenthesis here.

" But did you see Sir Isaac ? " she cried, abruptly.

" Sir Isaac ? " defended the startled Mr. Brumley. " Where ? "

" He was dodging about in the garden all the time."

" Dodging about the garden ! . . . I saw a sort of gardener—— "

"I'm sure I saw Him," said Lady Beach-Mandarin. "Positive. He hid away in the mushroom shed. The one you found locked."

"But my *dear* Lady Beach-Mandarin!" protested Mr. Brumley with the air of one who listens to preposterous suggestions. "What can make you think—— ?"

"Oh I *know* I saw him," said Lady Beach-Mandarin. "I know. He seemed all over the place. Like a Boy Scout. Didn't you see him too, Susan?"

Miss Sharsper was roused from deep preoccupation. "What, dear?" she asked.

"See Sir Isaac?"

"Sir Isaac?"

"Dodging about the garden when we went through it."

The novelist reflected. "I didn't notice," she said. "I was busy observing things.")

§ 6

Lady Beach-Mandarin's car passed through the open gates and was swallowed up in the dusty stream of traffic down Putney Hill; the great butler withdrew, the little manservant vanished, Mrs. Sawbridge and her elder daughter had hovered and now receded from the back of the hall; Lady Harman remained standing thoughtfully in the large Bulwer-Lyttonesque doorway of her house. Her face expressed a vague expectation. She waited to be addressed from behind.

Then she became aware of the figure of her husband standing before her. He had come out of the laurels in front. His pale face was livid with anger, his hair dishevelled, there was garden mould and greenness upon his knees and upon his extended hands.

She was startled out of her quiet defensiveness. "Why Isaac!" she cried. "Where have you been?"

It enraged him further to be asked so obviously unnecessary a question. He forgot his knightly chivalry.

"What the Devil do you mean," he cried, "by chasing me all round the garden?"

"Chasing you? All round the garden?"

"You heard me breaking my shins on that infernal flowerpot you put for me, and out you shot with all your pack of old women and chased me round the garden. What do you mean by it?"

"I didn't think you were in the garden."

"Any Fool could have told I was in the garden. Any Fool might have known I was in the garden. If I wasn't in the garden, then where the Devil was I? Eh? Where else could I be? Of course I was in the garden, and what you wanted was to hunt me down and make a fool of me. And look at me! Look, I say! Look at my hands!"

Lady Harman regarded the lord of her being and hesitated before she answered. She knew what she had to say would enrage him, but she had come to a point in their relationship when a husband's good temper is no longer a supreme consideration. "You've had plenty of time to wash them," she said.

"Yes," he shouted. "And instead I kept 'em to show you. I stayed out here to see the last of that crew for fear I might run against 'em in the house. Of all the infernal old women——"

His lips were providentially deprived of speech. He conveyed his inability to express his estimate of Lady Beach-Mandarin by a gesture of despair.

"If—if anyone calls and I am at home I have to receive them," said Lady Harman, after a moment's deliberation.

"Receiving them's one thing. Making a Fool of yourself——"

His voice was rising.

"Isaac," said Lady Harman, leaning forward and then in a low penetrating whisper, "*Snagsby!*"

(It was the name of the great butler.)

"*Damn* Snagsby!" hissed Sir Isaac, but dropping his voice and drawing near to her. What his voice lost in height it gained in intensity. "What I say is this, Ella, you oughtn't to have brought that old woman out into the garden at all——"

"She insisted on coming."

"You ought to have snubbed her. You ought to have done—anything. How the Devil was I to get away, once she was through the verandah? There I was! *Bagged!*"

"You could have come forward."

"What! And meet *her*!"

"*I* had to meet her."

Sir Isaac felt that his rage was being frittered away upon details. "If you hadn't gone fooling about looking at houses," he said, and now he stood very close to her and spoke with a confidential intensity, "you wouldn't have got that Holy Terror on our track, see? And now —here we are!"

He walked past her into the hall, and the little man-servant suddenly materialised in the middle of the space and came forward to brush him obsequiously. Lady Harman regarded that proceeding for some moments in a preoccupied manner and then passed slowly into the classical conservatory. She felt that in view of her engagements the discussion of Lady Beach-Mandarin was only just beginning.

§ 7

She reopened it herself in the long drawing-room into which they both drifted after Sir Isaac had washed the mould from his hands. She went to a French window, gathered courage, it seemed, by a brief contemplation of the garden, and turned with a little effort.

"I don't agree," she said, "with you about Lady Beach-Mandarin."

Sir Isaac appeared surprised. He had assumed the incident was closed. "*How?*" he asked compactly.

"I don't agree," said Lady Harman. "She seems friendly and jolly."

"She's a Holy Terror," said Sir Isaac. "I've seen her twice, Lady Harman."

"A call of that kind," his wife went on, " —when there are cards left and so on—has to be returned."

"You won't," said Sir Isaac.

Lady Harman took a blind-tassel in her hand,—she felt she had to hold on to something. "In any case," she said, "I should have to do that."

"In any case?"

She nodded. "It would be ridiculous not to. We—— It is why we know so few people—because we don't return calls. . . ."

Sir Isaac paused before answering. "We don't *want* to know a lot of people," he said. "And, besides—— Why! anybody could make us go running about all over London calling on them, by just coming and calling on us. No sense in it. She's come and she's gone, and there's an end of it."

"No," said Lady Harman, gripping her tassel more firmly. "I shall have to return that call."

"I tell you, you won't."

"It isn't only a call," said Lady Harman. "You see, I promised to go there to lunch."

"Lunch!"

"And to go to a meeting with her."

"Go to a meeting!"

"—of a society called the Social Friends. And something else. Oh! to go to the committee meetings of her Shakespear Dinners Movement."

"I've heard of that."

"She said you supported it—or else of course . . ."

Sir Isaac restrained himself with difficulty.

"Well," he said at last, "you'd better write and tell her you can't do any of these things; that's all."

He thrust his hands into his trousers pockets and walked to the French window next to the one in which she stood, with an air of having settled this business completely, and being now free for the tranquil contemplation of horticulture. But Lady Harman had still something to say.

"I am going to *all* these things," she said. "I said I would, and I will."

He didn't seem immediately to hear her. He made the little noise with his teeth that was habitual to him. Then he came towards her. "This is your infernal sister," he said.

Lady Harman reflected. "No," she decided. "It's myself."

"I might have known when we asked her here," said Sir Isaac with an habitual disregard of her judgments that was beginning to irritate her more and more. "You can't take on all these people. They're not the sort of people we want to know."

"I want to know them," said Lady Harman.

"I don't."

"I find them interesting," Lady Harman said. "And I've promised."

"Well you oughtn't to have promised without consulting me."

Her reply was the material of much subsequent reflection on the part of Sir Isaac. There was something in her manner . . .

"You see, Isaac," she said, "you kept so out of the way. . . ."

In the pause that followed her words, Mrs. Sawbridge appeared from the garden smiling with a determined amiability, and bearing a great bunch of the best roses (which Sir Isaac hated to have picked) in her hands.

CHAPTER THE FOURTH

THE BEGINNINGS OF LADY HARMAN

§ 1

LADY HARMAN had been married when she was just eighteen.

Mrs. Sawbridge was the widow of a solicitor who had been killed in a railway collision while his affairs, as she put it, were unsettled; and she had brought up her two daughters in a villa at Penge upon very little money, in a state of genteel protest. Ellen was the younger. She had been a sturdy dark-eyed doll-dragging little thing and had then shot up very rapidly. She had gone to a boarding-school at Wimbledon because Mrs. Sawbridge thought the Penge day-school had made Georgina opiniated and unladylike, besides developing her muscular system to an unrefined degree. The Wimbledon school was on less progressive lines, and anyhow Ellen grew taller and more feminine than her sister and by seventeen was already womanly, dignified and intensely admired by a number of schoolmates and a large circle of their cousins and brothers. She was generally very good and only now and then broke out with a venturesome enterprise that hurt nobody. She got out of a skylight, for example, and perambulated the roof in the moonshine to see how it felt and did one or two other little

74

things of a similar kind. Otherwise her conduct was admirable and her temper in those days was always contagiously good. That attractiveness which Mr. Brumley felt, was already very manifest, and a little hindered her in the attainment of other distinctions. Most of her lessons were done for her by willing slaves, and they were happy slaves because she abounded in rewarding kindnesses ; but on the other hand the study of English literature and music was almost forced upon her by the zeal of the two visiting Professors of these subjects.

And at seventeen, which is the age when girls most despise the boyishness of young men, she met Sir Isaac and filled him with an invincible covetousness. . . .

§ 2

The school at Wimbledon was a large, hushed, faded place presided over by a lady of hidden motives and great exterior calm named Miss Beeton Clavier. She was handsome without any improper attractiveness, an Associate in Arts of St. Andrew's University and a cousin of Mr. Blenker of the *Old Country Gazette*. She was assisted by several resident mistresses and two very carefully married visiting masters for music and Shakespear, and playground and shrubbery and tennis-lawn were all quite effectively hidden from the high-road. The curriculum included Latin Grammar—nobody ever got to the reading of books in that formidable tongue —French by an English lady who had been in France, Hanoverian German by an irascible native, the more seemly aspects of English history and literature, arithmetic, algebra, political economy and drawing. There was no hockey played within the precincts, science was taught without the clumsy apparatus or objectionable diagrams that are now so common, and stress was laid upon the carriage of the young ladies and the iniquity of speaking in raised voices. Miss Beeton Clavier deprecated the modern "craze for examinations," and released from such pressure her staff did not so much give courses of lessons as circle in a thorough-looking and patient manner about their subjects. This turn-spit quality was reflected in the school idiom ; one did not learn algebra or Latin or so forth, one *did* algebra, one was *put into* Latin. . . .

The girls went through this system of exercises and occupations, evasively and as it were *sotto voce*, making friends, making enemies, making love to one another, following instincts that urged them to find out something about life—in spite of the most earnest discouragement. . . . None of them believed for a moment that the school was preparing them for life. Most of them regarded it as a long inexplicable passage of blank, grey occupations through which they had to pass. Beyond was the sunshine.

Ellen gathered what came to her. She realized a certain beauty in music in spite of the biographies of great musicians, the technical enthusiasms and the general professionalism of her teacher ; the literature master directed her attention to memoirs and through these she caught gleams of understanding when the characters of history did for brief intervals cease to be rigidly dignified and institutional like Miss Beeton Clavier and became human—like schoolfellows. And one little spectacled mistress, who wore art dresses and adorned her class-room with flowers, took a great fancy to her, talked to her with much vagueness and emotion of High Aims, and lent her with an impressive furtiveness

the works of Emerson and Shelley and a pamphlet
by Bernard Shaw. It was a little difficult to understand what these writers were driving at, they were so
dreadfully clever, but it was clear they reflected
criticism upon the silences of her mother and the
rigidities of Miss Beeton Clavier.

In that suppressed and evasive life beneath the
outer forms and procedures of school and home, there
came glimmerings of something that seemed charged
with the promise of holding everything together, the
key, religion. She was attracted to religion, much
more attracted than she would confess even to herself,
but every circumstance in her training dissuaded her
from a free approach. Her mother treated religion
with a reverence that was almost indistinguishable
from huffiness. She never named the deity and she did
not like the mention of His name ; she threw a spell
of indelicacy over religious topics that Ellen never
thoroughly cast off. She put God among objectionable
topics—albeit a sublime one. Miss Beeton Clavier
sustained this remarkable suggestion. When she read
prayers in school she did so with the balanced
impartiality of one who offers no comment. She
seemed pained as she read and finished with a sigh.
Whatever she intended to convey, she conveyed that
even if the divinity was not all He should be, if, indeed,
He was a person almost primitive, having neither the
restraint nor the self-obliteration of a refined gentlewoman, no word of it should ever pass her lips. And so
Ellen as a girl never let her mind go quite easily into
this reconciling core of life, and talked of it only very
rarely and shyly with a few chosen coevals. It wasn't
very profitable talk. They had a guilty feeling, they
laughed a little uneasily, they displayed a fatal

proclivity to stab the swelling gravity of their souls with some forced and silly jest and so tumble back to ground again before they rose too high. . . .

Yet great possibilities of faith and devotion stirred already in the girl's heart. She thought little of God by day, but had a strange sense of Him in the starlight; never under the moonlight—that was in no sense divine—but in the stirring darkness of the stars. And it is remarkable that after a course of astronomical enlightenment by a visiting master and descriptions of masses and distances, incredible aching distances, then even more than ever she seemed to feel God among the stars. . . .

A fatal accident to a schoolfellow turned her mind for a time to the dark stillnesses of death. The accident happened away in Wales during the summer holidays; she saw nothing of it, she only knew of its consequence. Hitherto she had assumed it was the function of girls to grow up and go out from the grey intermediate state of school work into freedoms and realities beyond. Death happened, she was aware, to young people, but not she had thought to the people one knew. This termination came with a shock. The girl was no great personal loss to Ellen, they had belonged to different sets and classes, but the conception of her as lying very very still for ever was a haunting one. Ellen felt she did not want to be still for evermore in a confined space, with life and sunshine going on all about her and above her, and it quickened her growing appetite for living to think that she might presently have to be like that. How stifled one would feel!

It couldn't be like that.

She began to speculate about that future life upon which religion insists so much and communicates so

little. Was it perhaps in other planets, under those
wonderful, many-mooned, silver-banded skies? She
perceived more and more a kind of absurdity in
the existence all about her. Was all this world a
mere make-believe, and would Miss Beeton Clavier and
every one about her presently cast aside a veil?
Manifestly there was a veil. She had a very natural
disposition to doubt whether the actual circumstances
of her life were real. Her mother for instance was so
lacking in blood and fire, so very like the stiff paper
wrapping of something else. But if these things were
not real, what was real? What might she not presently
do? What might she not presently be? Perhaps
death had something to do with that. Was death
perhaps no more than the flinging off of grotesque
outer garments by the newly arrived guests at the feast
of living? She had that feeling that there might be
a feast of living.

These preoccupations were a jealously guarded secret,
but they gave her a quality of slight detachment that
added a dreaming dignity to her dark tall charm.

There were moments of fine, deep excitement that
somehow linked themselves in her mind with these
thoughts as being set over against the things of every
day. These too were moments quite different and
separate in quality from delight, from the keen appreciation of flowers or sunshine or little vividly living things.
Daylight seemed to blind her to them, as they blinded
her to starshine. They too had a quality of reference
to things large and remote, distances, unknown mysteries of light and matter, the thought of mountains,
cool white wildernesses and driving snowstorms, or great
periods of time. Such were the luminous transfigurations
that would come to her at the evening service in church.

The school used to sit in the gallery over against the organist, and for a year and more Ellen had the place at the corner from which she could look down the hazy candle-lit vista of the nave and see the congregation as ranks and ranks of dim faces and vaguely apprehended clothes, ranks that rose with a peculiar deep and spacious rustle to sing, and sang with a massiveness of effect she knew in no other music. Certain hymns in particular seemed to bear her up and carry her into another larger, more wonderful world : " Light's Abode, Celestial Salem " for example, a world of luminous spiritualized sensuousness. Of such a quality she thought the Heavenly City must surely be, away there and away. But this persuasion differed from those other mystical intimations in its detachment from any sense of the divinity. And remarkably mixed up with it and yet not belonging to it, antagonistic and kindred like a silver dagger stuck through a mystically illuminated parchment, was the angelic figure of a tall fair boy in a surplice who stood out amidst the choir below and sang, it seemed to her, alone.

She herself on these occasions of exaltation would be far too deeply moved to sing. She was inundated by a swimming sense of boundaries nearly transcended, as though she was upon the threshold of a different life altogether, the real enduring life, and as though if she could only maintain herself long enough in this shimmering exaltation she would get right over ; things would happen, things that would draw her into that music and magic and prevent her ever returning to everyday life again. There one would walk through music between great candles under eternal stars, hand-in-hand with a tall white figure. But nothing ever did happen to make her cross that boundary ; the hymn ceased, the "Amen" died away, as if a curtain fell. The congregation subsided. Reluctantly she would sink back into her seat. . . .

But all through the sermon, to which she never gave the slightest attention, her mind would feel mute and stilled, and she used to come out of church silent and preoccupied, returning unwillingly to the commonplaces of life. . . .

§ 3

Ellen met Sir Isaac—in the days before he was Sir Isaac—at the house of a school friend with whom she was staying at Hythe, and afterwards her mother and sister came down and joined her for a fortnight at a Folkestone boarding house. Mr. Harman had caught a chill while inspecting his North Wales branches and had come down with his mother to recuperate. He and his mother occupied a suite of rooms in the most imposing hotel upon the Leas. Ellen's friend's people were partners in a big flour firm and had a pleasant new æsthetic white and green house of roughcast and slates in the pretty country beyond the Hythe golf links, and Ellen's friend's father was deeply anxious to develop amiable arrangements with Mr. Harman. There was much tennis, much croquet, much cycling to the Hythe sea-wall and bathing from little tents and sitting about in the sunshine, and Mr. Harman had his first automobile with him—they were still something of a novelty in those days—and was urgent to take picnic parties to large lonely places on the downs.

There were only two young men in that circle, one was engaged to Ellen's friend's sister, and the other was bound to a young woman remote in Italy; neither was strikingly attractive and both regarded Harman with that awe tempered by undignified furtive derision which wealth and business capacity so often inspire in the young male. At first he was quiet and simply looked at her, as it seemed any one might look, then she perceived he looked at her intently and continuously, and was persistently close to her and seemed always to be trying to do things to please her and attract her attention. And then from the general behaviour of the women about her, her mother and Mrs. Harman and her friend's mother and her friend's sister, rather than from any one specific thing they said, it grew upon her consciousness that this important and fabulously wealthy person, who was also it seemed to her so modest and quiet and touchingly benevolent, was in love with her.

" Your daughter," said Mrs. Harman repeatedly to Mrs. Sawbridge, " is charming, perfectly charming."

" She's *such* a child," said Mrs. Sawbridge repeatedly in reply.

And she told Ellen's friend's mother apropos of Ellen's friend's engagement that she wanted all her daughters to marry for love, she didn't care what the man had so long as they loved each other, and meanwhile she took the utmost care that Isaac had undisputed access to the girl, was watchfully ready to fend off anyone else, made her take everything he offered and praised him quietly and steadily to her. She pointed out how modest and unassuming he was, in spite of the fact that he was " controlling an immense business " and in his own particular trade " a perfect Napoleon."

" For all one sees to the contrary he might be just a private gentleman. And he feeds thousands and thousands of people. . . ."

"Sooner or later," said Mrs. Harman, " I suppose Isaac will marry. He's been such a good son to me that I shall feel it dreadfully, and yet, you know, I wish I could see him settled. Then *I* shall settle—in a little house of my own somewhere. Just a little place. I don't believe in coming too much between son and daughter-in-law. . . ."

Harman's natural avidity was tempered by a proper modesty. He thought Ellen so lovely and so infinitely desirable—and indeed she was—that it seemed incredible to him that he could ever get her. And yet he had got most of the things in life he had really and urgently wanted. His doubts gave his love-making an eager, lavish and pathetic delicacy. He watched her minutely in an agony of appreciation. He felt ready to give or promise anything.

She was greatly flattered by his devotion and she liked the surprises and presents he heaped upon her extremely. Also she was sorry for him beyond measure. In the deep recesses of her heart was an oleographic ideal of a large brave young man with blue eyes, a wave in his fair hair, a wonderful tenor voice and —she could not help it, she tried to look away and not think of it—a broad chest. With him she intended to climb mountains. So clearly she could not marry Mr. Harman. And because of that she tried to be very kind indeed to him, and when he faltered that she could not possibly care for him, she reassured him so vaguely as to fill him with wild gusts of hope and herself with a sense of pledges. He told her one day between two sets of tennis—which he played with a certain tricky skill—that he felt that the very highest happiness he could ever attain would be to die at her feet. Presently her pity and her sense of responsibility had become so large and deep that the dream hero with the blue eyes was largely overlaid and hidden by them.

Then, at first a little indirectly and then urgently and with a voice upon the edge of tears, Harman implored her to marry him. She had never before in the whole course of her life seen a grown-up person on the verge of tears. She felt that the release of such deep fountains as that must be averted at any cost. She felt that for a mere schoolgirl like herself, a backward schoolgirl who had never really mastered quadratics, to cause these immense and tragic distresses was abominable. She was sure her former head-mistress would disapprove very highly of her. " I will make you a queen," said Harman, " I will give all my life to your happiness."

She believed he would.

She refused him for the second time but with a weakening certainty in a little white summer-house that gave a glimpse of the sea between green and wooded hills. She sat and stared at the sea after he had left her, through a mist of tears ; so pitiful did he seem. He had beaten his poor fists on the stone table and then caught up her hand, kissed it and rushed out. . . . She had not dreamt that love could hurt like that.

And all that night—that is to say for a full hour before her wet eyelashes closed in slumber—she was sleepless with remorse for the misery she was causing him.

The third time when he said with suicidal conviction that he could not live without her, she burst into tears of pity and yielded. And instantly, amazingly, with the famished swiftness of a springing panther he caught her body into his arms and kissed her on the lips. . . .

§ 4

They were married with every circumstance of splendour, with very expensive music, and portraits in the illustrated newspapers and a great glitter of favours and carriages. The bridegroom was most thoughtful and generous about the Sawbridge side of the preparations. Only one thing was a little perplexing. In spite of his impassioned impatience he delayed the wedding. Full of dark hints and a portentous secret, he delayed the wedding for twenty-five whole days in order that it should follow immediately upon the publication of the birthday honours list. And then they understood.

" You will be Lady Harman," he exulted; " *Lady* Harman. I would have given double. . . . I have had to back the *Old Country Gazette* and I don't care a rap. I'd have done anything. I'd have bought the rotten thing outright. . . . Lady Harman ! "

He remained loverlike until the very eve of their marriage. Then suddenly it seemed to her that all the people she cared for in the world were pushing her away from them towards him, giving her up, handing her over. He became—possessive. His abjection changed to pride. She perceived that she was going to be left tremendously alone with him, with an effect, as if she had stepped off a terrace on to what she believed to be land and had abruptly descended into very deep water. . . .

And while she was still feeling quite surprised by everything and extremely doubtful whether she wanted to go any further with this business, which was manifestly far more serious, out of all proportion

more serious, than anything that had ever happened
to her before—and *unpleasant*, abounding indeed in
crumpling indignities and horrible nervous stresses, it
dawned upon her that she was presently to be that
strange, grown-up and pre-occupied thing, a mother,
and that girlhood and youth and vigorous games,
mountains and swimming and running and leaping
were over for her as far as she could see for ever. . . .

Both the prospective grandmothers became
wonderfully kind and helpful and intimate, preparing
with gusto and an agreeable sense of delegated responsibility for the child that was to give them all the
pride of maternity again and none of its inconveniences.

CHAPTER THE FIFTH

THE WORLD ACCORDING TO SIR ISAAC

§ 1

HER marriage had carried Ellen out of the narrow world of home and school into another that had seemed at first vastly larger, if only on account of its freedom from the perpetual achievement of small economies. Hitherto the urgent necessity of these had filled life with irksome precautions and clipped the wings of every dream. This new life into which Sir Isaac led her by the hand promised not only that release but more light, more colour, more movement, more people. There was to be at any rate so much in the way of rewards and compensation for her pity of him.

She found the establishment at Putney ready for her. Sir Isaac had not consulted her about it, it had been his secret, he had prepared it for her with meticulous care as a surprise. They returned from a honeymoon in Skye in which the attentions of Sir Isaac and the comforts of a first-class hotel had obscured a marvellous background of sombre mountain and wide stretches of shining sea. Sir Isaac had been very fond and insistent and inseparable, and she was doing her best to conceal a strange distressful jangling of her nerves which she now feared might presently dispose her to

scream.   Sir Isaac had been goodness itself, but how
she craved now for solitude !   She was under the
impression now that they were going to his mother's
house in Highbury.   Then she thought he would have
to go away to business for part of the day at any rate,
and she could creep into some corner and begin to
think of all that had happened to·her in these short
summer months.

They were met at Euston by his motor-car.
"*Home*," said Sir Isaac, with a little gleam of excitement, when the more immediate luggage was aboard.

As they hummed through the West-End afternoon
Ellen became aware that he was whistling through his
teeth. It was his invariable indication of mental activity,
and her attention came drifting back from her idle
contemplation of the shoppers and strollers of Piccadilly
to link this already alarming symptom with the
perplexing fact that they were manifestly travelling
west.

" But this," she said presently, " is Knightsbridge."

" Goes to Kensington," he replied with attempted
indifference.

" But your mother doesn't live this way."

" *We* do," said Sir Isaac, shining at every point of
his face.

" But," she halted.   " Isaac !—where are we
going ? "

" Home," he said.

" You've not taken a house ? "

" Bought it."

" But,—it won't be ready ! "

" I've seen to that."

" Servants ! " she cried in dismay.

" That's all right."   His face broke into an excited

smile. His little eyes danced and shone. "Every-thing," he said.

"But the servants!" she said.

"You'll see," he said. "There's a butler—and everything."

"A butler!" He could now no longer restrain himself. "I was weeks," he said, "getting it ready. Weeks and weeks. . . . It's a house. . . . I'd had my eye on it before ever I met you. It's a real *good* house, Elly. . . ."

The fortunate girl-wife went on through Brompton to Walham Green with a stunned feeling. So women have felt in tumbrils. A nightmare of butlers, a galaxy of possible butlers, filled her soul.

No one was quite so big and formidable as Snagsby, towering up to receive her, upon the steps of the home her husband was so amazingly giving her.

The reader has already been privileged to see some-thing of this house in the company of Lady Beach-Mandarin. At the top of the steps stood Mrs. Crumble, the new and highly recommended cook-housekeeper in her best black silk flounced and expanded, and behind her peeped several neat maids in caps and aprons. A little valet-like under-butler appeared and tried to balance Snagsby by hovering two steps above him on the opposite side of the Victorian mediæval porch.

Assisted officiously by Snagsby and amidst the deferential unhelpful gestures of the under-butler, Sir Isaac handed his wife out of the car. "Everything all right, Snagsby?" he asked brusquely if a little breathless.

"Everything in order, Sir Isaac."

"And here;—this is her ladyship."

"I 'ope her ladyship 'ad a pleasant journey to 'er

new 'ome. I'm sure if I may presume, Sir Isaac, we shall all be very glad to serve her ladyship."

(Like all well-trained English servants, Snagsby always dropped as many h's as he could when conversing with his superiors. He did this as a mark of respect and to prevent social confusion, just as he was always careful to wear a slightly misfitting dress coat and fold his trousers so that they creased at the sides and had a wide flat effect in front.)

Lady Harman bowed a little shyly to his good wishes and was then led up to Mrs. Crumble, in a stiff black silk, who curtseyed with a submissive amiability to her new mistress. "I'm sure, me lady," she said. " I'm sure—— "

There was a little pause. " Here they are, you see, right and ready," said Sir Isaac, and then with an inspiration, " Got any tea for us, Snagsby ? "

Snagsby addressing his mistress inquired if he should serve tea in the garden or the drawing-room, and Sir Isaac decided for the garden.

" There's another hall beyond this," he said, and took his wife's arm, leaving Mrs. Crumble still bowing amiably before the hall table. And every time she bowed she rustled richly. . . .

" It's quite a big garden," said Sir Isaac.

§ 2

And so the woman who had been a girl three weeks ago, this tall, dark-eyed, slightly perplexed and very young-looking lady, was introduced to the home that had been made for her. She went about it with an alarmed sense of strange responsibilities, not in the least feeling that anything was being given to her. And

Sir Isaac led her from point to point full of the pride
and joy of new possession—for it was his first own
house as well as hers—rejoicing over it and exacting
gratitude.

" It's all right, isn't it ? " he asked looking up at her.

" It's wonderful.   I'd no idea."

" See," he said, indicating a great brass bowl of
perennial sunflowers on the landing, " your favourite
flower ! "

" My favourite flower ? "

" You said it was—in that book.   Perennial
sunflower."

She was perplexed and then remembered.

She understood now why he had said downstairs,
when she had glanced at a big photographic enlargement of a portrait of Doctor Barnardo, " your favourite
hero in real life."

He had brought her at Hythe one day a popular
Victorian device, a confession album, in which she had
had to write down on a neat rose-tinted page, her
favourite author, her favourite flower, her favourite
colour, her favourite hero in real life, her " pet
aversion," and quite a number of such particulars of
her subjective existence.   She had filled this page in a
haphazard manner late one night, and she was disconcerted to find how thoroughly her careless replies
had come home to roost.   She had put down " pink "
as her favourite colour because the page she was writing
upon suggested it, and the paper of the room was
pale pink, the curtains strong pink with a pattern of
paler pink and tied with large pink bows, and the
lamp shades, the bedspread, the pillow-cases, the
carpet, the chairs, the very crockery—everything but
the omnipresent perennial sunflowers—was pink.

Confronted with this realization, she understood that pink was the least agreeable of all possible hues for a bedroom. She perceived she had to live now in a chromatic range between rather underdone mutton and salmon. She had said that her favourite musical composers were Bach and Beethoven; she really meant it, and a bust of Beethoven materialized that statement, but she had made Doctor Barnardo her favourite hero in real life because his name also began with a B and she had heard someone say somewhere that he was a very good man. The predominance of George Eliot's pensive rather than delightful countenance in her bedroom and the array of all that lady's works in a lusciously tooled pink leather, was due to her equally reckless choice of a favourite author. She had said too that Nelson was her favourite historical character, but Sir Isaac with a delicate jealousy had perferred to have this heroic but regrettably immoral personality represented in his home only by an engraving of the Battle of Copenhagen. . . .

She stood surveying this room, and her husband watched her eagerly. She was, he felt, impressed at last ! . . .

Certainly she had never seen such a bedroom in her life. By comparison even with the largest of the hotel apartments they had occupied it was vast; it had writing-tables and a dainty bookcase and a blushing sofa, and dressing-tables and a bureau and a rose-red screen and three large windows. Her thoughts went back to the narrow little bedroom at Penge with which she had hitherto been so entirely content. Her own few little books, a photograph or so,—they'd never dare to come here, even if she dared to bring them.

"Here," said Sir Isaac, flinging open a white door, " is your dressing-room."

She was chiefly aware of a huge white bath standing on a marble slab under a window of crinkled pink-stained glass, and of a wide space of tiled floor with white fur rugs.

"And here," he said, opening a panel that was covered by wall paper, "is *my* door."

"Yes," he said to the question in her eyes, "that's my room. You got this one—for your own. It's how people do now. People of our position. . . . There's no lock."

He shut the door slowly again and surveyed the splendours he had made with infinite satisfaction.

"All right?" he said, "isn't it?" . . . He turned to the pearl for which the casket was made, and slipped an arm about her waist. His arm tightened.

"Got a kiss for me, Elly?" he whispered.

At this moment, a gong almost worthy of Snagsby summoned them to tea. It came booming in to them with a vast officious arrogance that brooked no denial. It made one understand the imperatives of the Last Trump, albeit with a greater dignity. . . . There was a little awkward pause.

"I'm so dirty and trainy," she said, disengaging herself from his arm. "And we ought to go to tea."

§ 3

The same exceptional aptitude of Sir Isaac for detailed administration that had relieved his wife from the need of furnishing and arranging a home, made the birth of her children and the organization of her nursery an almost detached affair for her. Sir Isaac went about in a preoccupied way, whistling between his teeth and planning with expert advice the equipment of an ideal nursery, and her mother and his mother became as it were voluminous clouds of uncommunicative wisdom and precaution. In addition the conversation of Miss Crump, the extremely skilled and costly nurse, who arrived a full Advent before the child, fresh from the birth of a viscount, did much to generalize whatever had remained individual of this thing that was happening. With so much intelligence focussed, there seemed to Lady Harman no particular reason why she should not do her best to think as little as possible about the impending affair, which meant for her, she now understood quite clearly, more and more discomfort culminating in an agony. The summer promised to be warm, and Sir Isaac took a furnished house for the great event in the hills behind Torquay. The maternal instinct is not a magic thing, it has to be evoked and developed, and I decline to believe it is indicative of any peculiar unwomanliness in Lady Harman that when at last she beheld her newly-born daughter in the hands of the experts, she moaned druggishly, "Oh! please take it away. Oh! Take it—away. Anywhere—anywhere."

It was very red and wrinkled and aged-looking and, except when it opened its mouth to cry, extraordinarily like its father. This resemblance disappeared—along with a crop of darkish red hair—in the course of a day or two, but it left a lurking dislike to its proximity in her mind long after it had become an entirely infantile and engaging baby.

§ 4

Those early years of their marriage were the happiest period of Sir Isaac's life.

He seemed to have everything that man could desire. He was still only just forty at his marriage; he had made for himself a position altogether dominant in the world of confectionery and popular refreshment, he had won a title, he had a home after his own heart, a beautiful young wife, and presently delightful children in his own image, and it was only after some years of contentment and serenity and with a certain incredulity that he discovered that something in his wife, something almost in the nature of discontent with her lot, was undermining and threatening all the comfort and beauty of his life.

Sir Isaac was one of those men whom modern England delights to honour, a man of unpretentious acquisitiveness, devoted to business and distracted by no æsthetic or intellectual interests. He was the only son of his mother, the widow of a bankrupt steam-miller, and he had been a delicate child to rear. He left Mr. Gambard's college at Ealing after passing the second-class examination of the College of Preceptors at the age of sixteen, to go into a tea-office as clerk without a salary, a post he presently abandoned for a clerkship in the office of a large refreshment catering firm. He attracted the attention of his employers by suggesting various administrative economies, and he was already drawing a salary of two hundred and fifty pounds a year when he was twenty-one. Many young men would have rested satisfied with so rapid an advancement, and would have devoted themselves to the amusements that are now considered so permissible to youth, but young Harman was made of sterner stuff, and it only spurred him to further efforts. He contrived to save a considerable proportion of his salary for some years, and at the age of twenty-seven he

started, in association with a firm of flour millers, the
International Bread and Cake Stores, which spread
rapidly over the country. They were not in any
sense of the word " International," but in a search for
inflated and inflating adjectives this word attracted
him most, and the success of the enterprise justified
his choice. Originally conceived as a syndicated
system of baker's shops running a specially gritty
and nutritious line of bread, the Staminal Bread, in
addition to the ordinary descriptions, it rapidly
developed a catering side, and in a little time there
were few centres of clerkly employment in London
or the Midlands where an International could not be
found supplying the midday scone or poached egg,
washed down by a cup of tea, or coffee, or lemonade.
It meant hard work for Isaac Harman. It drew lines
on his cheeks, sharpened his always rather pointed
nose to an extreme efficiency, greyed his hair, and gave
an acquired firmness to his rather retreating mouth.
All his time was given to the details of this development ; always he was inspecting premises, selecting
and dismissing managers, making codes of rules and
fines for his growing army of employees, organizing
and reorganizing his central offices and his central
bakeries, hunting up cheaper and cheaper supplies of
eggs and flour, and milk and ham, devising advertisements and agency developments. He had something
of an artist's passion in these things ; he went about, a
little bent and peaky, calculating and planning and
hissing through his teeth, and feeling not only that he
was getting on, but that he was getting on in the most
exemplary way. Manifestly, anybody in his line of
business who wanted to be leisurely, or to be generous,
who possessed any broader interests than the shop,

who troubled to think about the nation or the race or any of the deeper mysteries of life, was bound to go down before him. He dealt privately with every appetite —until his marriage no human being could have suspected him of any appetite but business—he disposed of every distracting impulse with unobtrusive decision ; and even his political inclination towards Radicalism sprang chiefly from an irritation with the legal advantages of landlordism natural to a man who is frequently leasing shops.

At school Sir Isaac had not been a particularly prominent figure ; his disposition at cricket to block and to bowl " sneaks " and " twisters " under-arm had raised his average rather than his reputation ; he had evaded fights and dramatic situations, and protected himself upon occasions of unavoidable violence by punching with his white knuckles held in a peculiar and vicious manner. He had always been a little insensitive to those graces of style, in action if not in art, which appeal so strongly to the commoner sort of English mind ; he played first for safety, and that assured, for the uttermost advantage. These tendencies became more marked with maturity. When he took up tennis for his health's sake he developed at once an ungracious service that had to be killed like vermin ; he developed an instinct for the deadest ball available, and his returns close up to the net were like assassinations. Indeed, he was inherently incapable of any vision beyond the express prohibitions and permissions of the rules of the games he played, or beyond the laws and institutions under which he lived. His idea of generosity was the undocumented and unqualified purchase of a person by payments made in the form of a gift.

And this being the quality of Sir Isaac's mind, it followed that his interpretations of the relationship of marriage were simple and strict. A woman, he knew, had to be wooed to be won, but when she was won, she was won. He did not understand wooing after that was settled. There was the bargain and her surrender. He on his side had to keep her, dress her, be kind to her, give her the appearances of pride and authority, and in return he had his rights and his privileges and undefined powers of control. That you know, by the existing rules is the reality of marriage where there are no settlements and no private property of the wife's. That is to say, it is the reality of marriage in ninety-nine cases out of the hundred. And it would have shocked Sir Isaac extremely, and as a matter of fact it did shock him, for any one to suggest the slightest revision of so entirely advantageous an arrangement. He was confident of his good intentions, and resolved to the best of his ability to make his wife the happiest of living creatures, subject only to reasonable acquiescences and general good behaviour.

Never before had he cared for anything so much as he did for her—not even for the International Bread and Cake Stores. He gloated upon her. She distracted him from business. He resolved from the outset to surround her with every luxury and permit her no desire that he had not already anticipated. Even her mother and Georgina, whom he thought extremely unnecessary persons, were frequent visitors to his house. His solicitude for her was so great that she found it difficult even to see her doctor except in his presence. And he bought her a pearl necklace that cost six hundred pounds. He was, in fact, one of those complete husbands who grow rare in these decadent days.

The social circle to which Sir Isaac introduced his wife was not a very extensive one. The business misadventures of his father had naturally deprived his mother of most of her friends; he had made only acquaintances at school, and his subsequent concentration upon business had permitted very few intimacies. Renewed prosperity had produced a certain revival of cousins, but Mrs. Harman, established in a pleasant house at Highbury, had received their attentions with a well-merited stiffness. His chief associates were his various business allies, and these and their wives and families formed the nucleus of the new world to which Ellen was gradually and temperately introduced. There were a few local callers, but Putney is now too deeply merged with London for this practice of the countryside to have any great effect upon a new-comer's visiting circle.

Perhaps Mr. Charterson might claim to be Sir Isaac's chief friend at the time of that gentleman's marriage. Transactions in sugar had brought them together originally. He was Sir Isaac's best man, and the new knight entertained a feeling of something very like admiration for him. Moreover, Mr. Charterson had very large ears, more particularly was the left one large, extraordinarily large and projecting upper teeth, which he sought vainly to hide beneath an extravagant moustache, and a harsh voice, characteristics that did much to allay the anxieties natural to a newly married man. Mr. Charterson was moreover adequately married to a large, attentive, enterprising, swarthy wife, and possessed a splendid house in Belgravia. Not quite so self-made as Sir Isaac, he was still sufficiently self-made to take a very keen interest in his own social advancement and in social advancement generally, and it was through him that Sir Isaac's attention had been first directed to those developing relations with politics that arise as a business grows to greatness. "I'm for Parliament," said Charterson. "Sugar's in politics, and I'm after it. You'd better come too, Harman. Those chaps up there, they'll play jiggery-pokery with sugar if we aren't careful. And it won't be only sugar, Harman!"

Pressed to expand this latter sentence, he pointed out to his friend that "any amount of interfering with employment" was in the air—"any amount."

"And besides," said Mr. Charterson, "men like us have a stake in the country, Harman. We're getting biggish people. We ought to do our share. I don't see the fun of leaving everything to the landlords and the lawyers. Men of our sort have got to make ourselves felt. We want a business government. Of course—one pays. So long as I get a voice in calling the tune I don't mind paying the piper a bit. There's going to be a lot of interference with trade. All this social legislation. And there's what you were saying the other day about these leases. . . ."

"I'm not much of a talker," said Harman. "I don't see myself gassing in the House."

"Oh! I don't mean going into Parliament," said Charterson. "That's for some of us, perhaps. . . . But come into the party, make yourself felt. . . ."

Under Charterson's stimulation it was that Harman joined the National Liberal Club, and presently went on to the Climax, and through him he came to know something of that inner traffic of arrangements and bargains which does so much to keep a great historical party together and maintain its vitality. For a time he was largely overshadowed by the sturdy Radicalism of Charterson, but presently as he understood this interesting game better, he embarked upon a line of his own. Charterson wanted a seat, and presently got it; his maiden speech on the Sugar Bounties won a compliment from Mr. Evesham; and Harman, who would have piloted a monoplane sooner than address the House, decided to be one of those silent influences that work outside our national assembly. He came to the help of an embarrassed Liberal weekly, and then, in a Fleet Street crisis, undertook the larger share of backing the *Old Country Gazette*, that important social and intellectual party organ. His knighthood followed almost automatically.

Such political developments introduced a second element into the intermittent social relations of the Harman household. Before his knighthood and marriage Sir Isaac had participated in various public banquets and private parties and little dinners in the vaults of the House and elsewhere, arising out of his political intentions, and with the appearance of a Lady Harman there came a certain urgency on the part of those who maintain in a state of hectic dullness the social activities of the great Liberal party. Horatio Blenker, Sir Isaac's editor, showed a disposition to be socially very helpful, and after Mrs. Blenker had called in a state of worldly instructiveness, there was a little dinner at the Blenkers' to introduce young Lady Harman to the great political world. It was the first dinner-party of her life, and she found it dazzling rather than really agreeable.

She felt very slender and young and rather unclothed about the arms and neck, in spite of the six hundred pound pearl necklace that had been given to her just as she stood before the mirror in her white-and-gold dinner dress ready to start. She had to look down at that dress ever and again and at her shining arms to remind herself that she wasn't still in school-girl clothes, and it seemed to her there was not another woman in the room who was not fairly entitled to send her off to bed at any moment. She had been a little nervous about the details of the dinner, but there was nothing strange or difficult but caviare, and in that case she waited for some one else to begin. The Chartersons were there, which was very reassuring, and the abundant flowers on the table were a sort of protection. The man on her right was very nice, gently voluble, and evidently quite deaf, so that she had merely to make kind respectful faces at him. He talked to her most of the time, and described the peasant costumes in Marken and Walcheren. And Mr. Blenker, with a fine appreciation of Sir Isaac's watchful temperament and his own magnetism, spoke to her three times and never looked at her once all through the entertainment.

A few weeks later they went to dinner at the Chartersons', and then she gave a dinner, which was arranged very skilfully by Sir Isaac and Snagsby and the cook-housekeeper, with a little outside help, and then came a big party reception at Lady Barleypound's, a multitudinous miscellaneous assembly in which the obviously wealthy rubbed shoulders with the obviously virtuous and the not quite so obviously clever. It was a great orgy of standing about and seeing the various Blenkers and the Cramptons and the Weston Massinghays and the Daytons and Mrs. Millingham with her quivering lorgnette and her last tame genius and Lewis, and indeed all the Tapirs and Tadpoles of Liberalism,

being tremendously active and influential and important throughout the evening. The house struck Ellen
as being very splendid, the great staircase particularly
so, and never before had she seen a great multitude of
people in evening dress. Lady Barleypound in the
golden parlour at the head of the stairs shook hands
automatically, lost it would seem in some amiable dream,
Mrs. Blapton and a daughter rustled across the gathering in a hasty vindictive manner and vanished, and a
number of handsome, glittering, dark-eyed, splendidly
dressed women kept together in groups and were
tremendously but occultly amused. The various
Blenkers seemed everywhere, Horatio in particular with
his large fluent person and his luminous tenor was like
a shop-walker taking customers to the departments : one
felt he was weaving all these immiscibles together into
one great wise Liberal purpose, and that he deserved
quite wonderful things from the party; he even
introduced five or six people to Lady Harman, looking
sternly over her head and restraining his charm as he
did so on account of Sir Isaac's feelings. The people
he brought up to her were not very interesting people,
she thought, but then that was perhaps due to her own
dreadful ignorance of politics. . . .

Lady Harman ceased even to dip into the vortex of
London society after March, and in June she went with
her mother and a skilled nurse to that beautiful
furnished house Sir Isaac had found near Torquay, in
preparation for the birth of their first little daughter.

§ 5

It seemed to her husband that it was both unreasonable and ungrateful of her to become a tearful young

woman after their union, and for a phase of some months she certainly was a tearful young woman, but his mother made it clear to him that this was quite a correct and permissible phase for her, as she was, and so he expressed his impatience with temperance, and presently she was able to pull herself together and begin to readjust herself to a universe that had seemed for a time almost too shattered for endurance. She resumed the process of growing up that her marriage had for a time so vividly interrupted, and if her school-days were truncated and the college phase omitted, she had at any rate a very considerable amount of fundamental experience to replace these now customary completions.

Three little girls she brought into the world in the first three years of her married life, then after a brief interval of indifferent health she had a fourth girl baby of a physique quite obviously inferior to its predecessors, and then, after—and perhaps as a consequence of—much whispered conversation of the two mothers-in-law, protests and tactful explanation on the part of the elderly and trustworthy family doctor and remarks of an extraordinary breadth (and made at table too, almost before the door had closed on Snagsby!) from Ellen's elder sister, there came a less reproductive phase. . . .

But by that time Lady Harman had acquired the habit of reading and the habit of thinking over what she read, and from that it is an easy step to thinking over oneself and the circumstances of one's own life. The one thing trains for the other.

Now the chief circumstance in the life of Lady Harman was Sir Isaac. Indeed as she grew to a clear consciousness of herself and her position, it seemed to her he was not so much a circumstance as a circumvallation. There wasn't a direction in which she could turn without immediately running up against him. He had taken possession of her extremely. And from her first resignation to this as an inevitable fact she had come, she hardly knew how, to a renewed disposition to regard this large and various universe beyond him and outside of him, with something of the same slight adventurousness she had felt before he so comprehensively happened to her. After her first phase of despair she had really done her best to honour the bargain she had rather unwittingly made and to love and to devote herself and be a loyal and happy wife to this clutching, hardbreathing little man who had got her, and it was the insatiable excesses of his demands quite as much as any outer influence that made her realize the impossibility of such a concentration.

His was a supremely acquisitive and possessive character, so that he insulted her utmost subjugations by an obtrusive suspicion and jealousy, he was jealous of her childish worship of her dead father, jealous of her disposition to go to church, jealous of the poet Wordsworth because she liked to read his sonnets, jealous because she loved great music, jealous when she wanted to go out; if she seemed passionless and she seemed more and more passionless he was jealous, and the slightest gleam of any warmth of temperament filled him with a vile and furious dread of dishonouring possibilities. And the utmost resolution to believe in him could not hide from her for ever the fact that his love manifested itself almost wholly as a parade of ownership and a desire, without kindliness, without any self-forgetfulness. All his devotion, his self-abjection, had been the mere qualms of a craving, the flush of eager courtship. Do as she would to overcome these realizations, forces within her stronger than herself, primordial forces with the welfare of all life in their keeping, cried out upon the meanness of his face, the ugly pointed nose and the thin compressed lips, the weak neck, the clammy hands, the ungainly nervous gestures, the tuneless whistling between the clenched teeth. He would not let her forget a single detail. Whenever she tried to look at any created thing, he thrust himself, like one of his own open-air advertisements, athwart the attraction.

As she grew up to an achieved womanhood—and it was even a physical growing-up, for she added more than an inch of stature after her marriage—her life became more and more consciously like a fencing match in which her vision flashed over his head and under his arms and this side of him and that, while with a toiling industry he fought to intercept it. And from the complete acceptance of her matrimonial submission, she passed on by almost insensible degrees towards a conception of her life as a struggle, that seemed at first entirely lonely and unsupported, to exist—*against* him.

In every novel as in every picture there must be an immense simplification, and so I tell the story of Lady Harman's changing attitude without any of those tangled leapings-forward or harkings-back, those moods and counter moods and relapses which made up the necessary course of her mind. But sometimes she was here and sometimes she was there, sometimes quite back to the beginning an obedient, scrupulously loyal and up-looking young wife, sometimes a wife concealing the humiliation of an unhappy choice in a spurious satisfaction and affection. And mixed up with widening spaces of criticism and dissatisfaction and hostility there were, you must understand, moments of real liking for this outrageous little man and streaks of an absurd maternal tenderness for him. They had been too close together to avoid that. She had a woman's affection of ownership too, and disliked to see him despised or bettered or untidy ; even those ridiculous muddy hands had given her a twinge of solicitude. . . .

And all the while she was trying to see the universe also, the great background of their two little lives, and to think what it might mean for her over and above their too obliterating relationship.

§ 6

It would be like counting the bacteria of an infection to trace how ideas of insubordination came drifting into Sir Isaac's Paradise. The epidemic is in the air. There is no Tempter nowadays, no definitive apple. The disturbing force has grown subtler, blows in now like a draught, creeps and gathers like the dust,—a disseminated serpent. Sir Isaac brought home his young, beautiful and rather crumpled and astonished Eve and by all his standards he was entitled to be happy ever afterwards. He knew of one danger, but against that he was very watchful. Never once for six long years did she have a private duologue with another male. But Mudie and Sir Jesse Boot sent parcels to the house unchecked, the newspaper drifted in not even censored ; the nurses who guided Ellen through the essential incidents of a feminine career talked of something called a " movement." And there was Georgina. . . .

The thing they wanted they called the Vote, but that demand so hollow, so eyeless, had all the terrifying effect of a mask. Behind that mask was a formless invincible discontent with the lot of womanhood. It wanted,—it was not clear what it wanted, but whatever it wanted, all the domestic instincts of mankind were against admitting there was anything it could want. That remarkable agitation had already worked up to the thunderous pitch, there had been demonstrations at Public Meetings, scenes in the Ladies' Gallery and something like rioting in Parliament Square before ever it occurred to Sir Isaac that this was a disturbance that touched his home. He had supposed suffragettes were ladies of all too certain an age with red noses and spectacles and a masculine style of costume, who wished to be hugged by policemen. He said as much rather knowingly and wickedly to Charterson. He could not understand any woman not coveting the privileges of Lady Harman. And then one day while Georgina and her mother were visiting them, as he was looking over the letters at the breakfast table according to his custom before giving them out, he discovered two identical newspaper packets addressed to his wife and his sister-in-law, and upon them were these words printed very plainly, " Votes for Women."

" Good Lord ! " he cried. " What's this ? It oughtn't to be allowed." And he pitched the papers at the waste-paper basket under the sideboard.

" I'll thank you," said Georgina, " not to throw away our *Votes for Women*. We subscribe to that."

" Eh ? " cried Sir Isaac.

" We're subscribers. Snagsby, just give us those papers." (A difficult moment for Snagsby.) He picked up the papers and looked at Sir Isaac.

" Put 'em down there," said Sir Isaac, waving to the sideboard and then in an ensuing silence handed two letters of no importance to his mother-in-law. His face was pale and he was breathless. Snagsby with an obvious tactfulness retired.

Sir Isaac watched the door close.

His remark pointedly ignored Georgina.

"What you been thinking about, Elly," he asked, "subscribing to *that* thing?"

"I wanted to read it."

"But you don't hold with all that Rubbish——"

"*Rubbish!*" said Georgina, helping herself to marmalade.

"Well, rot then, if you like," said Sir Isaac, unamiably and panting.

With that as Snagsby afterwards put it—for the battle raged so fiercely as to go on even when he presently returned to the room—"the fat was in the fire." The Harman breakfast-table was caught up into the Great Controversy with heat and fury like a tree that is overtaken by a forest fire. It burnt for weeks, and smouldered still when the first white heats had abated. I will not record the arguments of either side, they were abominably bad and you have heard them all time after time; I do not think that whatever side you have taken in this matter you would find much to please you in Sir Isaac's goadings or Georgina's repartees. Sir Isaac would ask if women were prepared to go as soldiers and Georgina would enquire how many years of service he had done or horrify her mother by manifest allusion to the agonies and dangers of maternity,—things like that. It gave a new interest to breakfast for Snagsby; and the peculiarly ladylike qualities of Mrs. Sawbridge, a gift for silent, pallid stiffness, a disposition, tactful but unsuccessful, to "change the subject," an air of being about to leave the room in disdain, had never shone with such baleful splendour. Our interest here is rather with the effect of these remarkable disputes, which echoed in Sir

Isaac's private talk long after Georgina had gone again, upon Lady Harman. He could not leave this topic of feminine emancipation alone, once it had been set going, and though Ellen would always preface her remarks by, " Of course Georgina goes too far," he worried her slowly into a series of definite insurgent positions. Sir Isaac's attacks on Georgina certainly brought out a good deal of absurdity in her positions, and Georgina at times left Sir Isaac without a leg to stand on, and the net result of their disputes as of most human controversies was not conviction for the hearer but release. Her mind escaped between them, and went exploring for itself through the great gaps they had made in the simple obedient assumptions of her girlhood. That question originally put in Paradise, " Why shouldn't we ? " came into her mind and stayed there. It is a question that marks a definite stage in the departure from innocence. Things that had seemed opaque and immutable appeared translucent and questionable. She began to read more and more in order to learn things and get a light upon things, and less and less to pass the time. Ideas came to her that seemed at first strange altogether and then grotesquely justifiable and then crept to a sort of acceptance by familiarity. And a disturbing intermittent sense of a general responsibility increased and increased in her.

You will understand this sense of responsibility which was growing up in Lady Harman's mind if you have felt it yourself, but if you have not then you may find it a little difficult to understand. You see it comes, when it comes at all, out of a phase of disillusionment. All children, I suppose, begin by taking for granted the rightness of things in general, the soundness of accepted standards, and many people

are at least so happy that they never really grow out
of this assumption.   They go to the grave with an
unbroken confidence that somewhere behind all the
immediate injustices and disorders of life, behind the
antics of politics, the rigidities of institutions, the
pressure of custom and the vagaries of law, there is
wisdom and purpose and adequate provision, they
never lose that faith in the human household they
acquired amongst the directed securities of home.   But
for more of us and more there comes a dissolution of
these assurances; there comes illumination as the day
comes into a candle-lit uncurtained room.   The warm
lights that once rounded off our world so completely
are betrayed for what they are, smoky and guttering
candles.   Beyond what once seemed a casket of dutiful
security is now a limitless and indifferent universe.
Ours is the wisdom or there is no wisdom; ours is the
decision or there is no decision.   That burthen is upon
each of us in the measure of our capacity.   The talent
has been given us and we may not bury it.

§ 7

And as we reckon up the disturbing influences
that were stirring Lady Harman out of that life of
acquiescences to which women are perhaps even more
naturally disposed than men, we may pick out the
conversation of Susan Burnet as something a little
apart from the others, as something with a peculiar
barbed pointedness of its own that was yet in other
respects very representative of a multitude of nudges
and nips and pricks and indications that life was giving
Lady Harman's awaking mind.   Susan Burnet was a
woman who came to renovate and generally do up the

Putney curtains and furniture and loose covers every spring ; she was Mrs. Crumble's discovery, she was sturdy and short and she had open blue eyes and an engaging simplicity of manner that attracted Lady Harman from the outset. She was stuck away in one of the spare bedrooms and there she was available for any one, so long, she explained, as they didn't fluster her when she was cutting out, with a flow of conversation that not even a mouth full of pins seemed to interrupt. And Lady Harman would go and watch Susan Burnet by the hour together and think what an enviably independent young woman she was, and listen with interest and something between horror and admiration to the various impressions of life she had gathered during a hardy and adventurous career.

Their early conversations were about Susan Burnet's business and the general condition of things in that world of upholsterers' young women in which Susan had lived until she perceived the possibilities of a "connexion," and set up for herself. And the condition of things in that world, as Susan described it, brought home to Lady Harman just how sheltered and limited her own upbringing had been. "It isn't right," said Susan, "the way they send girls out with fellers into empty houses. Naturally the men get persecuting them. They don't seem hardly able to help it, some of them, and I will say this for them, that a lot of the girls go more than half way with them, leading them on. Still there's a sort of man won't leave you alone. One I used to be sent out with and a married man too he was, Oh !—he used to give me a time. Why I've bit his hands before now, bit hard, before he'd leave go of me. It's my opinion the married men are worse than the single. Bolder they are. I pushed him over

a scuttle once and he hit his head against a bookcase.
I was fair frightened of him. 'You little devil,' he
says ; 'I'll be even with you yet. . . .' Oh! I've been
called worse things than that. . . . Of course a respectable girl gets through with it, but it's trying and
to some it's a sort of temptation. . . .'"

"I should have thought," reflected Lady Harman,
" you could have told some one."

" It's queer," said Susan ; " but it never seemed to
me the sort of thing a girl ought to go telling. It's a
kind of private thing. And besides, it isn't exactly
easy to tell. . . . I suppose the Firm didn't want to be
worried by complaints and disputes about that sort of
thing. And it isn't always easy to say just which of
the two is to blame."

" But how old are the girls they send out ? " asked
Lady Harman.

" Some's as young as seventeen or eighteen. It all
depends on the sort of work that's wanted to be
done. . . ."

" Of course a lot of them have to marry. . . ."

This lurid little picture of vivid happenings in
unoccupied houses and particularly of the prim,
industrious, capable Susan Burnet, biting aggressive
wrists, stuck in Lady Harman's imagination. She
seemed to be looking into hitherto unsuspected pits
of simple and violent living just beneath her feet.
Susan told some upholsteress love tales, real love tales,
with a warmth and honesty of passion in them that
seemed at once dreadful and fine to Lady Harman's
underfed imagination. Under encouragement Susan
expanded the picture, beyond these mere glimpses of
workshop and piece-work and furtive lust. It appeared
that she was practically the head of her family ; there

was a mother who had specialized in ill-health, a sister
of defective ability who stayed at home, a brother in
South Africa who was very good and sent home money,
and three younger sisters growing up. And father,
—she evaded the subject of father at first. Then
presently Lady Harman had some glimpses of an
earlier phase in Susan Burnet's life " before any of us
were earning money." Father appeared as a kindly,
ineffectual, insolvent figure struggling to conduct a
baker's and confectioner's business in Walthamstow,
mother was already specializing, there were various
brothers and sisters being born and dying. " How
many were there of you altogether?" asked Lady
Harman.

" Thirteen there was. Father always used to laugh
and say he'd had a fair baker's dozen. There was
Luke to begin with—— "

Susan began to count on her fingers and recite
braces of scriptural names.

She could only make up her tale to twelve. She
became perplexed. Then she remembered. " Of
course!" she cried: " there was Nicodemus. He was
still-born. I *always* forget Nicodemus, poor little
chap! But he came—was it sixth or seventh?—
seventh after Anna."

She gave some glimpses of her father and then
there was a collapse of which she fought shy. Lady
Harman was too delicate to press her to talk of that.

But one day in the afternoon Susan's tongue ran.

She was telling how first she went to work before
she was twelve.

" But I thought the board schools—— " said Lady
Harman.

" I had to go before the committee," said Susan.

" I had to go before the committee and ask to be let go to work. There they was, sitting round a table in a great big room, and they was as kind as anything, one old gentleman with a great white beard, he was as kind as could be. 'Don't you be frightened, my dear,' he says. 'You tell us why you want to go out working.' 'Well,' I says, '*somebody's* got to earn something,' and that made them laugh in a sort of fatherly way, and after that there wasn't any difficulty. You see it was after Father's Inquest, and everybody was disposed to be kind to us. 'Pity they can't all go instead of this educational Tommy Rot,' the old gentleman says. 'You learn to work, my dear'—and I did. . . ."

She paused.

" Father's inquest ? " said Lady Harman.

Susan seemed to brace herself to the occasion. " Father," she said, " was drowned. I know—I hadn't told you that before. He was drowned in the Lea. It's always been a distress and humiliation to us there had to be an Inquest. And they threw out things. . . . It's why we moved to Haggerston. It's the worst that ever happened to us in all our lives   Far worse. Worse than having the things sold or the children with scarlet fever and having to burn everything. . . . I don't like to talk about it. I can't help it but I don't. . . .

" I don't know why I talk to you as I do, Lady Harman, but I don't seem to mind talking to you. I don't suppose I've opened my mouth to any one about it, not for years—except to one dear friend I've got—her who persuaded me to be a church member. But what I've always said and what I will always say is this, that I don't believe any evil of Father, I don't believe, I won't ever believe he took his life. I won't even believe he was in drink. I don't know how he got in the river, but I'm certain it wasn't so. He was a weak man, was Father, I've never denied he was a weak man. But a harder working man than he was, never lived. He worried, anyone would have worried, seeing the worries he had. The shop wasn't paying as it was ; often we never tasted meat for weeks together, and then there came one of these Internationals, giving overweight and underselling. . . ."

" One of these Internationals ? "

" Yes, I don't suppose you've ever heard of them. They're in the poorer neighbourhoods chiefly. They sell teas and things mostly now but they began as bakers' shops and what they did was to come into a place and undersell until all the old shops were ruined and shut up. That was what they tried to do and Father hadn't no more chance amongst them than a mouse in a trap. . . . It was just like being run over. All the trade that stayed with us after a bit was Bad Debts. You can't blame people I suppose for going where they get more and pay less, and it wasn't till we'd all gone right away to Haggerston that they altered things and put the prices up again. Of course Father lost heart and all that. He didn't know what to do, he'd sunk all he had in the shop ; he just sat and moped about. Really,—he was pitiful. He wasn't able to sleep ; he used to get up at nights and go about downstairs. Mother says she found him once sweeping out the bakehouse at two o'clock in the morning. He got it into his head that getting up like that would help him. But I don't believe and I won't believe he wouldn't have seen it through if he could. Not to my dying day will I believe that. . . ."

Lady Harman reflected. " But couldn't he have got work again—as a baker ? "

"It's hard after you've had a shop. You see all the younger men've come on. They know the new ways. And a man who's had a shop and failed, he's lost heart. And these stores setting up make everything drivinger. They do things a different way. They make it harder for every one."

Both Lady Harman and Susan Burnet reflected in silence for a few seconds upon the International Stores. The sewing woman was the first to speak.

"Things like that," she said, "didn't ought to be. One shop didn't ought to be allowed to set out to ruin another. It isn't fair trading, it's a sort of murder. It oughtn't to be allowed. How was father to know ? . . ."

" 'There's got to be competition," said Lady Harman.

" I don't call that competition," said Susan Burnet.

" But,—I suppose they give people cheaper bread."

" They do for a time. Then when they've killed you they do what they like. . . . Luke—he's one of those who'll say anything—well, he used to say it was a regular Monopoly. But it's hard on people who've set out to live honest and respectable and bring up a family plain and decent to be pushed out of the way like that."

" I suppose it is," said Lady Harman.

" What was father to *do* ? " said Susan, and turned to Sir Isaac's arm-chair from which this discourse had distracted her.

And then suddenly, in a voice thick with rage, she burst out : " And then Alice must needs go and take their money. That's what sticks in *my* throat."

Still on her knees she faced about to Lady Harman.

"Alice goes into one of their Ho'burn branches as a waitress, do what I could to prevent her. It makes one mad to think of it. Time after time I've said to her, 'Alice,' I've said, 'sooner than touch their dirty money I'd starve in the street.' And she goes! She says it's all nonsense of me to bear a spite. Laughs at me! 'Alice,' I told her, 'it's a wonder the spirit of poor father don't rise up against you.' And she laughs. Calls that bearing a spite. . . . Of course she was little when it happened. She can't remember, not as I remember. . . ."

Lady Harman reflected for a time. "I suppose you don't know," she began, addressing Susan's industrious back; "you don't know who—who owns these International Stores?"

"I suppose it's some company," said Susan. "I don't see that it lets them off—being in a company."

§ 8

We have done much in the last few years to destroy the severe limitations of Victorian delicacy, and all of us, from princesses and prime-ministers' wives downward, talk of topics that would have been considered quite gravely improper in the nineteenth century. Nevertheless, some topics have, if anything, become more indelicate than they were, and this is especially true of the discussion of income, of any discussion that tends, however remotely, to inquire, Who is it at the base of everything who really pays in blood and muscle and involuntary submissions for *your* freedom and magnificence? This, indeed, is almost the ultimate

surviving indecency. So that it was with considerable
private shame and discomfort that Lady Harman
pursued even in her privacy the train of thought that
Susan Burnet had set going. It had been conveyed
into her mind long ago, and it had settled down there
and grown into a sort of security, that the International Bread and Cake Stores were a very important
contribution to Progress, and that Sir Isaac, outside
the gates of his home, was a very useful and beneficial
personage, and richly meriting a baronetcy. She
hadn't particularly analysed this persuasion, but she
supposed him engaged in a kind of daily repetition,
but upon modern scientific lines, of the miracle of the
loaves and fishes, feeding a great multitude that would
otherwise have gone hungry. She knew, too, from the
advertisements that flowered about her path through
life, that this bread in question was exceptionally clean
and hygienic; whole front pages of the *Daily
Messenger*, headed the " Fauna of Small Bakehouses,"
and adorned with a bordering of *Blatta orientalis*, the
common cockroach, had taught her that, and she knew
that Sir Isaac's passion for purity had also led to the
Old Country Gazette's spirited and successful campaign
for a non-party measure securing additional bakehouse
regulation and inspection. And her impression had
been that the growing and developing refreshment side
of the concern was almost a public charity; Sir Isaac
gave, he said, a larger, heavier scone, a bigger pat of
butter, a more elegant teapot, ham more finely cut and
less questionable pork-pies than any other system of
syndicated tea-shops. She supposed that whenever he
sat late at night going over schemes and papers, or
when he went off for days together to Cardiff or
Glasgow or Dublin, or such-like centres, or when he

became preoccupied at dinner and whistled thoughtfully through his teeth, he was planning to increase
the amount or diminish the cost of tea and cocoa-
drenched farinaceous food in the stomachs of that
section of our national adolescence which goes out
daily into the streets of our great cities to be fed.
And she knew his vans and catering were indispensable
to the British Army upon its manœuvres. . . .

Now the smashing up of the Burnet family by the
International Stores was disagreeably not in the picture
of these suppositions. And the remarkable thing is
that this one little tragedy wouldn't for a moment
allow itself to be regarded as an exceptional accident
in an otherwise fair vast development. It remained
obstinately a specimen—of the other side of the great
syndication.

It was just as if she had been doubting sub-
consciously all along. . . . In the silence of the night
she lay awake and tried to make herself believe that
the Burnet case was just a unique overlooked disaster,
that it needed only to come to Sir Isaac's attention to
be met by the fullest reparation. . . .

After all she did not bring it to Sir Isaac's
attention.

But one morning, while this phase of new doubts
was still lively in her mind, Sir Isaac told her he
was going down to Brighton, and then along the coast
road in a car to Portsmouth, to pay a few surprise
visits, and see how the machine was working. He
would be away a night, an unusual breach in his
habits.

" Are you thinking of any new branches, Isaac ? "

" I may have a look at Arundel."

" Isaac." She paused to frame her question

carefully. " I suppose there are some shops at Arundel now ? "

" I've got to see to that."

" If you open—— I suppose the old shops get hurt. What becomes of the people if they do get hurt ? "

" That's *their* look-out," said Sir Isaac.

" Isn't it bad for them ? "

" Progress is Progress, Elly."

" It *is* bad for them. I suppose—— Wouldn't it be sometimes kinder if you took over the old shop— made a sort of partner of him, or something ? "

Sir Isaac shook his head. " I want younger men," he said. " You can't get a move on the older hands."

" But, then, it's rather bad—— I suppose these little men you shut up,—some of them must have families."

" You're theorizing a bit this morning, Elly," said Sir Isaac, looking up over his coffee cup.

" I've been thinking—about these little people."

" Someone's been talking to you about my shops," said Sir Isaac, and stuck out an index finger. " If that's Georgina—— "

" It isn't Georgina," said Lady Harman, but she had it very clear in her mind that she must not say who it was.

" You can't make a business without squeezing somebody," said Sir Isaac. " It's easy enough to make a row about any concern that grows a bit. Some people would like to have every business tied down to a maximum turnover and so much a year profit. I dare say you've been hearing of these articles in the *London Lion*. Pretty stuff it is, too. This fuss about the little shopkeepers ; that's a new racket. I've had all that row about the waitresses before, and the yarn about the Normandy eggs, and all that, but I don't see that you need go reading it against me, and bringing it up at the breakfast-table. A business is a business, it isn't a charity, and I'd like to know where you and I would be if we didn't run the concern on business lines. . . . Why, that *London Lion* fellow came to me with the first two of those articles before the thing began. I could have had the whole thing stopped if I liked, if I'd chosen to take the back page of his beastly cover. That shows the stuff the whole thing is made of. That shows you. Why!—he's just a blackmailer, that's what he is. Much he cares for my waitresses if he can get the dibs. Little shopkeepers, indeed! I know 'em! Nice martyrs they are! There isn't one wouldn't *skin* all the others if he got half a chance. . . ."

Sir Isaac gave way to an extraordinary fit of nagging anger. He got up and stood upon the hearthrug to deliver his soul the better. It was an altogether unexpected and illuminating outbreak. He was flushed with guilt. The more angry and eloquent he became, the more profoundly thoughtful grew the attentive lady at the head of his table. . . .

When at last Sir Isaac had gone off in the car to Victoria, Lady Harman rang for Snagsby. "Isn't there a paper," she asked, "called the *London Lion*?"

"It isn't one I think your ladyship would like," said Snagsby, gently but firmly.

"I know. But I want to see it. I want copies of all the issues in which there have been articles upon the International Stores."

"They're thoroughly volgar, me lady," said Snagsby, with a large dissuasive smile.

"I want you to go out into London and get them now."

Snagsby hesitated and went. Within five minutes he reappeared with a handful of buff-covered papers.

"There 'appened to be copies in the pantry, me lady," he said. "We can't imagine 'ow they got there; someone must have brought them in, but 'ere they are quite at your service, me lady." He paused for a discreet moment. Something indescribably confidential came into his manner. "I doubt if Sir Isaac will quite like to 'ave them left about, me lady—after you done with them."

She was in a mood of discovery. She sat in the room that was all furnished in pink (her favourite colour) and read a bitter, malicious, coarsely written and yet insidiously credible account of her husband's business methods. Something within herself seemed to answer, "But didn't you know this all along?" That large conviction that her wealth and position were but the culmination of a great and honourable social service, a conviction that had been her tacit comfort during much distasteful loyalty seemed to shrivel and fade. No doubt the writer was a thwarted blackmailer; even her unaccustomed mind could distinguish a twang of some such vicious quality in his sentences; but that did not alter the realities he exhibited and exaggerated. There was a description of how Sir Isaac pounced on his managers that was manifestly derived from a manager he had dismissed. It was dreadfully like him. Convincingly like him. There was a statement of the wages he paid his girl assistants and long extracts from his code of rules and schedules of fines. . . .

When she put down the paper she was suddenly afflicted by a vivid vision of Susan Burnet's father, losing heart and not knowing what to do. She had an unreasonable feeling that Susan Burnet's father must have been a small, kindly, furry, bunnyish, little man. Of course there had to be progress and the survival of the fittest. She found herself weighing what she imagined Susan Burnet's father to be like, against the ferrety face, stooping shoulders and scheming whistle of Sir Isaac.

There were times now when she saw her husband with an extreme distinctness.

§ 9

As this cold and bracing realization that all was not right with her position, with Sir Isaac's business procedure and the world generally, took possession of Lady Harman's thoughts there came also with it and arising out of it quite a series of new moods and dispositions. At times she was very full of the desire " to do something," something that would, as it were, satisfy and assuage this growing uneasiness of responsibility in her mind. At times her consuming wish was not to assuage but escape from this urgency. It worried her and made her feel helpless, and she wanted beyond anything else to get back to that child's world where all experiences are adventurous and everything is finally right. She felt, I think, that it was a little unfair to her that this something within her should be calling upon her to take all sorts of things gravely—hadn't she been a good wife and brought four children into the world . . . ?

I am setting down here as clearly as possible what wasn't by any means clear in Lady Harman's mind. I am giving you side by side phases that never came side by side in her thoughts but which followed and ousted and obliterated one another. She had moods of triviality. She had moods of magnificence. She had moods of intense secret hostility to her urgent little husband, and moods of genial tolerance for everything there was in her life. She had moods, and don't we all have moods?—of scepticism and cynicism, much profounder than the conventions and limitations of novel-writing permit us to tell here. And for hardly any of these moods had she terms and recognitions. . .

It isn't a natural thing to keep on worrying about the morality of one's material prosperity. These are proclivities superinduced by modern conditions of the conscience. There is a natural resistance in every healthy human being to such distressful heart-searchings. Strong instincts battled in Lady Harman against this intermittent sense of responsibility that was beginning to worry her. An immense lot of her was for simply running away from these troublesome considerations, for covering herself up from them, for distraction.

And about this time she happened upon "Elizabeth and her German Garden," and was very greatly delighted and stimulated by that little sister of Montaigne. She was charmed by the book's fresh gaiety, by its gallant resolve to set off all the good things there are in this world, the sunshine and flowers and laughter, against the limitations and thwartings and disappointments of life. For a time it seemed to her that these brave consolations were solutions, and she was stirred by an imitative passion. How stupid had she not been to let life and Sir Isaac overcome her! She felt that she must make herself like Elizabeth, exactly like Elizabeth; she tried forthwith, and a certain difficulty she found, a certain deadness, she ascribed to the square modernity of her house and something in the Putney air. The house was too large, it dominated the garden and controlled her. She felt she must get away to some place that was chiefly exterior, in the sunshine, far from towns and struggling, straining, angry and despairing humanity, from syndicated shops and all the embarrassing challenges of life. Somehow there it would be possible to keep Sir Isaac at arm's length; and the ghost of Susan Burnet's father could be left behind to haunt the square rooms of the London house. And there she would live, horticultural, bookish, whimsical, witty, defiant, happily careless.

And it was this particular conception of evasion that had set her careering about the countryside in her car, looking for conceivable houses of refuge from this dark novelty of social and personal care, and that had driven her into the low long room of 'Black Strand and the presence of Mr. Brumley.

Of what ensued and the appearance and influence of Lady Beach-Mandarin and how it led among other things to a lunch invitation from that lady the reader has already been informed.

CHAPTER THE SIXTH

The Adventurous Afternoon

§ 1

You will perhaps remember that before I fell into this extensive digression about Lady Harman's upbringing, we had got to the entry of Mrs. Sawbridge into the house bearing a plunder of Sir Isaac's best roses. She interrupted a conversation of some importance. Those roses at this point are still unwithered and fragrant, and moreover they are arranged according to Mrs. Sawbridge's ideas of elegance about Sir Isaac's home . . . And Sir Isaac, when that conversation could be renewed, categorically forbade Lady Harman to go to Lady Beach-Mandarin's lunch and Lady Harman went to Lady Beach-Mandarin's lunch.

She had some peculiar difficulties in getting to that lunch.

It is necessary to tell certain particulars. They are particulars that will distress the delicacy of Mrs. Sawbridge unspeakably if ever she chances to read this book. But a story has to be told. You see Sir Isaac Harman had never considered it advisable to give his wife a private allowance. Whatever she wished to have, he maintained, she could have. The bill would afterwards be paid by his cheque on the first day of the month following the receipt of the bill. He found a generous pleasure in writing these cheques, and Lady Harman was magnificently housed, fed and adorned. Moreover, whenever she chose to ask for money he gave her money, usually double of what she demanded,—and often a kiss or so into the bargain. But after he had forbidden her to go to Lady Beach-Mandarin's so grave an estrangement ensued that she could not ask him for money. A door closed between them. And the crisis had come at an unfortunate moment. She possessed the sum of five shillings and eightpence.

She perceived quite early that this shortness of money would greatly embarrass the rebellion she contemplated. She was exceptionally ignorant of most worldly things, but she knew there was never yet a campaign without a war chest. She felt entitled to money. . . .

She planned several times to make a demand for replenishment with a haughty dignity; the haughty dignity was easy enough to achieve, but the demand was not A sensitive dread of her mother's sympathetic curiosity barred all thoughts of borrowing in that direction,—she and her mother "never discussed money matters." She did not want to get Georgina into further trouble. And besides, Georgina was in Devonshire.

Even to get to Lady Beach-Mandarin's became difficult under these circumstances. She knew that Clarence, though he would take her into the country quite freely, had been instructed, on account of Sir Isaac's expressed dread of any accident happening to her while alone, not to plunge with her into the vortex of London traffic. Only under direct orders from Sir Isaac would Clarence take her down Putney Hill; though she might go up and away—to anywhere. She knew nothing of pawnshops or any associated methods of getting cash advances, and the possibility of using the telephone to hire an automobile never occurred to her. But she was fully resolved to go. She had one advantage in the fact that Sir Isaac didn't know the precise date of the disputed engagement. When that arrived she spent a restless morning and dressed herself at last with great care. She instructed Peters, her maid, who participated in these preparations with a mild astonishment, that she was going out to lunch, asked her to inform Mrs Sawbridge of the fact and, outwardly serene, made a bolt for it down the staircase and across the hall. The great butler appeared ; she had never observed how like a large note of interrogation his forward contours could be.

" I shall be out to lunch, Snagsby," she said, and went past him into the sunshine.

She left a discreetly astonished Snagsby behind her.

(" Now where are we going out to lunch ? " said Snagsby presently to Peters.

" I've never known her so particular with her clothes," said the maid.

" Never before—not in the same way ; it's something new and special to this affair," Snagsby reflected. " I wonder now if Sir Isaac. . . ."

" One can't help observing things," said the maid, after a pause. " Mute though we be.")

Lady Harman had the whole five and eightpence with her. She had managed to keep it intact in her jewel case, declaring she had no change when any small demands where made on her.

With an exhilaration so great that she wanted sorely to laugh aloud she walked out through her big

open gates and into the general publicity of Putney
Hill. Why had she not done as much years ago?
How long she had been, working up to this obvious
thing! She hadn't been out in such complete possession of herself since she had been a schoolgirl. She
held up a beautifully gloved hand to a private motor-car
going downhill and then to an engaged taxi going up,
and then with a slightly dashed feeling, picked up her
skirt and walked observantly downhill. Her reason
dispelled a transitory impression that these two vehicles
were on Sir Isaac's side against her.

There was quite a nice taxi on the rank at the
bottom of the hill. The driver, a pleasant-looking
young man in a white cap, seemed to have been waiting
for her in particular; he met her timid invitation halfway and came across the road to her and jumped down
and opened the door. He took her instructions as
though they were after his own heart, and right in front
of her as she sat was a kind of tin cornucopia full of
artificial flowers that seemed like a particular attention
to her. His fare was two and eightpence and she gave
him four shillings. He seemed quite gratified by her
largesse, his manner implied he had always thought as
much of her, from first to last their relations had been
those of sunny contentment, and it was only as she
ascended the steps of Lady Beach-Mandarin's portico,
that it occurred to her that she now had insufficient
money for an automobile to take her home. But there
were railways and buses and all sorts of possibilities;
the day was an adventure; and she entered the drawing-
room with a brow that was beautifully unruffled. She
wanted to laugh still; it animated her eyes and lips
with the pleasantest little stir you can imagine.

"A-a-a-a-a-h!" cried Lady Beach-Mandarin in a

high note, and threw out—it had an effect of being
quite a number of arms—as though she was one of those
brass Indian goddesses one sees.

Lady Harman felt taken in at once to all that
capacious bosom involved and contained. . . .

§ 2

It was quite an amusing lunch.   But any lunch
would have been amusing to Lady Harman in the
excitement of her first act of deliberate disobedience.
She had never been out to lunch alone in all her life
before ; she experienced a kind of scared happiness, she
felt like someone at Lourdes who has just thrown
away crutches.   She was seated between a pink
young man with an eyeglass whose place was labelled
"Bertie Trevor" and who was otherwise unexplained,
and Mr. Brumley.   She was quite glad to see Mr.
Brumley again, and no doubt her eyes showed it.   She
had hoped to see him.   Miss Sharsper was sitting
nearly opposite to her, a real live novelist pecking
observations out of life as a hen pecks seeds amidst
scenery, and next beyond was a large-headed inattentive
fluffy person who was Mr. Keystone the well-known
critic. · And there was Agatha Alimony under a
rustling vast hat of green-black cock's feathers next to
Sir Markham Crosby, with whom she had been having
an abusive controversy in the *Times* and to whom quite
elaborately she wouldn't speak, and there was Lady
Viping with her lorgnette and Adolphus Blenker,
Horatio's younger and if possible more gentlemanly
brother—Horatio of the *Old Country Gazette* that is—
sole reminder that there was such a person as Sir Isaac
in the world.   Lady Beach-Mandarin's mother and the

Swiss governess and the tall but retarded daughter, Phyllis, completed the party. The reception was lively and cheering; Lady Beach-Mandarin enfolded her guests in generosities and kept them all astir like a sea-swell under a squadron, and she introduced Lady Harman to Miss Alimony by public proclamation right across the room because there were two lavish tables of bric-à-brac, a marble bust of old Beach-Mandarin and most of the rest of the party in the way. And at the table conversation was like throwing bread, you never knew whom you might hit or who might hit you. (But Lady Beach-Mandarin produced an effect of throwing whole loaves.) Bertie Trevor was one of those dancing young men who talk to a woman as though they were giving a dog biscuits, and mostly it was Mr. Brumley who did such talking as reached Lady Harman's ear.

Mr. Brumley was in very good form that day. He had contrived to remind her of all their Black Strand talk while they were still eating *Petites Bouchées à la Reine*. " Have you found that work yet ? " he asked and carried her mind to the core of her situation. Then they were snatched up into a general discussion of Bazaars. Sir Markham spoke of a great bazaar that was to be held on behalf of one of the many Shakespear Theatre movements that were then so prevalent. Was Lady Beach-Mandarin implicated ? Was anyone ? He told of novel features in contemplation. He generalized about bazaars and, with an air of having forgotten the presence of Miss Alimony, glanced at the Suffrage Bazaar—it was a season of bazaars. He thought poorly of the Suffrage Bazaar. The hostess intervened promptly with anecdotes of her own cynical daring as a Bazaar-seller, Miss Sharsper

offered fragments of a reminiscence about signing one
of her own books for a Bookstall, Blenker told a well-
known Bazaar anecdote brightly and well, and the
impending skirmish was averted.

While the Bazaar talk still whacked to and fro
about the table Mr. Brumley got at Lady Harman's
ear again. "Rather tantalizing these meetings at
table," he said. "It's like trying to talk while you
swim in a rough sea. . . ."

Then Lady Beach-Mandarin intervened with
demands for support for her own particular Bazaar
project and they were eating salad before there was a
chance of another word between them. "I must
confess that when I want to talk to people I like to get
them alone," said Mr. Brumley, and gave form to
thoughts that were already on the verge of crystallisa-
tion in her own mind. She had been recalling that
she had liked his voice before, noting something very
kindly and thoughtful and brotherly about his right
profile and thinking how much an hour's talk with him
would help to clear up her ideas.

"But it's so difficult to get one alone," said Lady
Harman, and suddenly an idea of the utmost daring
and impropriety flashed into her mind. She was on
the verge of speaking it forthwith and then didn't, she
met something in his eye that answered her own and
then Lady Beach-Mandarin was foaming over them like
a dam-burst over an American town.

"What do *you* think, Mr. Brumley?" demanded
Lady Beach-Mandarin.

"?"

"About Sir Markham's newspaper symposium.
They asked him what allowance he gave his wife. Sent
a prepaid reply telegram."

" But he hasn't got a wife ! "

" They don't stick at a little thing like that," said Sir Markham grimly.

" I think a husband and wife ought to have everything in common like the early Christians," said Lady Beach-Mandarin. " *We* always did," and so got the discussion afloat again off the sandbank of Mr. Brumley's inattention.

It was quite a good discussion and Lady Harman contributed an exceptionally alert and intelligent silence. Sir Markham distrusted Lady Beach-Mandarin's communism and thought that anyhow it wouldn't do for a financier or business man. He favoured an allowance. "So did Sir Joshua," said the widow Viping. This roused Agatha Alimony. "Allowance indeed!" she cried. "Is a wife to be on no better footing than a daughter? The whole question of a wife's financial autonomy needs reconsidering. . . ."

Adolphus Blenker became learned and lucid upon Pin-money and dowry and the customs of savage tribes, and Mr. Brumley helped with corroboration. . . .

Mr. Brumley managed to say just one other thing to Lady Harman before the lunch was over. It struck her for a moment as being irrelevant. "The gardens at Hampton Court," he said, "are delightful just now. Have you seen them? Autumnal fires. All the September perennials lifting their spears in their last great chorus. It's the *Götterdämmerung* of the year."

She was going out of the room before she appreciated his possible intention.

Lady Beach-Mandarin delegated Sir Markham to preside over the men's cigars and bounced and slapped her four ladies upstairs to the drawing-room. Her

mother disappeared and so did Phyllis and the
governess. Lady Harman heard a large aside to Lady
Viping : " Isn't she perfectly lovely ? " glanced to
discover the lorgnette in appreciative action, and then
found herself drifting into a secluded window-seat and
a duologue with Miss Agatha Alimony. Miss Alimony
was one of that large and increasing number of dusky,
grey-eyed ladies who go through life with an air of
darkly incomprehensible significance. She led off Lady
Harman as though she took her away to reveal unheard-
of mysteries and her voice was a contralto undertone
that she emphasized in some inexplicable way by the
magnetic use of her eyes. Her hat of cock's feathers
which rustled like familiar spirits greatly augmented
the profundity of her effect. As she spoke she
glanced guardedly at the other ladies at the end of
the room and from first to last she seemed undecided
in her own mind whether she was a conspirator or a
prophetess. She had heard of Lady Harman before,
she had been longing impatiently to talk to her all
through the lunch. " You are just what we want,"
said Agatha. " What who want ? " asked Lady
Harman, struggling against the hypnotic influence
of her interlocutor. " *We*," said Miss Agatha, " the
Cause. The G. S. W. S.

" We want just such people as you," she repeated,
and began in panting rhetorical sentences to urge the
militant cause.

For her it was manifestly· a struggle against " the
Men." Miss Alimony had no doubts of her sex. It had
nothing to learn, nothing to be forgiven, it was compact
of obscured and persecuted marvels, it needed only
revelation. " They know Nothing," she said of the
antagonist males, bringing deep notes out of the

melodious caverns of her voice; "they know *Nothing* of the Deeper Secrets of Woman's Nature." Her discourse of a general feminine insurrection fell in very closely with the spirit of Lady Harman's private revolt. "We want the Vote," said Agatha, "and we want the Vote because the Vote means Autonomy. And then——"

She paused voluminously. She had already used that word "Autonomy" at the lunch table and it came to her hearer to supply a long-felt want. Now she poured meanings into it, and Lady Harman with each addition realized more clearly that it was still a roomy sack for more. "A woman should be absolute mistress of herself," said Miss Alimony, "absolute mistress of her person. She should be free to develop——"

Germinating phrases these were in Lady Harman's ear.

She wanted to know about the Suffrage movement from some one less generously impatient than Georgina, for Georgina always lost her temper about it and to put it fairly *ranted*; this at any rate was serene and confident, and she asked tentative ill-formed questions and felt her way among Miss Alimony's profundities. She had her doubts, her instinctive doubts about this campaign of violence, she doubted its wisdom, she doubted its rightness, and she perceived, but she found it difficult to express her perception, that Miss Alimony wasn't so much answering her objections as trying to swamp her with exalted emotion. And if there was any flaw whatever in her attention to Miss Alimony's stirring talk, it was because she was keeping a little look-out in the tail of her eye for the reappearance of the men, and more particularly for the reappearance of Mr. Brumley with whom she had a peculiar feeling of uncompleted

relations. And at last the men came and she caught
his glance and saw that her feeling was reciprocated.

She was presently torn from Agatha, who gasped with
pain at the parting and pursued her with a sedulous gaze
as a doctor might watch an injected patient, she parted
with Lady Beach-Mandarin with a vast splash of
enthusiasm and mutual invitations, and Lady Viping
came and pressed her to come to dinner and rapped her
elbow with her lorgnette to emphasize her invitation.
And Lady Harman after a still moment for reflection
athwart which the word Autonomy flickered, accepted
this invitation also.

§ 3

Mr. Brumley hovered for a few moments in the hall
conversing with Lady Beach-Mandarin's butler, whom
he had known for some years and helped about a small
investment, and who was now being abjectly polite and
grateful to him for his attention. It gave Mr. Brumley
a nice feudal feeling to establish and maintain such relationships. The furry-eyed boy fumbled with the sticks
and umbrellas in the background and wondered if he
too would ever climb to these levels of respectful gilt-
tipped friendliness. Mr. Brumley hovered the more
readily because he knew Lady Harman was with the
looking-glass in the little parlour behind the dining-room
on her way to the outer world. At last she emerged.
It was instantly manifest to Mr. Brumley that she had
expected to find him there. She smiled frankly at him,
with the faintest admission of complicity in her smile.

"Taxi, milady?" said the butler.

She seemed to reflect. "No, I will walk." She

hesitated over a glove button. "Mr. Brumley, is there a Tube station near here?"

"Not two minutes. But can't I perhaps take you in a taxi?"

"I'd rather walk."

"I will show you——"

He found himself most agreeably walking off with her.

Still more agreeable things were to follow for Mr. Brumley.

She appeared to meditate upon a sudden idea. She disregarded some conversational opening of his that he forgot in the instant. "Mr. Brumley," she said, "I didn't intend to go directly home."

"I'm altogether at your service," said Mr. Brumley.

"At least," said Lady Harman with that careful truthfulness of hers, "it occurred to me during lunch that I wouldn't go directly home."

Mr. Brumley reined in an imagination that threatened to bolt with him.

"I want," said Lady Harman, "to go to Kensington Gardens, I think. This can't be far from Kensington Gardens—and I want to sit there on a green chair and—meditate —and afterwards I want to find a tube railway or something that will take me back to Putney. There is really no need for me to go directly home. . . . It's very stupid of me but I don't know my way about London as a rational creature should do. So will you take me and put me in a green chair and—tell me how afterwards I can find the Tube and get home. Do you mind?"

"All my time, so long as you want it, is at your service," said Mr. Brumley with convincing earnestness.

" And it's not five minutes to the gardens. And afterwards a taxi-cab——— "

" No," said Lady Harman mindful of her one-and-
eightpence, " I prefer a tube. But that we can talk
about later. You're sure, Mr. Brumley, I'm not invading
your time ? "

" I wish you could see into my mind," said Mr.
Brumley.

She became almost barefaced. " It is so true," she
said, " that at lunch one can't really talk to anyone.
And I've so wanted to talk to you. Ever since we met
before."

Mr. Brumley conveyed an unfeigned delight.

" Since then," said Lady Harman, " I've read your
Euphemia books." Then after a little unskilful pause,
" again." Then she blushed and added, " I *had* read
one of them, you know, before."

" Exactly," he said with an infinite helpfulness.

" And you seem so sympathetic, so understanding.
I feel that all sorts of things that are muddled in my
mind would come clear if I could have a really Good
Talk. To you. . . ."

They were now through the gates approaching the
Albert Memorial. Mr. Brumley was filled with an idea
so desirable that it made him fear to suggest it.

" Of course we can talk very comfortably here," he
said, " under these great trees. But I do so wish———
Have you seen those great borders at Hampton Court ?
The whole place is glowing, and in such sunshine as
this——— A taxi—will take us there under the hour.
If you are free until half-past five."

Why shouldn't she ?

The proposal seemed so outrageous to all the world
of Lady Harman that in her present mood she felt it

was her duty in the cause of womanhood to nerve herself and accept it. . . .

"I mustn't be later than half-past five."

"We could snatch a glimpse of it all and be back before then."

"In that case—— It would be very agreeable"

(*Why shouldn't she?* It would no doubt make Sir Isaac furiously angry—if he heard of it. But it was the sort of thing other women of her class did; didn't all the novels testify? She had a perfect right——

And besides, Mr. Brumley was so entirely harmless.)

§ 4

It had been Lady Harman's clear intention to have a luminous and illuminating discussion of the peculiar difficulties and perplexities of her position with Mr. Brumley. Since their first encounter this idea had grown up in her mind. She was one of those women who turn instinctively to men and away from women for counsel. There was to her perception something wise and kindly and reassuring in him; she felt that he had lived and suffered and understood and that he was ready to help other people to live, his heart she knew from his published works was buried with his dead Euphemia, and he seemed as near a thing to a brother and a friend as she was ever likely to meet. She wanted to tell him all this and then to broach her teeming and tangled difficulties, about her own permissible freedoms, about her social responsibilities, about Sir Isaac's business. But now as their taxi dodged through the traffic of Kensington High Street and went on its way past Olympia and so out westwards, she found it extremely difficult to fix her mind upon the large propositions with which it had been her intention to open. Do as she would to feel that this was a momentous occasion, she could not suppress, she could not ignore an obstinate and entirely undignified persuasion that she was having a tremendous lark. The passing vehicles, various motors, omnibuses, vans, carriages, the thronging pedestrians, the shops and houses, were all so distractingly interesting that at last she had to put it fairly to herself whether she hadn't better resign herself to the sensations of the present and reserve that sustained discussion for an interval she foresaw as inevitable on some comfortable seat under great trees at Hampton Court. You cannot talk well and penetratingly about fundamental things when you are in a not too well-hung taxi which is racing to get ahead of a vast red motor-omnibus. . . .

With a certain discretion Mr. Brumley had instructed the chauffeur to cross the river not at Putney but at Hammersmith, and so they went by Barnes station and up a still almost rural lane into Richmond Park, and there suddenly they were among big trees and bracken and red deer and it might have been a hundred miles from London streets. Mr. Brumley directed the driver to make a detour that gave them quite all the best of the park.

The mind of Mr. Brumley was also agreeably excited and dispersed on this occasion. It was an occasion of which he had been dreaming very frequently of late, he had invented quite remarkable dialogues during those dreams, and now he too was conversationally inadequate and with a similar feeling of unexpected adventure. He was now no more ready to go to the roots of things than Lady Harman. He talked on the way down chiefly of the route they were following, of the changes

in the London traffic due to motor traction and of the
charm and amenity of Richmond Park. And it was
only after they had arrived at Hampton Court and
dismissed the taxi and spent some time upon the
borders, that they came at last to a seat under a grove
beside a long piece of water bearing water lilies, and
sat down and made a beginning with the Good Talk.
Then indeed she tried to gather together the heads of
her perplexity and Mr. Brumley did his best to do
justice to the confidence she reposed in him. . . .

It wasn't at all the conversation he had dreamt of;
it was halting, it was inconclusive, it was full of a vague
dissatisfaction.

The roots of this dissatisfaction lay perhaps more
than anything else in her inattention to him—how
shall I say it?—as *Him*. Hints have been conveyed to
the reader already that for Mr. Brumley the universe
was largely a setting, a tangle, a maze, a quest enshrin-
ing at the heart of it and adumbrating everywhere, a
mystical Her, and his experience of this world had
pointed him very definitely to the conclusion that for
that large other half of mankind which is woman, the
quality of things was reciprocal and centred, for all the
appearances and pretences of other interests, in—Him.
And he was disposed to believe that the other things in
life, not merely the pomp and glories but the faiths and
ambitions and devotions, were all demonstrably little
more than posings and dressings of this great duality.
A large part of his own interests and of the interests of
the women he knew best, was the sustained and in some
cases recurrent discovery and elaboration of lights and
glimpses of Him or Her as the case might be, in various
definite individuals; and it was a surprise to him, it perplexed him to find that this lovely person, so beautifully

equipped for those mutual researches which constituted, he felt, the heart of life, was yet completely in
her manner unaware of this primary sincerity and looking quite simply, as it were, over him and through him
at such things as the ethics of the baking, confectionery
and refreshment trade and the limits of individual
responsibility in these matters. The conclusion that
she was "unawakened" was inevitable.

The dream of "awakening" this Sleeping Beauty
associated itself in a logical sequence with his interpretations. I do not say that such thoughts were clear in
Mr. Brumley's mind, they were not, but into this shape
the forms of his thoughts fell. Such things dimly felt
below the clear level of consciousness were in him. And
they gave his attempt to take up and answer the question
that perplexed her, something of the quality of an
attempt to clothe and serve hidden purposes. It could
not but be evident to him that the effort of Lady
Harman to free herself a little from her husband's
circumvallation and to disentangle herself a little from
the realities of his commercial life, might lead to such
a liberation as would leave her like a nascent element
ready to recombine. And it was entirely in the vein of
this drift of thought in him that he should resolve upon
an assiduous proximity against that moment of release
and awakening. . . .

I do not do Mr. Brumley as the human lover justice
if I lead you to suppose that he plotted thus clearly
and calculatingly. Yet all this was in his mind. All
this was in Mr. Brumley, but it wasn't Mr. Brumley.
Presented with it as a portrait of his mind, he would
have denied it indignantly—and, knowing it was there,
have grown a little flushed in his denials. Quite
equally in his mind was a simple desire to please her,

to do what she wished, to help her because she wanted help. And a quite keen desire to be clean and honest about her and everything connected with her, for his own sake as well as for her sake—for the sake of the relationship. . . .

So you have Mr. Brumley on the green seat under the great trees at Hampton Court, in his neat London clothes, his quite becoming silk-hat, above his neatly handsome and intelligent profile, with his gloves in his hand and one arm over the seat back, going now very earnestly and thoughtfully into the question of the social benefit of the International Bread and Cake Stores and whether it was possible for her to "do anything" to repair any wrongs that might have arisen out of that organization, and you will understand why there is a little flush in his cheek and why his sentences are a trifle disconnected and tentative and why his eye wanders now to the soft raven tresses about Lady Harman's ear, now to the sweet movement of her speaking lips and now to the gracious droop of her pose as she sits forward, elbow upon crossed knee and chin on glove, and jabs her parasol at the ground in her unaccustomed efforts to explain and discuss the difficulties of her position.

And you will understand too why it is that he doesn't deal with the question before him so simply and impartially as he seems to do. Obscuring this extremely interesting problem of a woman growing to man-like sense of responsibility in her social consequences, is the dramatic proclivity that makes him see all this merely as something which must necessarily weaken Lady Harman's loyalty and qualify her submission to Sir Isaac, that makes him want to utilize it and develop it in that direction. . . .

§ 5

Moreover so complex is the thought of man, there was also another stream of mental activity flowing in the darker recesses of Mr. Brumley's mind. Unobtrusively he was trying to count the money in his pockets and make certain estimates.

It had been his intention to replenish his sovereign purse that afternoon at his club and he was only reminded of this abandoned plan when he paid off his taxi at the gates of Hampton Court. The fare was nine and tenpence and the only piece of gold he had was a half-sovereign. But there was a handful of loose silver in his trouser pocket and so the fare and tip were manageable. " Will you be going back, sir? " asked the driver.

And Mr. Brumley reflected too briefly and committed a fatal error. " No," he said with his mind upon that loose silver. " We shall go back by train."

Now it is the custom with taxi-cabs that take people to such outlying and remote places as Hampton Court, to be paid off and to wait loyally until their original passengers return. Thereby the little machine is restrained from ticking out twopences which should go in the main to the absent proprietor, and a feeling of mutuality is established between the driver and his fare. But of course this cab being released presently found another passenger and went away. . . .

I have written in vain if I have not conveyed to you that Mr. Brumley was a gentleman of great and cultivated delicacy, that he liked the seemly and handsome side of things and dreaded the appearance of any flaw upon his prosperity as only a man trained in an English public school can do. It was intolerable to think of any hitch in this happy excursion which was to establish he knew not what confidence between himself and Lady Harman. From first to last he felt it had to go with an air—and what was the first class fare from Hampton Court to Putney—which latter station he believed was on the line from Hampton Court to London—and could one possibly pretend it was unnecessary to have tea? And so while Lady Harman talked about her husband's business—"our business" she called it—and shrank from ever saying anything more about the more intimate question she had most in mind, the limits to a wife's obedience, Mr. Brumley listened with these financial solicitudes showing through his expression and giving it a quality of intensity that she found remarkably reassuring. And once or twice they made him miss points in her remarks that forced him back upon that very inferior substitute for the apt answer, a judicious "Um."

(It would be quite impossible to go without tea, he decided. He himself wanted tea quite badly. He would think better when he had had some tea. . . .)

The crisis came at tea. They had tea at the inn upon the green that struck Mr. Brumley as being most likely to be cheap and which he pretended to choose for some trivial charm about the windows. And it wasn't cheap, and when at last Mr. Brumley was faced by the little slip of the bill and could draw his money from his pocket and look at it, he knew the worst and the worst was worse than he had expected. The bill was five shillings (Should he dispute it? Too ugly altogether, a dispute with a probably ironical waiter!) and the money in his hand amounted to four shillings and sixpence.

He acted surprise with the waiter's eye upon him. (Should he ask for credit? They might be frightfully disagreeable in such a cockney resort as this.) "Tut, tut," said Mr. Brumley, and then—a little late for it—resorted to and discovered the emptiness of his sovereign purse. He realized that this was out of the picture at this stage, felt his ears and nose and cheeks grow hot and pink. The waiter's colleague across the room became interested in the proceedings.

"I had no idea," said Mr. Brumley, which was a premeditated falsehood.

"Is anything the matter?" asked Lady Harman with a sisterly interest.

"My dear Lady Harman, I find myself—— Ridiculous position. Might I borrow half a sovereign?"

He felt sure that the two waiters exchanged glances. He looked at them,—a mistake again—and got hotter.

"Oh!" said Lady Harman and regarded him with frank amusement in her eyes. The thing struck her at first in the light of a joke. "I've only got one-and-eightpence. I didn't expect—— "

She blushed as beautifully as ever. Then she produced a small but plutocratic-looking purse and handed it to him.

"Most remarkable—inconvenient," said Mr. Brumley, opening the precious thing and extracting a shilling. "That will do," he said and dismissed the waiter with a tip of sixpence. Then with the open purse still in his hand, he spent much of his remaining strength trying to look amused and unembarrassed, feeling all the time that with his flushed face and in view of all the circumstances of the case he must be really looking very silly and fluffy.

"It's really most inconvenient," he remarked.

"I never thought of the—of this. It was silly of me," said Lady Harman.

"Oh no! Oh dear no! The silliness I can assure you is all mine. I can't tell you how entirely apologetic—— Ridiculous fix. And after I had persuaded you to come here."

"Still we were able to pay," she consoled him.

"But you have to get home!"

She hadn't so far thought of that. It brought Sir Isaac suddenly into the picture. "By half-past five," she said with just the faintest flavour of interrogation.

Mr. Brumley looked at his watch. It was ten minutes to five.

"Waiter," he said, "how do the trains run from here to Putney?"

"I don't *think*, sir, that we have any trains from here to Putney——"

An A.B.C Railway Guide was found and Mr. Brumley learnt for the first time that Putney and Hampton Court are upon two distinct and separate and, as far as he could judge by the time-table, mutually hostile branches of the South Western Railway, and that at the earliest they could not get to Putney before six o'clock.

Mr. Brumley was extremely disconcerted. He perceived that he ought to have kept his taxi. It amounted almost to a debt of honour to deliver this lady secure and untarnished at her house within the next hour. But this reflection did not in the least degree assist him to carry it out and as a matter of fact Mr. Brumley became flurried and did not carry it out. He was not used to being without money, it unnerved him, and he gave way to a kind of hectic *savoir faire*. He demanded a taxi of the waiter. He tried to evolve a taxi by will power alone.   He went out with Lady Harman and back towards the gates of Hampton Court to look for taxis.   Then it occurred to him that they might be losing the 5.25 up.   So they hurried over the bridge to the station.

He had a vague notion that he would be able to get tickets on credit at the booking office if he presented his visiting card.   But the clerk in charge seemed to find something uncongenial in his proposal.   He did not seem to like what he saw of Mr. Brumley through his little square window and Mr. Brumley found something slighting and unpleasant in his manner.   It was one of those little temperamental jars which happen to men of delicate sensibilities and Mr. Brumley tried to be reassuringly overbearing in his manner and then lost his temper and was threatening and so wasted precious moments what time Lady Harman waited on the platform, with a certain shadow of doubt falling upon her confidence in him, and watched the five-twenty-five gather itself together and start Londonward.   Mr. Brumley came out of the ticket office resolved to travel without tickets and carry things through with a high hand just as it became impossible to do so by that train, and then I regret to say he returned for some further haughty passages with the ticket clerk upon the duty of public servants to point out such oversights as his, that led to repartee and did nothing to help Lady Harman on her homeward way.

Then he discovered a current time-table and learnt that now even were all the ticket difficulties overridden he could not get Lady Harman to Putney before twenty minutes past seven, so completely is the South Western Railway not organized for conveying people from Hampton Court to Putney.   He explained this as well as he could to Lady Harman, and then led her out of the station in another last desperate search for a taxi.

"We can always come back for that next train," he said. "It doesn't go for half an hour."

"I cannot blame myself sufficiently," he said for the eighth or ninth time. . . .

It was already well past a quarter to six before Mr. Brumley bethought himself of the London County Council tramcars that run from the palace gates. Along these an ample four-pennyworth was surely possible and at the end would be taxis—— There *must* be taxis. The tram took them—but oh ! how slowly it seemed !—to Hammersmith by a devious route through interminable roads and streets, and long before they reached that spot twilight had passed into darkness, and all the streets and shops were flowering into light and the sense of night and lateness was very strong. After they were seated in the tram a certain interval of silence came between them and then Lady Harman laughed and Mr. Brumley laughed—there was no longer any need for him to be energetic and fussy—and they began to have that feeling of adventurous amusement which comes on the further side of desperation. But beneath the temporary elation Lady Harman was a prey to grave anxieties and Mr. Brumley could not help thinking he had made a tremendous ass of himself in that ticket clerk dispute. . . .

At Hammersmith they got out, two quite penniless travellers, and after some anxious moments found a taxi. It took them to Putney Hill. Lady Harman descended at the outer gates of her home and walked up the drive in the darkness while Mr. Brumley went on to his club and solvency again. It was five minutes past eight when he entered the hall of his club. . . .

§ 6

It had been Lady Harman's original intention to come home before four, to have tea with her mother and to inform her husband when he returned from the city of her entirely dignified and correct disobedience to his absurd prohibitions. Then he would have bullied at a disadvantage, she would have announced her intention of dining with Lady Viping and making the various calls and expeditions for which she had arranged and all would have gone well. But you see how far accident and a spirit of enterprise may take a lady from so worthy a plan, and when at last she returned to the Victorian baronial home in Putney it was very nearly eight and the house blazed with crisis from pantry to nursery. Even the elder three little girls, who were accustomed to be kissed good-night by their " boofer muvver," were still awake and—catching the subtle influence of the atmosphere of dismay about them—in tears. The very under-housemaids were saying : " Where *ever* can her ladyship 'ave got to ? "

Sir Isaac had come home that day at an unusually early hour and with a peculiar pinched expression that filled even Snagsby with apprehensive alertness. Sir Isaac had in fact returned in a state of quite unwonted venom. He had come home early because he wished to vent it upon Ellen, and her absence filled him with something of that sensation one has when one puts out a foot for the floor and instead a step drops one down —it seems abysmally.

" But where's she gone, Snagsby ? "

" Her ladyship *said* to lunch, Sir Isaac," said Snagsby.

"Good gracious! Where?"

"Her ladyship didn't *say*, Sir Isaac."

"But where? Where the devil——?"

"I have—'ave no means whatever of knowing, Sir Isaac."

He had a defensive inspiration.

"Perhaps Mrs. Sawbridge, Sir Isaac. . . ."

Mrs. Sawbridge was enjoying the sunshine upon the lawn. She sat in the most comfortable garden chair, held a white sunshade overhead, had the last new novel by Mrs. Humphry Ward upon her lap, and was engaged in trying not to wonder where her daughter might be. She beheld with a distinct blenching of the spirit Sir Isaac advancing towards her. She wondered more than ever where Ellen might be.

"Here!" cried her son-in-law. "Where's Ellen gone?"

Mrs. Sawbridge with an affected off-handedness was sure she hadn't the faintest idea.

"Then you *ought* to have," said Isaac. "She ought to be at home."

Mrs. Sawbridge's only reply was to bridle slightly.

"Where's she got to? Where's she gone? Haven't you any idea at all?"

"I was not favoured by Ellen's confidence," said Mrs. Sawbridge.

"But you *ought* to know," cried Sir Isaac. "She's your daughter. Don't you know anything of *either* of your daughters. I suppose you don't care where they are, either of them, or what mischief they're **up to**. Here's a man—comes home early to his tea—and no wife! After hearing all I've done at the club."

Mrs. Sawbridge stood up in order to be more dignified than a seated position permitted.

"It is scarcely my business, Sir Isaac," she said, "to know of the movements of your wife."

"Nor Georgina's apparently either. Good God! I'd have given a hundred pounds that this shouldn't have happened!"

"If you must speak to me, Sir Isaac, will you please kindly refrain from—from the deity——"

"Oh! shut it!" said Sir Isaac, blazing up to violent rudeness. "Why! Don't you know, haven't you an idea? The infernal foolery! Those tickets. She got those women—— Look here, if you go walking away with your nose in the air before I've done—— Look here! Mrs. Sawbridge, you listen to me—— Georgina. I'm speaking of Georgina."

The lady was walking now swiftly and stiffly towards the house, her face very pale and drawn, and Sir Isaac hurrying beside her in a white fury of expostulation. "I tell you," he cried, "Georgina—— "

There was something maddeningly incurious about her. He couldn't understand why she didn't even pause to hear what Georgina had done and what he had to say about it. A person so wrapped up in her personal and private dignity makes a man want to throw stones. Perhaps she knew of Georgina's misdeeds. Perhaps she sympathized. . . .

A sense of the house windows checked his pursuit of her ear. "Then go," he said to her retreating back. "*Go!* I don't care if you go for good. I don't care if you go altogether. If *you* hadn't had the upbringing of these two girls——"

She was manifestly out of earshot and in full yet almost queenly flight for the house. He wanted to say things about her. *To* someone. He was already saying things to the garden generally. What does one marry a wife for? His mind came round to Ellen again. Where had she got to? Even if she had gone out to lunch, it was time she was back. He went to his study and rang for Snagsby.

" Lady Harman back yet ? " he asked grimly.

" No, Sir Isaac."

" Why isn't she back ? "

Snagsby did his best. " Perhaps, Sir Isaac, her lady-ship has experienced—'as hexperienced a naxident. "

Sir Isaac stared at that idea for a moment. Then he thought, ' Someone would have telephoned .' " No, " he said, " she's out. That's where she is. And I suppose I can wait here, as well as I can, until she chooses to come home. Degenerate foolish nonsense. . . ! "

He whistled between his teeth like an escape of steam. Snagsby after the due pause of attentiveness, bowed respectfully and withdrew. . . .

He had barely time to give a brief outline of the interview to the pantry before a violent ringing summoned him again. Sir Isaac wished to speak to Peters, Lady Harman's maid. He wanted to know where Lady Harman had gone ; this being impossible, he wanted to know where Lady Harman had seemed to be going.

" Her Ladyship *seemed* to be going out to lunch, Sir Isaac," said Peters, her meek face irradiated by helpful intelligence.

" Oh *get* out ! said Sir Isaac. " *Get* out ! "

" Yes, Sir Isaac," said Peters and obeyed. . . .

" He's in a rare bait about her," said Peters to Snagsby downstairs.

" I'm inclined to think her ladyship will catch it pretty hot," said Snagsby.

" He can't *know* anything," said Peters.

" What about ? " asked Snagsby.

" Oh, *I* don't know," said Peters.   " Don't ask *me* about her. . . ."

About ten minutes later Sir Isaac was heard to break a little china figure of the goddess Kwannon, that had stood upon his study mantel-shelf.   The fragments were found afterwards in the fireplace. . . .

The desire for self-expression may become over-whelming.   After Sir Isaac had talked to himself about Georgina and Lady Harman for some time in his study, he was seized with a great longing to pour some of this spirited stuff into the entirely unsympathetic ear of Mrs. Sawbridge.   So he went about the house and garden looking for her, and being at last obliged to enquire about her, learnt from a scared defensive housemaid whom he cornered suddenly in the conservatory, that she had retired to her own room.   He went and rapped at her door but after one muffled " Who's that ? " he could get no further response.

" I want to tell you about Georgina," he said.

He tried the handle but the discreet lady within had turned the key upon her dignity.

" I want," he shouted, " to tell you about Georgina. . . .   GEORGINA !   Oh *damn !* "

Silence.

Tea awaited him downstairs.   He hovered about the drawing-room, making noises between his teeth.

" Snagsby," said Sir Isaac, " jest tell Mrs. Sawbridge I shall be obliged if she will come down to tea."

" Mrs. Sawbridge 'as a 'ead ache, Sir Isaac," said Mr. Snagsby with extreme blandness.   " She asked me to acquaint you.   She 'as ordered tea in 'er own apartment."

For a moment Sir Isaac was baffled. Then he had an inspiration. "Just get me the *Times*, Snagsby," he said.

He took the paper and unfolded it until a particular paragraph was thrown into extreme prominence. This he lined about with his fountain pen and wrote above it with a quivering hand, "These women's tickets were got by Georgina under false pretences from me." He handed the paper thus prepared back to Snagsby. "Just take this paper to Mrs. Sawbridge," he said, "and ask her what she thinks of it?"

But Mrs. Sawbridge tacitly declined this proposal for a correspondence *viâ* Snagsby.

§ 7

There was no excuse for Georgina.

Georgina had obtained tickets from Sir Isaac for the great party reception at Barleypound House, under the shallow pretext that she wanted them for "two spinsters from the country," for whose good behaviour she would answer, and she had handed them over to that organization of disorder which swayed her mind. The historical outrage upon Mr. Blapton was the consequence.

Two desperate and misguided emissaries had gone to the great reception, dressed and behaving as much as possible like helpful Liberal women; they had made their way towards the brilliant group of leading Liberals of which Mr. Blapton was the centre, assuming an almost Whig-like expression and bearing to mask the fires within, and had then suddenly accosted him. It was one of those great occasions when the rank and

file of the popular party is privileged to look upon
Court dress. The ministers and great people had
come on from Buckingham Palace in their lace and
legs. Scarlet and feathers, splendid trains and
mysterious ribbons and stars, gave an agreeable
intimation of all that it means to be in office to the
dazzled wives and daughters of the party stalwarts and
fired the ambition of innumerable earnest but earnestly
competitive young men. It opened the eyes of the
Labour leaders to the higher possibilities of Parliament.
And then suddenly came a stir, a rush, a cry of "Tear
off his epaulettes!" and outrage was afoot. And two
quite nice-looking young women!

It is unhappily not necessary to describe the scene
that followed. Mr. Blapton made a brave fight for
his epaulettes, fighting chiefly with his cocked hat,
which was bent double in the struggle. Mrs. Blapton
gave all the assistance true womanliness could offer
and, in fact, she boxed the ears of one of his assailants
very soundly. The intruders were rescued in an extremely torn and draggled condition from the indignant
statesmen who had fallen upon them by tardy but
decisive police. . . .

Such scenes sprinkle the recent history of England
with green and purple patches and the interest of this
particular one for us is only because of Georgina's
share in it. That was brought home to Sir Isaac, very
suddenly and disagreeably, while he was lunching at
the Climax Club with Sir Robert Charterson. A man
named Gobbin, an art critic or something of that sort,
one of those flimsy literary people who mar the solid
worth of so many great clubs, a man with a lot of hair
and the sort of loose tie that so often seems to be less
of a tie than a detachment from all decent restraints,

told him. Charterson was holding forth upon the outrage.

"That won't suit Sir Isaac, Sir Robert," said Gobbin presuming on his proximity.

Sir Isaac tried to give him the sort of look one gives to an unsatisfactory clerk.

"They went there with Sir Isaac's tickets," said Gobbin.

"They *never*——!"

"Horatio Blenker was looking for you in the hall. Haven't you seen him? After all the care they took. The poor man's almost in tears."

"They never had tickets of mine!" cried Sir Isaac stoutly and indignantly.

And then the thought of Georgina came like a blow upon his heart. . . .

In his flurry he went on denying. . . .

The subsequent conversation in the smoking-room was as red-eared and disagreeable for Sir Isaac as any conversation could be. "But how *could* such a thing have happened?" he asked in a voice that sounded bleached to him. "How could such a thing have come about?" Their eyes were dreadful. Did they guess? Could they guess? Conscience within him was going up and down shouting out, "Georgina, your sister-in-law, Georgina," so loudly that he felt the whole smoking-room must be hearing it. . . .

§ 8

As Lady Harman came up through the darkness of the drive to her home, she was already regretting very deeply that she had not been content to talk to Mr. Brumley in Kensington Gardens instead of accepting his picturesque suggestion of Hampton Court. There was an unpleasant waif-like feeling about this return. She was reminded of pictures published in the interests of Doctor Barnardo's philanthropies,—Dr. Barnardo her favourite hero in real life—in which wistful little outcasts creep longingly towards brightly lit but otherwise respectable homes. It wasn't at all the sort of feeling she would have chosen if she had had a choice of feelings. She was tired and dusty and as she came into the hall the bright light was blinding. Snagsby took her wrap. " Sir Isaac, me lady, 'as been enquiring for your ladyship," he communicated.

Sir Isaac appeared on the staircase.

" Good gracious, Elly ! " he shouted. " Where you been ? "

Lady Harman decided against an immediate reply. " I shall be ready for dinner in half an hour," she told Snagsby and went past him to the stairs.

Sir Isaac awaited her. " Where you been ? " he repeated as she came up to him.

A housemaid on the staircase and the second nursemaid on the nursery landing above shared Sir Isaac's eagerness to hear her answer. But they did not hear her answer, for Lady Harman with a movement that was all too reminiscent of her mother's in the garden, swept past him towards the door of her own room. He followed her and shut the door on the thwarted listeners.

" Here ! " he said, with a connubial absence of restraint. " Where the devil you been ? What the deuce do you think you've been getting up to ? "

She had been calculating her answers since the moment she had realized that she was to return home at a disadvantage. (It is not my business to blame her for a certain disingenuousness; it is my business simply to record it.) " I went out to lunch at Lady Beach-Mandarin's," she said. " I told you I meant to."

" Lunch ! " he cried. " Why, it's eight ! "

" I met —some people. I met Agatha Alimony. I have a perfect right to go out to lunch—— "

" You met a nice crew I'll bet. But that don't account for your being out to eight, does it ? With all the confounded household doing as it pleases ! "

" I went on—to see the borders at Hampton Court."

" With *her* ? "

" *Yes*," said Lady Harman. . . .

It wasn't what she had meant to happen. It was an inglorious declension from her comtemplated pose of dignified assertion. She was impelled to do her utmost to get away from this lie she had uttered at once, to eliminate Agatha from the argument by an emphatic generalization. " I've a perfect right," she said, suddenly nearly breathless, " to go to Hampton Court with anyone I please, talk about anything I like and stay there as long as I think fit."

He squeezed his thin lips together for a silent moment and then retorted. " You've got nothing of the sort, nothing of the sort. You've got to do your duty like everybody else in the world, and your duty is to be in this house controlling it—and not gossiping about London just where any silly fancy takes you."

" I don't think that *is* my duty," said Lady Harman after a slight pause to collect her forces.

" Of *course* it's your duty. You know it's your duty. You know perfectly well. It's only these rotten, silly, degenerate, decadent fools who've got ideas into you——" The sentence staggered under its load of adjectives like a camel under the last straw and collapsed. "*See?*" he said.

Lady Harman knitted her brows.

"I do my duty," she began.

But Sir Isaac was now resolved upon eloquence. His mind was full with the accumulations of an extremely long and bitter afternoon and urgent to discharge. He began to answer her and then a passion of rage flooded him. Suddenly he wanted to shout and use abusive expressions and it seemed to him there was nothing to prevent his shouting and using abusive expressions. So he did. "Call this your duty," he said, "gadding about with some infernal old suffragette——"

He paused to gather force. He had never quite let himself go to his wife before; he had never before quite let himself go to anyone. He had always been in every crisis just a little too timid to let himself go. But a wife is privileged. He sought strength and found it in words from which he had hitherto abstained. It was not a discourse to which print could do justice; it flickered from issue to issue. He touched upon Georgina, upon the stiffness of Mrs. Sawbridge's manner, upon the neurotic weakness of Georgina's unmarried state, upon the general decay of feminine virtue in the community, upon the laxity of modern literature, upon the dependent state of Lady Harman, upon the unfairness of their relations which gave her every luxury while he spent his days in arduous toil, upon the shame and annoyance in the eyes of his servants that her unexplained absence had caused him.

He emphasised his speech by gestures. He thrust out one rather large ill-shaped hand at her with two vibrating fingers extended. His ears became red, his nose red, his eyes seemed red and all about these points his face was wrathful white. His hair rose up into stiff scared listening ends. He had his rights, he had some *little* claim to consideration surely, he might be just nobody but he wasn't going to stand this much anyhow. He gave her fair warning. What was she, what did she know of the world into which she wanted to rush? He lapsed into views of Lady Beach-Mandarin—unfavourable views. I wish Lady Beach-Mandarin could have heard him. . . .

Ever and again Lady Harman sought to speak. This incessant voice confused and baffled her; she had a just attentive mind at bottom and down there was a most weakening feeling that there must indeed be some misdeed in her to evoke so impassioned a storm. She had a curious and disconcerting sense of responsibility for his dancing exasperation, she felt she was to blame for it, just as years ago she had felt she was to blame for his tears when he had urged her so desperately to marry him. Some irrational instinct made her want to allay him. It is the supreme feminine weakness, that wish to allay. But she was also clinging desperately to her resolution to proclaim her other forthcoming engagements. Her will hung on to that as a man hangs on to a mountain path in a thunderburst. She stood gripping her dressing-table and ever and again trying to speak. But whenever she did so Sir Isaac lifted a hand and cried almost threateningly : " You hear me out Elly ! You hear me out ! " and went on a little faster. . . .

(Limburger in his curious " *Sexuelle Unterschiede der Seele*," points out as a probably universal distinction between the sexes that when a man scolds a woman, if only he scolds loudly enough and long enough, conviction of sin is aroused, while in the reverse case the result is merely a murderous impulse.   This he further says is not understood by women, who hope by scolding to produce the similar effect upon men that they themselves would experience.   The passage is illustrated by figures of ducking stools and followed by some carefully analysed statistics of connubial crime in Berlin in the years 1901–2.   But in this matter let the student compare the achievement of Paulina in *The Winter's Tale* and reflect upon his own life.   And moreover it is difficult to estimate how far the twinges of conscience that Lady Harman was feeling were not due to an entirely different cause, the falsification of her position by the lie she had just told Sir Isaac.)

And presently upon this noisy scene in the great pink bedroom, with Sir Isaac walking about and standing and turning and gesticulating and Lady Harman clinging on to her dressing-table, and painfully divided between her new connections, her sense of guilty deception and the deep instinctive responsibilities of a woman's nature, came, like one of those rows of dots that are now so frequent and so helpful in the art of fiction, the surging, deep, assuaging note of Snagsby's gong : Booooooom. Boom. Booooooom. . . . .

" Damn it ! " cried Sir Isaac smiting at the air with both fists clenched and speaking as though this was Ellen's crowning misdeed, " and we aren't even dressed for dinner ! "

§ 9

Dinner had something of the stiffness of court ceremonial.

Mrs. Sawbridge, perhaps erring on the side of

discretion, had consumed a little soup and a wing of chicken in her own room. Sir Isaac was down first and his wife found him grimly astride before the great dining-room fire awaiting her. She had had her dark hair dressed with extreme simplicity and had slipped on a blue velvet tea-gown, but she had been delayed by a visit to the nursery, where the children were now flushed and uneasily asleep.

Husband and wife took their places at the genuine Sheraton dining-table—one of the very best pieces Sir Isaac had ever picked up—and were waited on with a hushed, scared dexterity by Snagsby and the footman.

Lady Harman and her husband exchanged no remarks during the meal; Sir Isaac was a little noisy with his soup as became a man who controls honest indignation, and once he complained briefly in a slightly hoarse voice to Snagsby about the state of one of the rolls. Between the courses he leant back in his chair and made faint sounds with his teeth. These were the only breach of the velvety quiet. Lady Harman was surprised to discover herself hungry, but she ate with thoughtful dignity and gave her mind to the attempted digestion of the confusing interview she had just been through.

It was a very indigestible interview.

On the whole her heart hardened again. With nourishment and silence her spirit recovered a little from its abasement, and her resolution to assert her freedom to go hither and thither and think as she chose renewed itself. She tried to plan some way of making her declaration so that she would not again be overwhelmed by a torrent of response. Should she speak to him at the end of dinner? Should she speak to him while Snagsby was in the room? But he might behave badly even with Snagsby in the room and she could not bear to think of him behaving badly to her in the presence of Snagsby. She glanced at him over the genuine old silver bowl of roses in the middle of the table—all the roses were good *new* sorts—and tried to estimate how he might behave under various methods of declaration.

The dinner followed its appointed ritual to the dessert. Came the wine and Snagsby placed the cigars and a little silver lamp beside his master.

She rose slowly with a speech upon her lips. Sir Isaac remained seated looking up at her with a mitigated fury in his little red-brown eyes.

The speech receded from her lips again.

" I think," she said after a strained pause, " I will go and see how mother is now."

" She's only shamming," said Sir Isaac belatedly to her back as she went out of the room.

She found her mother in a wrap before her fire and made her dutiful enquiries.

" It's only quite a *slight* headache," Mrs. Sawbridge confessed. " But Isaac was so upset about Georgina and about "— she flinched—" about—everything, that I thought it better to be out of the way."

" What exactly has Georgina done? "

" It's in the paper, dear. On the table there."

Ellen studied the *Times*.

" Georgina got them the tickets," Mrs. Sawbridge explained. " I wish she hadn't. It was so—so unnecessary of her."

There was a little pause as Lady Harman read. She put down the paper and asked her mother if she could do anything for her.

"I—I suppose it's all Right, dear, now?" Mrs. Sawbridge asked.

"Quite," said her daughter "You're sure I can do nothing for you, mummy?"

"I'm kept so in the dark about things."

"It's quite all right now, mummy."

"He went on—dreadfully."

"It was annoying—of Georgina."

"It makes my position so difficult. I do wish he wouldn't want to speak to me—about all these things. . . . Georgina treats me like a Perfect Nonentity and then he comes—— It's so inconsiderate. Starting Disputes. Do you know, dear, I really think—if I were to go for a little time to Bournemouth—— ?"

Her daughter seemed to find something attractive in the idea. She came to the hearthrug and regarded her mother with maternal eyes.

"Don't you *worry* about things, mummy," she said.

"Mrs. Bleckhorn told me of such a nice quiet boarding-house, almost looking on the sea. . . . One would be safe from Insult there. You know——" her voice broke for a moment, "he was Insulting, he *meant* to be Insulting. I'm—Upset. I've been thinking over it ever since."

§ 10

Lady Harman came out upon the landing. She felt absolutely without backing in the world. (If only she hadn't told a lie!) Then with an effort she directed her course downstairs to the dining-room.

(The lie had been necessary. It was only a detail. It mustn't blind her to the real issue.)

She entered softly and found her husband standing

before the fire plunged in gloomy thoughts. Upon the marble mantel-shelf behind him was a little glass; he had been sipping port in spite of the express prohibition of his doctor and the wine had reddened the veins of his eyes and variegated the normal pallor of his countenance with little flushed areas. "Hel-lo," he said looking up suddenly as she closed the door behind her.

For a moment there was something in their two expressions like that on the faces of men about to box.

"I want you to understand," she said, and then; "The way you behaved——"

There was an uncontrollable break in her voice. She had a dreadful feeling that she might be going to cry. She made a great effort to be cold and clear.

"I don't think you have a right—just because I am your wife—to control every moment of my time. In fact you haven't. And I have a right to make engagements. . . . I want you to know I am going to an afternoon meeting at Lady Beach-Mandarin's. Next week. And I have promised to go to Miss Alimony's to tea."

"Go on," he encouraged grimly.

"I am going to Lady Viping's to dinner, too; she asked me and I accepted. Later."

She stopped.

He seemed to deliberate. Then suddenly he thrust out a face of pinched determination.

"You *won't*, my lady," he said. "You bet your life you won't. *No!* So *now* then!"

And then gripping his hands more tightly behind him, he made a step towards her.

"You're losing your bearings, Lady Harman," he said, speaking with much intensity in a low earnest voice. " You don't seem to be remembering where you are. You come and you tell me you're going to do this and that. Don't you know, Lady Harman, that it's your wifely duty to obey, to do as I say, to behave as I wish." He brought out a lean index finger to emphasise his remarks. " And I am going to make you do it ! " he said.

" I've a perfect right," she repeated.

He went on, regardless of her words. " What do you think you can do, Lady Harman ? You're going to all these places—how ? Not in *my* motor-car, not with *my* money. You've not a thing that isn't mine, that *I* haven't given you. And if you're going to have a lot of friends I haven't got, where're they coming to see you ? Not in *my* house ! I'll chuck 'em out if I find 'em. I won't have 'em. I'll turn 'em out. See ? "

" I'm not a slave."

" You're a wife—and a wife's got to do what her husband wishes. You can't have two heads on a horse. And in *this* horse—this house I mean, the head's— *me !* "

" I'm not a slave and I won't be a slave."

" You're a wife and you'll stick to the bargain you made when you married me. I'm ready in reason to give you anything you want—if you do your duty as a wife should. Why !—I spoil you. But this going about on your own, this highty-flighty go-as-you-please, —no man on earth who's worth calling a man will stand it. I'm not going to begin to stand it. . . . You try it on. You try it, Lady Harman. . . . You'll come to your senses soon enough. See ? You start trying it on now—straight away. We'll make an experiment. We'll watch how it goes. Only don't expect me to give you any money, don't expect me to

help your struggling family, don't expect me to alter
my arrangements because of you. Let's keep apart
for a bit and you go your way and I'll go mine. And
we'll see who's sick of it first, we'll see who wants to
cry off."

"I came down here," said Lady Harman, " to give
you a reasonable notice——"

"And you found *I* could reason too," interrupted
Sir Isaac in a kind of miniature shout, "you found I
could reason too ! "

"You think—— Reason ! I *won't*," said Lady
Harman, and found herself in tears. By an enormous
effort she recovered something of her dignity and withdrew. He made no effort to open the door, but stood
a little hunchbacked and with a sense of rhetorical
victory surveying her retreat

§ 11

After Lady Harman's maid had left her that night,
she sat for some time in a low easy-chair before her fire,
trying at first to collect together into one situation all
the events of the day and then lapsing into that state of
mind which is not so much thinking as resting in the
attitude of thought. Presently, in a vaguely conceived
future, she would go to bed. She was stunned by the
immense dimensions of the row her simple act of
defiance had evoked.

And then came an incredible incident, so incredible
that next day she still had great difficulty in deciding
whether it was an actuality or a dream. She heard a
little very familiar sound. It was the last sound she
would have expected to hear and she turned sharply
when she heard it. The paper-covered door in the

wall of her husband's apartment opened softly, paused, opened some more and his little undignified head appeared. His hair was already tumbled from his pillow.

He regarded her steadfastly for some moments with an expression between shame and curiosity and smouldering rage, and then allowed his body, clad now in purple-striped pyjamas, to follow his head into her room. He advanced guiltily.

" Elly," he whispered. " Elly ! "

She caught her dressing-gown about her and stood up.

" What is it, Isaac," she asked, feeling curiously abashed at this invasion.

" Elly," he said, still in that furtive undertone. " *Make it up !* "

" I want my freedom," she said, after a little pause.

" Don't be *silly*, Elly," he whispered in a tone of remonstrance and advancing slowly towards her. " Make it up. Chuck all these ideas."

She shook her head.

" We've got to get along together. You can't go going about just anywhere. We've got—we've got to be reasonable."

He halted, three paces away from her. His eyes weren't sorrowful eyes, or friendly eyes ; they were just shiftily eager eyes. " Look here," he said. " It's all nonsense. . . . Elly, old girl ; let's—let's make it up."

She looked at him and it dawned upon her that she had always imagined herself to be afraid of him and that indeed she wasn't. She shook her head obstinately.

" It isn't reasonable," he said. " Here, we've been the happiest of people—— Anything in reason I'll let

you have." He paused with an effect of making an
offer.

"I want my autonomy," she said.

"Autonomy!" he echoed. "Autonomy! What's
autonomy? Autonomy!"

This strange word seemed first to hold him in
distressful suspense and then to infuriate him.

"I come in here to make it up," he said, with a
voice charged with griefs, "after all you've done, and
you go and you talk of autonomy!"

His feelings passed beyond words. An extremity
of viciousness flashed into his face. He gave vent to a
snarl of exasperation, "Ya-ap!" he said, he raised his
clenched fists and seemed on the verge of assault, and
then with a gesture between fury and despair, he wheeled
about and the purple-striped pyjamas danced in passionate retreat from her room.

"Autonomy! . . . ."

A slam, a noise of assaulted furniture, and then
silence.

Lady Harman stood for some moments regarding
the paper-covered door that had closed behind him.
Then she bared her white forearm and pinched it—
hard.

It wasn't a dream! This thing had happened.

§ 12

At a quarter to three in the morning, Lady Harman
was surprised to find herself wide awake. It was exactly
a quarter to three when she touched the stud of the
ingenious little silver apparatus upon the table beside
her bed which reflected a luminous clock-face upon the
ceiling. And her mind was no longer resting in the

attitude of thought but extraordinarily active. It was active, but as she presently began to realize it was not progressing. It was spinning violently round and round the frenzied figure of a little man in purple-striped pyjamas retreating from her presence, whirling away from her like something blown before a gale. That seemed to her to symbolize the completeness of the breach the day had made between her husband and herself.

She felt as a statesman might feel who had inadvertently—while conducting some trivial negotiations—declared war.

She was profoundly alarmed. She perceived ahead of her abundant possibilities of disagreeable things. And she wasn't by any means as convinced of the righteousness of her cause as a happy warrior should be. She had a natural disposition towards truthfulness and it worried her mind that while she was struggling to assert her right to these common social freedoms she should be tacitly admitting a kind of justice in her husband's objections by concealing the fact that her afternoon's companion was a man. She tried not to recognize the existence of a doubt, but deep down in her mind there did indeed lurk a weakening uncertainty about the right of a woman to free conversation with any man but her own. Her reason disowned that uncertainty with scorn. But it wouldn't go away for all her reason. She went about in her mind doing her utmost to cut that doubt dead. . . .

She tried to go back to the beginning and think it all out. And as she was not used to thinking things out, the effort took the form of an imaginary explanation to Mr. Brumley of the difficulties of her position. She framed phrases. " You see, Mr.

Brumley," she imagined herself to be saying, "I want to do my duty as a wife, I have to do my duty as a wife. But it's so hard to say just where duty leaves off and being a mere slave begins. I cannot believe that *blind* obedience is any woman's duty. A woman needs —autonomy." Then her mind went off for a time to a wrestle with the exact meaning of autonomy, an issue that had not arisen hitherto in her mind. . . . And as she planned out such elucidations, there grew more and more distinct in her mind a kind of idealized Mr. Brumley, very grave, very attentive, wonderfully understanding, saying illuminating helpful tonic things, that made everything clear, everything almost easy. She wanted someone of that quality so badly. The night would have been unendurable if she could not have imagined Mr. Brumley of that quality. And imagining him of that quality her heart yearned for him. She felt that she had been terribly inexpressive that afternoon, she had shirked points, misstated points, and yet he had been marvellously understanding. Ever and again his words had seemed to pierce right through what she had been saying to what she had been thinking. And she recalled with peculiar comfort a kind of abstracted calculating look that had come at times into his eyes, as though his thoughts were going ever so much deeper and ever so much further than her blundering questionings could possibly have taken them. He weighed every word, he had a guarded way of saying "Um. . . ."

Her thoughts came back to the dancing little figure in purple-striped pyjamas. She had a scared sense of irrevocable breaches. What would he do to-morrow? What should she do to-morrow? Would he speak to her at breakfast or should she speak first to him? . . .

She wished she had some money. If she could have foreseen all this she would have got some money before she began. . . .

So her mind went on round and round and the dawn was breaking before she slept again.

§ 13

Mr. Brumley, also, slept little that night. He was wakefully mournful, recalling each ungraceful incident of the afternoon's failure in turn and more particularly his dispute with the ticket clerk, and thinking over all the things he might have done—if only he hadn't done the things he had done. He had made an atrocious mess of things. He felt he had hopelessly shattered the fair fabric of impressions of him that Lady Harman had been building up, that image of a wise humane capable man to whom a woman would gladly turn; he had been flurried, he had been incompetent, he had been ridiculously incompetent, and it seemed to him that life was a string of desolating inadequacies and that he would never smile again.

The probable reception of Lady Harman by her husband never came within his imaginative scope. Nor did the problems of social responsibility that Lady Harman had been trying to put to him exercise him very greatly. The personal disillusionment was too strong for that.

About half-past four a faint ray of comfort came with the consideration that after all a certain practical incapacity is part of the ensemble of a literary artist, and then he found himself wondering what flowers of wisdom Montaigne might not have culled from such a day's experience; he began an imitative essay in his

head and he fell asleep upon this at last at about ten
minutes past five in the morning.

There were better things than this in the
composition of Mr. Brumley, we shall have to go deep
into these reserves before we have done with him, but
when he had so recently barked the shins of his self-
esteem they had no chance at all.

CHAPTER THE SEVENTH

LADY HARMAN LEARNS ABOUT HERSELF

§ 1

So it was that the great and long incubated quarrel between Lady Harman and her husband broke into active hostilities.

In spite of my ill-concealed bias in favour of Lady Harman I have to confess that she began this conflict rashly, planlessly, with no equipment and no definite end. Particularly I would emphasize that she had no definite end. She had wanted merely to establish a right to go out by herself occasionally, exercise a certain choice of friends, take on in fact the privileges of a grown-up person, and in asserting that she had never anticipated that the participation of the household would be invoked, or that a general breach might open between herself and her husband. It had seemed just a definite little point at issue, but at Sir Isaac's angry touch a dozen other matters that had seemed safely remote, matters she had never yet quite properly thought about, had been drawn into controversy. It was not only that he drew in things from outside; he evoked things within herself. She discovered she was disposed to fight not simply to establish certain liberties for herself but also—which had certainly not been in her mind before—to keep her husband away

176

from herself. Something latent in the situation had surprised her with this effect. It had arisen out of the quarrel like a sharpshooter out of an ambuscade. Her right to go out alone had now only the value of a mere pretext for far more extensive independence. The ultimate extent of these independences, she still dared not contemplate.

She was more than a little scared. She wasn't prepared for so wide a revision of her life as this involved. She wasn't at all sure of the rightfulness of her position. Her conception of the marriage contract at that time was liberal towards her husband. After all, didn't she owe obedience? Didn't she owe him a subordinate's co-operation? Didn't she in fact owe him the whole marriage service contract? When she thought of the figure of him in his purple-striped pyjamas dancing in a paroxysm of exasperation, that sense of responsibility which was one of her innate characteristics reproached her. She had a curious persuasion that she must be dreadfully to blame for provoking so ridiculous, so extravagant an outbreak. . . .

§ 2

She heard him getting up tumultuously and when she came down,—after a brief interview with her mother who was still keeping her room—she found him sitting at the breakfast-table eating toast and marmalade in a greedy malignant manner. The tentative propitiations of his proposal to make things up had entirely disappeared, he was evidently in a far profounder rage with her than he had been overnight. Snagsby too, that seemly domestic barometer, looked extraordinarily hushed and grave. She made a greeting-like noise and

Sir Isaac scrunched "morning" up amongst a crowded fierce mouthful of toast. She helped herself to tea and bacon and looking up presently discovered his eye fixed upon her with an expression of ferocious hatred. . . .

He went off in the big car, she supposed to London, about ten and she helped her mother to pack and depart by a train a little after midday. She made a clumsy excuse for not giving that crisp little trifle of financial assistance she was accustomed to, and Mrs. Sawbridge was anxiously tactful about the disappointment. They paid a visit of inspection and farewell to the nursery before the departure. Then Lady Harman was left until lunch to resume her meditation upon this unprecedented breach that had opened between her husband and herself. She was presently moved to write a little note to Lady Beach-Mandarin expressing her intention of attending a meeting of the Social Friends and asking whether the date was the following Wednesday or Thursday. She found three penny stamps in the bureau at which she wrote and this served to remind her of her penniless condition. She spent some time thinking out the possible consequences of that. How after all was she going to do things, with not a penny in the world to do them with?

Lady Harman was not only instinctively truthful but also almost morbidly honourable. In other words she was simple-minded. The idea of a community of goods between husband and wife had never established itself in her mind, she took all Sir Isaac's presents in the spirit in which he gave them, presents she felt they were on trust, and so it was that with a six-hundred-pound pearl necklace, a diamond tiara, bracelets, lockets, rings, chains and pendants of the most costly kind—there had been a particularly beautiful bracelet when Millicent was born, a necklace on account of Florence, a fan painted by Charles Conder for Annette and a richly splendid set of old Spanish jewellery— yellow sapphires set in gold—to express Sir Isaac's gratitude for the baby—with all sorts of purses, bags, boxes, trinkets and garments, with a bedroom and morning-room rich in admirable loot, and with endless tradespeople willing to give her credit it didn't for some time occur to her that there was any possible means of getting pocket-money except by direct demand from Sir Isaac. She surveyed her balance of two penny stamps and even about these she felt a certain lack of negociable facility.

She thought indeed that she might perhaps borrow money, but there again her paralysing honesty made her recoil from the prospect of uncertain repayment. And besides, from whom could she borrow ? . . .

It was on the evening of the second day that a chance remark from Peters turned her mind to the extensive possibilities of liquidation that lay close at hand. She was discussing her dinner dress with Peters, she wanted something very plain and high and unattractive, and Peters who disapproved of this tendency and was all for female wiles and propitiations, fell into an admiration of the pearl necklace. She thought perhaps by so doing she might induce Lady Harman to wear it, and if she wore it Sir Isaac might be a little propitiated, and if Sir Isaac was a little propitiated it would be much more comfortable for Snagsby and herself and everyone. She was reminded of a story of a lady who sold one and substituted imitation pearls, no one the wiser, and she told this to her mistress out of sheer garrulousness. "But if no one found out," said Lady Harman, "how do you know ? "

"Not till her death, me lady," said Peters, brushing, "when all things are revealed. Her husband, they say, made it a present of to another lady and the other lady, me lady, had it valued. . . ."

Once the idea had got into Lady Harman's head it stayed there very obstinately. She surveyed the things on the table before her with a slightly lifted eyebrow. At first she thought the idea of disposing of them an entirely dishonourable idea, and if she couldn't get it out of her head again at least she made it stand in a corner. And while it stood in a corner she began putting a price for the first time in her life first upon this coruscating object and then that. Then somehow she found herself thinking more and more whether among all these glittering possessions there wasn't something that she might fairly regard as absolutely her own. There were for example her engagement ring and, still more debateable, certain other pre-nuptial trinkets Sir Isaac had given her. Then there were things given her on her successive birthdays. A birthday present of all presents is surely one's very own? But selling is an extreme exercise of ownership. Since those early schooldays when she had carried on an unprofitable traffic in stamps she had never sold anything—unless we are to reckon that for once and for all she had sold herself.

Concurrently with these insidious speculations Lady Harman found herself trying to imagine how one sold jewels. She tried to sound Peters by taking up the story of the necklace again. But Peters was uninforming. "But where," asked Lady Harman, "could such a thing be done?"

"There are places, me lady," said Peters.

"But where?"

"In the West End, me lady. The West End is full of places—for things of that sort. There's scarcely anything you can't do there, me lady—if only you know how."

That was really all that Peters could impart.

"How *does* one sell jewels?" Lady Harman became so interested in this side of her perplexities that she did a little lose sight of those subtler problems of integrity that had at first engaged her. Do jewellers buy jewels as well as sell them? And then it came into her head that there were such things as pawnshops. By the time she had thought about pawnshops and tried to imagine one, her original complete veto upon any idea of selling had got lost to sight altogether. Instead there was a growing conviction that if ever she sold anything it would be a certain sapphire and diamond ring which she didn't like and never wore that Sir Isaac had given her as a birthday present two years ago. But of course she would never dream of selling anything; at the utmost she need but pawn. She reflected and decided that on the whole it would be wiser not to ask Peters how one pawned. It occurred to her to consult the *Encyclopædia Britannica* on the subject, but though she learnt that the Chinese pawnshops must not charge more than three per cent. per annum, that King Edward the Third pawned his jewels in 1338 and that Father Bernardino di Feltre who set up pawnshops in Assisi and Padua and Pavia was afterward canonized, she failed to get any very clear idea of the exact ritual of the process. And then suddenly she remembered that she knew a finished expert in pawnshop work in the person of Susan Burnet. Susan could tell her everything. She found some curtains in the study that needed replacement, consulted Mrs. Crumble and, with a view to economising her own resources, made that lady send off an urgent letter to Susan bidding her come forthwith.

§ 3

It has been said that Fate is a plagiarist. Lady Harman's Fate at any rate at this juncture behaved like a benevolent plagiarist who was also a little old-fashioned. This phase of speechless hostility was complicated by the fact that two of the children fell ill, or at least seemed for a couple of days to be falling ill. By all the rules of British sentiment this ought to have brought about a headlong reconciliation at the tumbled bedside. It did nothing of the sort; it merely wove fresh perplexities into the tangled skein of her thoughts.

On the day after her participation in that forbidden lunch Millicent, her eldest daughter, was discovered with a temperature of a hundred and one, and then Annette, the third, followed suit with a hundred. This carried Lady Harman post haste to the nursery, where to an unprecedented degree she took command. Latterly she had begun to mistrust the physique of her children and to doubt whether the trained efficiency of Mrs. Harblow the nurse wasn't becoming a little blunted at the edges by continual use. And the tremendous quarrel she had afoot made her keenly resolved not to let anything go wrong in the nursery and less disposed than she usually was to leave things to her husband's servants. She interviewed the doctor herself, arranged for the isolation of the two flushed and cross little girls, saw to the toys and amusements which she discovered had become a little flattened and disused by the servants' imperatives of tidying up and putting away, and spent the greater part of the next two days between the night and day nurseries.

She was a little surprised to find how readily she did this and how easily the once entirely authoritative Mrs. Harblow submitted. It was much the same surprise that growing young people feel when they reach some shelf that has hitherto been inaccessible. The crisis soon passed. At his first visit the doctor was a little doubtful whether the Harman nursery wasn't under the sway of measles, which were then raging in a particularly virulent form in London; the next day he inclined to the view that the trouble was merely a feverish cold, and before night this second view was justified by the disappearance of the " temperatures " and a complete return to normal conditions.

But as for that hushed reconciliation in the fevered presence of the almost sacrificial offspring, it didn't happen. Sir Isaac merely thrust aside the stiff silences behind which he masked his rage to remark: " This is what happens when wimmen go gadding about ! "

That much and glaring eyes and compressed lips and emphasizing fingers and then he had gone again.

Indeed rather than healing their widening breach this crisis did much to spread it into strange new regions. It brought Lady Harman to the very verge of realizing how much of instinct and how much of duty held her the servant of the children she had brought into the world, and how little there mingled with that any of those factors of pride and admiration that go to the making of heroic maternal love. She knew what is expected of a mother, the exalted and lyrical devotion, and it was with something approaching terror that she perceived that certain things in these children of hers she *hated.* It was her business she knew to love them blindly; she lay awake at night in infinite dismay realizing she did nothing of the sort. Their weakness held her more than anything else, the invincible pathos of their little limbs in discomfort so that she was ready to die she felt to give them ease. But so she would have been held, she was assured, by the little children of anybody if they had fallen with sufficient helplessness into her care.

Just how much she didn't really like her children she presently realized when in the feeble irascibility of their sickness they fell quarrelling. They became— horrid. Millicent and Annette being imprisoned in their beds it seemed good to Florence when she came back from the morning's walk, to annex and hide a selection of their best toys. She didn't take them and play with them, she hid them with an industrious earnestness in a box window-seat that was regarded as peculiarly hers, staggering with armfuls across the nursery floor. Then Millicent by some equally mysterious agency divined what was afoot and set up a clamour for a valued set of doll's furniture, which immediately provoked a similar outcry from little Annette for her Teddy Bear. Followed woe and uproar. The invalids insisted upon having every single toy they possessed brought in and put upon their beds; Florence was first disingenuous and then surrendered her loot with passionate howlings. The Teddy Bear was rescued from Baby after a violent struggle in which one furry hind leg was nearly twisted off. It jars upon the philoprogenitive sentiment of our time to tell of these things and still more to record that all four, stirred by possessive passion to the profoundest depths of their beings, betrayed to an unprecedented degree in their little sharp noses, their flushed faces, their earnest eyes, their dutiful likeness to Sir Isaac. He peeped from under Millicent's daintily knitted brows and gestured with Florence's dimpled fists. It was as if God had tried to make him into four cherubim and as if in spite of everything he was working through.

Lady Harman toiled to pacify these disorders, gently, attentively, and with a faint dismay in her dark eyes. She bribed and entreated and marvelled at mental textures so unlike her own. Baby was squared with a brand new Teddy Bear, a rare sort, a white one, which Snagsby went and purchased in the Putney High Street and brought home in his arms, conferring such a lustre upon the deed that the lower orders, the very street-boys, watched him with reverence as he passed. Annette went to sleep amidst a discomfort of small treasures and woke stormily when Mrs. Harblow tried to remove some of the spikier ones. And Lady Harman went back to her large pink bedroom and meditated for a long time upon these things and tried to remember whether in her own less crowded childhood with Georgina, either of them had been quite so inhumanly hard and grasping as these feverish little mites in her nursery. She tried to think she had been, she tried to think that all children were such little distressed lumps of embittered individuality, and she did what she could to overcome the queer feeling that this particular clutch of offspring had been foisted upon her and weren't at all the children she could now imagine and desire,—gentle children, sweet spirited children. . . .

§ 4

Susan Burnet arrived in a gusty mood and brought new matter for Lady Harman's ever broadening consideration of the wifely position. Susan, led by a newspaper placard, had discovered Sir Isaac's relations to the International Bread and Cake Stores.

" At first I thought I wouldn't come," said Susan. " I really did. I couldn't hardly believe it. And then I thought, ' it isn't *her*. It can't be *her!* ' But I'd never have dreamt before that I could have been brought to set foot in the house of the man who drove poor father to ruin and despair. . . . You've been so kind to me. . . ."

Susan's simple right-down mind stopped for a moment with something very like a sob, baffled by the contradictions of the situation.

" So I came," she said, with a forced bright smile.

" I'm glad you came," said Lady Harman. " I wanted to see you. And you know, Susan, I know very little— very little indeed—of Sir Isaac's business."

" I quite believe it, my lady. I've never for one moment thought *you*—— I don't know how to say it, my lady."

" And indeed I'm not," said Lady Harman, taking it as said.

" I knew you weren't," said Susan, relieved to be so understood.

And the two women looked perplexedly at one another over the neglected curtains Susan had come to " see to," and shyness just snatched back Lady Harman from her impulse to give Susan a sisterly kiss. Nevertheless Susan who was full of wise intuitions felt that kiss that was never given, and in the remote world of unacted deeds returned it with effusion.

"But it's hard," said Susan, "to find one's own second sister mixed up in a strike, and that's what it's come to last week. They've struck, all the International waitresses have struck, and last night in Piccadilly they were standing on the kerb and picketing and her among them. With a crowd cheering. . . And me ready to give my right hand to keep that girl respectable!"

And with a volubility that was at once tumultuous and effective, Susan sketched in the broad outlines of the crisis that threatened the dividends and popularity of the International Bread and Cake Stores. The unsatisfied demands of that bright journalistic enterprise, *The London Lion*, lay near the roots of the trouble. *The London Lion* had stirred it up. But it was only too evident that *The London Lion* had merely given a voice and form and cohesion to long smouldering discontents.

Susan's account of the matter had that impartiality which comes from intellectual incoherence, she hadn't so much a judgment upon the whole as a warring mosaic of judgments. It was talking upon Post Impressionist lines, talking in the manner of Picasso. She had the firmest conviction that to strike against employment, however ill-paid or badly conditioned, was a disgraceful combination of folly, ingratitude and general wickedness, and she had an equally strong persuasion that the treatment of the employees of the International Bread and Cake Stores was such as no reasonably spirited person ought to stand. She blamed her sister extremely and sympathized with her profoundly, and she put it all down in turn to *The London Lion*, to Sir Isaac, and to a small round-faced person called Babs Wheeler, who appeared to be the strike leader and

seemed always to be standing on tables in the branches,
or clambering up to the lions in Trafalgar Square, or
being cheered in the streets.

But there could be no mistaking the quality of Sir
Isaac's " International " organization as Susan's dabs of
speech shaped it out. It was indeed what we all of us
see everywhere about us, the work of the base energetic
mind, raw and untrained, in possession of the keen
instruments of civilization, the peasant mind allied and
blended with the Ghetto mind, grasping and acquisitive,
clever as a Norman peasant or a Jew pedlar is clever, and
beyond that outrageously stupid and ugly.   It was a new
view and yet the old familiar view of her husband, but
now she saw him not as little eager eyes, a sharp nose,
gaunt gestures and a leaden complexion, but as shops
and stores and rules and cash registers and harsh
advertisements and a driving merciless hurry to get—to
get anything and everything, money, monopoly, power,
prominence, whatever any other human being seemed
to admire or seemed to find desirable, a lust rather
than a living soul. Now that her eyes were at last
opened Lady Harman, who had seen too little heretofore
now saw too much ; she saw all that she had not seen,
with an excess of vision, monstrous, caricatured.   Susan
had already dabbed in the disaster of Sir Isaac's
unorganized competitors going to the wall—for charity
or the state to neglect or bandage as it might chance—
the figure of that poor little " Father," moping hopelessly before his " accident " symbolized that ; and now
she gave in vivid splotches of allusion, glimpses of the
business machine that had replaced those shattered
enterprises and carried Sir Isaac to the squalid glory of
a Liberal honours list,—the carefully balanced antago-
nisms and jealousies of the girls and the manageresses,

those manageresses who had been obliged to invest little bunches of savings as guarantees and who had to account for every crumb and particle of food stock that came to the branch, and the hunt for cases and inefficiency by the inspectors, who had somehow to justify a salary of two hundred a year, not to mention a percentage of the fines they inflicted.

"There's all that business of the margarine," said Susan. "Every branch gets its butter under weight,— the water squeezes out—and every branch has over weight margarine. Of course the rules say that mixing's forbidden and if they get caught they go, but they got to pay-in for that butter, and it's setting a snare for their feet. People who've never thought to cheat, when they get it like that, day after day, they cheat, my lady. . . . And the girls get left food for rations. There's always trouble, it's against what the rules say, but they get it. Of course it's against the rules, but what can a manageress do?—if the waste doesn't fall on them, it falls on her. She's tied there with her savings. . . . Such driving, my lady, it's against the very spirit of God. It makes scoffers point. It makes people despise law and order. There's Luke, he gets bitterer and bitterer; he says that it's in the Word we mustn't muzzle the ox that treadeth out the corn, but these Stores, he says, they'd muzzle the ox and keep it hungry and make it work a little machine, he says, whenever it put down its head in the hope of finding a scrap. . . ."

So Susan, bright-eyed, flushed and voluble, pleading the cause of that vague greatness in humanity that would love, that would loiter, that would think, that would if it could give us art, delight and beauty, that turns blindly and stumblingly towards joy, towards intervals, towards the mysterious things of the spirit, against all this sordid strenuousness, this driving destructive association of hard-fisted peasant soul and Ghetto greed, this fool's " efficiency," that rules our world to-day.

Then Susan lunged for a time at the waitress life her sister led. " She has 'er 'ome with us, but some—they haven't homes."

" They make a fuss about all this White Slave Traffic," said Susan, " but if ever there were white slaves it's the girls who work for a living and keep themselves respectable. And nobody wants to make an example of the men who get rich out of *them*. . . ."

And after some hearsay about the pressure in the bake-houses and the accidents to the van-men, who worked on a speeding-up system that Sir Isaac had adopted from an American business specialist, Susan's mental discharge poured out into the particulars of the waitresses' strike and her sister's share in that. " She *would* go into it," said Susan, " she let herself be drawn in. I asked her never to take the place. Better Service, I said, a thousand times. I begged her, I could have begged her on my bended knees. . . ."

The immediate cause of the strike it seemed was the exceptional disagreeableness of one of the London district managers. " He takes advantage of his position," repeated Susan with face aflame, and Lady Harman was already too wise about Susan's possibilities to urge her towards particulars. . . .

Now as Lady Harman listened to all this confused effective picturing of the great catering business which was the other side of her husband and which she had taken on trust so long, she had in her heart a quite unreasonable feeling of shame that she should listen at all, a shyness, as though she was prying, as though this

really did not concern her.   She knew she had to listen
and still she felt beyond her proper jurisdiction.   It
is against instinct, it is with an enormous reluctance that
women are bringing their quick emotions, their flashing
unstable intelligences, their essential romanticism, their
inevitable profound generosity into the world of politics
and business.   If only they could continue believing
that all that side of life is grave and wise and admirably
managed for them they would.   It is not in a day or a
generation that we shall un-specialize women.   It is a
wrench nearly as violent as birth for them to face out
into the bleak realization that the man who goes out for
them into business, into affairs, and returns so comfortably loaded with housings and wrappings and trappings
and toys, isn't, as a matter of fact, engaged in benign
creativeness while he is getting these desirable things.

§ 5

Lady Harman's mind was so greatly exercised by
Susan Burnet's voluminous confidences that it was only
when she returned to her own morning room that she
recalled the pawning problem.   She went back to Sir
Isaac's study and found Susan with all her measurements
taken and on the very edge of departure.

" Oh Susan ! " she said.

She found the matter a little difficult to broach.
Susan remained in an attitude of respectful expectation.

" I wanted to ask you," said Lady Harman, and then
broke off to shut the door.   Susan's interest increased.

" You know, Susan," said Lady Harman with an air
of talking about commonplace things, " Sir Isaac is very
rich and—of course—very generous. . . .   But sometimes one feels, one wants a little money of one's own."

"I think I can understand that, my lady," said Susan.

"I knew you would," said Lady Harman, and then with a brightness that was slightly forced, "I can't always get money of my own. It's difficult—sometimes."

And then blushing vividly: "I've got lots of *things*. . . . Susan, have you ever pawned anything?"

And so she broached it.

"Not since I got fairly into work," said Susan; "I wouldn't have it. But when I was little we were always pawning things. Why! we've pawned kettles! . . ."

She flashed three reminiscences.

Meanwhile Lady Harman produced a little glittering object and held it between finger and thumb. "If I went into a pawnshop near here," she said, "it would seem so odd. . . . This ring, Susan, must be worth thirty or forty pounds. And it seems so silly when I have it that I should really be wanting money. . . ."

Susan displayed a peculiar reluctance to handle the ring. "I've never," she said, "pawned anything valuable—not valuable like that. Suppose—suppose they wanted to know how I had come by it."

"It's more than Alice earns in a year," she said. "It's—— " she eyed the glittering treasure; "it's a queer thing for me to have."

A certain embarrassment arose between them. Lady Harman's need of money became more apparent. "I'll do it for you," said Susan, "indeed I'll do it. But—— There's one thing—— "

Her face flushed hotly. "It isn't that I want to make difficulties. But people in our position—we aren't like people in your position. It's awkward sometimes to explain things. You've got a good character, but people

don't know it. You can't be too careful. It isn't
sufficient—just to be honest. If I take that—— If
you were just to give me a little note—in your hand-
writing—on your paper—just asking me—— I don't
suppose I need show it to anyone. . . ."

"I'll write the note," said Lady Harman. A new
set of uncomfortable ideas was dawning upon her. "But
Susan—— You don't mean that anyone, anyone who's
really honest—might get into trouble ? "

"You can't be too careful," said Susan, manifestly
resolved not to give our highly civilized state half a
chance with her.

§ 6

The problem of Sir Isaac and just what he was doing
and what he thought he was doing and what he meant
to do increased in importance in Lady Harman's mind
as the days passed by. He had an air of being
malignantly up to something and she could not imagine
what this something could be. He spoke to her very
little but he looked at her a great deal. He had more
and more of the quality of a premeditated imminent
explosion. . . .

One morning she was standing quite still in the
drawing-room thinking over this now almost oppressive
problem of why the situation did not develop further
with him, when she became aware of a thin flat unusual
book upon the small side table near the great arm-chair
at the side of the fire. He had been reading that
overnight and it lay obliquely—it might almost have
been left out for her.

She picked it up. It was *The Taming of the Shrew*
in that excellent folio edition of Henley's which makes

each play a comfortable thin book apart. A curiosity
to learn what it was had drawn her husband to English
Literature made her turn over the pages. *The Taming
of the Shrew* was a play she knew very slightly. For
the Harmans though deeply implicated like most other
rich and striving people in plans for honouring the
immortal William, like most other people found scanty
leisure to read him.

As she turned over the pages a pencil mark caught
her eye. Thence words were underlined and further
accentuated by a deeply scored line in the margin.

> " But for my bonny Kate, she must with me.
> Nay ; look not big, nor stamp, nor stare, nor fret ;
> I will be master of what is mine own :
> She is my goods, my chattels ; she is my house,
> She is my household stuff, my field, my barn,
> My horse, my ox, my ass, my any thing :
> And here she stands, touch her whoever dare ;
> I'll bring mine action on the proudest He,
> That stops my way in Padua."

With a slightly heightened colour Lady Harman
read on and presently found another page slashed with
Sir Isaac's approval. . . .

Her face became thoughtful. Did he mean to
attempt—Petruchio ? He could never dare. There
were servants, there were the people one met, the
world. . . . He would never dare. . . .

What a strange play it was ! Shakespear of course
was wonderfully wise, the crown of English wisdom, the
culminating English mind,—or else one might almost
find something a little stupid and clumsy. . . . Did
women nowadays really feel like these Elizabethan wives
who talked—like girls, very forward girls indeed, but
girls of sixteen ? . . .

She read the culminating speech of Katherine and now she had so forgotten Sir Isaac she scarcely noted the pencil line that endorsed the immortal words.

"Thy husband is thy Lord, thy Life, thy Keeper,
  Thy Head, thy Sovereign ; one who cares for thee,
  And for thy maintenance commits his body
  To painful labour both by sea and land,
  To watch the night in storms, the day in cold,
  While thou liest warm at home, secure and safe ;
  And craves no other tribute at thy hands
  But love, fair looks, and true obedience ;
  Too little payment for so great a debt.
  Such duty as the Subject owes the Prince,
  Even such a woman oweth to her husband ;
  And when she is froward, peevish, sullen, sour,
  And not obedient to his honest will,
  What is she but a foul contending Rebel
  And graceless traitor to her loving Lord ?
  I am ashamed that women are so simple
  To offer war, where they should kneel for peace ;

    .   .   .   .   .

  My mind has been as big as one of yours,
  My heart as great ; my reason, haply, more,
  To bandy word for word and frown for frown.
  But now I see our lances are but straws ;
  Our strength is weak, our weakness past compare,
  Seeming that most which we indeed least are. . . ."

She wasn't indignant. Something in these lines took hold of her protesting imagination.

She knew that so she could have spoken of a man.

But that man,—she apprehended him as vaguely as an Anglican bishop apprehends God. He was obscured altogether by shadows ; he had only one known characteristic, that he was totally unlike Sir Isaac. And the play was false she felt in giving this speech to a broken woman. Such things are not said by broken

women. Broken women do no more than cheat and lie.
But so a woman might speak out of her unconquered
wilfulness, as a queen might give her lover a kingdom
out of the fullness of her heart.

§ 7

The evening after his wife had had this glimpse into
Sir Isaac's mental processes he telephoned that Charterson and Horatio Blenker were coming home to dinner
with him. Neither Lady Charterson nor Mrs. Blenker
were to be present; it was to be a business conversation
and not a social occasion, and Lady Harman he desired
should wear her black and gold with just a touch of
crimson in her hair. Charterson wanted a word or two
with the flexible Horatio on sugar at the London docks,
and Sir Isaac had some vague ideas that a turn might
be given to the public judgment upon the waitresses
strike, by a couple of Horatio's thoughtful yet gentlemanly articles. And in addition Charterson seemed to
have something else upon his mind; he did not tell as
much to Sir Isaac but he was weighing the possibilities
of securing a controlling share in the *Daily Spirit*,
which simply didn't know at present where it was upon
the sugar business, and of installing Horatio's brother,
Adolphus, as its editor. He wanted to form some idea
from Horatio of what Adolphus might expect before he
approached Adolphus.

Lady Harman wore the touch of crimson in her
hair as her husband had desired, and the table was
decorated simply with a big silver bowl of crimson roses.
A slight shade of apprehension in Sir Isaac's face
changed to approval at the sight of her obedience.

After all perhaps she was beginning to see the commonsense of her position.

Charterson struck her as looking larger, but then whenever she saw him he struck her as looking larger. He enveloped her hand in a large amiable paw for a minute and asked after the children with gusto. The large teeth beneath his discursive moustache gave him the effect of a perennial smile to which his asymmetrical ears added a touch of waggery. He always betrayed a fatherly feeling towards her as became a man who was married to a handsome wife old enough to be her mother. Even when he asked about the children he did it with something of the amused knowingness of assured seniority, as if indeed he knew all sorts of things about the children that she couldn't as yet even begin to imagine. And though he confined his serious conversation to the two other men, he would ever and again show himself mindful of her and throw her some friendly enquiry, some quizzically puzzling remark. Blenker as usual treated her as if she were an only very indistinctly visible presence to whom an effusive yet inattentive politeness was due. He was clearly nervous almost to the pitch of jumpiness. He knew he was to be spoken to about the sugar business directly he saw Charterson, and he hated being spoken to about the sugar business. He had his code of honour. Of course one has to make concessions to one's proprietors, but he could not help feeling that if only they would consent to see his really quite obvious gentlemanliness more clearly it would be better for the paper, better for the party, better for them, far better for himself. He wasn't altogether a fool about that sugar ; he knew how things lay. They ought to trust him more. His nervousness betrayed itself in many little ways. He crumbled his bread constantly until, thanks to Snagsby's assiduous replacement he had made quite a pile of crumbs, he dropped his glasses in the soup—a fine occasion for Snagsby's *sang-froid*—and he forgot not to use a fish knife with the fish as Lady Grove directs and tried when he discovered his error to replace it furtively on the table cloth. Moreover he kept on patting the glasses on his nose—after Snagsby had whisked his soup plate away, rescued, wiped and returned them to him—until that feature glowed modestly at such excesses of attention, and the soup and sauces and things bothered his fine blond moustache unusually. So that Mr. Blenker what with the glasses, the napkin, the food and the things seemed as restless as a young sparrow. Lady Harman did her duties as hostess in the quiet key of her sombre dress, and until the conversation drew her out into unexpected questionings she answered rather than talked, and she did not look at her husband once throughout the meal.

At first the talk was very largely Charterson. He had no intention of coming to business with Blenker until Lady Harman had given place to the port and the man's nerves were steadier. He spoke of this and that in the large discursive way men use in clubs and it was past the fish before the conversation settled down upon the topic of business organization and Sir Isaac, a little warmed by champagne, came out of the uneasily apprehensive taciturnity into which he had fallen in the presence of his wife. Horatio Blenker was keenly interested in the idealization of commercial syndication, he had been greatly stirred by a book of Mr. Gerald Stanley Lee's called *Inspired Millionaires* which set out to show just what magnificent airs rich men might give themselves, and he had done his best to catch its tone and to find *Inspired Millionaires* in Sir Isaac and

Charterson and to bring it to their notice and to the notice of the readers of the *Old Country Gazette*. He felt that if only Sir Isaac and Charterson would see getting rich as a Great Creative Act it would raise their tone and his tone and the tone of the *Old Country Gazette* tremendously. It wouldn't of course materially alter the methods or policy of the paper but it would make them all feel nobler, and Blenker was of that finer clay that does honestly want to feel nobler. He hated pessimism and all that criticism and self-examination that makes weak men pessimistic, he wanted to help weak men and be helped himself, he was all for that school of optimism that would have each dunghill was a well upholstered throne, and his nervous, starry contributions to the talk were like patches of water ranunculuses trying to flower in the overflow of a sewer.

Because you know it is idle to pretend that the talk of Charterson and Sir Isaac wasn't a heavy flow of base ideas; they hadn't even the wit to sham very much about their social significance. They cared no more for the growth, the stamina, the spirit of the people whose lives they dominated than a rat cares for the stability of the house it gnaws. They *wanted* a broken-spirited people. They were in such relations wilfully and offensively stupid, and I do not see why we people who read and write books should pay this stupidity merely because it is prevalent even the mild tribute of an ironical civility. Charterson talked of the gathering trouble that might lead to a strike of the transport workers in London docks, and what he had to say, he said,—he repeated it several times—was, "*Let* them strike. We're ready. The sooner they strike the better. Devonport's a Man and this time we'll *beat* 'em. . . ."

He expanded generally on strikes. "It's a question practically whether we are to manage our own businesses or whether we're to have them managed for us. *Managed* I say ! . . ."

"They know nothing of course of the details of organization," said Blenker, shining with intelligence and looking quickly first to the 'right and then to the left. "Nothing."

Sir Isaac broke out into confirmatory matter. There was an idea in his head that this talk might open his wife's eyes to some sense of the magnitude of his commercial life, to the wonder of its scale and quality. He compared notes with Charterson upon a speeding-up system for delivery vans invented by an American specialist and it made Blenker flush with admiration and turn as if for sympathy to Lady Harman to realize how a modification in a tail-board might mean a yearly saving in wages of many thousand pounds. "The sort of thing they don't understand," he said. And then Sir Isaac told of some of his own little devices. He had recently taken to having the returns of percentage increase and decrease from his various districts printed on postcards and circulated monthly among the district managers, postcards endorsed with such stimulating comments in red type as "Well done Cardiff !" or "What ails Portsmouth ?"— the results had been amazingly good ; "neck and neck work," he said, "everywhere"—and thence they passed to the question of confidential reports and surprise inspectors. Thereby they came to the rights and wrongs of the waitress strike.

And then it was that Lady Harman began to take a share in the conversation.

She interjected a question. "Yes," she said suddenly,

and her interruption was so unexpected that all three
men turned their eyes to her.   " But how much do the
girls get a week ? "

" I thought," she said to some confused explanations
by Blenker and Charterson, " that gratuities were
forbidden."

Blenker further explained that most of the girls of
the class Sir Isaac was careful to employ lived at home.
Their income was " supplementary."

" But what happens to the others who don't live at
home, Mr. Blenker ? " she asked.

" Very small minority," said Mr. Blenker reassuring
himself about his glasses.

" But what do they do ? "

Charterson couldn't imagine whether she was going
on in this way out of sheer ignorance or not.

" Sometimes their fines make big unexpected holes
in their week's pay," she said.

Sir Isaac made some indistinct remark about " utter
nonsense."

" It seems to me to be driving them straight upon
the streets."

The phrase was Susan's.   Its full significance wasn't
at that time very clear to Lady Harman and it was
only when she had uttered it that she realized from
Horatio Blenker's convulsive start just what a blow she
had delivered at that table.   His glasses came off
again.   He caught them and thrust them back, he
seemed to be holding his nose on, holding his face on,
preserving those carefully arranged features of himself
from hideous revelations ; his free hand made weak
movements with his dinner napkin.   He seemed to be
holding it in reserve against the ultimate failure of his
face.   Charterson surveyed her through an immense

pause open-mouthed; then he turned his large now frozen amiability upon his host. "These are Awful questions," he gasped, "rather beyond Us don't you think?" and then magnificently; "Harman, things are looking pretty Queer in the Far East again. I'm told there are chances—of revolution—even in Pekin. . . ."

Lady Harman became aware of Snagsby's arm and his steady well-trained breathing beside her as, tenderly almost but with a regretful disapproval, he removed her plate. . .

§ 8

If Lady Harman had failed to remark at the time the deep impression her words had made upon her hearers, she would have learnt it later from the extra-ordinary wrath in which Sir Isaac as soon as his guests had departed, visited her. He was so angry he broke the seal of silence he had set upon his lips. He came raging into the pink bedroom through the paper-covered door as if they were back upon their old intimate footing. He brought a flavour of cigars and manly refreshment with him, his shirt front was a little splashed and crumpled and his white face was variegated with flushed patches.

"What ever d'you mean," he cried, " by making a fool of me in front of those fellers? . . . What's my business got to do with you?"

Lady Harman was too unready for a reply.

"I ask you what's my business got to do with you? It's *my* affair, *my* side. You got no more right to go shoving your spoke into that than—anything. See? What do *you* know of the rights and wrongs of business? How can *you* tell what's right and what

isn't right? And the things you came out with—the
things you came out with! Why Charterson—after
you'd gone Charterson said, she doesn't know, she can't
know what she's talking about! A decent woman!
a *lady!* talking of driving girls on the street. You
ought to be ashamed of yourself! You aren't fit to
show your face. . . . It's these damned papers and
pamphlets, all this blear-eyed stuff, these decadent
novels and things putting narsty thoughts, *narsty dirty*
thoughts into decent women's heads. It ought to be
rammed back down their throats, it ought to be put a
stop to!"

Sir Isaac suddenly gave way to woe. "What have
I *done?*" he cried, "what have I done? Here's everything going so well! We might be the happiest of
couples! We're rich, we got everything we want. . . .
And then you go harbouring these ideas, fooling about
with rotten people, taking up with Socialism——
Yes, I tell you—Socialism!"

His moment of pathos ended. "NO?" he shouted
in an enormous voice.

He became white and grim. He emphasized his
next words with a shaken finger.

"It's got to end, my lady. It's going to end sooner
than you expect. That's all! . . ."

He paused at the papered door. He had a popular
craving for a vivid curtain and this he felt was just a
little too mild.

"It's going to end," he repeated and then with
great violence, with almost alcoholic violence, with the
round eyes and shouting voice and shaken fist and
blaspheming violence of a sordid, thrifty peasant
enraged, "it's going to end a Damned Sight sooner
than you expect."

CHAPTER THE EIGHTH

Sir Isaac as Petruchio

§ 1

Twice had Sir Isaac come near to betraying the rapid
and extensive preparations for the subjugation of his
wife, that he hid behind his silences. He hoped that
their estrangement might be healed by a certain display
of strength and decision. He still refused to let himself
believe that all this trouble that had arisen between
them, this sullen insistence upon unbecoming freedoms
of intercourse and movement, this questioning spirit
and a gaucherie of manner that might almost be
mistaken for an aversion from his person, were due to
any essential evil in her nature ; he clung almost
passionately to the alternative that she was the victim
of those gathering forces of discontent, of that
interpretation which can only be described as decadent
and that veracity which can only be called immodest,
that darken the intellectual skies of our time, a sweet
thing he held her still though touched by corruption, a
prey to " idees," " idees " imparted from the poisoned
mind of her sister, imbibed from the carelessly edited
columns of newspapers, from all too laxly censored
plays, from " blear-eyed " books—how he thanked the
Archbishop of York for that clever expressive epithet !
—from the careless talk of rashly admitted guests, from

the very atmosphere of London. And it had grown clearer and clearer to him that his duty to himself and the world and her was to remove her to a purer, simpler air, beyond the range of these infections, to isolate her and tranquillize her and so win her back again to that acquiescence, that entirely hopeless submissiveness that had made her so sweet and dear a companion for him in the earlier years of their married life. Long before Lady Beach-Mandarin's crucial luncheon, his deliberate foreseeing mind had been planning such a retreat, Black Strand even at his first visit had appeared to him in the light of a great opportunity, and the crisis of their quarrel did but release that same torrential energy which had carried him to a position of Napoleonic predominance in the world of baking, light catering and confectionery, into the channels of a scheme already very definitely formed in his mind.

His first proceeding after the long hours of sleepless passion that had followed his wife's Hampton Court escapade, had been to place himself in communication with Mr. Brumley. He learnt at Mr. Brumley's club that that gentleman had slept there overnight and had started but a quarter of an hour before, back to Black Strand. Sir Isaac in hot pursuit and gathering force and assistance in mid flight reached Black Strand by midday.

It was with a certain twinge of the conscience that Mr. Brumley perceived his visitor, but it speedily became clear that Sir Isaac had no knowledge of the guilty circumstances of the day before. He had come to buy Black Strand—incontinently, that was all. He was going, it became clear at once, to buy it with all its fittings and furnishings as it stood, lock, stock and barrel. Mr. Brumley, concealing that wild elation, that

sense of a joyous rebirth, that only the liquidation
of nearly all one's possessions can give, was firm but
not excessive. Sir Isaac haggled as a wave breaks and
then gave in and presently they were making a memo-
randum upon the pretty writing-desk beneath the
traditional rose Euphemia had established there when
Mr. Brumley was young and already successful.

This done, and it was done in less than fifteen
minutes, Sir Isaac produced a rather crumpled young
architect from the motor-car as a conjurer might
produce a rabbit from a hat, a builder from Aleham
appeared astonishingly in a dog-cart—he had been
summoned by telegram—and Sir Isaac began there and
then to discuss alterations, enlargements and, more
particularly, with a view to his nursery requirements,
the conversion of the empty barn into a nursery wing
and its connexion with the house by a corridor across
the shrubbery.

" It will take you three months," said the builder
from Aleham. " And the worst time of the year
coming."

" It won't take three weeks—if I have to bring down
a young army from London to do it," said Sir Isaac.

" But such a thing as plastering—— "

" We won't have plastering."

" There's canvas and paper, of course," said the
young architect.

" There's canvas and paper," said Sir Isaac. " And
those new patent building units, so far as the corridor
goes. I've seen the ads."

." We can whitewash 'em. They won't show much,"
said the young architect.

" Oh if you do things in *that* way," said the builder
from Aleham with bitter resignation. . . .

§ 2

The morning dawned at last when the surprise was ripe. It was four days after Susan's visit, and she was due again on the morrow with the money that would enable her employer to go to Lady Viping's now imminent dinner. Lady Harman had had to cut the Social Friends' meeting altogether, but the day before the surprise Agatha Alimony had come to tea in her jobbed car, and they had gone together to the committee meeting of the Shakespear Dinner Society. Sir Isaac had ignored that defiance, and it was an unusually confident and quite unsuspicious woman who descended in a warm October sunshine to the surprise. In the breakfast-room she discovered an awe-stricken Snagsby standing with his plate-basket before her husband, and her husband wearing strange unusual tweeds and gaiters,—buttoned gaiters, and standing a-straddle,—unusually a-straddle, on the hearthrug.

"That's enough, Snagsby," said Sir Isaac, at her entrance. "Bring it all."

She met Snagsby's eye, and it was portentous.

Latterly Snagsby's eye had lost the assurance of his former days. She had noted it before, she noted it now more than ever; as though he was losing confidence, as though he was beginning to doubt, as though the world he had once seemed to rule grew insecure beneath his feet. For a moment she met his eye; it might have been a warning he conveyed, it might have been an appeal for sympathy, and then he had gone. She looked at the table. Sir Isaac had breakfasted acutely.

In silence, among the wreckage and with a certain

wonder growing, Lady Harman attended to her needs.

Sir Isaac cleared his throat.

She became aware that he had spoken. " What did you say, Isaac?" she asked, looking up. He seemed to have widened his straddle almost dangerously, and he spoke with a certain conscious forcefulness.

" We're going to move out of this house, Elly," he said. " We're going down into the country right away."

She sat back in her chair and regarded his pinched and determined visage.

" What do you mean?" she asked.

" I've bought that house of Brumley's,—Black Strand. We're going to move down there—*now*. I've told the servants. . . . When you've done your breakfast you'd better get Peters to pack your things. The big car's going to be ready at half-past ten."

Lady Harman reflected.

" To-morrow evening," she said, " I was going out to dinner at Lady Viping's."

" Not my affair—seemingly," said Sir Isaac with irony. "Well, the car's going to be ready at half-past ten."

" But that dinner—— ! "

" We'll think about it when the time comes."

Husband and wife regarded each other.

" I've had about enough of London," said Sir Isaac. " So we're going to shift the scenery. See?"

Lady Harman felt that one might adduce good arguments against this course if only one knew of them.

Sir Isaac had a bright idea. He rang.

"Snagsby," he said, "just tell Peters to pack up Lady Harman's things. . . ."

"*Well!*" said Lady Harman, as the door closed on Snagsby. Her mind was full of confused protest, but she had again that entirely feminine and demoralizing conviction that if she tried to express it she would weep or stumble into some such emotional disaster. If now she went upstairs and told Peters *not* to pack——!

Sir Isaac walked slowly to the window, and stood for a time staring out into the garden.

Extraordinary bumpings began overhead in Sir Isaac's room. No doubt somebody was packing something. . . .

Lady Harman realized with a deepening humiliation that she dared not dispute before the servants, and that he could. "But the children——" she said at last.

"I've told Mrs. Harblow," he said, over his shoulder. "Told her it was a bit of a surprise." He turned, with a momentary lapse into something like humour. "You see," he said, "it *is* a bit of a surprise."

"But what are you going to do with this house?"

"Lock it all up for a bit. . . . I don't see any sense in living where we aren't happy. Perhaps down there we shall manage better. . . ."

It emerged from the confusion of Lady Harman's mind that perhaps she had better go to the nursery, and see how things were getting on there. Sir Isaac watched her departure with a slightly dubious eye, made little noises with his teeth for a time, and then went towards the telephone.

In the hall she found two strange young men in green aprons assisting the under-butler to remove the hats and overcoats and such-like personal material into a motor-van outside. She heard two of the house-maids scurrying upstairs. "'Arf an hour," said one, " isn't what I call a proper time to pack a box in."

In the nursery the children were disputing furiously what toys were to be taken into the country.

Lady Harman was a very greatly astonished woman. The surprise had been entirely successful.

§ 3

It has been said, I think, by Limburger, in his already cited work, that nothing so excites and prevails with woman as rapid and extensive violence, sparing and yet centring upon herself, and certainly it has to be recorded that, so far from being merely indignant, and otherwise a helplessly pathetic spectacle, Lady Harman found, though perhaps she did not go quite so far as to admit to herself that she found, this vehement flight from the social, moral, and intellectual contaminations of London an experience not merely stimulating but entertaining. It lifted her delicate eyebrows. Something, it may have been a sense of her own comparative immobility amid this sudden extra-ordinary bustle of her home, put it into her head that so it was long ago that Lot must have bundled together his removable domesticities.

She made one attempt at protest. " Isaac," she said, " isn't all this rather ridiculous——— "

" Don't speak to me ! " he answered, waving her off. " Don't speak to me ! You should have spoken before, Elly. *Now*,—things are happening."

The image of Black Strand as, after all, a very pleasant place indeed returned to her. She adjudicated upon the nursery difficulties, and then went in a dream-like state of mind to preside over her own more personal packing. She found Peters exercising all that indecisive helplessness which is characteristic of ladies' maids the whole world over.

It was from Peters she learnt that the entire house-hold, men and maids together, was to be hurled into Surrey. "Aren't they all rather surprised?" asked Lady Harman.

"Yes, m'm," said Peters on her knees, "but of course if the drains is wrong the sooner we all go the better."

(So that was what he had told them.)

A vibration and a noise of purring machinery out-side drew the lady to the window, and she discovered that at least four of the large motor-vans from the International Stores were to co-operate in the trek. There they were waiting, massive and uniform. And then she saw Snagsby in his alpaca jacket *running* towards the house from the gates. Of course he was running only very slightly indeed, but still he was running, and the expression of distress upon his face convinced her that he was being urged to unusual and indeed unsuitable tasks under the immediate personal supervision of Sir Isaac. . . . Then from round the corner appeared the under butler or at least the legs of him going very fast, under a pile of shirt boxes and things belonging to Sir Isaac. He dumped them into the nearest van and heaved a deep sigh and returned houseward after a remorseful glance at the windows.

A violent outcry from baby, who, with more than her customary violence was making her customary

morning protest against being clad, recalled Lady
Harman from the contemplation of these exterior
activities. . . .

The journey to Black Strand was not accomplished
without misadventure; there was a puncture near
Farnham, and as Clarence with a leisurely assurance
entertained himself with the Stepney, they were passed
first by the second car with the nursery contingent,
which went by in a shrill chorus, crying, " *We-e-e*
shall get there first, *We-e-e* shall get there first," and
then by a large hired car all agog with housemaids and
Mrs. Crumble and with Snagsby, as round and
distressed as the full moon, and the under butler,
cramped and keen beside the driver. There followed
the leading International Stores car, and then the
Stepney was on and they could hasten in pursuit. . . .

And at last they came to Black Strand, and when
they saw Black Strand it seemed to Lady Harman that
the place had blown out a huge inflamed red cheek and
lost its pleasant balance altogether. " *Oh !* " she cried,

It was the old barn flushed by the strain of adaptation
to a new use, its comfortable old wall ruptured by half-
a dozen brilliant new windows, a light red chimney stack
at one end. From it a vividly artistic corridor ran to
the house and the rest of the shrubbery was all trampled
and littered with sheds, bricks, poles and material
generally. Black Strand had left the hands of the
dilettante school and was in the grip of those vigorous
moulding forces that are shaping our civilization to-day.

The jasmine wig over the porch had suffered a
strenuous clipping; the door might have just come out of
prison. In the hall the Carpaccio copies still glowed,
but there were dust sheets over most of the furniture
and a plumber was moving his things out with that

eleventh hour reluctance so characteristic of plumbers.
Mrs. Rabbit, a little tearful, and dressed for departure
very respectably in black was giving the youngest and
least experienced housemaid a faithful history of Mr.
Brumley's earlier period. "'Appy we all was," said
Mrs. Rabbit, " as Birds in a Nest."

Through the windows two of the Putney gardeners
were busy replacing Mr. Brumley's doubtful roses by
recognized sorts, the *right* sorts. . . .

" I've been doing all I can to make it ready for
you," said Sir Isaac at his wife's ear, bringing a curious
reminiscence of the first home-coming to Putney into
her mind.

§ 4

" And now," said Sir Isaac with evident premeditation and a certain deliberate amiability, " now we got
down here, now we got away a bit from all those
London things with nobody to cut in between us, me
and you can have a bit of a talk, Elly, and see what it's
all about."

They had lunched together in the little hall-dining
room,—the children had had a noisily cheerful picnic
in the kitchen with Mrs. Harblow, and now Lady
Harman was standing at the window surveying the
ravages of rose replacement.

She turned towards him. " Yes," she said. I
think—I think we can't go on like this. "

" *I* can't," said Sir Isaac, " anyhow."

He too came and stared at the rose planting.

" If we were to go up there—among the pine
woods "—he pointed with his head at the dark

background of Euphemia's herbaceous borders—" we shouldn't hear quite so much of this hammering. . . ."

Husband and wife walked slowly in the afternoon sunlight across the still beautiful garden. Each was gravely aware of an embarrassed incapacity for the task they had set themselves. They were going to talk things over. Never in their lives had they really talked to each other clearly and honestly about anything. Indeed it is scarcely too much to say that neither had ever talked about anything to anyone. She was too young, her mind was now growing up in her and feeling its way to conscious expression, and he had never before wanted to express himself. He did now want to express himself. For behind his rant and fury Sir Isaac had been thinking very hard indeed during the last three weeks about his life and her life and their relations; he had never thought so much about anything except his business economics. So far he had either joked at her, talked " silly " to her, made, as they say, " remarks," or vociferated. That had been the sum of their mental intercourse, as indeed it is the sum of the intercourse of most married couples. His attempt to state his case to her had so far always flared into rhetorical outbreaks. But he was discontented with these rhetorical outbreaks. His dispositions to fall into them made him rather like a nervous sepia that cannot keep its ink sac quiet while it is sitting for its portrait. In the earnestness of his attempt at self-display he vanished in his own outpourings.

He wanted now to reason with her simply and persuasively. He wanted to say quietly impressive and convincing things in a low tone of voice and make her abandon every possible view except his view. He walked now slowly meditating the task before him,

making a faint thoughtful noise with his teeth, his
head sunken in the collar of the motor overcoat he wore
because of a slight cold he had caught. And he had
to be careful about colds because of his constitutional
defect. She too felt she had much to say. Much too
she had in her mind that she couldn't say, because this
strange quarrel had opened unanticipated things for
her; she had found and considered repugnances in her
nature she had never dared to glance at hitherto. . . .

Sir Isaac began rather haltingly when they had
reached a sandy, ant-infested path that ran slantingly
up among the trees. He affected a certain perplexity.
He said he did not understand what it was his wife was
" after," what she " thought she was doing " in " making
all this trouble "; he wanted to know just what it was
she wanted, how she thought they ought to live, just
what she considered his rights were as her husband and
just what she considered were her duties as his wife—if,
that is, she considered she had any duties. To these
enquiries Lady Harman made no very definite reply;
their estrangement instead of clearing her mind had on
the whole perplexed it more, by making her realize the
height and depth and extent of her possible separation
from him. She replied therefore with an unsatisfactory
vagueness; she said she wanted to feel that she
possessed herself, that she was no longer a child, that
she thought she had a right to read what she chose, see
what people she liked, go out a little by herself, have a
certain independence—she hesitated, " have a certain
definite allowance of my own."

" Have I ever refused you money ? " cried Sir Isaac
protesting.

" It isn't that," said Lady Harman ; " it's the
feeling—— "

"The feeling of being able to—defy—anything I say," said Sir Isaac with a note of bitterness. "As if I didn't understand!"

It was beyond Lady Harman's powers to express just how that wasn't the precise statement of the case.

Sir Isaac, reverting to his tone of almost elaborate reasonableness, expanded his view that it was impossible for husband and wife to have two different sets of friends;—let alone every other consideration, he explained, it wasn't convenient for them not to be about together, and as for reading or thinking what she chose he had never made any objection to anything unless it was "decadent rot" that any decent man would object to his womanfolk seeing, rot she couldn't understand the drift of—fortunately. Blear-eyed humbug. . . . He checked himself on the verge of an almost archiepiscopal outbreak in order to be patiently reasonable again. He was prepared to concede that it would be very nice if Lady Harman could be a good wife and also an entirely independent person, very nice, but the point was—his tone verged on the ironical— that she couldn't be two entirely different people at the same time.

"But you have your friends," she said, "you go away alone——"

"That's different," said Sir Isaac with a momentary note of annoyance. "It's business. It isn't that I want to."

Lady Harman had a feeling that they were neither of them gaining any ground. She blamed herself for her lack of lucidity. She began again, taking up the matter at a fresh point. She said that her life at present wasn't full, that it was only half a life, that it was just home and marriage and nothing else; he had his business, he went out into the world, he had politics and—"all sorts of things"; she hadn't these interests; she had nothing in the place of them——

Sir Isaac closed this opening rather abruptly by telling her that she should count herself lucky she hadn't, and again the conversation was suspended for a time.

"But I want to know about these things," she said.

Sir Isaac took that musingly.

"There's things go on," she said; "outside home. There's social work, there's interests—— Am I never to take any part—in that?"

Sir Isaac still reflected.

"There's one thing," he said at last, "I want to know. We'd better have it out—*now*."

But he hesitated for a time.

"Elly!" he blundered, "you aren't—you aren't getting somehow—not fond of me?"

She made no immediate reply.

"Look here!" he said in an altered voice. "Elly! there isn't something below all this? There isn't something been going on that I don't know?"

Her eyes with a certain terror in their depths questioned him.

"Something," he said, and his face was deadly white—"*Some other man, Elly?*"

She was suddenly crimson, a flaming indignation.

"Isaac!" she said, "what do you *mean*? How can you *ask* me such a thing?"

"If it's that!" said Sir Isaac, his face suddenly full of malignant force, "I'll—— But I'd *kill* you. . . .

"If it isn't that," he went on searching his mind; "why should a woman get restless? Why should she want to go away from her husband, go meeting other people, go gadding about? If a woman's satisfied, she's satisfied. She doesn't harbour fancies. . . . All this grumbling and unrest. Natural for your sister, but why should you? You've got everything a woman needs, husband, children, a perfectly splendid home, clothes, good jewels and plenty of them, respect! Why should you want to go out after things? It's mere spoilt-childishness. Of course you want to wander out —and if there isn't a man——"

He caught her wrist suddenly. "There isn't a man?" he demanded.

"Isaac!" she protested in horror.

"Then there'll be one. You think I'm a fool, you think I don't know anything all these literary and society people know. I *do* know. I know that a man and a woman have got to stick together, and if you go straying—you may think you're straying after the moon or social work or anything—but there's a strange man waiting round the corner for every woman and a strange woman for every man. Think *I've* had no temptations? . . . Oh! I *know*, I *know*. What's life or anything but that? and it's just because we've not gone on having more children, just because we listened to all those fools who said you were overdoing it, that all this fretting and grumbling began. We've got on to the wrong track, Elly, and we've got to get back to plain wholesome ways of living. See? That's what I've come down here for and what I mean to do. We've got to save ourselves. I've been too—too modern and all that. I'm going to be a husband as a husband should. I'm going to protect you from these idees—protect you from your own self. . . . And that's about where we stand, Elly, as I make it out."

He paused with the effect of having delivered himself of long premeditated things.

Lady Harman essayed to speak. But she found that directly she set herself to speak she sobbed and began weeping. She choked for a moment. Then she determined she would go on, and if she must cry, she must cry. She couldn't let a disposition to tears seal her in silence for ever.

" It isn't " she said, " what I expected—of life. It isn't—— "

" It's what life is," Sir Isaac cut in.

" When I think," she sobbed, "of what I've lost—— "

" *Lost !* " cried Sir Isaac. " Lost ! Oh come now, Elly, I like that. What !—*lost.* Hang it ! You got to look facts in the face. You can't deny—— Marrying like this,—you made a jolly good thing of it."

" But the beautiful things, the noble things ! "

" *What's* beautiful ? " cried Sir Isaac in protesting scorn. " *What's* noble ? ROT ! Doing your duty if you like and being sensible, that's noble and beautiful, but not fretting about and running yourself into danger. You've got to have a sense of humour, Elly, in this life—— " He created a quotation. " As you make your bed—so shall you lie."

For an interval neither of them spoke. They crested the hill, and came into view of that advertisement board she had first seen in Mr. Brumley's company. She halted, and he went a step further and halted too. He recalled his ideas about the board. He had meant to have them all altered but other things had driven it from his mind. . . .

" Then you mean to imprison me here," said Lady Harman to his back. He turned about.

"It isn't much like a prison. I'm asking you to stay here—and be what a wife *should* be."

"I'm to have no money."

"That's—that depends entirely on yourself. You know that well enough."

She looked at him gravely.

"I won't stand it," she said at last with a gentle deliberation.

She spoke so softly that he doubted his hearing. "*What?*" he asked sharply.

"I won't stand it," she repeated. "No."

"But—what can you do?"

"I don't know," she said, after a moment of grave consideration.

For some moments his mind hunted among possibilities.

"It's me that's standing it," he said. He came closely up to her. He seemed on the verge of rhetoric. He pressed his thin white lips together. "Standing it! when we might be so happy," he snapped, and shrugged his shoulders and turned with an expression of mournful resolution towards the house again. She followed slowly.

He felt that he had done all that a patient and reasonable husband could do. *Now*—things must take their course.

§ 5

The imprisonment of Lady Harman at Black Strand lasted just one day short of a fortnight.

For all that time except for such interludes as the urgent needs of the strike demanded, Sir Isaac devoted himself to the siege. He did all he could to make her

realize how restrainedly he used the powers the law
vests in a husband, how little he forced upon her the
facts of marital authority and wifely duty. At times
he sulked, at times he affected a cold dignity, and at
times a virile anger swayed him at her unsubmissive
silences. He gave her little peace in that struggle, a
struggle that came to the edge of physical conflict.
There were moments when it seemed to her that
nothing remained but that good old-fashioned connubial institution, the tussle for the upper hand, when
with a feminine horror she felt violence shouldering her
shoulder or contracting ready to grip her wrist. Against
violence she doubted her strength, was filled with a
desolating sense of yielding nerve and domitable
muscle. But just short of violence Sir Isaac's spirit
failed him. He would glower and bluster, half threaten,
and retreat. It might come to that at last but at
present it had not come to that.

She could not understand why she had neither
message nor sign from Susan Burnet, but she hid that
anxiety and disappointment under her general dignity.

She spent as much time with the children as she
could, and until Sir Isaac locked up the piano she
played, and was surprised to find far more in Chopin
than she had ever suspected in the days when she had
acquired a passable dexterity of execution. She found,
indeed, the most curious things in Chopin, emotional
phrases, that stirred and perplexed and yet pleased
her. . . .

The weather was very fine and open that year. A
golden sunshine from October passed on into November
and Lady Harman spent many of these days amidst the
pretty things the builder from Aleham had been too
hurried to desecrate, dump, burn upon, and flatten into

indistinguishable mire, after the established custom of builders in gardens since the world began. She would sit in the rockery where she had sat with Mr. Brumley and recall that momentous conversation, and she would wander up the pinewood slopes behind, and she would spend long musing intervals among Euphemia's perennials, thinking sometimes, and sometimes not so much thinking as feeling the warm tendernesses of nature and the perplexing difficulties of human life. With an amused amazement Lady Harman reflected as she walked about the pretty borders and the little patches of lawn and orchard that in this very place she was to have realized an imitation of the immortal "Elizabeth" and have been wise, witty, gay, defiant, gallant and entirely successful with her "Man of Wrath." Evidently there was some temperamental difference, or something in her situation, that altered the values of the affair. It was clearly a different sort of man for one thing. She didn't feel a bit gay, and her profound and deepening indignation with the alternative to this stagnation was tainted by a sense of weakness and incapacity.

She came very near surrender several times. There were afternoons of belated ripened warmth, a kind of summer that had been long in the bottle, with a certain lassitude in the air and a blue haze among the trees, that made her feel the folly of all resistances to fate. Why, after all, shouldn't she take life as she found it, that is to say, as Sir Isaac was prepared to give it to her? He wasn't really so bad, she told herself. The children—their noses were certainly a little sharp, but there might be worse children. The next might take after herself more. Who was she to turn upon her appointed life and declare it wasn't good

enough ? Whatever happened the world was still full
of generous and beautiful things, trees, flowers, sunset
and sunrise, music and mist and morning dew. . . .
And as for this matter of the sweated workers, the
harshness of the business, the ungracious competition,
suppose if instead of fighting her husband with her
weak powers, she persuaded him. She tried to imagine
just exactly how he might be persuaded. . . .

She looked up and discovered with an extraordinary
amazement Mr. Brumley with eager gestures and a
flushed and excited visage hurrying towards her across
the croquet lawn.

§ 6

Lady Viping's dinner-party had been kept waiting
exactly thirty-five minutes for Lady Harman. Sir
Isaac, with a certain excess of zeal, had intercepted the
hasty note his wife had written to account for her
probable absence. The party was to have centred
entirely upon Lady Harman, it consisted either of people
who knew her already, or of people who were to have
been specially privileged to know her, and Lady Viping
telephoned twice to Putney before she abandoned hope.
" It's disconnected," she said, returning in despair from
her second struggle with the great public service.
" They can't get a reply."

" It's that little wretch," said Lady Beach-Mandarin.
" He hasn't let her come. *I* know him."

" It's like losing a front tooth," said Lady Viping,
surveying her table as she entered the dining-room.

" But surely—she would have written," said Mr.
Brumley, troubled and disappointed, regarding an aching
gap to the left of his chair, a gap upon which a pathetic

little card bearing Lady Harman's name still lay obliquely.

Naturally the talk tended to centre upon the Harmans. And naturally Lady Beach-Mandarin was very bold and outspoken and called Sir Isaac quite a number of vivid things. She also aired her views of the marriage of the future which involved a very stringent treatment of husbands indeed. "Half his property and half his income," said Lady Beach-Mandarin, "paid into her separate banking account."

"But," protested Mr. Brumley, "would men marry under those conditions?"

"Men will marry anyhow," said Lady Beach-Mandarin, "under *any* conditions."

"Exactly Sir Joshua's opinion," said Lady Viping.

All the ladies at the table concurred and only one cheerful bachelor barrister dissented. The other men became gloomy and betrayed a distaste for this general question. Even Mr. Brumley felt a curious faint terror and had for a moment a glimpse of the possibilities that might lie behind the Vote. Lady Beach-Mandarin went bouncing back to the particular instance. At present, she said, witness Lady Harman, women were slaves, pampered slaves if you will, but slaves. As things were now there was nothing to keep a man from locking up his wife, opening all her letters, dressing her in sack-cloth, separating her from her children. Most men, of course, didn't do such things, they were amenable to public opinion, but Sir Isaac was a jealous little Ogre. He was a gnome who had carried off a princess. . . .

She threw out projects for assailing the Ogre. She would descend to-morrow morning upon the Putney house, a living flamboyant writ of Habeas Corpus. Mr. Brumley, who had been putting two and two together, was abruptly moved to tell of the sale of Black Strand. "They may be there," he said.

" He's carried her off," cried Lady Beach-Mandarin on a top note. " It might be the eighteenth century for all he cares. But if it's Black Strand,—I'll go to Black Strand. . . ."

But she had to talk about it for a week before she actually made her raid, and then, with an instinctive need for an audience, she took with her a certain Miss Garradice, one of those mute, emotional nervous spinsters who drift detachedly, with quick sudden movements, glittering eyeglasses and a pent-up imminent look, about our social system. There is something about this type of womanhood—it is hard to say—almost as though they were the bottled souls of departed buccaneers grown somehow virginal. She came with Lady Beach-Mandarin quietly, almost humorously, and yet it was as if the pirate glittered dimly visible through the polished glass of her erect exterior.

" Here we are ! " said Lady Beach-Mandarin, staring astonished at the once familiar porch. " Now for it ! "

She descended and assailed the bell herself and Miss Garradice stood beside her with the light of combat in her eyes and glasses and cheeks.

" Shall I offer to take her for a drive ! "

" *Let's*," said Miss Garradice in an enthusiastic whisper. " *Right away ! For ever.*"

" *I will*," said Lady Beach-Mandarin, and nodded desperately.

She was on the point of ringing again when Snagsby appeared.

He stood with a large obstructiveness in the doorway. "Lady 'Arman, my lady," he said with a well-trained deliberation, " is not a Tome."

"Not at home!" queried Lady Beach-Mandarin.

"Not a Tome, my lady," repeated Snagsby invincibly.

"But—when will she be at home?"

"I can't say, my lady."

"Is Sir Isaac——?"

"Sir Isaac, my lady, is not a Tome. Nobody is a Tome, my lady."

"But we've come from London!" said Lady Beach-Mandarin.

"I'm very sorry, my lady."

"You see, I want my friend to see this house and garden."

Snagsby was visibly disconcerted. "I 'ave no instructions, my lady," he tried.

"Oh, but Lady Harman would never object——"

Snagsby's confusion increased. He seemed to be wanting to keep his face to the visitors and at the same time glance over his shoulder. "I will," he considered, "I will enquire, my lady." He backed a little, and seemed inclined to close the door upon them. Lady Beach-Mandarin was too quick for him. She got herself well into the open doorway. "And of whom are you going to enquire?"

A large distress betrayed itself in Snagsby's eye. "The 'ousekeeper," he attempted. "It falls to the 'ousekeeper, my lady."

Lady Beach-Mandarin turned her face to Miss Garradice, shining in support. "Stuff and nonsense," she said, "of course we shall come in." And with a wonderful movement that was at once powerful and perfectly lady-like this intrepid woman—"butted" is not the word—collided herself with Snagsby and hurled him backward into the hall. Miss Garradice followed closely behind and at once extended herself in open order on Lady Beach-Mandarin's right. " Go and enquire," said Lady Beach-Mandarin with a sweeping gesture of her arm. " Go and enquire."

For a moment Snagsby surveyed the invasion with horror and then fled precipitately into the recesses of the house.

" Of *course* they're at home ! " said Lady Beach-Mandarin. " Fancy that — that — that *navigable* — trying to shut the door on us ! "

For a moment the two brightly excited ladies surveyed each other and then Lady Beach-Mandarin, with a quickness of movement wonderful in one so abundant, began to open first one and then another of the various doors that opened into the long hall-living-room. At a peculiar little cry from Miss Garradice she turned from a contemplation of the long low study in which so much of the Euphemia books had been written, to discover Sir Isaac behind her, closely followed by an agonized Snagsby.

" A–a–a–a–h ! " she cried, with both hands extended, " and so you've come in, Sir Isaac ! That's perfectly delightful. This is my friend Miss Garradice, who's *dying* to see anything you've left of poor Euphemia's garden. And *how* is dear Lady Harman ? "

For some crucial moments Sir Isaac was unable to speak and regarded his visitors with an expression that was unpretendingly criminal.

Then he found speech. " You can't," he said. " It—can't be managed." He shook his head ; his lips were whitely compressed.

" But all the way from London, Sir Isaac ! "

" Lady Harman's ill," lied Sir Isaac. " She mustn't be disturbed. Everything has to be kept quiet. See ?

Not even shouting. Not even ordinarily raised voices. A voice like yours—might kill her. That's why Snagsby here said we were not at home. We aren't at home—not to anyone."

Lady Beach-Mandarin was baffled.

" Snagsby," said Sir Isaac, " open that door."

" But can't I see her—just for a moment ? "

Sir Isaac's malignity had softened a little at the prospect of victory. " Absolutely impossible," he said. " Everything disturbs her, every tiny thing. You—— You'd be certain to."

Lady Beach-Mandarin looked at her companion and it was manifest that she was at the end of her resources. Miss Garradice after the fashion of highly strung spinsters suddenly felt disappointed in her leader. It wasn't, her silence intimated, for her to offer suggestions.

The ladies were defeated. When at last that stiff interval ended their dresses rustled doorward, and Sir Isaac broke out into the civilities of a victor. . . .

It was only when they were a mile away from Black Strand that fluent speech returned to Lady Beach-Mandarin. " The little—Crippen," she said. " He's got her locked up in some cellar. . . . Horrid little face he has ! He looked like a rat at bay."

" I think perhaps if we'd done *differently*," said Miss Garradice in a tone of critical irresponsibility.

" I'll write to her. That's what I'll do," said Lady Beach-Mandarin contemplating her next step. " I'm really—concerned. And didn't you feel—something sinister. That butler-man's expression—a kind of round horror."

That very evening she told it all—it was almost the trial trip of the story—to Mr. Brumley. . . .

Sir Isaac watched their departure furtively from the study window and then ran out to the garden. He went right through into the pine woods beyond and presently, far away up the slopes, he saw his wife loitering down towards him, a gracious white tallness touched by a ray of sunlight—and without a suspicion of how nearly rescue had come to her.

§ 7

So you see under what excitement Mr. Brumley came down to Black Strand.

Luck was with him at first and he forced the defence with ridiculous ease.

" Lady Harman, sir, is not a Tome," said Snagsby.

" Ah ! " said Mr. Brumley, with all the assurance of a former proprietor, " then I'll just have a look round the garden," and was through the green door in the wall and round the barn end before Snagsby's mind could function. That unfortunate man went as far as the green door in pursuit and then with a gesture of despair retreated to the pantry and began cleaning all his silver to calm his agonized spirit. He could pretend perhaps that Mr. Brumley had never rung at the front door at all. If not——

Moreover Mr. Brumley had the good fortune to find Lady Harman quite unattended and pensive upon the little seat that Euphemia had placed for the better seeing of her herbaceous borders.

" Lady Harman ! " he said rather breathlessly, taking both her hands with an unwonted assurance and then sitting down beside her, " I am so glad to see you. I came down to see you—to see if I couldn't be of any service to you."

" It's so kind of you to come," she said, and her dark eyes said as much or more. She glanced round and he too glanced round for Sir Isaac.

" You see," he said. " I don't know. . . . I don't want to be impertinent. . . . But I feel—if I can be of any service to you. . . . I feel perhaps you want help here. I don't want to seem to be taking advantage of a situation. Or making unwarrantable assumptions. But I want to assure you—I would willingly die—if only I could do anything. . . . Ever since I first saw you."

He said all this in a distracted way, with his eyes going about the garden for the possible apparition of Sir Isaac, and all the time his sense of possible observers made him assume an attitude as though he was engaged in the smallest of small talk. Her colour quickened at the import of his words, and emotion, very rich and abundant emotion, its various factors not altogether untouched perhaps by the spirit of laughter, lit her eyes. She doubted a little what he was saying and yet she had anticipated that somehow, someday, in quite other circumstances, Mr. Brumley might break into some such strain.

" You see," he went on with a quality of appeal in his eyes, " there's so little time to say things—without possible interruption. I feel you are in difficulties and I want to make you understand—— We—— Every beautiful woman, I suppose, has a sort of right to a certain sort of man. I want to tell you—I'm not really presuming to make love to you—but I want to tell you I am altogether yours, altogether at your service. I've had sleepless nights. All this time I've been thinking about you. I'm quite clear, I haven't a doubt, I'll do anything for you, without reward, without return, I'll be your devoted brother, anything, if only you'll make use of me. . . ."

Her colour quickened. She looked around and still no one appeared. "It's so kind of you to come like this," she said. "You say things—— But I *have* felt that you wanted to be brotherly. . . ."

"Whatever I *can* be," assured Mr. Brumley.

"My situation here," she said, her dark frankness of gaze meeting his troubled eyes. "It's so strange and difficult. I don't know what to do. I don't know —what I *want* to do. . . ."

"In London," said Mr. Brumley, "they think— they say—you have been taken off—brought down here—to a sort of captivity."

"I *have*," admitted Lady Harman with a note of recalled astonishment in her voice.

"If I can help you to escape——!"

"But where can I escape?"

And one must admit that it is a little difficult to indicate a correct refuge for a lady who finds her home intolerable. Of course there was Mrs. Sawbridge, but Lady Harman felt that her mother's disposition to lock herself into her bedroom at the slightest provocation made her a weak support for a defensive fight, and in addition that boarding-house at Bournemouth did not attract her. Yet what other wall in all the world was there for Lady Harman to set her back against? During the last few days Mr. Brumley's mind had been busy with the details of impassioned elopements conducted in the most exalted spirit, but now in the actual presence of the lady these projects did in the most remarkable manner vanish.

"Couldn't you," he said at last, "go somewhere?" And then with an air of being meticulously explicit.

"I mean, isn't there somewhere, where you might safely go?"

(And in his dreams he had been crossing high passes with her; he had halted suddenly and stayed her mule. In his dream because he was a man of letters and a poet it was always a mule, never a *train de luxe*. "Look," he had said, "below there,—*Italy!*—the country you have never seen before.")

"There's nowhere," she answered.

"Now *where?*" asked Mr. Brumley, "and how?" with the tone and something of the gesture of one who racks his mind. "If you only trust yourself to me—— Oh! Lady Harman, if I dared ask it——"

He became aware of Sir Isaac walking across the lawn towards them. . . .

The two men greeted each other with a reasonable cordiality. "I wanted to see how you were getting on down here," said Mr. Brumley, "and whether there was anything I could do for you."

"We're getting on all right," said Sir Isaac with no manifest glow of gratitude.

"You've altered the old barn—tremendously."

"Come and see it," said Sir Isaac. "It's a wing."

Mr. Brumley remained seated. "It was the first thing that struck me, Lady Harman. This evidence of Sir Isaac's energy."

"Come and look over it," Sir Isaac persisted.

Mr. Brumley and Lady Harman rose together.

"One's enough to show him that," said Sir Isaac.

"I was telling Lady Harman how much we missed her at Lady Viping's, Sir Isaac."

"It was on account of the drains," Sir Isaac explained. "You can't—it's foolhardy to stay a day when the drains are wrong, dinners or no dinners."

" You know *I* was extremely sorry not to come to
Lady Viping's. I hope you'll tell her. I wrote."

But Mr. Brumley didn't remember clearly enough
to make any use of that.

" Everybody naturally *is* sorry on an occasion of
that sort," said Sir Isaac. " But you come and see
what we've done in that barn. In three weeks. They
couldn't have got it together in three months ten years
ago. It's—system."

Mr. Brumley still tried to cling to Lady Harman.
" Have you been interested in this building?" he
asked.

" I still don't understand the system of the corridor,"
she said, rising a little belatedly to the occasion. " I
will come."

Sir Isaac regarded her for a moment with a dubious
expression and then began to explain the new method of
building with large prepared units and shaped pieces of
reinforced concrete instead of separate bricks that Messrs.
Prothero & Cuthbertson had organized and which had
enabled him to create this artistic corridor so simply. It
was a rather uncomfortable three-cornered conversation,
Sir Isaac addressed his exposition exclusively to Mr.
Brumley and Mr. Brumley made repeated ineffectual
attempts to bring Lady Harman, and Lady Harman
made repeated ineffectual attempts to bring herself, into
a position in the conversation.

Their eyes met, the glow of Mr. Brumley's declarations remained with them, but neither dared risk any
phrase that might arouse Sir Isaac's suspicions or escape
his acuteness. And when they had gone through the
new additions pretty thoroughly—the plumbers were still
busy with the barn bath-room—Sir Isaac asked Mr.
Brumley if there was anything more he would like to see.

In the slight pause that ensued Lady Harman suggested
tea. But tea gave them no opportunity of resuming
their interrupted conversation, and as Sir Isaac's invincible determination to shadow his visitor until he
was well off the premises became more and more unmistakable,—he made it quite ungraciously unmistakable,
—Mr. Brumley's inventiveness failed. One thing came
to him suddenly, but it led to nothing of any service
to him.

"But I heard you were dangerously ill, Lady
Harman!" he cried. "Lady Beach-Mandarin called
here——"

"But when?" asked Lady Harman, astonished over
the tea-things.

"But you *know* she called!" said Mr. Brumley and
looked in affected reproach at Sir Isaac."

"I've not been ill at all!"

"Sir Isaac told her."

"Told her I was ill!"

"Dangerously ill. That you couldn't bear to be
disturbed."

"But *when*, Mr. Brumley?"

"Three days ago."

They both looked at Sir Isaac who was sitting on
the music stool and eating a piece of tea-cake with a
preoccupied air. He swallowed and then spoke
thoughtfully—in a tone of detached observation.
Nothing but a slight reddening of the eyes betrayed
any unusual feeling in him.

"It's my opinion," he said, "that that old lady—
Lady Beach-Mandarin I mean—doesn't know what she's
saying half the time. She says—oh! remarkable
things. Saying *that* for example!"

"But did she call on me?"

"She called. I'm surprised you didn't hear. And she was all in a flurry for going on. . . . Did you come down, Mr. Brumley, to see if Lady Harman was ill?"

"That weighed with me."

"Well,—you see she isn't," said Sir Isaac and brushed a stray crumb from his coat. . . .

Mr. Brumley was at last impelled gateward and Sir Isaac saw him as far as the high-road.

"Good-bye!" cried Mr. Brumley with excessive amiability.

Sir Isaac with soundless lips made a good-bye like gesture.

"And now," said Sir Isaac to himself with extreme bitterness, "now to see about getting a dog."

"Bull mastiff?" said Sir Isaac developing his idea as he went back to Lady Harman. "Or perhaps a Thoroughly Vicious collie?"

"How did that chap get in?" he demanded. "What had he got to say to you?"

"He came in—to look at the garden," said Lady Harman. "And of course he wanted to know if I had been well—because of Lady Viping's party. And I suppose because of what you told Lady Beach-Mandarin."

Sir Isaac grunted doubtfully. He thought of Snagsby and of all the instructions he had given Snagsby. He turned about and went off swiftly and earnestly to find Snagsby. . . .

Snagsby lied. But Sir Isaac was able to tell from the agitated way in which he was cleaning his perfectly clean silver at that unseasonable hour that the wretched man was lying.

§ 8

Quite a number of words came to the lips of Mr.
Brumley as he went unwillingly along the pleasant
country road that led from Black Strand to the railway
station.   But the word he ultimately said showed how
strongly the habits of the gentlemanly *littérateur*
prevailed in him.   It was the one inevitable word for
his mood,—" Baffled ! "

Close upon its utterance came the weak irritation
of the impotent man.   " What the *devil ?* " cried Mr.
Brumley.

Some critical spirit within him asked him urgently
why he was going to the station, what he thought he
was doing, what he thought he had done, and what
he thought he was going to do.   To all of which
questions Mr. Brumley perceived he had no adequate
reply.

Earlier in the day he had been inspired by a vague
yet splendid dream of large masterful liberations
achieved.   He had intended to be very disinterested, very
noble, very firm, and so far as Sir Isaac was concerned,
a trifle overbearing.   You know now what he said and
did.   " Of course if we could have talked for a little
longer," he said.   From the stormy dissatisfaction of
his retreat this one small idea crystallized, that he had
not   talked   enough   without   disturbance   to   Lady
Harman.   The thing he had to do was to talk to her
some more.   To go on with what he had been saying.
That thought arrested his steps.   On that hypothesis
there was no reason whatever why he should go on to the
station and London.   Instead—— He stopped short,
saw a convenient gate ahead, went to it, seated himself

upon its topmost rail and attempted a calm survey of
the situation.   He had somehow to continue that
conversation with Lady Harman.

Was it impossible to do that by going back to the
front door of Black Strand?   His instinct was against
that course.   He knew that if he went back now openly
he would see nobody but Sir Isaac or his butler. He must
therefore not go back openly.   He must go round now
and into the pine-woods at the back of Black Strand ;
thence he must watch the garden and find his opportunity of speaking to the imprisoned lady.   There was
something at once attractively romantic and repellantly
youthful about this course of action.   Mr. Brumley
looked at his watch, then he surveyed the blue clear
sky overhead, with just one warm tinted wisp of cloud.
It would be dark in an hour and it was probable that
Lady Harman had already gone indoors for the day.
Might it be possible after dark to approach the
house?   No one surely knew the garden so well as he.

Of course this sort of thing is always going on in
romances ; in the stories of that last great survivor of
the Stevensonian tradition, H. B. Marriott Watson, the
heroes are always creeping through woods, tapping at
windows, and scaling house-walls, but Mr. Brumley as
he sat on his gate became very sensible of his own
extreme inexperience in such adventures.   And yet anything seemed in his present mood better than going
back to London.

Suppose he tried his luck !

He knew of course the lie of the land about Black
Strand very well indeed and his harmless literary social
standing gave him a certain freedom of trespass.   He
dropped from his gate on the inner side and taking a
bridle path through a pine-wood was presently out upon

the moorland behind his former home.   He struck the
high-road that led past the Staminal Bread Board and
was just about to clamber over the barbed wire on his left
and make his way through the trees to the crest that
commanded the Black Strand garden when he perceived a man in a velveteen coat and gaiters strolling
towards him.   He decided not to leave the road until
he was free from observation.   The man was a
stranger, an almost conventional gamekeeper, and he
endorsed Mr. Brumley's remark upon the charmingness
of the day with guarded want of enthusiasm.   Mr.
Brumley went on for some few minutes, then halted,
assured himself that the stranger was well out of sight
and returned at once towards the point where high-
roads were to be left and adventure begun.   But he
was still some yards away when he became aware of
that velveteen-coated figure approaching again.
"Damn!" said Mr. Brumley and slacked his eager
paces.   This time he expressed a view that the weather
was extremely mild.   "Very," said the man in velveteen
with a certain lack of respect in his manner.

It was no good turning back again.   Mr. Brumley
went on slowly, affected to botanize, watched the man
out of sight and immediately made a dash for the pine-
woods, taking the barbed wire in a manner extremely
detrimental to his left trouser leg.   He made his way
obliquely up through the trees to the crest from which
he had so often surveyed the shining ponds of Aleham.
There he paused to peer back for that gamekeeper—
whom he supposed in spite of reason to be stalking
him—to recover his breath and to consider his further
plans.   The sunset was very fine that night, a great red
sun was sinking towards acutely outlined hill-crests, the
lower nearer distances were veiled in lavender mists

and three of the ponds shone like the fragments of a shattered pink topaz. But Mr. Brumley had no eye for landscape. . . .

About two hours after nightfall Mr. Brumley reached the railway station. His trousers and the elbow of his coat bore witness to a second transit of the barbed-wire fence in the darkness, he had manifestly walked into a boggy place and had some difficulty in recovering firm ground and he had also been sliding in a recumbent position down a bank of moist ferruginous sand. Moreover he had cut the palm of his left hand. There was a new strange stationmaster who regarded him without that respect to which he had grown accustomed. He received the information that the winter train service had been altered and that he would have to wait forty-five minutes for the next train to London with the resignation of a man already chastened by misfortune and fatigue. He went into the waiting-room and after a vain search for the poker— the new stationmaster evidently kept it in a different place—sat down in front of an irritatingly dull fire banked up with slack, and nursed his damaged hand and meditated on his future plans.

His plans were still exactly in the state in which they had been when Sir Isaac parted from him at the gate of Black Strand. They remained in the same state for two whole days. Throughout all that distressing period his general intention of some magnificent intervention on behalf of Lady Harman remained unchanged, it produced a number of moving visions of flights at incredible speeds in (recklessly hired) motorcars of colossal power,—most of the purchase money for Black Strand was still uninvested at his bank— of impassioned interviews with various people, of a divorce court with a hardened judge congratulating the manifestly quite formal co-respondent on the moral beauty of his behaviour, but it evolved no sort of concrete practicable detail upon which any kind of action might be taken. And during this period of indecision Mr. Brumley was hunted through London by a feverish unrest. When he was in his little flat in Pont Street he was urged to go to his club, when he got to his club he was urged to go anywhere else, he called on the most improbable people and as soon as possible fled forth again, he even went to the British Museum and ordered out a lot of books on matrimonial law. Long before that great machine had disgorged them for him he absconded and this neglected, this widowed pile of volumes still standing to his account only came back to his mind in the middle of the night suddenly and disturbingly while he was trying to remember the exact words he had used in his brief conversation with Lady Harman. . . .

§ 9

Two days after Mr. Brumley's visit Susan Burnet reached Black Strand. She too had been baffled for a while. For some week or more she couldn't discover the whereabouts of Lady Harman and lived in the profoundest perplexity. She had brought back her curtains to the Putney house in a large but luggable bundle, they were all made and ready to put up and she found the place closed and locked, in the charge of a caretaker whose primary duty it was to answer no questions. It needed several days of thought and amazement, and a vast amount of " I wonder," and " I just would like to know," before it occurred to Susan that if she wrote to Lady Harman at the Putney address the letter might be forwarded. And even then she almost wrecked the entire enterprise by mentioning the money, and it was by a quite exceptional inspiration that she thought after all it was wiser not to say that but to state that she had finished the curtains and done everything (underlined) that Lady Harman had desired. Sir Isaac read it and tossed it over to his wife. " Make her send her bill," he remarked.

Whereupon Lady Harman set Mrs. Crumble in motion to bring Susan down to Black Strand. This wasn't quite easy because as Mrs. Crumble pointed out they hadn't the slightest use for Susan's curtains there, and Lady Harman had to find the morning light quite intolerable in her bedroom—she always slept with window wide open and curtains drawn back—to create a suitable demand for Susan's services. But at last Susan came, too humbly invisible for Sir Isaac's attention, and directly she found Lady Harman alone in the room with her, she produced a pawn ticket and twenty pounds. " I 'ad to give all sorts of particulars," she said. " It was a job. But I did it. . . ."

The day was big with opportunity, for Sir Isaac had been unable to conceal the fact that he had to spend the morning in London. He had gone up in the big car and his wife was alone, and so, with Susan upstairs still deftly measuring for totally unnecessary hangings, Lady Harman was able to add a fur stole and a muff and some gloves to her tweed gardening costume, walk unchallenged into the garden and from the garden into the wood and up the hillside and over the crest and down to the high-road and past that great advertisement of Staminal Bread and so for four palpitating miles, to the railway station and the outer world.

She had the good fortune to find a train imminent,—
the twelve-seventeen. She took a first-class ticket for
London and got into a compartment with another
woman because she felt it would be safer.

§ 10

Lady Harman reached Miss Alimony's flat at half-
past three in the afternoon. She had lunched rather
belatedly and uncomfortably in the Waterloo Refreshment Room and she had found out that Miss Alimony
was at home through the telephone. "I want to see
you urgently," she said, and Miss Alimony received her
in that spirit. She was hatless but she had a great
cloud of dark fuzzy hair above the grey profundity of
her eyes and she wore an artistic tea-gown that in spite
of a certain looseness at neck and sleeve emphasized
the fine lines of her admirable figure. Her flat was
furnished chiefly with books and rich oriental hangings
and vast cushions and great bowls of scented flowers.
On the mantel-shelf was the crystal that amused her
lighter moments and above it hung a circular allegory
by Florence Swinstead, very rich in colour, the
Awakening of Woman, in a heavy gold frame. Miss
Alimony conducted her guest to an armchair, knelt
flexibly on the hearthrug before her, took up a small
and elegant poker with a brass handle and a spear-
shaped service end of iron and poked the fire.

The service end came out from the handle and fell
into the grate. "It always does that," said Miss
Alimony charmingly. "But never mind." She warmed
both hands at the blaze. "Tell me all about it," she
said, softly.

Lady Harman felt she would rather have been told all about it. But perhaps that would follow.

"You see," she said, "I find—— My married life—— "

She halted. It *was* very difficult to tell.

"Everyone," said Agatha, giving a fine firelit profile, and remaining gravely thoughtful through a little pause.

"Do you mind," she asked abruptly, "if I smoke."

When she had completed her effect with a delicately flavoured cigarette, she encouraged Lady Harman to proceed.

This Lady Harman did in a manner do. She said her husband left her no freedom of mind or movement, gave her no possession of herself, wanted to control her reading and thinking. "He insists—— " she said.

"Yes," said Miss Agatha sternly blowing aside her cigarette smoke. "They all insist."

"He insists," said Lady Harman, "on seeing all my letters, choosing all my friends. I have no control over my house or my servants, no money except what he gives me."

"In fact you are property."

"I'm simply property."

"A harem of one. And all *that* is within the provisions of the law!"

"How any woman can marry!" said Miss Agatha, after a little interval. "I sometimes think that is where the true strike of the sex ought to begin. If none of us married! If we said all of us, 'No,—definitely—we refuse this bargain! It is a man-made contract. We have had no voice in it. We decline.' Perhaps it will come to that. And I knew that you, you with that quiet beautiful penetration in your eyes

would come to see it like that. The first task, after
the vote is won, will be the revision of that contract.
The very first task of our Women Statesmen. . . ."

She ceased and revived her smouldering cigarette
and mused blinking through the smoke. She seemed
for a time almost lost to the presence of her guest in a
great daydream of womanstatecraft.

"And so," she said, "you've come, as they all
come,—to join us."

"*Well*," said Lady Harman in a tone that made
Agatha turn eyes of surprise upon her.

"Of course," continued Lady Harman, "I suppose—
I shall join you; but as a matter of fact you see, what
I've done to-day has been to come right away. . . .
You see I am still in my garden tweeds. . . . There it
was down there, a sort of stalemate. . . ."

Agatha sat up on her heels.

"But my dear!" she said, "you don't mean you've
run away?"

"Yes,—I've run away."

"But—run away!"

"I sold a ring and got some money and here I am!"

"But—what are you going to do?"

"I don't know. I thought you perhaps—might
advise."

"But—a man like your husband! He'll pursue
you!"

"If he knows where I am, he will," said Lady
Harman.

"He'll make a scandal. My dear! are you wise?
Tell me, tell me exactly, *why* have you run away? I
didn't understand at all—that you had run away."

"Because," began Lady Harman and flushed hotly.
"It was impossible," she said.

Miss Alimony regarded her deeply. " I wonder," she said.

" I feel," said Lady Harman, " if I stayed, if I gave in—— I mean after—after I had once—rebelled. Then I should just be—a wife—ruled, ordered—— "

" It wasn't your place to give in," said Miss Alimony and added one of those parliament touches that creep more and more into feminine phraseology ; " I agree to that—*nemine contradicente.* But—I *wonder. . . .*"

She began a second cigarette and thought in profile again.

" I think, perhaps, I haven't explained, clearly, how things are," said Lady Harman, and commenced a rather more explicit statement of her case. She felt she had not conveyed and she wanted to convey to Miss Alimony that her rebellion was not simply a desire for personal freedom and autonomy, that she desired these things because she was becoming more and more aware of large affairs outside her home life in which she ought to be not simply interested but concerned, that she had been not merely watching the workings of the business that made her wealthy, but reading books about socialism, about social welfare that had stirred her profoundly. . . . " But he won't even allow me to know of such things," she said. . . .

Miss Alimony listened a little abstractedly.

Suddenly she interrupted. " Tell me," she said, " one thing. . . . I confess," she explained, " I've no business to ask. But if I'm to advise—— If my advice is to be worth anything. . . ."

" Yes ? " asked Lady Harman.

" Is there—— Is there someone else ? "

" Someone else ? " Lady Harman was crimson.

" On *your* side ! "

" Someone else on my side ? "

" I mean—someone. A man perhaps ? Some man that you care for ? More than you do for your husband ? . . ."

"*I can't imagine*," whispered Lady Harman, "*any-thing*——" And left her sentence unfinished. Her breath had gone. Her indignation was profound.

" Then I can't understand why you should find it so important to come away."

Lady Harman could offer no elucidation.

" You see," said Miss Alimony, with an air of expert knowledge, " our case against our opponents is just exactly their great case against us. They say to us when we ask for the Vote, ' the Woman's Place is the Home.' ' Precisely,' we answer, ' the Woman's Place *is* the Home. *Give* us our Homes ! ' Now *your* place is your home—with your children. That's where you have to fight your battle. Running away—for you it's simply running away."

" But—— If I stay I shall be beaten." Lady Harman surveyed her hostess with a certain dismay. " Do you understand, Agatha ? I *can't* go back."

" But my dear ! What else can you do ? What had you thought ? "

" You see," said Lady Harman, after a little struggle with that childish quality in her nerves that might, if it wasn't controlled, make her eyes brim. " You see, I didn't expect you quite to take this view. I thought perhaps you might be disposed—— If I could have stayed with you here, only for a little time, I could have got some work or something——"

" It's so dreadful," said Miss Alimony, sitting far

back with the relaxation of infinite regrets.   "It's dreadful."

"Of course if you don't see it as I do——"

"I can't," said Miss Alimony.   "I can't."

She turned suddenly upon her visitor and grasped her knees with her shapely hands.   "Oh let me implore you! Don't run away. Please for my sake, for all our sakes, for the sake of Womanhood, don't run away! Stay at your post. You mustn't run away. You must *not*. If you do, you admit everything. Everything. You must fight in your home. It's *your* home. That is the great principle you must grasp,—it's not his. It's there your duty lies.   And there are your children —*your* children, your little ones! Think if you go— there may be a fearful fuss —proceedings. Lawyers—a search. Very probably he will take all sorts of proceedings.   It will be a Matrimonial Case. How can I be associated with that? We mustn't mix up Women's Freedom with Matrimonial Cases. Impossible! We *dare* not! A woman leaving her husband! Think of the weapon it gives our enemies. If once other things complicate the Vote,—the Vote is lost.   After all our self-denial, after all our sacrifices. . . . You see! Don't you *see*? . . .

"*Fight!*" she summarized after an eloquent interval.

"You mean," said Lady Harman,—"You think I ought to go back."

Miss Alimony paused to get her full effect. "*Yes*," she said in a profound whisper and endorsed it, "Oh so much so!—yes."

"Now?"

"Instantly."

For an interval neither lady spoke. It was the visitor at last who broke the tension.

"Do you think," she asked in a small voice and with the hesitation of one whom no refusal can surprise, "you could give me a cup of tea?"

Miss Alimony rose with a sigh and a slow unfolding rustle. "I forgot," she said. "My little maid is out."

Lady Harman left alone sat for a time staring at the fire with her eyes rather wide and her eyebrows raised as though she mutely confided to it her infinite astonishment. This was the last thing she had expected. She would have to go to some hotel. Can a woman stay alone at an hotel? Her heart sank. Inflexible forces seemed to be pointing her back to home—and Sir Isaac. He would be a very triumphant Sir Isaac, and she'd not have much heart left in her. . . . "I *won't* go back," she whispered to herself. "Whatever happens I *won't* go back. . . ."

Then she became aware of the evening newspaper Miss Alimony had been reading. The headline, "Suffrage Raid on Regent Street," caught her eye. A queer little idea came into her head. It grew with tremendous rapidity. She put out a hand and took up the paper and read.

She had plenty of time to read because her hostess not only got the tea herself but went during that process to her bedroom and put on one of those hats that have contributed so much to remove the stigma of dowdiness from the suffrage cause, as an outward and visible sign that she was presently ceasing to be at home. . . .

Lady Harman found an odd fact in the report before her. "One of the most difficult things to buy at the present time in the West End of London," it ran, "is a hammer. . . ."

Then a little further: "The magistrate said it

was impossible to make discriminations in this affair. All the defendants must have a month's imprisonment. . . ."

When Miss Alimony returned Lady Harman put down the paper almost guiltily.

Afterwards Miss Alimony recalled that guilty start, and the still more guilty start that had happened, when presently she went out of the room again and returned with a lamp, for the winter twilight was upon them. Afterwards, too, she was to learn what had become of the service end of her small poker, the little iron club, which she missed almost as soon as Lady Harman had gone. . . .

Lady Harman had taken that grubby but convenient little instrument and hidden it in her muff, and she had gone straight out of Miss Alimony's flat to the Post Office at the corner of Jago Street, and there, with one simple effective impact, had smashed a ground-glass window, the property of His Majesty King George the Fifth. And having done so, she had called the attention of a youthful policeman, fresh from Yorkshire, to her offence, and after a slight struggle with his incredulity and a visit to the window in question, had escorted him to the South Hampsmith police-station, and had there made him charge her. And on the way she explained to him with a new-found lucidity why it was that women should have votes.

And all this she did from the moment of percussion onward, in a mood of exaltation entirely strange to her, but, as she was astonished to find, by no means disagreeable. She found afterwards that she only remembered very indistinctly her selection of the window and her preparations for the fatal blow, but that the effect of the actual breakage remained extraordinarily vivid upon her memory. She saw with extreme distinctness both as it was before and after the breakage, first as a rather irregular grey surface, shining in the oblique light of a street lamp, and giving pale phantom reflections of things in the street, and then as it was after her blow. It was all visual impression in her memory; she could not recollect afterwards if there had been any noise at all. Where there had been nothing but a milky dinginess a thin-armed, irregular star had flashed into being, and a large triangular piece at its centre, after what seemed an interminable indecision, had slid, first covertly downward, and then fallen forward at her feet and shivered into a hundred fragments. . . .

Lady Harman realized that a tremendous thing had been done—irrevocably. She stared at her achievement open-mouthed. The creative lump of iron dropped from her hand. She had a momentary doubt whether she had really wanted to break that window at all; and then she understood that this business had to be seen through, and seen through with neatness and dignity; and that wisp of regret vanished absolutely in her concentration upon these immediate needs.

§ 11

Some day, when the arts of the writer and illustrator are more closely blended than they are to-day, it will be possible to tell of all that followed this blow, with an approach to its actual effect. Here there should stand a page showing simply and plainly the lower half of the window of the Jago Street Post Office, a dark, rather grimy pane, reflecting the light of a street lamp—and *broken*. Below the pane would come a band of evilly painted woodwork, a corner of letter-box, a foot or so of brickwork, and then the pavement with a dropped lump of iron. That would be the sole content of this page, and the next page would be the same, but very slightly fainter, and across it would be printed a dim sentence or so of explanation. The page following that would show the same picture again, but now several lines of type would be visible, and then, as one turned over, the smashed window would fade a little, and the printed narrative, still darkened and dominated by it, would nevertheless resume. One would read on how Lady Harman returned to convince the incredulous young Yorkshireman of her feat, how a man with a barrow-load of bananas volunteered comments, and how she went in custody, but with the extremest dignity, to the police-station. Then, with some difficulty, because that imposed picture would still prevail over the letterpress, and because it would be in small type, one would learn how she was bailed out by Lady Beach-Mandarin, who was clearly the woman she ought to have gone to in the first place, and who gave up a dinner with a duchess to entertain her, and how Sir Isaac, being too torn by his feelings to come near her, spent the evening in a frantic attempt to keep the whole business out of the papers. He could not manage it. The magistrate was friendly next morning, but inelegant in his friendly expedients; he remanded Lady Harman until her mental condition could be inquired into, but among her fellow-defendants—there had been quite an epidemic of window-smashing that evening—Lady Harman shone pre-eminently sane. She said she had

broken this window because she was assured that
nothing would convince people of the great dissatisfaction of women with their conditions except such
desperate acts, and when she was reminded of her four
daughters she said it was precisely the thought of how
they too would grow up to womanhood that had made
her strike her blow. The statements were rather the
outcome of her evening with Lady Beach-Mandarin
than her own unaided discoveries, but she had honestly
assimilated them, and she expressed them with a
certain simple dignity.

Sir Isaac made a pathetic appearance before the
court, and Lady Harman was shocked to see how worn
he was with distress at her scandalous behaviour. He
looked a broken man. That curious sense of personal
responsibility, which had slumbered throughout the
Black Strand struggle, came back to her in a flood, and
she had to grip the edge of the dock tightly to
maintain her self-control. Unaccustomed as he was
to public speaking, Sir Isaac said in a low, sorrow-
laden voice, he had provided himself with a written
statement dissociating himself from the views his wife's
rash action might seem to imply, and expressing his
own opinions upon woman's suffrage and the relations
of the sexes generally, with especial reference to
contemporary literature. He had been writing it most
of the night. He was not, however, permitted to read
this, and he then made an unstudied appeal for the
consideration and mercy of the court. He said Lady
Harman had always been a good mother and a faithful
wife; she had been influenced by misleading people
and bad books and publications, the true significance
of which she did not understand, and if only the court
would regard this first offence leniently he was ready

to take his wife away and give any guarantee that might be specified that it should not recur. The magistrate was sympathetic and kindly, but he pointed out that this window-breaking had to be stamped out, and that it could only be stamped out by refusing any such exception as Sir Isaac desired. And so Sir Isaac left the court widowed for a month, a married man without a wife, and terribly distressed.

All this and more one might tell in detail, and how she went to her cell, and the long tedium of her imprisonment, and how deeply Snagsby felt the disgrace, and how Miss Alimony claimed her as a convert to the magic of her persuasions, and many such matters—there is no real restraint upon a novelist fully resolved to be English and Gothic and unclassical except obscure and inexplicable instincts. But these obscure and inexplicable instincts are at times imperative, and on this occasion they insist that here must come a break, a pause, in the presence of this radiating gap in the Postmaster-General's glass, and the phenomenon of this gentle and beautiful lady, the mother of four children, grasping in her gloved hand, and with a certain amateurishness, a lumpish poker-end of iron.

We make the pause by ending the chapter here and by resuming the story at a fresh point—with an account of various curious phases in the mental development of Mr. Brumley.

CHAPTER THE NINTH

MR. BRUMLEY IS TROUBLED BY DIFFICULT IDEAS

§ 1

THEN as that picture of a post office pane, smashed and with a large hole knocked clean through it, fades at last upon the reader's consciousness, let another and a kindred spectacle replace it. It is the carefully cleaned and cherished window of Mr. Brumley's mind, square and tidy and as it were "frosted" against an excess of light, and in that also we have now to record the most jagged and all devastating fractures.

Little did Mr. Brumley reckon when first he looked up from his laces at Black Strand, how completely that pretty young woman in the dark furs was destined to shatter all the assumptions that had served his life.

But you have already had occasion to remark a change in Mr. Brumley's bearing and attitude that carries him far from the kindly and humorous conservatism of his earlier work. You have shared Lady Harman's astonishment at the ardour of his few stolen words in the garden, an astonishment that not only grew but flowered in the silences of her captivity, and you know something of the romantic impulses, more at least than she did, that gave his appearance at the little local railway station so belated and so disreputable a

254

flavour. In the chilly ill-flavoured solitude of her prison cell and with a mind quickened by meagre and distasteful fare, Lady Harman had ample leisure to reflect upon many things, she had already fully acquainted herself with the greater proportion of Mr. Brumley's published works, and she found the utmost difficulty in reconciling the flushed impassioned quality of his few words of appeal, with the moral assumptions of his published opinions. On the whole she was inclined to think that her memory had a little distorted what he had said. In this however she was mistaken; Mr. Brumley had really been proposing an elopement and he was now entirely preoccupied with the idea of rescuing, obtaining and possessing Lady Harman for himself as soon as the law released her.

One may doubt whether this extensive change from a humorous conservatism to a primitive and dangerous romanticism is to be ascribed entirely to the personal charm, great as it no doubt was, of Lady Harman; rather did her tall soft dark presence come to release a long accumulating store of discontent and unrest beneath the polished surfaces of Mr. Brumley's mind. Things had been stirring in him for some time; the later Euphemia books had lacked much of the freshness of their precursors and he had found it increasingly hard, he knew not why, to keep up the lightness, the geniality, the friendly badinage of successful and accepted things, the sunny disregard of the grim and unamiable aspects of existence, that were the essential merits of that Optimistic Period of our literature in which Mr. Brumley had begun his career. With every justification in the world Mr. Brumley had set out to be an optimist, even in the *Granta* his work had been distinguished by its gay yet steadfast superficiality, and his early success, his rapid popularity, had done much to turn this early disposition into a professional attitude. He had determined that for all his life he would write for comfortable untroubled people in the character of a light-spirited, comfortable, untroubled person, and that each year should have its book of connubial humour, its travel in picturesque places, its fun and its sunshine, like roses budding in succession on a stem. He did his utmost to conceal from himself the melancholy realization that the third and the fourth roses were far less wonderful than the first and the second, and that by continuing the descending series a rose might be attained at last that was almost unattractive, but he was already beginning to suspect that he was getting less animated and a little irritable when Euphemia very gently and gracefully but very firmly and rather enigmatically died, and after an interval of tender and tenderly expressed regrets he found himself, in spite of the most strenuous efforts to keep bright and kindly and optimistic in the best style, dull and getting duller—he could disguise the thing no longer. And he weighed more. Six—eight—eleven pounds more. He took a flat in London, dined and lunched out lightly but frequently, sought the sympathetic friendship of several charming ladies, and involved himself deeply in the affairs of the Academic Committee. Indeed he made a quite valiant struggle to feel that optimism was just where it always had been and everything all right and very bright with him and with the world about him. He did not go under without a struggle. But as Max Beerbohm's caricature—the 1908 one I mean—brought out all too plainly, there was in his very animation, something of the alert liveliness of the hunted man. Do what he would he had a terrible irrational feeling

that things, as yet scarce imagined things, were after
him and would have him. Even as he makes his point,
even as he gesticulates airily, with his rather distinctively
North European nose Beerbohmically enlarged and his
sensitive nostril in the air, he seems to be looking at
something he does not want to look at, something
conceivably pursuing, out of the corner of his eye.

The thing that was assailing Mr. Brumley and
making his old established humour and tenderness seem
dull and opaque and giving this new uneasy quality to
his expression was of course precisely the thing that Sir
Isaac meant when he talked about "idees" and their
disturbing influence upon all the once assured tranquil-
lities and predominances of Putney life. It was
criticism breaking bounds.

As a basis and substance for the tissue of whimsi-
cally expressed happiness and confident appreciation of
the good things of life, which Mr. Brumley had set
before himself as his agreeable—and it was to be hoped
popular and profitable—life-task, certain assumptions
had been necessary. They were assumptions he had
been very willing to make and which were being made
in the most exemplary way by the writers who were
succeeding all about him at the commencement of his
career. And these assumptions had had such an air
then of being quite trustworthy, as being certain to
wash and wear ! Already nowadays it is difficult to get
them stated ; they have become incredible while still
too near to justify the incredibility that attaches to
history. It was assumed, for example, that in the
institutions, customs and culture of the middle Victorian
period, humanity had, so far as the broad lines of things
are concerned, achieved its goal. There were of course
still bad men and women—individually—and classes one

had to recognize as "lower," but all the main things were right, general ideas were right; the law was right, institutions were right, Consols and British Railway Debentures were right and were going to keep right for ever. The Abolition of Slavery in America had been the last great act which had inaugurated this millennium. Except for individual instances the tragic intensities of life were over now and done with; there was no more need for heroes and martyrs; for the generality of humanity the phase of genial comedy had begun. There might be improvements and refinements ahead, but social, political and economic arrangement were now in their main outlines settled for good and all; nothing better was possible and it was the agreeable task of the artist and the man of letters to assist and celebrate this establishment. There was to be much editing of Shakespear and Charles Lamb, much delightful humour and costume romance, and an Academy of refined Fine Writers would presently establish belles-lettres on the reputable official basis, write *finis* to creative force and undertake the task of stereotyping the language. Literature was to have its once terrible ferments reduced to the quality of a helpful pepsin. Ideas were dead—or domesticated. The last wild idea, in an impoverished and pitiful condition, had been hunted down and killed in the mobbing of "The Woman Who Did." For a little time the world did actually watch a phase of English writing that dared nothing, penetrated nothing, suppressed everything and aspired at most to Charm, creep like a transitory patch of sunlight across a storm-rent universe. And vanish. . . .

At no time was it a perfectly easy task to pretend that the crazy makeshifts of our legal and political

systems, the staggering accidents of economic relationship, the festering disorder of contemporary philosophy
and religious teaching, the cruel and stupid bed of King
Og that is our last word in sexual adjustment, really
constituted a noble and enduring sanity, and it became
less and less so with the acute disillusionments that arose
out of the Boer War. The first decade of the twentieth
century was for the English a decade of badly sprained
optimism. Our Empire was nearly beaten by a handful
of farmers amidst the jeering contempt of the whole
world—and we felt it acutely for several years. We
began to question ourselves. Mr. Brumley found his
gay but entirely respectable irresponsibility harder and
harder to keep up as that decade wore on. And close
upon the South African trouble came that extraordinary
new discontent of women with a woman's lot which we
have been observing as it reached and troubled the life
of Lady Harman. Women who had hitherto so
passively made the bulk of that reading public which
sustained Mr. Brumley and his kind—they wanted
something else !

And behind and beneath these immediately disconcerting things still more sinister hintings and
questionings were beginning to pluck at contentment.
In 1899 nobody would have dreamt of asking and in
1909 even Mr. Brumley was asking, " Are things going
on much longer ? " A hundred little incidents conspired
to suggest that a Christianity that had, to put it
mildly, shirked the Darwinian challenge, had no longer
the palliating influence demanded of a national religion,
and that down there in the deep levels of labour where
they built railways to carry Mr. Brumley's food and
earn him dividends, where they made engines and
instruments and textiles and drains for his little needs,

there was a new, less bounded discontent, a grimmer spirit, something that one tried in vain to believe was only the work of " agitators," something that was to be pacified no longer by the thin pretences of liberalism, something that might lead ultimately—optimism scarcely dared to ask whither. . . .

Mr. Brumley did his best to resist the influence of these darkening ideas. He tried to keep it up that everything was going well and that most of these shadows and complaints were the mischief of a few incurably restless personalities. He tried to keep it up that to belong to the working class was a thoroughly jolly thing—for those who were used to it. He declared that all who wanted to alter our laws or our ideas about property or our methods of production were envious and base and all who wanted any change between the sexes, foolish or vicious. He tried to go on disposing of socialists, agitators, feminists, women's suffragists, educationists and every sort of reformer with a good-humoured contempt. And he found an increasing difficulty in keeping his contempt sufficiently good-humoured. Instead of laughing down at folly and failure, he had moments when he felt that he was rather laughing up—a little wryly at monstrous things impending. And since ideas are things of atmosphere and the spirit, insidious wolves of the soul, they crept up to him and gnawed the insides out of him even as he posed as their manful antagonist.

Insensibly Mr. Brumley moved with his times. It is the necessary first phase in the break-up of any system of unsound assumptions that a number of its votaries should presently set about padding its cutting corners and relieving the harsh pressure of its injustices by exuberances of humour and sentimentality. Mr.

Brumley became charitable and romantic,—orthodox still but charitable and romantic. He was all for smashing with the generalization, but now in the particular instance he was more and more for forgiveness. One finds creeping into the later Euphemia books a Bret-Harte-like doctrine that a great number of bad women are really good and a persuasion in the ' Raffles ' key that a large proportion of criminals are really very picturesque and admirable fellows. One wonders how far Mr. Brumley's less ostensible life was softening in harmony with this exterior change, this tender twilight of principle. He wouldn't as yet face the sterner fact that most people who are condemned by society, whether they are condemned justly or not, are by the very gregariousness of man's nature debased, and that a law or custom that stamps you as bad makes you bad. A great state should have high and humane and considerate laws nobly planned, nobly administered and needing none of these shabby little qualifications *sotto voce*. To find goodness in the sinner and justification in the outcast is to condemn the law, but as yet Mr. Brumley's heart failed where his intelligence pointed towards that conclusion. He hadn't the courage to revise his assumptions about right and wrong to that extent ; he just allowed them to get soft and sloppy. He waded, where there should be firm ground. He waded toward wallowing. This is a perilous way of living and the sad little end of Euphemia, flushed and coughing, left him no doubt in many ways still more exposed to the temptations of the sentimental byway and the emotional gloss. Happily this is a book about Lady Harman and not an exhaustive monograph upon Mr. Brumley. We will at least leave him the refuge of a few shadows.

Occasionally he would write an important signed review for the *Twentieth Century* or the *Hebdomadal Review*, and on one such occasion he took in hand several studies of contemporary conditions by various 'New Witnesses,' 'Young Liberals,' *New Age* rebels and associated insurgent authors. He intended to be rather kindly with them, rather disillusioned, quite sympathetic but essentially conventional and conservative and sane. He sat at a little desk near the drooping Venus, under the benediction of Euphemia's posthumous rose, and turned over the pages of one of the least familiar of the group. The stuff was written with a crude force that at times became almost distinguished, but with a bitterness that he felt he must reprove. And suddenly he came upon a passionate tirade against the present period. It made him nibble softly with his lips at the top of his fountain pen as he read.

" We live," said the writer, " in a second Byzantine age, in one of those multitudinous accumulations of secondary interests, of secondary activities and conventions and colossal intricate insignificances, that lie like dust heaps in the path of the historian. The true history of such periods is written in bank books and cheque counterfoils and burnt to save individual reputations ; it sneaks along under a thousand pretences, it finds its mole-like food and safety in the dirt ; its outer forms remain for posterity, a huge débris of unfathomable riddles."

" Hm ! " said Mr. Brumley. " He slings it out. And what's this ? "

" A civilization arrested and decayed, waiting through long inglorious ages of unscheduled crime, unchallenged social injustice, senseless luxury, mercenary politics and universal vulgarity and weakness, for the long overdue scavenging of the Turk."

"I wonder where the children pick up such language," whispered Mr. Brumley with a smile.

But presently he had pushed the book away and was thinking over this novel and unpleasant idea that perhaps after all his age didn't matter as some ages have mattered and as he had hitherto always supposed it did matter. Byzantine, with the gold of life stolen and the swans changed to geese? Of course always there had been a certain qualification upon heroes, even Cæsar had needed a wreath, but at any rate the age of Cæsar had mattered. Kings no doubt might be more kingly and the issues of life plainer and nobler, but this had been true of every age. He tried to weigh values against values, our past against our present, temperately and sanely. Our art might perhaps be keener for beauty than it seemed to be, but still—it flourished. And our science at least was wonderful—wonderful. There certainly this young detractor of existing things went astray. What was there in Byzantium to parallel with the electric light, the electric tram, wireless telegraphy, aseptic surgery? Of course this about "unchallenged social injustice" was nonsense. Rant. Why! we were challenging social injustice at every general election—plainly and openly. And crime! What could the man mean about unscheduled crime? Mere words! There was of course a good deal of luxury, but not *wicked* luxury, and to compare our high-minded and constructive politics with the mere conflict of unscrupulous adventurers about that semi-oriental throne! It was nonsense!

"This young man must be spanked," said Mr. Brumley and, throwing aside an open illustrated paper in which a full length portrait of Sir Edward Carson faced a picture of the King and Queen in their robes sitting

side by side under a canopy at the Coronation Durbar,
he prepared himself to write in an extremely salutary
manner about the follies of the younger generation, and
incidentally to justify his period and his professional
contentment.

§ 2

One is reminded of those houses into which the
white ants have eaten their way; outwardly still fair
and solid, they crumble at the touch of a hand. And
now you will begin to understand those changes of
bearing that so perplexed Lady Harman, that sudden
insurgence of flushed half-furtive passion in the garden,
through the thin pretences of a liberal friendship.
His hollow honour had been gripped and had given
way.

He had begun so well. At first Lady Harman had
occupied his mind in the properest way. She was
another man's wife and sacred—according to all
honourable standards, and what he wanted was merely
to see more of her, talk to her, interest her in himself,
share whatever was available outside her connubial
obligations,—and think as little of Sir Isaac as possible.

How quickly the imaginative temperament of Mr.
Brumley enlarged that to include a critical hostility to
Sir Isaac, we have already recorded. Lady Harman was
no longer simply a charming, suppressed young wife,
crying out for attentive development; she became an
ill-treated beautiful woman—misunderstood. Still
scrupulously respecting his own standards, Mr. Brumley
embarked upon the dangerous business of inventing just
how Sir Isaac might be outraging them, and once his
imagination had started to hunt in that field, it speedily

brought in enough matter for a fine state of moral indignation, a white heat of not altogether justifiable chivalry. Assisted by Lady Beach-Mandarin Mr. Brumley had soon converted the little millionaire into a matrimonial ogre to keep an anxious lover very painfully awake at nights. Because by that time and quite insensibly he had become an anxious lover—with all the gaps in the thread of realities that would have made him that, quite generously filled up from the world of reverie.

Moral indignation is jealousy with a halo. It is the peculiar snare of the perplexed orthodox, and soon Mr. Brumley was in a state of nearly unendurable moral indignation with Sir Isaac for a hundred exaggerations of what he was and of what conceivably he might have done to his silent yet manifestly unsuitably mated wife. And now that romantic streak which is as I have said the first certain symptom of decay in a system of moral assumptions began to show itself in Mr. Brumley's thoughts and conversation. "A marriage like that," said Mr. Brumley to Lady Beach-Mandarin, "isn't a marriage. It flouts the True Ideal of Marriage. It's slavery—following a kidnapping. . . ."

But this is a wide step from the happy optimism of the Cambridge days. What becomes of the sanctity of marriage and the institution of the family when respectable gentlemen talk of something called "True Marriage," as non-existent in relation to a lady who is already the mother of four children? I record this lapsing of Mr. Brumley into romanticism without either sympathy or mitigation. The children, it presently became apparent, were not "true" children. "Forced upon her," said Mr. Brumley. "It makes one ill to think of it!" It certainly very nearly made him ill.

And as if these exercises in distinction had inflamed his conscience Mr. Brumley wrote two articles in the *Hebdomadal* denouncing impure literature, decadence, immorality, various recent scandalous instances, and the suffragettes, declaring that woman's place was the home and that " in a pure and exalted monogamy lies the sole unitary basis for a civilized state." The most remarkable thing about this article is an omission. That Sir Isaac's monogamy with any other instances that might be akin to it was not pure and exalted, and that it needed—shall we call it readjustment? is a view that in this article Mr. Brumley conspicuously doesn't display. It's as if for a moment, pen in hand, he had eddied back to his old absolute positions. . .

In a very little while Mr. Brumley and Lady Beach-Mandarin had almost persuaded each other that Sir Isaac was applying physical torture to his proudly silent wife, and Mr. Brumley was no longer dreaming and glancing at but steadily facing the possibility of a pure-minded and handsomely done elopement to " free " Lady Harman, that would be followed in due course by a marriage, a " true marriage " on a level of understanding far above any ordinary respectable wedding, amidst universal sympathy and admiration and the presence of all the very best people. In these antici-pations he did rather remarkably overlook the absence of any sign of participation on the part of Lady Harman in his own impassioned personal feelings, and he overlooked still more remarkably as possible objections to his line of conduct, Millicent, Florence, Annette and Baby. These omissions no doubt simpli-fied but also greatly falsified his outlook.

This proposal that all the best people shall applaud the higher rightness that was to be revealed in his projected elopement, is in the very essence of the romantic attitude. All other people are still to remain under the law. There is to be nothing revolutionary. But with exceptional persons under exceptional conditions——

Mr. Brumley stated his case over and over again to his utmost satisfaction, and always at great moral altitudes and with a kind of transcendent orthodoxy. The more difficult any aspect of the affair appeared from the orthodox standpoint the more valiantly Mr. Brumley soared; if it came to his living with Lady Harman for a time before they could be properly married amidst picturesque foreign scenery in a little *casa* by the side of a stream, then the water in that stream was to be quite the purest water conceivable and the scenery and associations as morally faultless as a view that had passed the exacting requirements of Mr. John Ruskin. And Mr. Brumley was very clear in his mind that what he proposed to do was entirely different in quality even if it was similar in form from anything that anyone else had ever done who had ever before made a scandal or appeared in the divorce court. This is always the way in such cases—always. The scandal was to be a noble scandal, a proud scandal, one of those instances of heroical love that turn misdemeanours—admittedly misdemeanours—into edifying marvels.

This was the state of mind to which Mr. Brumley had attained when he made his ineffectual raid upon Black Strand, and you will remark about it, if you are interested in the changes in people's ideas that are going on to-day, that although he was prepared to make the most extensive glosses in this particular instance upon the commonly accepted rules of what is right and proper, he was not for a moment prepared to accord the terrible gift of an independent responsibility to Lady Harman. In that direction lay regions that Mr. Brumley had still to explore. Lady Harman he considered was married wrongly and disastrously and this he held to be essentially the fault of Sir Isaac— with perhaps some slight blame attaching to Lady Harman's mother. The only path of escape he could conceive as yet for Lady Harman lay through the chivalry of some other man. That a woman could possibly rebel against one man without the sympathy and moral maintenance of another was still outside the range of Mr. Brumley's understanding. It is still outside the range of most men's understandings—and of a great many women's. If he generalized at all from these persuasions it was in the direction that in the interests of " true marriage " there should be greater facilities for divorce and also a kind of respectable-iza-tion of divorce. Then these " false marriages " might be rectified without suffering. The reasons for divorce he felt should be extended to include things not generally reprehensible, and chivalrous people coming into court should be protected from the indelicate publicity of free reporting. . . .

§ 3

Mr. Brumley was still contemplating rather inconclusively the possibility of a long and intimate talk leading up to and preparing for an elopement with Lady Harman, when he read of her Jago Street escapade and of her impending appearance at the South Hampsmith police court. He was astonished. The

more he contemplated the thing the greater became
his astonishment.

Even at the first impact he realized that the line
she had taken wasn't quite in the picture with the line
he had proposed for her. He felt—left out. He felt
as though a door had slammed between himself and
affairs to which he had supposed himself essential. He
could not understand why she had done this thing
instead of coming straight to his flat and making use
of all that chivalrous service she surely knew was at her
disposal. This self-reliance, this direct dealing with
the world, seemed to him, even in the height of his
concern, unwomanly, a deeper injury to his own
abandoned assumptions than any he had contemplated.
He felt it needed explanation, and he hurried to secure
an elbowed unsavory corner in the back of the court in
order to hear her defence. He had to wait through
long stuffy spaces of time before she appeared. There
were half a dozen other window smashers,—plain or at
least untidy-looking young women. The magistrate
told them they were silly and the soul of Mr. Brumley
acquiesced. One tried to make a speech, and it was
such a poor speech—squeaky. . . .

When at last Lady Harman entered the box—the
strangest place it seemed for her—he tried to emerge
from the jostling crowd about him into visibility, to
catch her eye, to give her the support of his devoted
presence. Twice at least she glanced in his direction
but gave no sign of seeing him. He was surprised that
she could look without fear or detestation, indeed once
with a gesture of solicitude, at Sir Isaac. She was
astonishingly serene. There seemed to be just the
faintest shadow of a smile about her lips as the stipen-
diary explained the impossibility of giving her anything

less than a month. An uneasy object like the smashed remains of a colossal box of bonbons that was riding out a gale, down in the middle of the court, turned round at last completely and revealed itself as the hat of Lady Beach-Mandarin, but though Mr. Brumley waved his hand he could not even make that lady aware of his presence. A powerful rude criminal-looking man who stood in front of him and smelt grossly of stables, would not give him a fair chance of showing himself, and developed a strong personal hostility to him on account of his alleged "shoving about." It would not he felt be of the slightest help to Lady Harman for him to involve himself in a personal struggle with a powerful and powerfully flavoured criminal.

It was all very dreadful.

After the proceedings were over and Lady Harman had been led away into captivity, he went out and took a taxi in an agitated distraught manner to Lady Beach-Mandarin's house.

"She meant," said Lady Beach-Mandarin, "to have a month's holiday from him and think things out. And she's got it."

Perhaps that was it. Mr. Brumley could not tell, and he spent some days in that state of perplexity which, like the weariness that heralds a cold, marks so often the onset of a new series of ideas. . . .

Why hadn't she come to him? Had he after all rather overloaded his memory of her real self with imaginative accessories? Had she really understood what he had been saying to her in the garden? Afterwards when he had met her eyes as he and she went over the new wing with Sir Isaac she had so manifestly— and, when one came to think of it, so tranquilly—seemed to understand. . . .

It was such an extraordinary thing to go smashing a window like that—when there he was at hand ready to help her. She knew his address ? Did she ? For a moment Mr. Brumley cherished that wild surmise. Was that perhaps it ? But surely she could have looked in the Telephone Directory or Who's Who. . . .

But if that was the truth of the matter she would have looked and behaved differently in court—quite differently. She would have been looking for him. She would have seen him. . . .

It was queer too to recall what she had said in court about her daughters. . . .

Could it be, he had a frightful qualm, that after all —he wasn't the man ? How little he knew of her really. . . .

" This wretched agitation," said Mr. Brumley, trying to flounder away anyhow from these disconcerting riddles ; " it seems to unbalance them all."

But he found it impossible to believe that Lady Harman was seriously unbalanced.

§ 4

And if Mr. Brumley's system of romantically distorted moral assumptions was shattered by Lady Harman's impersonal blow at a post office window when all the rules seemed to require her to fly from the oppression of one man to the chivalry of another, what words can convey the devastating effect upon him of her conduct after her release ? To that crisis he had been looking forward continually ; to record the variety of his expectations would fill a large volume, but throughout them all prevailed one general idea, that when she came out of prison her struggle with her husband would be resumed, and that this would give Mr. Brumley such extraordinary opportunities of displaying his devotion that her response, which he was now beginning to suspect might be more reluctant than his earlier dreams had assumed, was ultimately inevitable. In all these dreams and meditations that response figured as the crown. He had to win and possess Lady Harman. The idea had taken hold of his busy yet rather pointless life, had become his directing object. He was full of schemes for presently arresting and captivating her imagination. He was already convinced that she cared for him ; he had to inflame interest and fan liking into the fire of passion. And with a mind so occupied, Mr. Brumley wrote this and that and went about his affairs. He spent two days and a night at Margate visiting his son at his preparatory school, and he found much material for musing in the question of just how the high romantic affairs ahead of him would affect this delicately intelligent boy. For a time perhaps he might misjudge his father. . . . He spent a week-end with Lady Viping and stayed on until Wednesday and then he came back to London. His plans were still unformed when the day came for Lady Harman's release, and indeed beyond an idea that he would have her met at the prison gates by an enormous bunch of snowy-white and crimson chrysanthemums he had nothing really concrete at all in his mind.

She had, however, been released stealthily a day before her time, and this is what she had done. She had asked that—of all improbable people !—Sir Isaac's mother should meet her, the biggest car had come to the prison gates, and she had gone straight down with Mrs. Harman to her husband—who had taken a chill

and was in bed drinking Contrexéville water—at Black
Strand.

As these facts shaped themselves in answer to the
blanched inquiries of Mr. Brumley his amazement grew.
He began to realize that there must have been a
correspondence during her incarceration, that all sorts
of things had been happening while he had been
dreaming, and when he went round to Lady Beach-
Mandarin, who was just packing up to be the life and
soul of a winter-sports party at a nice non-Lunnite
hotel at Lenzerheide, he learnt particulars that chilled
him to the marrow. "They've made it up," said Lady
Beach-Mandarin.

"But how?" gasped Mr. Brumley, with his soul
in infinite distress. "But how?"

"The Ogre, it seems, has come to see that bullying
won't do. He's given in tremendously. He's let her
have her way with the waitress strike and she's going to
have an allowance of her own and all kinds of things.
It's settled. It's his mother and that man Charterson
talked him over. You know—his mother came to me—
as her friend. For advice. Wanted to find out what
sort of things we might have been putting in her head.
She said so. A curious old thing—vulgar but—*wise*.
I liked her. He's her darling—and she just knows
what he is. . . . He doesn't like it but he's taken his
dose. The thought of her going to prison again—— !
He's let her do anything rather than that. . . ."

"And she's gone to him!"

"Naturally," said Lady Beach-Mandarin with what
he felt to be deliberate brutality. Surely she must have
understood——

"But the waitress strike—what has it got to do with
the waitress strike?"

" She cared—tremendously."

" *Did* she ? "

" Tremendously. And they all go back and the system of inspection is being altered, and he's even forgiven Babs Wheeler. It made him ill to do it but he did."

" And she's gone back to him."

" Like Godiva," said Lady Beach-Mandarin with that sweeping allusiveness that was part of her complicated charm.

§ 5

For three days Mr. Brumley was so staggered by these things that it did not occur to him that it was quite possible for him to see Lady Harman for himself and find out just how things stood. He remained in London with an imagination dazed. And as it was the Christmas season and as George Edmund in a rather expectant holiday state had now come up from Margate, Mr. Brumley went in succession to the Hippodrome, to Peter Pan and to an exhibition at Olympia, assisted at an afternoon display of the kinemacolor at La Scala Theatre, visited Hamley's and lunched George Edmund once at the Criterion and twice at the Climax Club, while thinking of nothing in all the world but the incalculable strangeness of women. George Edmund thought him a very passive leadable parent indeed, less querulous about money matters and altogether much improved. The glitter and colour of these various entertainments reflected themselves upon the surface of that deep flood of meditation, hook-armed wooden-legged pirates, intelligent elephants, ingenious but extremely expensive toys, flickering processions, comic turns, snatches of popular music and George Edmund's way of eating an orange, pictured themselves on his mind confusedly without in any way deflecting its course. Then on the fourth day he roused himself, gave George Edmund ten shillings to get himself a cutlet at the Café Royal and do the cinematographs round and about the West End, and so released reached Aleham in time for a temperate lunch. He chartered the Aleham car to take him to Black Strand and arrived there about a quarter past three, in a great effort to feel himself a matter-of-course visitor.

It ought to be possible to record that Mr. Brumley's mind was full of the intensest sense of Lady Harman during that journey and of nothing else, but as a matter of fact his mind was now curiously detached and reflective, the tensions and expectation of the past month and the astonishment of the last few days had worked themselves out and left him as it were the passive instrument of the purpose of his more impassioned moods. This distressed lover approached Black Strand in a condition of philosophical lassitude.

The road from Aleham to Black Strand is a picturesque old English road, needlessly winding and badly graded, wriggling across a heathy wilderness with occasional pine woods. Something in that familiar landscape—for his life had run through it since first he and Euphemia on a tandem bicycle and altogether very young had sought their ideal home in the South of England—set his mind swinging and generalizing. How freshly youthful he and Euphemia had been when first he came along that road, how crude, how full of happy expectations of success; it had been as bright and it was now as completely gone as the sunsets they had seen together.

How great a thing life is! How much greater than any single romance, or any individual affection! Since those days he had grown, he had succeeded, he had suffered in a reasonable way of course, still he could recall with a kind of satisfaction tears and deep week-long moods of hopeless melancholy—and he had changed. And now dominating this landscape, filling him with new emotions and desires and perplexing intimations of ignorance and limitations he had never suspected in his youth, was this second figure of a woman. She was different from Euphemia. With Euphemia everything had been so simple and easy; until that slight fading, that fatigue of entire success and satisfaction, of the concluding years. He and Euphemia had always kept it up that they had no thought in the world except for one another. . . . Yet if that had been true, why hadn't he died when she did. He hadn't died—with remarkable elasticity. Clearly in his case there had been these unexplored, unsuspected hinterlands of possibility towards which Lady Harman seemed now to be directing him. It came to him that afternoon as an entirely fresh thought that there might also have been something in Euphemia beyond their simple, so charmingly treated relationship. He began to recall moments when Euphemia had said perplexing little things, had looked at him with an expression that was unexpected, had been—difficult. . . .

I write of Mr. Brumley to tell you things about him and not to explain him. It may be that the appetite for thorough good talks with people grows upon one, but at any rate it did occur to Mr. Brumley on his way to talk to Lady Harman, it occurred to him as a thing distressingly irrevocable that he could now never have a thorough good talk with Euphemia about certain neglected things between them. It would have helped him so much. . . .

His eyes rested as he thought of these things upon the familiar purple hill crests, patched that afternoon with the lingering traces of a recent snowstorm, the heather slopes, the dark mysterious woods, the patches of vivid green where a damp and marshy meadow or so broke the moorland surface. To-day in spite of the sun there was a bright blue-white line of frost to the northward of every hedge and bank, the trees were dripping down the white edgings of the morning into the pine-needle mud at their feet; he had seen it so like this before; years hence he might see it all like this again; all this great breezy countryside had taken upon itself a quality of endurance, as though it would still be real and essential in his mind when Lady Harman had altogether passed again. It would be real when he himself had passed away, and in other costumes and other vehicles fresh Euphemias and new crude George Brumleys would come along, feeling in the ultimate bright new wisdom of youth that it was all for them— a subservient scenery, when really it was entirely indifferent in its careless permanence to all their hopes and fancies. . . .

§ 6

Mr. Brumley's thoughts on the permanence of landscape and the mutability of human affairs were more than a little dashed when he came within sight of Black Strand and perceived that once cosily beautiful little home clipped and extended, its shrubbery wrecked and the old barn now pierced with windows and adorned — for its new chimneys were not working very well—by several efficient novelties in chimney cowls. Up the slopes behind Sir Isaac had extended his boundaries, and had been felling trees and levelling a couple of tennis courts for next summer.

Something was being done to the porch, and the jasmine had been cleared away altogether. Mr. Brumley could not quite understand what was in progress; Sir Isaac he learnt afterwards had found a wonderful bargain in a real genuine Georgian portal of great dignity and simplicity in Aleham, and he was going to improve Black Strand by transferring it thither—with the utmost precaution and every piece numbered—from its original situation. Mr. Brumley stood among the preparatory débris of this and rang a quietly resolute electric bell, which was answered no longer by Mrs. Rabbit but by the ample presence of Snagsby.

Snagsby in that doorway had something of the preposterous effect of a very large face beneath a very small hat. He had to Mr. Brumley's eye a restored look, as though his self-confidence had been thoroughly done up since their last encounter. Bygones were bygones. Mr. Brumley was admitted as one is admitted to any normal home. He was shown into the little study-drawing-room with the stepped floor, which had been so largely the scene of his life with Euphemia, and he was left there for the better part of a quarter of an hour before his hostess appeared.

The room had been changed very little. Euphemia's solitary rose had gone, and instead there were several bowls of beaten silver scattered about, each filled with great chrysanthemums from London. Sir Isaac's jackdaw acquisitiveness had also overcrowded the corner beyond the fireplace with a very fine and genuine Queen Anne cabinet; there were a novel by Elizabeth Robins and two or three feminist and socialist works lying on the table which would certainly not have been visible, though they might have been in the house, during the Brumley régime. Otherwise things were very much as they always had been.

A room like this, thought Mr. Brumley among much other mental driftage, is like a heart,—so long as it exists it must be furnished and tenanted. No matter what has been, however bright and sweet and tender, the spaces still cry aloud to be filled again. The very essence of life is its insatiability. How complete all this had seemed in the moment when first he and Euphemia had arranged it. And indeed how complete life had seemed altogether at seven-and-twenty. Every year since then he had been learning—or at any rate unlearning. Until at last he was beginning to realize he had still everything to learn. . . .

The door opened and the tall dark figure of Lady Harman stood for a moment in the doorway before she stepped down into the room.

She had always the same effect upon him, the effect of being suddenly remembered. When he was away from her he was always sure that she was a beautiful woman, and when he saw her again he was always astonished to see how little he had borne her beauty in mind. For a moment they regarded one another silently. Then she closed the door behind her and came towards him.

All Mr. Brumley's philosophizing had vanished at the sight of her. His spirit was reborn within him. He thought of her and of his effect upon her, vividly, and of nothing else in the world.

She was paler he thought beneath her dusky hair, a little thinner and graver. . . .

There was something in her manner as she advanced towards him that told him he mattered to her, that his coming there was something that moved her imagination as well as his own. With an almost impulsive movement she held out both her hands to him, and with an inspiration as sudden he took them and kissed them. When he had done so he was ashamed of his temerity; he looked up to meet in her dark eyes the scared shyness of a fallow deer. She suddenly remembered to withdraw her hands, and it became manifest to both of them that the incident must never have happened. She went to the window, stood almost awkwardly for a moment looking out of it, then turned. She put her hands on the back of the chair and stood holding it.

"I knew you would come to see me," she said.

"I've been very anxious about you," he said, and on that their minds rested through a little silence.

"You see," he explained, "I didn't know what was happening to you. Or what you were doing."

"After asking your advice," she said.

"Exactly."

"I don't know why I broke that window. Except I think that I wanted to get away."

"But why didn't you come to me?"

"I didn't know where you were. And besides—— I didn't somehow want to come to you."

"But wasn't it wretched in prison? Wasn't it miserably cold? I used to think of you of nights in some wretched ill-aired cell. . . . You. . . ."

"It *was* cold," she admitted. "But it was very good for me. It was quiet. The first few days seemed endless; then they began to go by quickly. Quite quickly at last. And I came to think. In the day there was a little stool where one sat. I used to sit on that and brood and try to think things out—all sorts of things I've never had the chance to think about before."

" Yes," said Mr. Brumley.

" All this," she said.

" And it has brought you back here ! " he said, with something of the tone of one who has a right to enquire, with some flavour too of reproach.

"You see," she said after a little pause, " during that time it was possible to come to understandings. Neither I nor my husband had understood the other. In that interval it was possible—to explain.

" Yes. You see, Mr. Brumley, we—we both misunderstood. It was just because of that and because I had no one who seemed able to advise me that I turned to you. A novelist always seems so wise in these things. He seems to know so many lives. One can talk to you as one can scarcely talk to anyone ; you are a sort of doctor—in these matters. And it was necessary— that my husband should realize that I had grown up and that I should have time to think just how one's duty and one's—freedom have to be fitted together. . . . And my husband is ill. He has been ill, rather short of breath—the doctor thinks it is asthma—for some time, and all the agitation of this business has upset him and made him worse. He is upstairs now— asleep. Of course if I had thought I should make him ill I could never have done any of this. But it's done now and here I am, Mr. Brumley, back in my place. With all sorts of things changed. Put right. . . ."

" I see," said Mr. Brumley stupidly.

Her speech was like the falling of an opaque curtain upon some romantic spectacle. She stood there, almost defensively behind her chair as she made it. There was a quality of premeditation in her words, yet something in her voice and bearing made him feel that she knew just how it covered up and extinguished his dreams and impulses. He heard her out and then suddenly his spirit rebelled against her decision. " No ! " he cried.

She waited for him to go on.

" You see," he said, " I thought that it was just that you wanted to get away—— That this life was intolerable—— That you were—— Forgive me if I seem to be going beyond—going beyond what I ought to be thinking about you. Only, why should I pretend ? I care, I care for you tremendously. And it seemed to me that you didn't love your husband, that you were enslaved and miserable. I would have done anything to help you —anything in the world, Lady Harman. I know— it may sound ridiculous—there have been times when I would have faced death to feel you were happy and free. I thought all that, I felt all that,—and then —then you come back here. You seem not to have minded. As though I had misunderstood. . . ."

He paused and his face was alive with an unwonted sincerity. His self-consciousness had for a moment fallen from him.

" I know," she said, " it *was* like that. I knew you cared. That is why I have so wanted to talk to you. It looked like that. . . ."

She pressed her lips together in that old familiar hunt for words and phrases.

" I didn't understand, Mr. Brumley, all there was in my husband or all there was in myself. I just saw his hardness and his—his hardness in business. It's become so different now. You see, I forgot he has bad health. He's ill ; I suppose he was getting ill

then. Instead of explaining himself—he was—excited
and—unwise. And now——"

"Now I suppose he has—explained," said Mr.
Brumley slowly and with infinite distaste. "Lady
Harman, *what* has he explained?"

"It isn't so much that he has explained, Mr.
Brumley," said Lady Harman, "as that things have
explained themselves."

"But how, Lady Harman? How?"

"I mean about my being a mere girl, almost a
child when I married him. Naturally he wanted to
take charge of everything and leave nothing to me.
And quite as naturally he didn't notice that now I
am a woman, grown up altogether. And it's been
necessary to do things. And naturally, Mr. Brumley,
they shocked and upset him. But he sees now so
clearly, he wrote to me, such a fair letter—an unusual
letter—quite different from when he talks—it surprised
me, telling me he wanted me to feel free, that he
meant to make me—to arrange things that is, so that
I should feel free and more able to go about as I
pleased. It was a *generous* letter, Mr. Brumley.
Generous about all sorts of affairs that there had been
between us. He said things, quite kind things, not
like the things he has ever said before——"

She stopped short and then began again.

"You know, Mr. Brumley, it's so hard to tell
things without telling other things that somehow are
difficult to tell. Yet if I don't tell you them, you
won't know them and then you won't be able to
understand in the least how things are with us."

Her eyes appealed to him.

"Tell me," he said, "whatever you think fit."

"When one has been afraid of anyone and felt they

were ever so much stronger and cruel and hard than one is and one suddenly finds they aren't. It alters everything."

He nodded, watching her.

Her voice fell nearly to a whisper. " Mr. Brumley," she said, " when I came back to him—you know he was in bed here—instead of scolding me—he *cried*. He cried like a vexed child. He put his face into the pillow—just misery. . . . I'd never seen him cry—at least only once—long ago. . . ."

Mr Brumley looked at her flushed and tender face and it seemed to him that indeed he could die for her quite easily.

" I saw how hard I had been," she said. " In prison I'd thought of that, I'd thought women mustn't be hard, whatever happens to them. And when I saw him like that I knew at once how true that was. . . . He begged me to be a good wife to him. No !—he just said, ' Be a wife to me,' not even a good wife— and then he cried. . . ."

For a moment or so Mr. Brumley didn't respond. " I see," he said at last. " Yes."

" And there were the children—such helpless little things. In the prison I worried about them. I thought of things for them. I've come to feel—they are left too much to nurses and strangers. . . . And then you see he has agreed to nearly everything I had wanted. It wasn't only the personal things—I was anxious about those silly girls—the strikers. I didn't want them to be badly treated. It distressed me to think of them. I don't think you know how it distressed me. And he—he gave way upon all that. He says I may talk to him about the business, about the way we do our business—the kindness of it I mean.

And this is why I am back here. Where else *could* I be?"

"No," said Mr. Brumley still with the utmost reluctance. "I see. Only——"

He paused downcast and she waited for him to speak.

"Only it isn't what I expected, Lady Harman. I didn't think that matters could be settled by such arrangements. It's sane, I know, it's comfortable and kindly. But I thought—Oh! I thought of different things, quite different things from all this. I thought of you who are so beautiful caught in a loveless passionless world. I thought of the things there might be for you, the beautiful and wonderful things of which you are deprived. . . . Never mind what I thought! Never mind! You've made your choice. But I thought that you didn't love, that you couldn't love—this man. It seemed to me that you felt too—that to live as you are doing—with him—was a profanity. Something—I'd give everything I have, everything I am, to save you from. Because—because I care. . . . I misunderstood you. I suppose you can—do what you are doing."

He jumped to his feet as he spoke and walked three paces away and turned to utter his last sentences. She too stood up.

"Mr. Brumley," she said weakly, "I don't understand. What do you mean? I have to do what I am doing. He—he is my husband."

He made a gesture of impatience. "Do you understand nothing of *love*?" he cried.

She pressed her lips together and remained still and silent, dark against the casement window.

There came a sound of tapping from the room above. Three taps and again three taps.

Lady Harman made a little gesture as though she would put this sound aside.

"Love," she said at last. "It comes to some people. It happens. It happens to young people. . . . But when one is married——"

Her voice fell almost to a whisper. "One must not think of it," she said. "One must think of one's husband and one's duty. Life cannot begin again, Mr. Brumley."

The taps were repeated, a little more urgently.

"That is my husband," she said.

She hesitated through a little pause. "Mr. Brumley," she said, "I want friendship so badly, I want some one to be my friend. I don't want to think of things—disturbing things—things I have lost—things that are spoilt. *That*—that which you spoke of; what has it to do with me?"

She interrupted him as he was about to speak.

"Be my friend. Don't talk to me of impossible things. Love! Mr. Brumley, what has a married woman to do with love? I never think of it. I never read of it. I want to do my duty. I want to do my duty by him and by my children and by all the people I am bound to. I want to help people, weak people, people who suffer. I want to help him to help them. I want to stop being an idle, useless, spending woman. . . ."

She made a little gesture of appeal with her hands.

"Oh!" he sighed, and then, "You know if I can help you—— Rather than distress you——"

Her manner changed. It became confidential and urgent.

"Mr. Brumley," she said, "I must go up to my husband. He will be impatient. And when I tell

him you are here he will want to see you. . . . You
will come up and see him?"

Mr. Brumley sought to convey the struggle within
him by his pose.

"I will do what you wish, Lady Harman," he said,
with an almost theatrical sigh.

He closed the door after her and was alone in his
former study once more. He walked slowly to his old
writing-desk and sat down in his familiar seat. Presently
he heard her footfalls across the room above. Mr.
Brumley's mind under the stress of the unfamiliar and
the unexpected was now lapsing rapidly towards the
theatrical. "My *God!*" said Mr. Brumley.

He addressed that friendly memorable room in
tones that mingled amazement and wrong. "He is
her husband!" he said, and then: "The power of
words!" . . .

§ 7

It seemed to Mr. Brumley's now entirely disordered
mind that Sir Isaac, propped up with cushions upon a
sofa in the upstairs sitting-room, white-faced, wary and
very short of breath, was like Proprietorship enthroned.
Everything about him referred deferentially to him.
Even his wife dropped at once into the position of a
beautiful satellite. His illness, he assured his visitor
with a thin-lipped emphasis, was "quite temporary,
quite the sort of thing that might happen to anyone."
He had had a queer little benumbing of one leg, "just a
trifle of nerve fag did it," and the slight asthma that
came and went in his life had taken advantage of his
condition to come again with a little beyond its usual
aggressiveness. "Elly is going to take me off to

Marienbad next week or the week after," he said.
" I shall have a cure and she'll have a treat, and we
shall come back as fit as fiddles." The incidents of the
past month were to be put on a facetious footing it
appeared. " It's a mercy they didn't crop her hair,"
he said, apropos of nothing and with an air of dry
humour. No further allusion was made to Lady
Harman's incarceration.

He was dressed in a lama wool bedroom suit and
his resting leg was covered by a very splendid and
beautiful fur rug. All Euphemia's best and gayest
cushions sustained his back. The furniture had been
completely rearranged for his comfort and convenience.
Close to his hand was a little table with carefully selected
remedies and aids and helps and stimulants, and the
latest and best of the light fiction of the day was tossed
about between the table, the couch and the floor. At
the foot of the couch Euphemia's bedroom writing-
table had been placed, and over this there were scattered
traces of the stenographer who had assisted him to
wipe off the day's correspondence. Three black
cylinders and other appliances in the corner witnessed
that his slight difficulty in breathing could be relieved
by oxygen, and his eyes were regaled by a great abundance of London flowers at every available point in the
room. Of course there were grapes, fabulous looking
grapes.

Everything conspired to give Sir Isaac and his
ownership the centre of the picture. Mr. Brumley had
been brought upstairs to him, and the tea table, with
scarcely a reference to any one else, was arranged by
Snagsby conveniently to his hand. And Sir Isaac
himself had a confidence—the assurance of a man who
has been shaken and has recovered. Whatever tears

he had ever shed had served their purpose and were forgotten. "Elly" was his and the house was his and everything about him was his—he laid his hand upon her once when she came near him, his possessiveness was so gross—and the strained suspicion of his last meeting with Mr. Brumley was replaced now by a sage and wizened triumph over anticipated and arrested dangers.

Their party was joined by Sir Isaac's mother, and the sight of her sturdy, swarthy, and rather dignified presence flashed the thought into Mr. Brumley's mind that Sir Isaac's father must have been a very blond and very nosey person indeed. She was homely and practical and contributed very usefully to a conversation that remained a trifle fragmentary and faintly uncomfortable to the end.

Mr. Brumley avoided as much as he could looking at Lady Harman, because he knew Sir Isaac was alert for that, but he was acutely aware of her presence dispensing the tea and moving about the room, being a good wife. It was his first impression of Lady Harman as a good wife and he disliked the spectacle extremely. The conversation hovered chiefly about Marienbad, drifted away and came back again. Mrs. Harman made several confidences that provoked the betrayal of a strain of irritability in Sir Isaac's condition. "We're all looking forward to this Marienbad expedition," she said. "I do hope it will turn out well. Neither of them have ever been abroad before— and there's the difficulty of the languages."

"Ow," snarled Sir Isaac, with a glance at his mother that was almost vicious and a lapse into Cockney intonations and phrases that witnessed how her presence recalled his youth, "It'll *go* all right, mother. *You* needn't fret."

"Of course they'll have a courier to see to their things, and go train de luxe and all that," Mrs. Harman explained with a certain gusto. "But still it's an adventure, with him not well, and both as I say more like children than grown-up people."

Sir Isaac intervened with a crushing clumsiness to divert this strain of explanation, with questions about the quality of the soil in the wood where the ground was to be cleared and levelled for his tennis lawns.

Mr. Brumley did his best to behave as a man of the world should. He made intelligent replies about the sand, he threw out obvious but serviceable advice upon travel upon the continent of Europe, and he tried not to think that this was the way of living into which the sweetest, tenderest, most beautiful woman in the world had been trapped. He avoided looking at her until he felt it was becoming conspicuous, a negative stare. Why had she come back again? Fragmentary phrases she had used downstairs came drifting through his mind. "I never think of it. I never read of it." And she so made for beautiful love and a beautiful life! He recalled Lady Beach-Mandarin's absurdly apt, absurdly inept, "like Godiva," and was suddenly impelled to raise the question of those strikers.

"Your trouble with your waitresses is over, Sir Isaac?"

Sir Isaac finished a cup of tea audibly and glanced at his wife. "I never meant to be hard on them," he said, putting down his cup. "Never. The trouble blew up suddenly. One can't be all over a big business everywhere all at once, more particularly if one is worried about other things. As soon as I had time to look into it I put things right. There was misunderstandings on both sides."

He glanced up again at Lady Harman. (She was standing behind Mr. Brumley so that he could not see her but—did their eyes meet ?)

" As soon as we are back from Marienbad," Sir Isaac volunteered, " Lady Harman and I are going into all that business thoroughly."

Mr. Brumley concealed his intense aversion for this association under a tone of intelligent interest. " Into— I don't quite understand—what business ? "

" Women employees in London—Hostels—all that kind of thing. Bit more sensible than suffragetting, eh Elly ? "

" Very interesting," said Mr. Brumley with a hollow cordiality, " Very."

" Done on business lines, mind you," said Sir Isaac, looking suddenly very sharp and keen ; " done on proper business lines, there's no end of a change possible. And it's a perfectly legitimate outgrowth from such popular catering as ours. It interests me."

He made a little whistling noise with his teeth at the end of this speech.

" I didn't know Lady Harman was disposed to take up such things," he said. " Or I'd have gone into them before."

" He's going into them now," said Mrs. Harman, " heart and soul. Why ! we have to take his temperature over it, to see he doesn't work himself up into a fever." Her manner became reasonable and confidential. She spoke to Mr. Brumley as if her son was slightly deaf. " It's better than his fretting," she said. . . .

§ 8

Mr. Brumley returned to London in a state of extreme mental and emotional unrest. The sight of Lady Harman had restored all his passion for her, the all too manifest fact that she was receding beyond his reach stirred him with unavailing impulses towards some impossible extremity of effort. She had filled his mind so much that he could not endure the thought of living without hope of her. But what hope was there of her? And he was jealous, detestably jealous, so jealous that in that direction he did not dare to let his mind go. He sawed at the bit and brought it back, or he would have had to writhe about the carriage. His thoughts ran furiously all over the place to avoid that pit. And now he found himself flashing at moments into wild and hopeless rebellion against the institution of marriage, of which he had hitherto sought always to be the dignified and smiling champion against the innovator, the over-critical and the young. He had never rebelled before. He was so astonished at the violence of his own objection that he lapsed from defiance to an incredulous examination of his own novel attitude. "It's not *true* marriage I object to," he told himself. "It's this marriage like a rat trap, alluring and scarcely unavoidable, so that in we all go, and then with no escape—unless you tear yourself to rags. No escape. . . ."

It came to him that there was at least one way out for Lady Harman : *Sir Isaac might die !* . . .

He pulled himself up presently, astonished and dismayed at the activities of his own imagination. Among other things he had wondered if by any chance

Lady Harman had ever allowed her mind to travel in this same post-mortem direction. At times surely the thing must have shone upon her as a possibility, a hope. From that he had branched off to a more general speculation. How many people were there in the world, nice people, kind people, moral and delicate-minded people, to whom the death of another person means release from that inflexible barrier—possibilities of secretly desired happiness, the realization of crushed and forbidden dreams? He had a vision of human society, like the vision of a night landscape seen suddenly in a lightning flash, as of people caught by couples in traps and quietly hoping for one another's deaths. " Good Heavens ! " said Mr. Brumley, " what are we coming to," and got up in his railway compartment—he had it to himself—and walked up and down its narrow limits until a jolt over a point made him suddenly sit down again. " Most marriages are happy," said Mr. Brumley, like a man who has fallen into a river and scrambles back to safety. " One mustn't judge by the exceptional cases. . . .

" Though of course there are—a good many—exceptional cases." . . .

He folded his arms, crossed his legs, frowned and reasoned with himself,—resolved to dismiss post-mortem speculations—absolutely.

He was not going to quarrel with the institution of marriage. That was going too far. He had never been able to see the beginnings of reason in sexual anarchy, never. It is against the very order of things. Man is a marrying animal just as much as he was a fire-making animal; he goes in pairs like mantel ornaments ; it is as natural for him to marry and to exact and keep good faith—if need be with a savage jealousy, as it is for him to have lobes to his ears and hair under his armpits. These things jar with the dream perhaps; the gods on painted ceilings have no such ties, acting beautifully by their very nature; and here on the floor of the world one had them and one had to make the best of them. . . . Are we making the best of them? Mr. Brumley was off again. That last thought opened the way to speculative wildernesses, and into these Mr. Brumley went wandering with a novel desperate enterprise to find a kind of marriage that would suit him.

He began to reform the marriage laws. He did his utmost not to think especially of Lady Harman and himself while he was doing so. He would just take up the whole question and deal with it in a temperate reasonable way. It was so necessary to be reasonable and temperate in this question—and not to think of death as a solution. Marriages to begin with were too easy to make and too difficult to break; countless girls—Lady Harman was only a type—were married long before they could know the beginnings of their own minds. We wanted to delay marriage—until the middle twenties, say. Why not? Or if by the infirmities of humanity one must have marriage before then, there ought to be some especial opportunity of rescinding it later. (Lady Harman ought to have been able to rescind her marriage.) What ought to be the marriageable age in a civilized community? When the mind was settled into its general system of opinions, Mr. Brumley thought, and then lapsed into a speculation whether the mind didn't keep changing and developing all through life; Lady Harman's was certainly still doing so. . . . This pointed to logical consequences of an undesirable sort. . . .

(Some little mind-slide occurred just at this point and he found himself thinking that perhaps Sir Isaac might last for years and years, might even outlive a wife exhausted by nursing. And anyhow to wait for death! To leave the thing one loved in the embrace of the moribund!)

He wrenched his thoughts back as quickly as possible to a disinterested reform of the marriage laws. What had he decided so far? Only for more deliberation and a riper age in marrying. Surely that should appeal even to the most orthodox. But that alone would not eliminate mistakes and deceptions altogether. (Sir Isaac's skin had a peculiar, unhealthy look.) There ought in addition to be the widest facilities for divorce possible. Mr. Brumley tried to draw up a schedule in his head of the grounds for divorce that a really civilized community would entertain. But there are practical difficulties. Marriage is not simply a sexual union, it is an economic one of a peculiarly inseparable sort,—and there are the children. And jealousy! Of course so far as economics went, a kind of marriage settlement might meet most of the difficulties, and as for the children, Mr. Brumley was no longer in that mood of enthusiastic devotion to children that had made the birth of George Edmund so tremendous an event. Children, alone, afforded no reason for indissoluble lifelong union. Face the thing frankly. How long was it absolutely necessary for people to keep a home together for their children? The prosperous classes, the best classes in the community, packed the little creatures off to school at the age of nine or ten. One might overdo—we were overdoing in our writing nowadays this—philoprogenitive enthusiasm. . . .

He found himself thinking of George Meredith's idea of Ten Year Marriages. . . .

His mind recoiled to Sir Isaac's pillowed-up possession. What flimsy stuff all this talk of altered marriage was! These things did not even touch the essentials of the matter. He thought of Sir Isaac's thin lips and wary knowing eyes. What possible divorce law could the wit of man devise that would release a desired woman from that—grip? Marriage was covetousness made law. As well ask such a man to sell all his goods and give to the poor as expect the Sir Isaacs of this world to relax the matrimonial subjugation of the wife. Our social order is built on jealousy, sustained by jealousy, and those brave schemes we evolve in our studies for the release of women from ownership,— and for that matter for the release of men too,—they will not stand the dusty heat of the market-place for a moment, they wilt under the first fierce breath of reality. Marriage and property are the twin children of man's individualistic nature; only on these terms can he be drawn into societies. . . .

Mr. Brumley found his little scheme for novelties in marriage and divorce lying dead and for the most part stillborn in his mind; himself in despair. To set to work to alter marriage in any essential point was, he realized, as if an ant should start to climb a thousand feet of cliff. This great institution rose upon his imagination like some insurmountable sierra, blue and sombre, between himself and the life of Lady Harman and all that he desired. There might be a certain amount of tinkering with matrimonial law in the next few years, of petty tinkering that would abolish a few pretences and give ease to a few amiable people, but if he were to come back to life a thousand years hence he felt he

would still find the ancient gigantic barrier, crossed
perhaps by a dangerous road, pierced perhaps by a
narrow tunnel or so but in all its great essentials the
same, between himself and Lady Harman. It wasn't
that it was rational, it wasn't that it was justifiable,
but it was one with the blood in one's veins and the
rain-cloud in the sky, a necessity in the nature of
present things. Before mankind emerged from the
valley of these restraints—if ever they did emerge—
thousands of generations must follow one another,
there must be tens of thousands of years of struggle
and thought and trial, in the teeth of prevalent
habit and opinion—and primordial instincts. A new
humanity. . . .

His heart sank to hopelessness.

Meanwhile? Meanwhile we had to live our lives.

He began to see a certain justification for the
hidden cults that run beneath the fair appearances of
life, those social secrecies by which people—how could
one put it?—people who do not agree with established
institutions, people, at any rate not merely egoistic and
jealous as the crowd is egoistic and jealous, hide and
help one another to mitigate the inflexible austerities
of the great unreason.

Yes, Mr. Brumley had got to a phrase of that
quality for the undiscriminating imperatives of the
fundamental social institution. You see how a particular situation may undermine the assumptions of a mind
originally devoted to uncritical acceptances. He still
insisted it was a necessary great unreason, absolutely
necessary—for the mass of people, a part of them, a
natural expression of them, but he could imagine the
possibility—of 'understandings' . . . . Mr. Brumley
was very vague about those understandings, those

mysteries of the exalted that were to filch happiness
from the destroying grasp of the crude and jealous.
He had to be vague. For secret and noble are ideas
like oil and water ; you may fling them together with
all the force of your will but in a little while they will
separate again.

For a time this dream of an impossible secrecy was
uppermost in Mr. Brumley's meditations. It came into
his head with the effect of a discovery that always
among the unclimbable barriers of this supreme institution there had been,—caves. He had been reading
Anatole France recently and the lady of *Le Lys Rouge*
came into his thoughts. There was something in
common between Lady Harman and the Countess
Martin, they were tall and dark and dignified, and Lady
Harman was one of those rare women who could have
carried the magnificent name of Thérèse. And there in
the setting of Paris and Florence was a whole microcosm
of love, real but illicit, carried out as it were secretly
and tactfully, beneath the great shadow of the cliff.
But he found it difficult to imagine Lady Harman in
that. Or Sir Isaac playing Count Martin's part. . . .

How different were those Frenchwomen, with their
afternoons vacant except for love, their detachment,
their lovers, those secret, convenient, romantically furnished flats, that compact explicit business of *l'amour !*
He had indeed some moments of regret that Lady
Harman wouldn't go into that picture. She was
different—if only in her simplicity. There was something about these others that put them whole worlds
apart from her, who was held so tethered from all
furtive adventure by her filmy tentacles of responsibility,
her ties and strands of relationship, her essential
delicacy. That momentary vision of Ellen as the

Countess Martin broke up into absurdities directly he looked at it fully and steadfastly. From thinking of the two women as similar types he passed into thinking of them as opposites; Thérèse, hard, clear, sensuous, secretive, trained by a brilliant tradition in the technique of connubial betrayal, was the very antithesis of Ellen's vague but invincible veracity and openness. Not for nothing had Anatole France made his heroine the daughter of a grasping financial adventurer. . . .

Of course the cave is a part of the mountain. . . .

His mind drifted away to still more general speculations, and always he was trying not to see the figure of Sir Isaac, grimly and yet meanly resolute—in possession. Always too like some open-mouthed yokel at a fair who knows nothing of the insult chalked upon his back, he disregarded how he himself coveted and desired and would if he could have gripped. He forgot his own watchful attention to Euphemia in the past, nor did he think what he might have been if Lady Harman had been his wife. It needed the chill veracities of the small hours to bring him to that. He thought now of crude egotism as having Sir Isaac's hands and Sir Isaac's eyes and Sir Isaac's position. He forgot any egotism he himself was betraying.

All the paths of enlightenment he thought of, led to Lady Harman.

§ 9

That evening George Edmund, who had come home with his mind aglitter with cinematograph impressions, found his father a patient but inattentive listener. For indeed Mr. Brumley was not listening at all; he was thinking and thinking. He made noises like

" Ah ! " and " Um," at George Edmund and patted
the boy's shoulder kindly and repeated words un-
intelligently, such as, " Red Indians, Eh ! " or " Came
out of the water backwards ! My eye ! "

Sometimes he made what George Edmund regarded
as quite footling comments. Still George Edmund had
to tell some one and there was no one else to tell. So
George Edmund went on talking and Mr. Brumley
went on thinking.

§ 10

Mr. Brumley could not sleep at all until it was
nearly five. His intelligence seemed to be making up
at last for years of speculative restraint. In a world
for the most part given up to slumber Mr. Brumley
may be imagined as clambering hand over fist in the
silences, feverishly and wonderfully overtaking his age.
In the morning he got up pallid and he shaved badly,
but he was a generation ahead of his own Euphemia
series, and the school of charm and quiet humour and
of letting things slide with a kind of elegant donnishness,
had lost him for ever. . . .

And among all sorts of things that had come to
him in that vast gulf of nocturnal thinking was some
vivid self-examination. At last he got to that. He
had been dragged down to very elemental things
indeed by the manifest completeness of Lady Harman's
return to her husband. He had had at last to look at
himself starkly for the male he was, to go beneath the
gentlemanly airs, the refined and elegant virilities of
his habitual poses. Either this thing was unendurable
—there were certainly moments when it came near to
being unendurable—or it was not. On the whole and

excepting mere momentary paroxysms it was not, and
so he had to recognize and he did recognize with the
greatest amazement that there could be something
else besides sexual attraction and manœuvring and
possession between a beautiful woman and a man like
himself. He loved Lady Harman, he loved her, he
now began to realize just how much, and she could
defeat him and reject him as a conceivable lover, turn
that aside as a thing impossible, shame him as the
romantic school would count shame and still command
him with her confident eyes and her friendly extended
hands. He admitted he suffered, let us rather say he
claimed to suffer the heated torments of a passionate
nature, but he perceived like fresh air and sunrise
coming by blind updrawn and opened window into a
fœtid chamber, that also he loved her with a clean and
bodiless love, was anxious to help her, was anxious
now—it was a new thing—to understand her, to
reassure her, to give unrequited what once he had
sought rather to seem to give in view of an imagined
exchange.

He perceived too in these still hours how little he
had understood her hitherto. He had been blinded,—
obsessed. He had been seeing her and himself and the
whole world far too much as a display of the eternal
dualism of sex, the incessant pursuit. Now with his
sexual imaginings newly humbled and hopeless, with a
realization of her own tremendous minimization of that
fundamental of romance, he began to see all that there
was in her personality and their possible relations
outside that. He saw how gravely and deeply serious
was her fine philanthropy, how honest and simple and
impersonal her desire for knowledge and understandings.
There is the brain of her at least, he thought, far out

of Sir Isaac's reach. She wasn't abased by her surrenders, their simplicity exalted her, showed her innocent and himself a flushed and congested soul. He perceived now with the astonishment of a man newly awakened just how the great obsession of sex had dominated him—for how many years? Since his early undergraduate days. Had he anything to put beside her own fine detachment? Had he ever since his manhood touched philosophy, touched a social question, thought of anything human, thought of art, or literature or belief, without a glancing reference of the whole question to the uses of this eternal hunt? During that time had he ever talked to a girl or woman with an unembarrassed sincerity? He stripped his pretences bare ; the answer was no. His very refinements had been no more than indicative fig-leaves. His conservatism and morality had been a mere dalliance with interests that too brutal a simplicity might have exhausted prematurely. And indeed hadn't the whole period of literature that had produced him been, in its straining purity and refinement, as it were one glowing, one illuminated fig-leaf, a vast conspiracy to keep certain matters always in mind by conspicuously covering them away? But this wonderful woman —it seemed—she hadn't them in mind ! She shamed him if only by her trustful unsuspiciousness of the ancient selfish game of Him and Her that he had been so ardently playing. . . . He idealized and worshipped this clean blindness. He abased himself before it.

"No," cried Mr. Brumley suddenly in the silence of the night, " I will rise again. I will rise again by love out of these morasses. . . . She shall be my goddess and by virtue of her I will end this incessant irrational craving for women. . . . I will be her friend and her faithful friend."

He lay still for a time and then he said in a whisper very humbly : "*God help me.*"

He set himself in those still hours which are so endless and so profitable to men in their middle years, to think how he might make himself the perfect lover instead of a mere plotter for desire, and how he might purge himself from covetousness and possessiveness and learn to serve.

And if very speedily his initial sincerity was tinged again with egotism and if he drowsed at last into a portrait of himself as beautifully and admirably self-sacrificial, you must not sneer too readily at him, for so God has made the soul of Mr. Brumley and otherwise it could not do.

CHAPTER THE TENTH

Lady Harman comes out

§ 1

The treaty between Lady Harman and her husband which was to be her Great Charter, the constitutional basis of her freedoms throughout the rest of her married life, had many practical defects.   The chief of these was that it was largely undocumented ; it had been made piecemeal, in various ways, at different times and for the most part indirectly through diverse intermediaries. Charterson had introduced large vaguenesses by simply displaying more of his teeth at crucial moments, Mrs. Harman had conveyed things by hugging and weeping that were afterwards discovered to be indistinct ; Sir Isaac writing from a bed of sickness had frequently been totally illegible.   One cannot therefore detail the clauses of this agreement or give its provisions with any great precision ; one can simply intimate the kind of understanding that had had an air of being arrived at. The working interpretations were still to come.

Before anything else it was manifestly conceded by Lady Harman that she would not run away again, and still more manifest that she undertook to break no more windows or do anything that might lead to a second police court scandal.   And she was to be a true and faithful wife and comfort, as a wife should be, to Sir

Isaac. In return for that consideration and to ensure its continuance Sir Isaac came great distances from his former assumption of a matrimonial absolutism. She was to be granted all sorts of small autonomies,—the word autonomy was carefully avoided throughout but its spirit was omnipresent.

She was in particular to have a banking account for her dress and personal expenditure into which Sir Isaac would cause to be paid a hundred pounds monthly and it was to be private to herself alone until he chose to go through the cashed cheques and counterfoils. She was to be free to come and go as she saw fit, subject to a punctual appearance at meals, the comfort and dignity of Sir Isaac and such specific engagements as she might make with him. She might have her own friends, but there the contract became a little misty ; a time was to come when Sir Isaac was to betray a conviction that the only proper friends that a woman can have are women. There were also non-corroborated assurances as to the privacy of her correspondence. The second Rolls-Royce car was to be entirely at her service and Clarence was to be immediately supplemented by a new and more deferential man, and as soon as possible assisted to another situation and replaced. She was to have a voice in the further furnishing of Black Strand and in the arrangement of its garden. She was to read what she chose and think what she liked within her head without too minute or suspicious an examination by Sir Isaac, and short of flat contradiction at his own table she was to be free to express her own opinions in any manner becoming a lady. But more particularly if she found her ideas infringing upon the management or influence of the International Bread and Cake Stores, she was to convey her objections and ideas in the first instance privately and confidentially to Sir Isaac.

Upon this point he displayed a remarkable and creditable sensitiveness. His pride in that organization was if possible greater than his original pride in his wife, and probably nothing in all the jarring of their relationship had hurt him more than her accessibility to hostile criticism and the dinner-table conversation with Charterson and Blenker that had betrayed this fact. He began to talk about it directly she returned to him. His protestations and explanations were copious and heartfelt. It was perhaps the chief discovery made by Lady Harman at this period of reconstruction that her husband's business side was not to be explained completely as a highly energetic and elaborate avarice. He was no doubt acquisitive and retentive and mean-spirited, but these were merely the ugly aspects of a disposition that involved many other factors. He was also incurably a schemer. He liked to fit things together, to dove-tail arrangements, to devise economies, to spread ingeniously into new fields, he had a love of organization and contrivance as disinterested as an artist's love for the possibilities of his medium. He would rather have made a profit of ten per cent. out of a subtly planned shop than thirty by an unforeseen accident. He wouldn't have cheated to get money for the world. He knew he was better at figuring out expenditures and receipts than most people and he was as touchy about his reputation for this kind of cleverness as any poet or painter for his fame. Now that he had awakened to the idea that his wife was capable of looking into and possibly even understanding his business, he was passionately anxious to show her just how wonderfully he had done it all, and when he perceived she was in her large, unskilled, helpless way, intensely concerned for all the vast multitude of incompetent or partially competent young women who floundered about in badly paid employment in our great cities, he grasped at once at the opportunity of recovering her lost interest and respect by doing some brilliant feats of contrivance in that direction. Why shouldn't he? He had long observed with a certain envy the admirable advertisement such firms as Lever and Cadbury and Burroughs & Wellcome gained from their ostentatiously able and generous treatment of their workpeople, and it seemed to him conceivable that in the end it might not be at all detrimental to his prosperity to put his hand to this long neglected piece of social work. The Babs Wheeler business had been a real injury in every way to the International Bread and Cake Stores and even if he didn't ultimately go to all the lengths his wife seemed to contemplate, he was resolved at any rate that an affair of that kind should not occur again. The expedition to Marienbad took with it a secretary who was also a stenographer. A particularly smart young inspector and Graper, the staff manager, had brisk four-day holidays once or twice for consultation purposes; Sir Isaac's rabbit-like architect was in attendance for a week and the Harmans returned to Putney with the first vivid greens of late March,—for the Putney Hill house was to be reopened and Black Strand reserved now for week-end and summer use—with plans already drawn out for four residential Hostels in London primarily for the girl waitresses of the International Stores who might have no homes or homes at an inconvenient distance, and, secondarily, if any vacant accommodation remained over, for any other employed young women of the same class. . . .

§ 2

Lady Harman came back to England from the pine-woods and bright order and regimen and foreign novelty of their Bohemian Kur-Ort, in a state of renewed perplexity. Already that undocumented Magna Charta was manifestly not working upon the lines she had anticipated. The glosses Sir Isaac put upon it were extensive and remarkable and invariably in the direction of restricting her liberties and resuming controls she had supposed abandoned.

Marienbad had done wonders for him; his slight limp had disappeared, his nervous energy was all restored; except for a certain increase in his natural irritability and occasional panting fits, he seemed as well as he had ever been. At the end of their time at the Kur he was even going for walks. Once he went halfway up the Podhorn on foot. And with every increment in his strength his aggressiveness increased, his recognition of her new freedoms was less cordial and her sense of contrition and responsibility diminished. Moreover, as the scheme of those Hostels, which had played so large a part in her conception of their reconciliation, grew more and more definite, she perceived more and more that it was not certainly that fine and humanizing thing she had presumed it would be. She began to feel more and more that it might be merely an extension of Harman methods to cheap boarding-houses for young people. But faced with a mass of detailed concrete projects and invited to suggest modifications she was able to realize for the first time how vague, how ignorant and incompetent her wishes had been, how much she had to understand

and how much she had to discover before she could meet Sir Isaac with his " I'm doing it all for you, Elly. If you don't like it, you tell me what you don't like and I'll alter it. But just vague doubting! One can't do anything with vague doubting."

She felt that once back in England out of this picturesque toylike German world she would be able to grasp realities again and deal with these things. She wanted advice, she wanted to hear what people said of her ideas. She would also, she imagined, begin to avail herself of those conceded liberties which their isolation together abroad and her husband's constant need of her presence had so far prevented her from tasting. She had an idea that Susan Burnet might prove suggestive about the Hostels.

And moreover, if now and then she could have a good talk with someone understanding and intelligent, someone she could trust, someone who cared enough for her to think with her and for her. . . .

§ 3

We have traced thus far the emergence of Lady Harman from that state of dutiful subjection and social irresponsibility which was the lot of woman in the past to that limited, ill-defined and quite unsecured freedom which is her present condition. And now we have to give an outline of the ideas of herself and her uses and what she had to do, which were forming themselves in her mind. She had made a determination of herself, which carried her along the lines of her natural predisposition, to duty, to service. There she displayed that acceptance of responsibility which is so much more often a feminine than a masculine habit of thinking. But she brought to the achievement of this determination a discriminating integrity of mind that is more frequently masculine than feminine. She wanted to know clearly what she was undertaking and how far its consequences would reach and how it was related to other things.

Her confused reading during the last few years and her own observation and such leakages of fact into her life as the talk of Susan Burnet, had all contributed to her realization that the world was full of needless discomfort and hardships and failure, due to great imperfectly apprehended injustices and maladjustments in the social system, and recently it had been borne in upon her, upon the barbed point of the *London Lion* and the quick tongue of Susan, that if any particular class of people was more answerable than any other for these evils, it was the people of leisure and freedom like herself, who had time to think, and the directing organizing people like her husband, who had power to change. She was called upon to do something, at times the call became urgent, and she could not feel any assurance which it was of the many vague and conflicting suggestions that came drifting to her that she had to do. Her idea of Hostels for the International waitresses had been wrung out of her prematurely during her earlier discussions with her husband. She did not feel that it was anything more than a partial remedy for a special evil. She wanted something more general than that, something comprehensive enough to answer completely so wide a question as "What ought I to be doing with all my life?" In the honest simplicity of her nature she wanted to find an answer to that. Out of the confusion of voices about us she hoped to be able to disentangle directions

for her life. Already she had been reading voraciously;
while she was still at Marienbad she had written to
Mr. Brumley and he had sent her books and papers,
advanced and radical in many cases, that she might
know, "What are people thinking?"

Many phrases from her earlier discussions with
Sir Isaac stuck in her mind in a curiously stimulating
way and came back to her as she read. She recalled
him, for instance, with his face white and his eyes red
and his flat hand sawing at her, saying: "I dessay I'm
all wrong, I dessay I don't know anything about anything and all those chaps you read, Bernud Shaw, and
Gosworthy, and all the rest of them are wonderfully
clever; but you tell me, Elly, what they say we've got
to do! You tell me that. You go and ask some of
those chaps just what they want a man like me to
do. . . . They'll ask me to endow a theatre or run a
club for novelists or advertise the lot of them in the
windows of my International Stores or something.
And that's about all it comes to. You go and see if
I'm not right. They grumble and they grumble; I
don't say there's not a lot to grumble at, but give me
something they'll back themselves for all they're worth
as good to get done. . . . That's where I don't agree
with all these idees. They're Wind, Elly, Weak wind
at that."

It is distressing to record how difficult it was for
Lady Harman to form even the beginnings of a disproof
of that. Her life through all this second phase of
mitigated autonomy was an intermittent pilgrimage in
search of that disproof. She could not believe that
things as they were, this mass of hardships, cruelties,
insufficiencies and heartburnings were the ultimate
wisdom and possibility of human life, yet when she

went from them to the projects that would replace or change them she seemed to pass from things of overwhelming solidity to matters more thin and flimsy than the twittering of sparrows on the gutter. So soon as she returned to London she started upon her search for a solution ; she supplemented Mr. Brumley's hunt for books with her own efforts, she went to meetings—sometimes Sir Isaac took her, once or twice she was escorted by Mr. Brumley, and presently her grave interest and her personal charm had gathered about her a circle of companionable friends. She tried to talk to people and made great efforts to hear people who seemed authoritative and wise and leaderlike, talking.

There were many interruptions to this research, but she persevered. Quite early she had an illness that ended in a miscarriage, an accident for which she was by no means inconsolable, and before she had completely recovered from that Sir Isaac fell ill again, the first of a series of relapses that necessitated further foreign travel—always in elaborately comfortable trains with maid, courier, valet, and secretary, to some warm and indolent southward place. And few people knew how uncertain her liberties were. Sir Isaac was the victim of an increasing irritability, at times he had irrational outbursts of distrust that would culminate in passionate outbreaks and scenes that were truncated by an almost suffocating breathlessness. On several occasions he was on the verge of quarrelling violently with her visitors, and he would suddenly oblige her to break engagements, pour abuse upon her and bring matters back to the very verge of her first revolt. And then he would break her down by pitiful appeals. The cylinders of oxygen would be resorted to, and he would emerge from the crisis, rather rueful, tamed and quiet for the time.

He was her chief disturbance. Her children were healthy children and fell in with the routines of governess and tutor that their wealth provided. She saw them often, she noted their increasing resemblance to their father, she did her best to soften the natural secretiveness and aggressiveness of their manners, she watched their teachers and intervened whenever the influences about them seemed to her to need inter-vention, she dressed them and gave them presents and tried to believe she loved them, and as Sir Isaac's illness increased she took a larger and larger share in the direction of the household. . . .

Through all these occupations and interruptions and immediacies she went trying to comprehend and at times almost believing she comprehended life, and then the whole spectacle of this modern world of which she was a part would seem to break up again into a multitude of warring and discordant fragments having no conceivable common aim or solution. Those moments of unifying faith and confidence, that glowed so bravely and never endured, were at once tantalizing and sustaining. She could never believe but that ultimately she would not grasp and hold—some-thing. . . .

Many people met her and liked her and sought to know more of her ; Lady Beach-Mandarin and Lady Viping were happy to be her social sponsors, the Blenkers and the Chartersons met her out and woke up cautiously to this new possibility ; her emergence was rapid in spite of the various delays and interruptions I have mentioned and she was soon in a position to realize just how little one meets when one meets a number of people and how little one hears when one has much conversation. Her mind was presently crowded with confused impressions of pleasant men evading her agreeably and making out of her gravities an opportunity for bright sayings, and of women being vaguely solemn and quite indefinite.

She went into the circle of movements, was tried over by Mrs. Hubert Plessington, she questioned this and that promoter of constructive schemes, and instead of mental meat she was asked to come upon committees and sounded for subscriptions. On several occasions, escorted by Mr. Brumley—some instinct made her conceal or minimize his share in these expeditions to her husband—she went as inconspicuously as possible to the backs of public meetings in which she understood great questions were being discussed or great changes inaugurated. Some public figures she even followed up for a time, distrusting her first impressions.

She became familiar with the manners and bearing of our platform class, with the solemn dummy-like chairman or chairwoman, saying a few words, the alert secretary or organizer, the prominent figures sitting with an air of grave responsibility, generously acting an intelligent attention to others until the moment came for them themselves to deliver. Then with an ill-concealed relief some would come to the footlights, some leap up in their places with a tenoring eagerness, some would be facetious and some speak with neuralgic effort, some were impertinent, some propitiatory, some dull, but all were—disappointing, disappointing. God was not in any of them. A platform is no setting for the shy processes of an honest human mind,—we are all strained to artificiality

in the excessive glare of attention that beats upon us
there. One does not exhibit opinions at a meeting,
one acts them, the very truth must rouge its cheeks
and blacken its eyebrows to tell, and to Lady Harman
it was the acting chiefly and the make-up that was
visible. They didn't grip her, they didn't lift her, they
failed to convince her even of their own belief in what
they supported.

§ 4

But occasionally among the multitude of conversations that gave her nothing, there would come some
talk that illuminated and for the time almost reconciled
her to the effort and the loss of time and distraction
her social expeditions involved. One evening at one
of Lady Tarvrille's carelessly compiled parties she
encountered Edgar Wilkins the novelist and got the
most suggestive glimpses of his attitude towards
himself and towards the world of intellectual ferment
to which he belonged. She had been taken down by
an amiable but entirely uninteresting permanent official
who when the time came turned his stereotyped talk
over to the other side of him with a quite mechanical
indifference, and she was left for a little while in
silence until Wilkins had disengaged himself.

He was a flushed man with untidy hair, and he
opened at once with an appeal to her sympathies.

"Oh! Bother!" he said. "I say,—I've eaten
that mutton. I didn't notice. One eats too much at
these affairs. One doesn't notice at the time and then
afterwards one finds out."

She was a little surprised at his gambit and could
think of nothing but a kindly murmur.

"Detestable thing," he said ; "my body."

"But surely not," she tried and felt as she said it that was a trifle bold.

"You're all right," he said making her aware he saw her. "But I've this thing that wheezes and fattens at the slightest excuse and—it encumbers me—bothers me to take exercise. . . . But I can hardly expect you to be interested in my troubles, can I ?"

He made an all too manifest attempt to read her name on the slip of card that lay before her among the flowers and as manifestly succeeded. "We people who write and paint and all that sort of thing are a breed of insatiable egotists, Lady Harman. With the least excuse. Don't you think so ?"

"Not—not exceptionally," she said.

"Exceptionally," he insisted.

"It isn't my impression," she said. "You're—franker."

"But someone was telling me—you've been taking impressions of us lately. I mean all of us people who go flapping ideas about in the air. Somebody—was it Lady Beach-Mandarin ?—was saying you'd come out looking for Intellectual Heroes—and found Bernard Shaw. . . . But what could you have expected ?"

"I've been trying to find out and understand what people are thinking. I want ideas."

"It's disheartening, isn't it ?"

"It's—perplexing sometimes."

"You go to meetings, and try to get to the bottom of Movements, and you want to meet and know the people who write the wonderful things? Get at the wonderful core of it ?"

"One feels there are things going on."

"Great illuminating things."

" Well—yes."

" And when you see those great Thinkers and Teachers and Guides and Brave Spirits and High Brows generally—— "

He laughed and stopped just in time on the very verge of taking pheasant.

" Oh, take it away," he cried sharply.

" We've all been through that illusion, Lady Harman," he went on.

" But I don't like to think—— Aren't Great Men after all—great ? "

" In their ways, in their places—Yes. But not if you go up to them and look at them. Not at the dinner table, not in their beds. . . . What a time of disillusionment you must have had !

" You see, Lady Harman," he said, leaning back from his empty plate, inclining himself confidentially to her ear and speaking in a privy tone ; " it's in the very nature of things that we—if I may put myself into the list—we ideologists, should be rather exceptionally loose and untrustworthy and disappointing men. Rotters—to speak plain contemporary English. If you come to think of it, it has to be so."

" But—— " she protested.

He met her eye firmly. " It has to be."

" Why ? "

" The very qualities that make literature entertaining, vigorous, inspiring, revealing, wonderful, beautiful and—all that sort of thing, make its producers—if you will forgive the word again—rotters."

She smiled and lifted her eyebrows protestingly.

" Sensitive nervous tissue," he said with a finger up to emphasize his words. " Quick responsiveness to stimulus, a vivid, almost uncontrollable, expressiveness; that's what you want in your literary man."

"Yes," said Lady Harman following cautiously. "Yes, I suppose it is."

"Can you suppose for a moment that these things conduce to self-control, to reserve, to consistency, to any of the qualities of a trustworthy man? . . . Of course you can't. And so we *aren't* trustworthy, we *aren't* consistent. Our virtues are our vices. . . . *My* life," said Mr. Wilkins still more confidentially, " won't bear examination. But that's by the way. It need not concern us now."

"But Mr. Brumley?" she asked on the spur of the moment.

"I'm not talking of him," said Wilkins with careless cruelty. "He's restrained. I mean the really imaginative people, the people with vision, the people who let themselves go. You see now why they are rotten, why they must be rotten. (No! No! take it away. I'm talking.) I feel so strongly about this, about the natural and necessary disreputableness of everybody who produces reputable writing—and for the matter of that, art generally—that I set my face steadily against all these attempts that keep on cropping up to make Figures of us. We aren't Figures, Lady Harman; it isn't our line. Of all the detestable aspects of the Victorian period surely that disposition to make Figures of its artists and literary men was the most detestable. Respectable Figures—Examples to the young. The suppressions, the coverings up that had to go on, the white-washing of Dickens,—who was more than a bit of a rip, you know, the concealment of Thackeray's mistresses. Did you know he had mistresses? Oh rather! And so on. It's like that bust of Jove—or Bacchus was it?—they pass off as Plato, who probably looked like any other literary Grub. That's why I won't have anything to do with these Academic developments that my friend Brumley —Do you know him by the way?—goes in for. He's the third man down——— You *do* know him. And he's giving up the Academic Committee, is he? I'm glad he's seen it at last. What *is* the good of trying to have an Academy and all that, and put us in uniform and make out we are Somebodies, and respectable enough to be shaken hands with by George and Mary, when as a matter of fact we are, by our very nature, a collection of miscellaneous scandals——— We *must* be. Bacon, Shakespear, Byron, Shelley—all the stars. . . . No, Johnson wasn't a star, he was a character by Boswell. . . . Oh! great things come out of us, no doubt, our arts are the vehicles of wonder and hope, the world is dead without these things we produce, but that's no reason why—why the mushroom-bed should follow the mushrooms into the soup, is it? Perfectly fair image. (No, take it away)."

He paused and then jumped in again as she was on the point of speaking.

"And you see even if our temperaments didn't lead inevitably to our—dipping rather, we should still have to—*dip*. Asking a writer or a poet to be seemly and Academic and so on, is like asking an eminent surgeon to be stringently decent. It's—you see, it's incompatible. Now a king or a butler or a family solicitor—if you like."

He paused again.

Lady Harman had been following him with an attentive reluctance.

"But what are we to do," she asked, "we people

who are puzzled by life, who want guidance and ideas and—help, if—if all the people we look to for ideas are——"

"Bad characters."

"Well, — it's your theory, you know — bad characters?"

Wilkins answered with the air of one who carefully disentangles a complex but quite solvable problem. "It doesn't follow," he said, "that because a man is a bad character he's not to be trusted in matters where character—as we commonly use the word—doesn't come in. These sensitives, these—would you mind if I were to call myself an Æolian Harp?—these Æolian Harps; they can't help responding to the winds of heaven. Well,—listen to them. Don't follow them, don't worship them, don't even honour them, but listen to them. Don't let anyone stop them from saying and painting and writing and singing what they want to. Freedom, canvas and attention, those are the proper honours for the artist, the poet and the philosopher. Listen to the noise they make, watch the stuff they produce, and presently you will find certain things among the multitude of things that are said and shown and put out and published, something—light in *your* darkness, —a writer for you, something for you. Nobody can have a greater contempt for artists and writers and poets and philosophers than I, oh! a squalid crew they are, mean, jealous, pugnacious, disgraceful in love, *disgraceful*—but out of it all comes the greatest serenest thing, the mind of the world, Literature. Nasty little midges, yes,—but fireflies—carrying light for the darkness. . . ."

His face was suddenly lit by enthusiasm and she wondered that she could have thought it rather heavy and commonplace. He stopped abruptly and glanced beyond her at her other neighbour who seemed on the verge of turning to them again. " If I go on," he said with a voice suddenly dropped, " I shall talk loud."

" You know," said Lady Harman, in a halty under-tone, " you—you are too hard upon—upon clever people, but it is true. I mean it is true in a way. . . ."

" Go on, I understand exactly what you are saying."

" I mean, there *are* ideas. It's just that, that is so—so——— I mean they seem never to be just there and always to be present."

" Like God. Never in the flesh—now. A spirit everywhere. You think exactly as I do, Lady Harman. It is just that. This is a great time, so great that there is no chance for great men. Every chance for great work. And we're doing it. There is a wind—blowing out of heaven. And when beautiful people like yourself come into things——— "

" I try to understand," she said. " I want to understand. I want—I want not to miss life."

He was on the verge of saying something further and then his eyes wandered down the table and he stopped short.

He ended his talk as he had begun it with " Bother ! Lady Tarvrille, Lady Harman, is trying to catch your eye."

Lady Harman turned her face to her hostess and answered her smile. Wilkins caught at his chair and stood up.

" It would have been jolly to have talked some more," he said.

" I hope we shall."

" Well ! " said Wilkins, with a sudden hardness in his eyes and she was swept away from him.

She found no chance of talking to him upstairs, Sir Isaac came for her early; but she went in hope of another meeting.

It did not come. For a time that expectation gave dinners and luncheon parties a quite appreciable attraction. Then she told Agatha Alimony. " I've never met him but that once," she said.

" One doesn't meet him now," said Agatha, darkly.

" But why ? "

Deep significance came into Miss Alimony's eyes. " My dear," she whispered, and glanced about them. " Don't you *know* ? "

Lady Harman was a radiant innocence.

And then Miss Alimony began in impressive undertones, with awful omissions like pits of darkness and with such richly embroidered details as serious spinsters enjoy, adding, indeed, two quite new things that came to her mind as the tale unfolded, and, naming no names and giving no chances of verification or reply, handed on the fearful and at that time extremely popular story of the awful wickedness of Wilkins the author.

Upon reflection Lady Harman perceived that this explained all sorts of things in their conversation and particularly the flash of hardness at the end.

Even then, things must have been hanging over him. . . .

§ 5

And while Lady Harman was making these meritorious and industrious attempts to grasp the significance of life and to get some clear idea of her social duty, the developments of those Hostels she had started— she now felt so prematurely—was going on. There were times when she tried not to think of them, turned her back on them, fled from them, and times when they and what she ought to do about them and what they ought to be and what they ought not to be, filled her mind to the exclusion of every other topic. Rigorously and persistently Sir Isaac insisted they were hers, asked her counsel, demanded her appreciation, presented as it were his recurring bill for them.

Five of them were being built, not four but five. There was to be one, the largest, in a conspicuous position in Bloomsbury near the British Museum, one in a conspicuous position looking out upon Parliament Hill, one conspicuously placed upon the Waterloo Road near St. George's Circus, one at Sydenham, and one in the Kensington Road which was designed to catch the eye of people going to and fro to the various exhibitions at Olympia.

In Sir Isaac's study at Putney there was a huge and rather splendid-looking morocco portfolio on a stand, and this portfolio bore in excellent gold lettering the words, International Bread and Cake Hostels. It was her husband's peculiar pleasure after dinner to take her to turn over this with him; he would sit pencil in hand, while she, poised at his request upon the arm of his chair, would endorse a multitude of admirable modifications and suggestions. These hostels were to be done—indeed they were being done—by Sir Isaac's tame architect, and the interlacing yellow and mauve tiles, and the Doulton ware mouldings that were already familiar to the public as the uniform of the Stores, were to be used upon the façades of the new institutions. They were to be boldly labelled

INTERNATIONAL HOSTELS

right across the front.

The plans revealed in every case a site depth as great as the frontage, and the utmost ingenuity had been used to utilize as much space as possible. "Every room we get in," said Sir Isaac, "adds one to the denominator in the cost ; " and carried his wife back to her schooldays. At last she had found sense in fractions. There was to be a series of convenient and spacious rooms on the ground floor, a refectory, which might be cleared and used for meetings—"dances," said Lady Harman. "Hardly the sort of thing we want 'em to get up to," said Sir Isaac—various offices, the matron's apartments—"We ought to begin thinking about matrons," said Sir Isaac ;—a bureau, a reading-room and a library—"We can pick good, serous stuff for them," said Sir Isaac, "instead of their filling their heads with trash "—one or two workrooms with tables for cutting out and sewing; this last was an idea of Susan Burnet's. Upstairs there was to be a beehive of bedrooms, floor above floor, and each floor as low as the building regulations permitted. There were to be long dormitories with cubicles at three-and-sixpence a week—make your own beds—and separate rooms at prices ranging from four-and-sixpence to seven-and-sixpence. Every three cubicles and every bedroom had lavatory basins with hot and cold water ; there were pull-out drawers under the beds and a built-in chest of drawers, a hanging cupboard, a looking-glass and a radiator in each cubicle, and each floor had a box-room. It was ship-shape.

"A girl can get this cubicle for three-and-six a week," said Sir Isaac, tapping the drawing before him with his pencil. "She can get her breakfast with a bit of bacon or a sausage for two shillings a week, and she can get her high tea, with cold meat, good potted salmon, shrimp paste, jam and cetera, for three-and-six a week. Say her bus fares and lunch out mean another four shillings. That means she can get along on about twelve-and-six a week, comfortable, read the papers, have a book out of the library. . . . There's nothing like it to be got now for twice the money. The sort of thing they have now is one room, dingy, badly fitted, extra for coals. . . .

"That's the answer to your problem, Elly," he said. "There we are. Every girl who doesn't live at home can live here—with a matron to keep her eye on her. . . . And properly run, Elly, properly run the thing's going to pay two or three per cent.—let alone the advertisement for the Stores. . . .

"We can easily make these Hostels obligatory on all our girls who don't live at their own homes," he said. "That ought to keep them off the streets, if anything can. I don't see how even Miss Babs Wheeler can have the face to strike against that.

"And then we can arrange with some of the big firms, drapers' shops and all that sort of thing near each hostel to take over most of our other cubicle space. A lot of them—overflow.

"Of course we'll have to make sure the girls get in at night." He reached out for a ground floor plan of the Bloomsbury establishment which was to be the first built. "If," he said, "we were to have a sort of porter's lodge with a book—and make 'em ring a bell after eleven say—just here. . . ."

He took out a silver pencil case and got to work.

Lady Harman's expression as she leant over him, became thoughtful.

There were points about this project that gave her the greatest misgivings ; that matron, keeping her eye

on the girls, that carefully selected library, the porter's
bell, these casual allusions to "discipline" that set her
thinking of scraps of the Babs Wheeler controversy.
There was a regularity, an austerity about this project
that chilled her, she hardly knew why. Her own
vague intentions had been an amiable, hospitable,
agreeably cheap establishment to which the homeless
feminine employees in London could resort freely and
cheerfully, and it was only very slowly that she perceived that her husband was by no means convinced of
the spontaneity of their coming. He seemed always
glancing at methods for compelling them to come in
and oppressions when that compulsion had succeeded.
There had already hovered over several of these
anticipatory evenings, his very manifest intention to
have very carefully planned "Rules." She felt there
lay ahead of them much possibility for divergence of
opinion about these "Rules." She foresaw a certain
narrowness and hardness. She herself had made her
fight against the characteristics of Sir Isaac and—
perhaps she was lacking in that aristocratic feeling
which comes so naturally to most successful middle-
class people in England—she could not believe that
what she had found bad and suffocating for herself
could be agreeable and helpful for her poorer sisters.

It occurred to her to try the effect of the scheme
upon Susan Burnet. Susan had such a knack of
seeing things from unexpected angles. She contrived
certain operations upon the study blinds, and then
broached the business to Susan casually in the course
of an enquiry into the welfare of the Burnet family.

Susan was evidently prejudiced against the idea.

"Yes," said Susan after various explanations and
exhibitions, "but where's the home in it?"

" 'The whole thing is a home."

" Barracks *I* call it," said Susan. " Nobody ever felt at home in a room coloured up like that—and no curtains, nor valances, nor toilet covers, nor anywhere where a girl can hang a photograph or anything. What girl's going to feel at home in a strange place like that ? "

" They ought to be able to hang up photographs," said Lady Harman, making a mental note of it.

" And of course there'll be all sorts of Rules."

" *Some* rules."

" Homes, real homes don't have Rules. And I daresay—Fines."

" No, there shan't be any Fines," said Lady Harman quickly. " I'll see to that."

" You got to back up rules somehow—once you got 'em," said Susan. " And when you get a crowd, and no father and mother, and no proper family feeling, I suppose there's got to be Rules."

Lady Harman pointed out various advantages of the project.

" I'm not saying it isn't cheap and healthy and social," said Susan, " and if it isn't too strict I expect you'll get plenty of girls to come to it, but at the best it's an Institution, Lady Harman. It's going to be an Institution. That's what it's going to be."

She held the front elevation of the Bloomsbury Hostel in her hand and reflected.

" Of course for my part, I'd rather lodge with nice struggling believing Christian people anywhere than go into a place like that. It's the feeling of freedom, of being yourself and on your own. Even if the water wasn't laid on and I had to fetch it myself. . . . If girls were paid properly there wouldn't be any need

of such places, none at all. It's the poverty makes
'em what they are. . . . And after all, somebody's got
to lose the lodgers if this place gets them. Suppose
this sort of thing grows up all over the place, it'll just
be the story of the little bakers and little grocer and
all those people over again. Why in London there are
thousands of people just keep a home together by
letting two or three rooms or boarding someone—and
it stands to reason, they'll have to take less or lose the
lodgers if this kind of thing's going to be done.
Nobody isn't going to build a Hostel for them."

"No," said Lady Harman, "I never thought of
them."

"Lots of 'em haven't anything in the world but
their bits of furniture and their lease and there they
are stuck and tied. There's Aunt Hannah, Father's
sister, she's like that. Sleeps in the basement and
works and slaves, and often I've had to lend her ten
shillings to pay the rent with, through her not being
full. This sort of place isn't going to do much good
to her."

Lady Harman surveyed the plan rather blankly.
" I suppose it isn't."

" And then if you manage this sort of place easy
and attractive, it's going to draw girls away from their
homes. There's girls like Alice who'd do anything to
get a bit of extra money to put on their backs and
seem to think of nothing but chattering and laughing
and going about. Such a place like this would be fine
fun for Alice; in when she liked and out when she
liked, and none of us to ask her questions. She'd be
just the sort to go, and mother who's had the
upbringing of her, how's she to make up for Alice's
ten shillings what she pays in every week? There's

lots like Alice. She's not bad isn't Alice, she's a good
girl and a good-hearted girl; I will say that for her,
but she's shallow, say what you like she's shallow, she's
got no thought and she's wild for pleasure, and sometimes it seems to me that that's as bad as being bad
for all the good it does to anyone else in the world, and
so I tell her. But of course she hasn't seen things as
I've seen them and doesn't feel as I do about all these
things. . . ."

Thus Susan.

Her discourse so puzzled Lady Harman that she
bethought herself of Mr. Brumley and called in his
only too readily accorded advice. She asked him to
tea on a day when she knew unofficially that Sir Isaac
would be away, she showed him the plans and sketched
their probable development. Then with that charming
confidence of hers in his knowledge and ability she put
her doubts and fears before him. What did he really
think of these places? What did he think of Susan
Burnet's idea of ruined lodging-house keepers? " I
used to think our stores were good things," she said.
" Is this likely to be a good thing at all?"

Mr. Brumley said " Um " a great number of times
and realized that he was a humbug. He fenced with
her and affected sagacity for a time and suddenly he
threw down his defences and confessed he knew as little
of the business as she did. " But I see it is a complex
question and—it's an interesting one too. May I
enquire into it for you? I think I might be able to
hunt up a few particulars. . . ."

He went away in a glow of resolution.

Georgina was about the only intimate who regarded
the new development without misgiving.

" You think you're going to do all sorts of things

with these Hostels, Ella," she said, " but as a matter of
fact they're bound to become just exactly what we've
always wanted."

" And what may that be ? " asked Mrs. Sawbridge
over her macramé work.

" Strongholds for a garrison of suffragettes," said
Georgina with the light of the Great Insane Movement
in her eyes and a ringing note in her voice. " Fort
Chabrols for women."

§ 6

For some months in a negative and occasionally
almost negligent fashion Mr. Brumley had been living
up to his impassioned resolve to be an unselfish lover
of Lady Harman. He had been rather at loose ends
intellectually, deprived of his old assumptions and
habitual attitudes and rather chaotic in the matter of
his new convictions. He had given most of his pro-
ductive hours to the writing of a novel which was to be
an entire departure from the Euphemia tradition.
The more he got on with this, the more clearly he
realized that it was essentially insignificant. When he
re-read what he had written he was surprised by
crudities where he had intended sincerities and rhetoric
where the scheme had demanded passion. What was
the matter with him ? He was stirred that Lady
Harman should send for him, and his inability to deal
with her perplexities deepened his realization of the
ignorance and superficiality he had so long masked
even from himself beneath the tricks and pretensions
of a gay scepticism. He went away fully resolved to
grapple with the entire Hostel question, and he put

the patched and tortured manuscript of the new novel aside with a certain satisfaction to do this.

The more he reflected upon the nature of this study he proposed for himself the more it attracted him. It was some such reality as this he had been wanting. He could presently doubt whether he would ever go back to his novel-writing again, or at least to the sort of novel-writing he had been doing hitherto. To invent stories to save middle-aged prosperous middle-class people from the distresses of thinking, is surely no work for a self-respecting man. Stevenson in the very deeps of that dishonourable traffic had realized as much and likened himself to a *fille de joie*, and Haggard, of the same school and period, had abandoned blood and thunder at the climax of his success for the honest study of agricultural conditions. The newer successes were turning out work, less and less conventional and agreeable and more and more stiffened with facts and sincerities. . . . He would show Lady Harman that a certain debonair quality he had always affected, wasn't incompatible with a powerful grasp of general conditions. . . . And she wanted this done. Suppose he did it in a way that made him necessary to her. Suppose he did it very well.

He set to work, and understanding as you do a certain quality of the chameleon in Mr. Brumley's moral nature, you will understand that he worked through a considerable variety of moods. Sometimes he worked with disinterested passion and sometimes he was greatly sustained by this thought that here was something that would weave him in with the gravities of her life and give him perhaps a new inlet to intimacy. And presently a third thing came to his help, and that was the discovery that the questions arising out of this attempt to realize the importance of those Hostels, were in themselves very fascinating questions for an intelligent person.

Because before you have done with the business of the modern employé, you must, if you are an intelligent person, have taken a view of the whole vast process of social reorganization that began with the development of factory labour and big towns, and which is even now scarcely advanced enough for us to see its general trend. For a time Mr. Brumley did not realize the magnitude of the thing he was looking at; when he did, theories sprouted in his mind like mushrooms and he babbled with mental excitement. He came in a state of the utmost lucidity to explain his theories to Lady Harman, and they struck that lady at the time as being the most illuminating suggestions she had ever encountered. They threw an appearance of order, of process, over a world of trade and employment and competition that had hitherto seemed too complex and mysterious for any understanding.

"You see," said Mr. Brumley—they had met that day in Kensington Gardens and they were sitting side by side upon green chairs near the frozen writhings of Physical Energy—"You see, if I may lecture a little, putting the thing as simply as possible, the world has been filling up new spaces ever since the discovery of America; all the period from then to about 1870, let us say, was a period of rapid increase of population in response to new opportunities of living and new fulnesses of life in every direction. During that time, four hundred years of it roughly, there was a huge development of family life; to marry and rear a quite considerable family became the chief business of everybody, celibacy grew rare, monasteries and nunneries which

had abounded vanished like things dissolving in a flood
and even the priests became Protestant against celibacy
and took unto themselves wives and had huge families.
The natural checks upon increase, famine and pestilence,
were lifted by more systematized communication and by
scientific discovery ; and altogether and as a consequence
the world now has probably three or four times the
human population it ever carried before. Everywhere
in that period the family prevailed again, the prospering
multiplying household ; it was a return to the family,
to the reproductive social grouping of early barbaric
life, and naturally all the thought of the modern world
which has emerged since the fifteenth century falls into
this form. So I see it, Lady Harman. The generation
of our grandfathers in the opening nineteenth century
had two shaping ideas, two forms of thought, the family
and progress, not realizing that that very progress
which had suddenly reopened the doors of opportunity for the family that had revived the ancient
injunction to increase and multiply and replenish the
earth, might presently close that door again and declare
the world was filled. But that is what is happening
now. The doors close. That immense swarming and
multiplying of little people is over, and the forces of
social organization have been coming into play now,
more and more for a century and a half, to produce
new wholesale ways of doing things, new great organizations, organizations that invade the autonomous family
more and more, and are perhaps destined ultimately to
destroy it altogether and supersede it. At least it is so
I make my reading of history in these matters."

"Yes," said Lady Harman, with knitted brows.
"Yes," and wondered privately whether it would be
possible to get from that opening to the matter of her

Hostels before it was time for her to return for Sir Isaac's tea.

Mr. Brumley continued to talk with his eyes fixed as it were upon his thoughts. "These things, Lady Harman, go on at different paces in different regions. I will not trouble you with a discussion of that, or of emigration, of any of the details of the vast proliferation that preceded the present phase. Suffice it, that now all the tendency is back towards restraints upon increase, to an increasing celibacy, to a fall in the birth-rate and in the average size of families, to—to a release of women from an entire devotion to a numerous offspring, and so at last to the supersession of those little family units that for four centuries have made up the substance of social life and determined nearly all our moral and sentimental attitudes. The autonomy of the family is being steadily destroyed, and it is being replaced by the autonomy of the individual in relation to some syndicated economic effort."

" I think," said Lady Harman slowly, arresting him by a gesture, " if you could make that about autonomy a little clearer. . . ."

Mr. Brumley did. He went on to point out with the lucidity of a University Extension lecturer what he meant by these singular phrases. She listened intelligently but with effort. He was much too intent upon getting the thing expressed to his own satisfaction to notice any absurdity in his preoccupation with these theories about the population of the world in the face of her immediate practical difficulties. He declared that the onset of this new phase in human life, the modern phase, wherein there was apparently to be no more " proliferating," but instead a settling down of population towards a stable equilibrium, became apparent first with the expropriation of the English peasantry and the birth of the factory system and machine production. " Since that time one can trace a steady substitution of wholesale and collective methods for household and family methods. It has gone far with us now. Instead of the woman drawing water from a well, the pipes and taps of the water company. Instead of the home-made rushlight, the electric lamp. Instead of home-spun, ready-made clothes. Instead of home-brewed, the brewer's cask. Instead of home-baked, first the little baker and then, clean and punctual, the International Bread and Cake Stores. Instead of the child learning at its mother's knee, the compulsory elementary school. Flats take the place of separate houses. Instead of the little holding, the big farm, and instead of the children working at home, the factory. Everywhere synthesis. Everywhere the little independent proprietor gives place to the company and the company to the trust. You follow all this, Lady Harman ? "

" Go on," she said, encouraged by that transitory glimpse of the Stores in his discourse.

" Now London—and England generally—had its period of expansion and got on to the beginnings at least of this period of synthesis that is following it, sooner than any other country in the world ; and because it was the first to reach the new stage it developed the characteristics of the new stage with a stronger flavour of the old than did such later growths of civilization as New York or Bombay or Berlin. That is why London and our British big cities generally are congestions of little houses, little homes, while the newer great cities run to apartments and flats. We hadn't grasped the logical consequences of what we were in for so completely as the people abroad did who caught it later, and that is why, as we began to develop our new floating population of mainly celibate employees and childless people, they had mostly to go into lodgings, they went into the homes that were intended for families as accessories to the family, and they were able to go in because the families were no longer so numerous as they used to be. London is still largely a city of landladies and lodgings, and in no other part of the world is there so big a population of lodgers. And this business of your Hostels is nothing more nor less than the beginning of the end of that. Just as the great refreshment caterers have mopped up the ancient multitude of coffee-houses and squalid little special feeding arrangements of the days of Tittlebat Titmouse and Dick Swiveller, so now your Hostels are going to mop up the lodging-house system of London. Of course there are other and kindred movements. Naturally. The Y.W.C.A., the Y.M.C.A., the London Girls Club Union and so forth are all doing kindred work."

" But what, Mr. Brumley, what is to become of the landladies ?" asked Lady Harman.

Mr. Brumley was checked in mid theory.

" I hadn't thought of the landladies," he said, after a short pause.

"They worry me," said Lady Harman.

" Um," said Mr. Brumley, thrown out.

" Do you know the other day I went into Chelsea, where there are whole streets of lodgings, and—I suppose it was wrong of me, but I went and pretended to be looking for rooms for a girl clerk I knew, and I saw—Oh ! no end of rooms. And such poor old women, such dingy, worked-out, broken old women, with a kind of fearful sharpness, so eager, so dreadfully eager to get that girl clerk who didn't exist. . . ."

She looked at him with an expression of pained enquiry.

"That," said Mr. Brumley, "that I think is a question, so to speak, for the social ambulance. If perhaps I might go on—— That particular difficulty we might consider later. I think I was talking of the general synthesis."

"Yes," said Lady Harman. "And what is it exactly that is to take the place of these isolated little homes and these dreary little lodgings? Here are we, my husband and I, rushing in with this new thing, just as he rushed in with his stores thirty years ago and overset little bakers and confectioners and refreshment dealers by the hundred. Some of them—poor dears—they—— I don't like to think. And it wasn't a good thing he made after all,—only a hard sort of thing. He made all those shops of his—with the girls who strike and say they are sweated and driven. . . . And now here we are making a kind of barrack place for people to live in!"

She expressed the rest of her ideas with a gesture of the hands.

"I admit the process has its dangers," said Mr. Brumley. "It's like the supersession of the small holdings by the *latifundia* in Italy. But that's just where our great opportunity comes in. These synthetic phases have occurred before in the world's history and their history is a history of lost opportunities. . . . But need ours be?"

She had a feeling as though something had slipped through her fingers.

"I feel," she said, "that it is more important to

me than anything else in life, that these Hostels, anyhow, which are springing so rapidly from a chance suggestion of mine, shouldn't be lost opportunities."

"Exactly," said Mr. Brumley, with the gesture of one who recovers a thread. "That is just what I am driving at."

The fingers of his extended hand felt in the warm afternoon air for a moment, and then he said "Ah!" in a tone of recovery while she waited respectfully for the resumed thread.

"You see," he said, "I regard this process of synthesis, this substitution of wholesale and collective methods for homely and individual ones as, under existing conditions, inevitable—inevitable. It's the phase we live in, it's to this we have to adapt ourselves. It is as little under your control or mine as the movement of the sun through the zodiac. Practically, that is. And what we have to do is not, I think, to sigh for lost homes and the age of gold and spade husbandry, and pigs and hens in the home, and so on, but to make this new synthetic life tolerable for the mass of men and women, hopeful for the mass of men and women, a thing developing and ascending. That's where your Hostels come in, Lady Harman; that's where they're so important. They're a pioneer movement. If they succeed—and things in Sir Isaac's hands have a way of succeeding at any rate to the paying point—then there'll be a headlong rush of imitations, imitating your good features, imitating your bad features, deepening a groove. . . . You see my point?"

"Yes," she said. "It makes me—more afraid than ever."

"But hopeful," said Mr. Brumley, presuming to

lay his hand for an instant on her arm. "It's big enough to be inspiring."

"But I'm afraid," she said.

"It's laying down the lines of a new social life—no less. And what makes it so strange, so typical, too, of the way social forces work nowadays, is that your husband, who has all the instinctive insistence upon every right and restriction of the family relation in his private life, who is narrowly, passionately *for* the home in his own case, who hates all books and discussion that seem to touch it, should in his business activities be striking this tremendous new blow at the ancient organization. For that, you see, is what it amounts to."

"Yes," said Lady Harman slowly. "Yes. Of course, he doesn't know. . . ."

Mr. Brumley was silent for a little while. "You see," he resumed, "at the worst this new social life may become a sort of slavery in barracks; at the best —it might become something very wonderful. My mind's been busy now for days thinking just how wonderful the new life might be. Instead of the old bickering, crowded family home, a new home of comrades. . . ."

He made another pause, and his thoughts ran off upon a fresh track.

"In looking up all these things I came upon a queer little literature of pamphlets and so forth, dealing with the case of the shop assistants. They have a great grievance in what they call the living-in system. The employers herd them in dormitories over the shops, and usually feed them by gaslight in the basements; they fine them and keep an almost intolerable grip upon them; make them go to bed at

half-past ten, make them go to church on Sundays,—
all sorts of petty tyrannies. The assistants are
passionately against this, but they've got no power
to strike. Where could they go if they struck? Into
the street. Only people who live out and have homes
of their own to sulk in *can* strike. Naturally, therefore, as a preliminary to any other improvement in the
shop assistant's life, these young people want to live
out. Practically that's an impossible demand at
present, because they couldn't get lodgings and live
out with any decency at all on what it costs their
employers to lodge and feed them *in*. Well, here you
see a curious possibility for your Hostels. You open
the prospect of a living-out system for shop assistants.
But just in the degree in which you choose to interfere
with them, regulate them, bully and deal with them
wholesale through their employers, do you make
the new living-out method approximate to the
living-in. *That's* a curious side development, isn't
it?"

Lady Harman appreciated that.

"That's only the beginning of the business.
There's something more these Hostels might touch.
. . ."

Mr. Brumley gathered himself together for the new
aspect. "There's marriage," he said.

"One of the most interesting and unsatisfactory
aspects of the life of the employee to-day—and you
know the employee is now in the majority in the adult
population—is this. You see, we hold them celibate.
We hold them celibate for a longer and longer period;
the average age at marriage rises steadily; and so long
as they remain celibate we are prepared with some sort
of ideas about the future development of their social

life, clubs, hostels, living-in, and so forth. But at present we haven't any ideas at all about the adaptation of the natural pairing instinct to the new state of affairs. Ultimately the employee marries; they hold out as long as they possibly can, but ultimately they have to. They have to, even in the face of an economic system that holds out no prospects of anything but insecurity and an increasing chance of trouble and disaster to the employee's family group. What happens is that they drop back into a distressful, crippled, insecure imitation of the old family life as one had it in what I might call the multiplying periods of history. They start a home,—they dream of a cottage, but they drift to a lodging, and usually it isn't the best sort of lodging, for landladies hate wives and the other lodgers detest babies. Often the young couple doesn't have babies. You see, they are more intelligent than peasants, and intelligence and fecundity vary reciprocally," said Mr. Brumley.

" You mean ? " interrupted Lady Harman softly.

" There is a world-wide fall in the birthrate. People don't have the families they did."

" Yes," said Lady Harman. " I understand now."

" And the more prosperous or the more sanguine take these suburban little houses, these hutches that make such places as Hendon nightmares of monotony, or go into ridiculous jerry-built sham cottages in some Garden Suburb, where each young wife does her own housework and pretends to like it. They have a sort of happiness for a time, I suppose; the woman stops all outside work, the man, very much handicapped, goes on competing against single men. Then— nothing more happens. Except difficulties. The world goes dull and grey for them. They look about for a lodger, perhaps. Have you read Gissing's *Paying Guest?* . . ."

" I suppose," said Lady Harman, " I suppose it is like that. One tries not to think it is so."

" One needn't let oneself believe that dullness is unhappiness," said Mr. Brumley. " I don't want to paint things sadder than they are. But it's not a fine life, it's not a full life, that life in a Neo-Malthusian suburban hutch."

" Neo—— ? " asked Lady Harman.

" A mere phrase," said Mr. Brumley hastily. " The extraordinary thing is that, until you set me looking into these things with your questions, I've always taken this sort of thing for granted, as though it couldn't be otherwise. Now I seem to see with a kind of freshness. I'm astounded at the muddle of it, the waste and aimlessness of it. And here again it is, Lady Harman, that I think your opportunity comes in. With these Hostels as they might be projected now, you seem to have the possibility of a modernized, more collective and civilized family life than the old close congestion of the single home, and I see no reason at all why you shouldn't carry that collective life on to the married stage. As things are now these little communities don't go beyond the pairing—and out they drift to find the homestead they will never possess. What has been borne in upon me more and more forcibly as I have gone through your—your nest of problems, is the idea that the new social—association, that has so extensively replaced the old family group, might be carried on right through life, that it might work in with all sorts of other discontents and bad adjustments. . . . The life of the women in these

little childless or one-or-two-child homes is more unsatisfactory even than the man's."

Mr. Brumley's face flushed with enthusiasm and he
wagged a finger to emphasize his words. "Why not
make Hostels, Lady Harman, for married couples?
Why not try that experiment so many people have talked
about of the conjoint kitchen and refectory, the
conjoint nursery, the collective social life, so that the
children who are single children or at best children
in small families of two or three, may have the advantages of playfellows, and the young mothers still, if they
choose, continue to have a social existence and go on
with their professional or business work? That's the
next step your Hostels might take. . . . Incidentally
you see this opens a way to a life of relative freedom for
the woman who is married. . . . I don't know if you
have read Mrs. Stetson. Yes, Charlotte Perkins Gilman
Stetson. . . . Yes, *Woman and Economics*, that's the
book.

"I know," Mr. Brumley went on, "I seem to be
opening out your project like a concertina, but I want
you to see just how my thoughts have been going about
all this. I want you to realize I haven't been idle
during these last few weeks. I know it's a far cry from
what the Hostels are to all these ideas of what they
might begin to be, I know the difficulties in your way
—all sorts of difficulties. But when I think just how
you stand at the very centre of the moulding forces in
these changes . . ."

He dropped into an eloquent silence.

Lady Harman looked thoughtfully at the sunlight
under the trees.

"You think," she said, "that it comes to as much as
all this."

" More," said Mr. Brumley.

" I was frightened before. *Now*—— You make me feel as though someone had put the wheel of a motor car in my hand, started it and told me to steer. . . ."

§ 7

Lady Harman went home from that talk in a taxi, and on the way she passed the building operations in Kensington Road. A few weeks ago it had been a mere dusty field of operation for the house-wreckers; now its walls were already rising to the second storey. She realized how swiftly nowadays the search for wisdom can be outstripped by reinforced concrete.

§ 8

It was only by slow degrees and rather in the absence of a more commanding interest than through any invincible quality in their appeal to her mind that these Hostels became in the next three years the grave occupation of Lady Harman's thoughts and energies. She yielded to them reluctantly. For a long time she wanted to look over them and past them and discover something—she did not know what—something high and domineering to which it would be easy to give herself. It was difficult to give herself to the Hostels. In that Mr. Brumley, actuated by a mixture of more or less admirable motives, did his best to assist her. These Hostels alone he thought could give them something upon which they could meet, give them a common interest and him a method of service and companionship. It threw the qualities of duty and justification over their more or less furtive meetings, their little expeditions together, their quiet frequent association.

Together they made studies of the Girls' Clubs which are scattered about London, supplementary homes that have in such places as Walworth and Soho worked small miracles of civilization. These institutions appealed to a lower social level than the one their Hostels were to touch, but they had been organized by capable and understanding minds and Lady Harman found in one or two of their evening dances and in the lunch she shared one morning with a row of cheerful young factory girls from Soho just that quality of concrete realization for which her mind hungered. Then Mr. Brumley took her once or twice for evening walks, just when the stream of workers is going home; he battled his way with her along the footpath of Charing Cross Railway Bridge from the Waterloo side, they swam in the mild evening sunshine of September against a trampling torrent of bobbing heads, and afterwards they had tea together in one of the International Stores near the Strand, where Mr. Brumley made an unsuccessful attempt to draw out the waitress on the subject of Babs Wheeler and the recent strike. The young woman might have talked freely to a man alone or freely to Lady Harman alone but the combination of the two made her shy. The bridge experience led to several other expeditions, to see home-going on the tube, at the big railway termini, on the train—and once they followed up the process to Streatham and saw how the people pour out of the train at last and scatter—until at last they are just isolated individuals running up steps, diving into basements. And then it occurred to Mr. Brumley that he knew someone who would take them over " Gerrard," that huge telephone exchange, and there Lady Harman saw how the National Telephone Company, as it was in those days, had a care for its staff, the pleasant club rooms, the rest room, and stood in that queer rendez-vous of messages, where the " Hello " girl sits all day, wearing a strange metallic apparatus over ear and mouth, watching small lights that wink significantly at her and perpetually pulling out and slipping in and releasing little flexible strings that seem to have a resilient volition of their own. They hunted out Mrs. Barnet and heard her ideas about conjoint homes for spinsters in the Garden Suburb. And then they went over a Training College for elementary teachers and visited the Post Office and then came back to more unobtrusive contemplation, from the customer's little table, of the ministering personalities of the International Stores.

There were times when all these things seen, seemed to fall into an entirely explicable system under Mr. Brumley's exposition, when they seemed to be giving and most generously giving the clearest indications of what kind of thing the Hostels had to be, and times when this all vanished again and her mind became confused and perplexed. She tried to express just what it was she missed to Mr. Brumley. " One doesn't," she said, " see all of them and what one sees isn't what we have to do with. I mean we see them dressed up and respectable and busy and then they go home and the door shuts. It's the home that we are going to alter and replace—and what is it like ? " Mr. Brumley took her for walks in Highbury and the newer parts of Hendon and over to Clapham. " I want to go inside those doors," she said.

" That's just what they won't let you do," said Mr. Brumley. " Nobody visits but relations—and

prospective relations, and the only other social intercourse is over the garden wall. Perhaps I can find
books——"

He got her novels by Edwin Pugh and Pett Ridge
and Frank Swinnerton and George Gissing. They didn't
seem to be attractive homes. And it seemed remarkable
to her that no woman had ever given the woman's view
of the small London home from the inside. . . .

She overcame her own finer scruples and invaded
the Burnet household. Apart from fresh aspects of
Susan's character in the capacity of a hostess she gained
little light from that. She had never felt so completely
outside a home in her life as she did when she was in
the Burnets' parlour. The very tablecloth on which
the tea was spread had an air of being new and
protective of familiar things ; the tea was manifestly
quite unlike their customary tea, it was no more
intimate than the confectioner's shop window from
which it mostly came ; the whole room was full of the
muffled cries of things hastily covered up and specially
put away. Vivid oblongs on the faded wallpaper
betrayed even a rearrangement of the pictures. Susan's
mother was a little dingy woman, wearing a very smart
new cap to the best of her ability ; she had an air of
having been severely shaken up and admonished, and
her general bearing confessed only too plainly how
shattered those preparations had left her. She watched
her capable daughter for cues. Susan's sisters displayed a disposition to keep their backs against
something and at the earliest opportunity to get into
the passage and leave Susan and her tremendous visitor
alone but within earshot. They started convulsively
when they were addressed and insisted on " your
ladyship." Susan had told them not to but they

would. When they supposed themselves to be un-
observed they gave themselves up to the impassioned
inspection of Lady Harman's costume. Luke had fled
into the street, and in spite of various messages conveyed
to him by the youngest sister he refused to enter until
Lady Harman had gone again and was well out of the
way. And Susan was no longer garrulous and at her
ease ; she had no pins in her mouth and that perhaps
hampered her speech ; she presided flushed and bright-
eyed in a state of infectious nervous tension. Her
politeness was awful. Never in all her life had Lady
Harman felt her own lack of real conversational power
so acutely. She couldn't think of a thing that mightn't
be construed as an impertinence and that didn't remind
her of district visiting. Yet perhaps she succeeded
better than she supposed.

"What a family you have had ! " she said to Mrs.
Burnet. "I have four little girls, and I find them as
much as we can manage."

"You're young yet, my ladyship," said Mrs. Burnet,
" and they aren't always the blessings they seem to be.
It's the rearing's the difficulty."

"They're all such healthy-looking—people."

"I wish we could get hold of Luke, my ladyship,
and show you '*im*. He's that sturdy. And yet when
'e was a little feller——"

She was launched for a time on those details that
were always so dear to the mothers of the past order
of things. Her little spate of reminiscences was the
only interlude of naturalness in an afternoon of
painfully constrained behaviour. . . .

Lady Harman returned a trifle shamefacedly from
this abortive dip into realities to Mr. Brumley's
speculative assurance.

§ 9

While Lady Harman was slowly accustoming her mind to this idea that the development of those Hostels was her appointed career in life, so far as a wife may have a career outside her connubial duties, and while she was getting insensibly to believe in Mr. Brumley's theory of their exemplary social importance, the Hostels themselves with a haste that she felt constantly was premature, were achieving a concrete existence. They were developing upon lines that here and there disregarded Mr. Brumley's ideas very widely; they gained in practicality what perhaps they lost in social value, through the entirely indirect relations between Mr. Brumley on the one hand and Sir Isaac on the other. For Sir Isaac manifestly did not consider and would have been altogether indisposed to consider Mr. Brumley as entitled to plan or suggest anything of the slightest importance in this affair, and whatever of Mr. Brumley reached that gentleman reached him in a very carefully transmitted form as Lady Harman's own unaided idea. Sir Isaac had sound Victorian ideas about the place of literature in life. If anyone had suggested to him that literature could supply ideas to practical men he would have had a choking fit, and he regarded Mr. Brumley's sedulous attentions to these hostel schemes with feelings, the kindlier elements of whose admixture was a belief that ultimately he would write some elegant and respectful approval of the established undertaking.

The entire admixture of Sir Isaac's feelings towards Mr. Brumley was by no means kindly. He disliked any man to come near Lady Harman, any man at all;

he had a faint uneasiness even about waiters and hotel porters and the clergy. Of course he had agreed she should have friends of her own and he couldn't very well rescind that without something definite to go upon. But still this persistent follower kept him uneasy. He kept this uneasiness within bounds by reassuring himself upon the point of Lady Harman's virtuous obedience, and so reassured he was able to temper his distrust with a certain contempt. The man was in love with his wife; that was manifest enough, and dangled after her. . . . Let him dangle. What after all did he get for it? . . .

But occasionally he broke through this complacency, betrayed a fitful ingenious jealousy, interfered so that she missed appointments and had to break engagements. He was now more and more a being of pathological moods. The subtle changes of secretion that were hardening his arteries, tightening his breath and poisoning his blood, reflected themselves upon his spirit in an uncertainty of temper and exasperating fatigues and led to startling outbreaks. Then for a time he would readjust himself, become in his manner reasonable again, become accessible.

He was the medium through which this vision that was growing up in her mind of a reorganized social life, had to translate itself, as much as it could ever translate itself, into reality. He called these hostels her hostels, made her the approver of all he did, but he kept every particle of control in his own hands. All her ideas and desires had to be realized by him. And his attitudes varied with his moods; sometimes he was keenly interested in the work of organization and then he terrified her by his bias towards acute economies, sometimes he was resentful at the burthen of the whole thing, sometimes he seemed to scent Brumley or at least some moral influence behind her mind and met her suggestions with a bitter resentment as though any suggestion must needs be a disloyalty to him. There was a remarkable outbreak upon her first tentative proposal that the hostel system might ultimately be extended to married couples.

He heard her with his lips pressing tighter and tighter together until they were yellow white and creased with a hundred wicked little horizontal creases. Then he interrupted her with silent gesticulations. Then words came.

"I never did, Elly," he said. "I never did. Reely —there are times when you ain't rational. Married couples who're assistants in shops and places!"

For a little while he sought some adequate expression of his point of view.

"Nice thing to go keeping a place for these chaps to have their cheap bits of skirt in," he said at last.

Then further: "If a man wants a girl let him work himself up until he can keep her. Married couples indeed!"

He began to expand the possibilities of the case with a quite unusual vividness. "Double beds in each cubicle, I suppose," he said, and played for a time about this fancy. . . . "Well, to hear such an idea from you of all people, Elly. I never did."

He couldn't leave it alone. He had to go on to the bitter end with the vision she had evoked in his mind. He was jealous, passionately jealous, it was too only manifest, of the possible happinesses of these young people. He was possessed by that instinctive hatred for the realized love of others which lies at the base of so much of our moral legislation. The bare thought—whole corridors of bridal chambers!—made his face white and his hand quiver. *His* young men and young women! The fires of a hundred Vigilance Committees blazed suddenly in his reddened eyes. He might have been a concentrated society for preventing the rapid multiplication of the unfit. The idea of facilitating early marriages was manifestly shameful to him, a disgraceful service to render, a job for Pandarus. What was she thinking of? Elly of all people! Elly who had been as innocent as driven snow before Georgina came interfering!

It ended in a fit of abuse and a panting seizure, and for a day or so he was too ill to resume the discussion, to do more than indicate a disgusted aloofness. . . .

And then it may be the obscure chemicals at work within him changed their phase of reaction. At any rate he mended, became gentler, was more loving to his wife than he had been for some time and astonished her by saying that if she wanted Hostels for married couples, it wasn't perhaps so entirely unreasonable. Selected cases, he stipulated, it would have to be and above a certain age limit, sober people. " It might even be a check on immorality," he said, " properly managed. . . ."

But that was as far as his acquiescence went and Lady Harman was destined to be a widow before she saw the foundation of any Hostel for young married couples in London.

§ 10

The reinforced concrete rose steadily amidst Lady Harman's questionings and Mr. Brumley's speculations. The Harmans returned from a recuperative visit to

Kissingen, to which Sir Isaac had gone because of a
suspicion that his Marienbad specialist had failed to
cure him completely in order to get him back again,
to find the first of the five hostels nearly ripe for
its opening. There had to be a manageress and a staff
organized and neither Lady Harman nor Mr. Brumley
were prepared for that sort of business. A number
of abler people however had become aware of the
opportunities of the new development and Mrs. Hubert
Plessington, that busy publicist, got the Harmans to a
helpful little dinner, before Lady Harman had the
slightest suspicion of the needs that were now so
urgent. There shone a neat compact widow, a Mrs.
Pembrose, who had buried her husband some eighteen
months ago after studying social questions with him
with great éclat for ten happy years, and she had done
settlement work and Girls' Club work and had perhaps
more power of organization—given a suitable director
to provide for her lack of creativeness, Mrs. Plessington
told Sir Isaac, than any other woman in London.
Afterwards Sir Isaac had an opportunity of talking
to her; he discussed the suffrage movement with
her and was pleased to find her views remarkably
sympathetic with his own. She was, he declared, a
sensible woman, anxious to hear a man out and
capable, it was evident, of a detachment from feminist
particularism rare in her sex at the present time.
Lady Harman had seen less of the lady that evening,
she was chiefly struck by her pallor, by a kind of
animated silence about her, and by the deep impression
her capabilities had made on Mr. Plessington, who had
hitherto seemed to her to be altogether too overworked in admiring his wife to perceive the points of
any other human being. Afterwards Lady Harman

was surprised to hear from one or two quite separate people that Mrs. Pembrose was the only possible person to act as general director of the new hostels. Lady Beach-Mandarin was so enthusiastic in the matter that she made a special call. " You've known her a long time ? " said Lady Harman.

" Long enough to see what a chance she is ! " said Lady Beach-Mandarin.

Lady Harman perceived equivocation. " Now how long is that really ? " she said.

" Count not in years, nor yet in moments on a dial," said Lady Beach-Mandarin with a fine air of quotation. " I'm thinking of her quiet strength of character. Mrs. Plessington brought her round to see me the other afternoon."

" Did she talk to you ? "

" I saw, my dear, I saw."

A vague aversion from Mrs. Pembrose was in some mysterious way strengthened in Lady Harman by this extraordinary convergence of testimony. When Sir Isaac mentioned the lady with a kind of forced casualness at breakfast as the only conceivable person for the work of initiation and organization that lay before them, Lady Harman determined to see more of her. With a quickened subtlety she asked her to tea. " I have heard so much of your knowledge of social questions and I want you to advise me about my work," she wrote, and then scribbled a note to Mr. Brumley to call and help her judgments.

Mrs. Pembrose appeared dressed in dove colour with a neat bonnetesque straw hat to match. She had a pale slightly freckled complexion, little hard blue-grey eyes with that sort of nose which redeems a squarish shape by a certain delicacy of structure; her

chin was long and protruding and her voice had a
wooden resonance and a ghost of a lisp. Her talk had
a false consecutiveness due to the frequent use of the
word "Yes." Her bearing was erect and her manner
guardedly alert.

From the first she betrayed a conviction that Mr.
Brumley was incidental and unnecessary and that her
real interest lay with Sir Isaac. She might almost
have been in possession of special information upon
that point.

"Yes," she said, "I'm rather specially *up* in this
sort of question. I worked side by side with my poor
Frederick all his life, we were collaborators, and this
question of the urban distributive employee was one
of his special studies. Yes, he would have been
tremendously interested in Sir Isaac's project."

"You know what we are doing?"

"Everyone is interested in Sir Isaac's enterprise.
Naturally. Yes, I think I have a fairly good idea of
what you mean to do. It's a great experiment."

"You think it is likely to answer?" said Mr.
Brumley.

"In Sir Isaac's hands it is *very* likely to answer,"
said Mrs. Pembrose with her eye steadily on Lady
Harman.

There was a little pause. "Yes, now you wrote of
difficulties and drawing upon my experience. Of course
just now I'm quite at Sir Isaac's disposal."

Lady Harman found herself thrust perforce into
the rôle of her husband's spokeswoman. She asked
Mrs. Pembrose if she knew the exact nature of the
experiment they contemplated.

Mrs. Pembrose hadn't a doubt she knew. Of course
for a long time and more especially in the Metropolis

where the distances were so great and increasing so rapidly, there had been a gathering feeling not only in the catering trade, but in very many factory industries, against the daily journey to employment and home again. It was irksome and wasteful to everyone concerned, there was a great loss in control, later hours of beginning, uncertain service. " Yes, my husband calculated the hours lost in London every week, hours that are neither work nor play, mere tiresome stuffy journeying. It made an enormous sum. It worked out at hundreds of working lives per week." Sir Isaac's project was to abolish all that, to bring his staff into line with the drapers and grocers who kept their assistants on the living-in system. . . .

" I thought people objected to the living-in system," said Mr. Brumley.

" There's an agitation against it on the part of a small Trade Union of Shop Assistants," said Mrs. Pembrose. " But they have no real alternative to propose."

" And this isn't Living In," said Mr. Brumley.

" Yes, I think you'll find it is," said Mrs. Pembrose with a nice little expert smile.

" Living-in isn't *quite* what we want," said Lady Harman slowly and with knitted brows, seeking a method of saying just what the difference was to be.

" Yes, not perhaps in the strictest sense," said Mrs. Pembrose giving her no chance, and went on to make fine distinctions. Strictly speaking, living-in meant sleeping over the shop and eating underneath it, and this hostel idea was an affair of a separate house and of occupants who would be assistants from a number of shops. " Yes, collectivism, if you like," said Mrs.

Pembrose. But the word collectivisim, she assured them, wouldn't frighten her, she was a collectivist, a socialist, as her husband had always been. The day was past when socialist could be used as a term of reproach. " Yes, instead of the individual employer of labour, we already begin to have the collective employer of labour, with a labour bureau—and so on. We share them. We no longer compete for them. It's the keynote of the time."

Mr. Brumley followed this with a lifted eyebrow. He was still new to these modern developments of collectivist ideas, this socialism of the employer.

The whole thing Mrs. Pembrose declared was a step forward in civilization, it was a step in the organization and discipline of labour. Of course the unruly and the insubordinate would cry out. But the benefits were plain enough, space, light, baths, association, reasonable recreations, opportunies for improvement—— "

" But freedom ? " said Mr. Brumley.

Mrs. Pembrose inclined her head a little on one side, looked at him this time and smiled the expert smile again. " If you knew as much as I do of the difficulties of social work," she said, " you wouldn't be very much in love with freedom."

" But—it's the very substance of the soul ! "

" You must permit me to differ," said Mrs. Pembrose, and for weeks afterwards Mr. Brumley was still seeking a proper polite retort to that difficult counterstroke. It was such a featureless reply. It was like having your nose punched suddenly by a man without a face.

They descended to a more particular treatment of the problems ahead. Mrs. Pembrose quoted certain precedents from the Girls' Club Union.

"The people Lady Harman contemplates—entertaining," said Mr. Brumley, "are of a slightly more self-respecting type than those young women."

"It's largely veneer," said Mrs. Pembrose. . . .

"Detestable little wretch," said Mr. Brumley when at last she had departed. He was very uncomfortable. "She's just the quintessence of all one fears and dreads about these new developments, she's perfect—in that way—self-confident, arrogant, instinctively aggressive, with a tremendous class contempt. There's a multitude of such people about who hate the employed classes, who *want* to see them broken in and subjugated. I suppose that kind of thing is in humanity. Every boy's school has louts of that kind, who love to torment fags for their own good, who spring upon a chance smut on the face of a little boy to scrub him painfully, who have a kind of lust to dominate under the pretence of improving. I remember—— But never mind that now. Keep that woman out of things or your hostels work for the devil."

"Yes," said Lady Harman. "Certainly she shall not——. No."

But there she reckoned without her husband.

"I've settled it," he said to her at dinner two nights later.

"What?"

"Mrs. Pembrose."

"You've not made her——?"

"Yes, I have. And I think we're very lucky to get her."

"But—Isaac! I don't want her!"

"You should have told me that before, Elly. I've made an agreement."

She suddenly wanted to cry. "But—— You said I should manage these Hostels myself."

"So you shall, Elly.   But we must have somebody. When we go abroad and all that and for all the sort of business stuff and looking after things that you can't do. We've *got* to have her.   She's the only thing going of her sort."

"But—I don't like her."

"Well," cried Sir Isaac, "why in goodness couldn't you tell me that before, Elly ?   I've been and engaged her."

She sat pale-faced staring at him with wide open eyes in which tears of acute disappointment were shining.   She did not dare another word because of her trick of weeping.

"It's all right, Elly," said Sir Isaac.   "How touchy you are !   Anything you want about these Hostels of yours, you've only got to tell me and it's done."

§ 11

Lady Harman was still in a state of amazement at the altered prospects of her hostels when the day arrived for the formal opening of the first of these in Blooms-bury.   They made a little public ceremony of it in spite of her reluctance, and Mr. Brumley had to witness things from out of the general crowd and realize just how completely he wasn't in it, in spite of all his efforts. Mrs. Pembrose was modestly conspicuous, like the unexpected in all human schemes.   There were several reporters present, and Horatio Blenker who was going to make a loyal leader about it, to be followed by one or two special articles for the *Old Country Gazette.*

Horatio had procured Mrs. Blapton for the opening after some ineffectual angling for the Princess Adeline, and the thing was done at half-past three in the

afternoon. In the bright early July sunshine outside
the new building there was a crimson carpet down on
the pavement and an awning above it, there was a great
display of dog-daisies at the windows and on the steps
leading up to the locked portals, an increasing number
of invited people lurked shyly in the ground-floor rooms
ready to come out by the back way and cluster expec-
tantly when Mrs. Blapton arrived, Graper the staff
manager and two assistants in dazzling silk hats seemed
everywhere, the rabbit-like architect had tried to look
doggish in a huge black silk tie and only looked more
like a rabbit than ever, and there was a steady driftage
of small boys and girls, nurses with perambulators, cab
touts, airing grandfathers and similar unemployed
people towards the promise of the awning, the carpet
and the flowers. The square building in all its bravery
of Doulton ware and yellow and mauve tiles and its
great gilt inscription

INTERNATIONAL HOSTELS

above the windows of the second storey seemed typical
of all those modern forces that are now invading and
dispelling the ancient residential peace of Bloomsbury.

Mrs. Blapton appeared only five minutes late,
escorted by Bertie Trevor and her husband's spare
secretary. Graper became so active at the sight of her
that he seemed more like some beast out of the Apoca-
lypse with seven hands and ten hats than a normal human
being; he marshalled the significant figures into their
places, the door was unlocked without serious difficulty,
and Lady Harman found herself in the main corridor
beside Mr. Trevor and a little behind Mrs. Blapton,

engaged in being shown over the new creation. Sir Isaac (driven by Graper at his elbow) was in immediate attendance on the great political lady, and Mrs. Pembrose, already with an air of proprietorship, explained glibly on her other hand. Close behind Lady Harman came Lady Beach-Mandarin, expanding like an appreciative gas in a fine endeavour to nestle happily into the whole big place, and with her were Mrs. Hubert Plessington and Mr. Pope, one of those odd people who are called publicists because one must call them something, and who take chairs and political sides and are vice-presidents of everything and organize philanthropies, write letters to the papers and cannot let the occasion pass without saying a few words and generally prevent the institutions of this country from falling out of human attention. He was a little abstracted in his manner, every now and then his lips moved as he imagined a fresh turn to some classic platitude; anyone who knew him might have foretold the speech into which he presently broke. He did this in the refectory where there was a convenient step up at the end. Beginning with the customary confession of incontinence, "could not let the occasion pass," he declared that he would not detain them long, but he felt that everyone there would agree with him that they shared that day in no slight occasion, no mean enterprise, that here was one of the most promising, one of the most momentous, nay! he would go further and add with due deference to them all, one of the most pregnant of social experiments in modern social work. In the past he had himself—if he might for a moment allow a personal note to creep into his observations, he himself had not been unconnected with industrial development.— (Querulous voice, "Who the devil is that?" and

whispered explanations on the part of Horatio Blenker:
" Pope—very good man—East Purblow Experiment—
Payment in Kind instead of Wages—Yes "). . . .

Lady Harman ceased to listen to Mr. Pope's strained
but not unhappy tenor. She had heard him before, and
she had heard his like endlessly. He was the larger
moiety of every public meeting she had ever attended.
She had ceased even to marvel at the dull self-satisfac-
tion that possessed him. To-day her capacity for
marvelling was entirely taken up by the details of
this extraordinary reality which had sprung from her
dream of simple, kindly, beautiful homes for distressed
and overworked young women ; nothing in the whole of
life had been so amazing since that lurid occasion when
she had been the agonized vehicle for the entry of Miss
Millicent Harman upon this terrestrial scene. It was all
so entirely what she could never have thought possible.
A few words from other speakers followed, Mrs. Blapton,
with the young secretary at hand to prompt, said something, and Sir Isaac was poked forwards to say, " Thank
you very much. It's all my wife's doing, really. . . .
Oh dash it ! Thank you very much." It had the effect
of being the last vestige of some more elaborate piece
of eloquence that had suddenly disintegrated in his
mind.

" And now, Elly," he said, as their landaulette took
them home, " you're beginning to have your hostels."

" Then they *are* my hostels ? " she asked abruptly.

" Didn't I say they were ? " The satisfaction of his
face was qualified by that fatigued irritability that
nowadays always followed any exertion or excitement.

" If I want things done ? If I want things
altered ? "

"Of course you may, of course you may. What's the matter with you, Elly? What's been putting ideers into your head. You got to have a directress to the thing; you must have a woman of education who knows a bit about things to look after the matrons and so on. Very likely she isn't everything you want. She's the only one we could get, and I don't see——. Here I go and work hard for a year and more getting these things together to please you, and then suddenly you don't like 'em. There's a lot of the spoilt child in you, Elly—first and last. There they are. . . ."

They were silent for the rest of the journey to Putney, both being filled with incommunicable things.

§ 12

And now Lady Harman began to share the trouble of all those who let their minds pass out of the circle of their immediate affections with any other desire save interest and pleasure. Assisted in this unhappy development by the sedulous suggestions of Mr. Brumley she had begun to offend against the most sacred law in our sensible British code, she was beginning to take herself and her hostels seriously, and think that it mattered how she worked for them and what they became. She tried to give all the attention her children's upbringing, her husband's ailments and the general demands of her household left free, to this complex, elusive, puzzling and worrying matter. Instead of thinking that these hostels were just old hostels and that you start them and put in a Mrs. Pembrose and feel very benevolent and happy and go away, she had come to realize partly by dint of her own conscientious thinking and partly through Mr. Brumley's strenuous resolve that she should not take Sir Isaac's gift horse without the most exhaustive examination of its quality, that this new work, like most new things in human life, was capable not only of admirable but of altogether detestable consequences, and that it rested with her far more than with any other human being to realize the former and avoid the latter. And directly one has got to this critical pose towards things, just as one ceases to be content with things anyhow and to want them precisely somehow, one begins to realize just how intractable, confused and disingenuous are human affairs. Mr. Brumley had made himself see and had made her see how inevitable these big wholesale ways of doing things, these organizations and close social co-operations, have become unless there is to be a social disintegration and set back, and he had also brought himself and her to realize how easily they may develop into a new servitude, how high and difficult is the way towards methods of association that will ensure freedom and permit people to live fine individual lives. Every step towards organization raises a crop of vices peculiar to itself, fresh developments of the egotism and greed and vanity of those into whose hands there falls control, fresh instances of that hostile pedantry which seems so natural to officials and managers, insurgencies and obstinacies and suspicions on the part of every one. The poor lady had supposed that when one's intentions were obviously benevolent every one helped. She only faced the realities of this task that she had not so much set for herself as had happened to her, after dreadful phases of disillusionment and dismay.

" These hostels," said Mr. Brumley in his most

prophetic mood, " can be made free, fine things—or not
—just as all the world of men we are living in, could
be made a free, fine world. And it's our place to see
they are that. It's just by being generous and giving
ourselves, helping without enslaving, and giving without exacting gratitude, planning and protecting with
infinite care, that we bring that world nearer. . . .
Since I've known you I've come to know such things
are possible. . . ."

The Bloomsbury hostel started upon its career with
an embarrassing difficulty. The young women of the
International Stores Refreshment Departments for
whom these institutions were primarily intended displayed what looked extremely like a concerted indis-
position to come in. They had been circularized and
informed that henceforth, to ensure the " good social
tone " of the staff, all girls not living at home with
their parents or close relations would be expected to
reside in the new hostels. There followed an attractive
account of the advantages of the new establishment.
In drawing up this circular with the advice of Mrs.
Pembrose, Sir Isaac had overlooked the fact that his
management was very imperfectly informed just where
the girls did live, and that after its issue it was very
improbable that it would be possible to find out this
very necessary fact. But the girls seemed to be
unaware of this ignorance at headquarters, Miss Babs
Wheeler was beginning to feel a little bored by good
behaviour and crave for those dramatic cessations at
the lunch hour, those speeches, with cheers, from a
table top, those interviews with reporters, those flushed
and eager councils of war and all the rest of that good
old crisis feeling that had previously ended so happily.
Mr. Graper came to his proprietor headlong, Mrs.

Pembrose was summoned and together they contemplated the lamentable possibility of this great
social benefit they had done the world being discredited
at the outset by a strike of the proposed beneficiaries.
Sir Isaac fell into a state of vindictiveness and was with
difficulty restrained by Mr. Graper from immediately
concluding the negotiations that were pending with
three great Oxford Street firms that would have given
over the hostels to their employees and closed them
against the International girls for ever.

Even Mrs. Pembrose couldn't follow Sir Isaac in
that, and remarked : " As I understand it, the whole
intention was to provide proper housing for our own
people first and foremost."

" And haven't we provided it, *damn* them ? " said
Sir Isaac in white desperation. . . .

It was Lady Harman who steered the newly
launched institutions through these first entanglements. It was her first important advantage in the
struggle that had hitherto been going relentlessly
against her. She now displayed her peculiar gift,
a gift that indeed is unhappily all too rare among
philanthropists, the gift of not being able to classify
the people with whom she was dealing, but of continuing to regard them as a multitude of individualized
souls as distinct and considerable as herself. That
makes no doubt for slowness and " inefficiency " and
complexity in organization, but it does make for
understandings. And now, through a little talk with
Susan Burnet about her sister's attitude upon the
dispute, she was able to take the whole situation in the
flank.

Like many people who are not easily clear, Lady
Harman when she was clear acted with very considerable

decision, which was perhaps none the less effective because of the large softnesses of her manner.

She surprised Sir Isaac by coming of her own accord into his study, where with an altogether novel disfavour he sat contemplating the detailed plans for the Sydenham Hostel. "I think I've found out what the trouble is," she said.

"What trouble?"

"About my hostel."

"How do you know?"

"I've been finding out what the girls are saying."

"They'd say anything."

"I don't think they're clever enough for that," said Lady Harman after consideration. She recovered her thread. "You see, Isaac, they've been frightened by the Rules. I didn't know you had printed a set of Rules."

"One must *have* rules, Elly."

"In the background," she decided. "But you see these Rules—were made conspicuous. They were printed in two colours on wall cards just exactly like that list of rules and scale of fines you had to withdraw—— "

"I know," said Sir Isaac, shortly.

"It reminded the girls. And that circular that seems to threaten them if they don't give up their lodgings and come in. And the way the front is got up to look just exactly like one of the refreshment-room branches—it makes them feel it will be unhome-like, and that there will be a kind of repetition in the evening of all the discipline and regulations they have to put up with during the day."

"Have to put up with!" murmured Sir Isaac.

"I wish that had been thought of sooner. If we

had made the places look a little more ordinary and called them Osborne House or something a little old-fashioned like that, something with a touch of the Old Queen about it and all that kind of thing."

" We can't go to the expense of taking down all those big gilt letters just to please the fancies of Miss Babs Wheeler."

" It's too late now to do that, perhaps. But we could do something, I think, to remove the suspicions— . . . I want, Isaac—— I think—— " She pulled herself together to announce her determination. " I think if I were to go to the girls and meet a delegation of them, and just talk to them plainly about what we mean by this hostel."

" *You* can't go making speeches."

" It would just be talking to them."

" It's such a Come Down," said Sir Isaac, after a momentary contemplation of the possibility.

For some time they talked without getting very far from these positions they had assumed. At last Sir Isaac shifted back upon his expert. " Can't we talk about it to Mrs. Pembrose ? She knows more about this sort of business than we do."

" I'm not going to talk to Mrs. Pembrose," said Lady Harman, after a little interval. Some unusual quality in her quiet voice made Sir Isaac lift his eyes to her face for a moment.

So one Saturday afternoon, Lady Harman had a meeting with a roomful of recalcitrant girls at the Regent Street Refreshment Branch, which looked very odd to her with grey cotton wrappers over everything and its blinds down, and for the first time she came face to face with the people for whom almost in spite of herself she was working. It was a meeting summoned by the

International Branch of the National Union of Waitresses and Miss Babs Wheeler and Mr. Graper were so to speak the north and south poles of the little group upon the improvised platform from which Lady Harman was to talk to the gathering. She would have liked the support of Mr. Brumley, but she couldn't contrive any unostentatious way of bringing him into the business without putting it upon a footing that would have involved the appearance of Sir Isaac and Mrs. Pembrose and—everybody. And essentially it wasn't to be everybody. It was to be a little talk.

Lady Harman rather liked the appearance of Miss Babs Wheeler, and met more than an answering approval in that insubordinate young woman's eye. Miss Wheeler was a minute swaggering person, much akimbo, with a little round blue-eyed innocent face that shone with delight at the lark of living. Her three companions who were in the lobby with her to receive and usher in Lady Harman seemed just as young, but they were relatively unilluminated except by their manifest devotion to their leader. They displayed rather than concealed their opinion of her as a "dear" and a "fair wonder." And the meeting generally it seemed to her was a gathering of very human young women, rather restless, then agog to see her and her clothes, and then somehow allayed by her appearance and quite amiably attentive to what she had to say. A majority were young girls dressed with the cheap smartness of the suburbs, the rest were for the most part older and dingier, and here and there were dotted young ladies of a remarkable and questionable smartness. In the front row, full of shy recognitions and a little disguised by an unfamiliar hat was Susan's sister Alice.

As Lady Harman had made up her mind that she

was not going to deliver a speech she felt no diffidence in speaking. She was far too intent on her message to be embarrassed by any thought of the effect she was producing. She talked as she might have talked in one of her easier moods to Mr. Brumley. And as she talked it happened that Miss Babs Wheeler and quite a number of the other girls present watched her face and fell in love with her.

She began with her habitual prelude. " You see," she said, and stopped and began again. She wanted to tell them and with a clumsy simplicity she told them how these Hostels had arisen out of her desire that they should have something better than the uncomfortable lodgings in which they lived. They weren't a business enterprise, but they weren't any sort of charity. " And I wanted them to be the sort of place in which you would feel quite free. I hadn't any sort of intention of having you interfered with. I hate being interfered with myself, and I understand just as well as anyone can that you don't like it either. I wanted these Hostels to be the sort of place that you might perhaps after a time almost manage and run for yourselves. You might have a committee or something. . . . Only you know it isn't always easy to do as one wants. Things don't always go in this world as one wants them to go—particularly if one isn't clever." She lost herself for a moment at that point, and then went on to say she didn't like the new rules. They had been drawn up in a hurry and she had only read them after they were printed. All sorts of things in them——

She seemed to be losing her theme again, and Mr. Graper handed her the offending card, a big varnished wall placard, with eyelets and tape complete.

She glanced at it. For example, she said, it wasn't her idea to have fines. (Great and long continued applause.) There was something she had always disliked about fines. (Renewed applause.) But these rules could easily be torn up. And as she said this and as the meeting broke into acquiescence again it occurred to her that there was the card of rules in her hands, and nothing could be simpler than to tear it up there and then. It resisted her for a moment, she compressed her lips and then she had it in halves. This tearing was so satisfactory to her that she tore it again and then again. As she tore it, she had a pleasant irrational feeling that she was tearing Mrs. Pembrose, Mr. Graper's face betrayed his shocked feelings, and the meeting which had become charged with a strong desire to show how entirely it approved of her, made a crowning attempt at applause. They hammered umbrellas on the floor, they clapped hands, they rattled chairs and gave a shrill cheer. A chair was broken.

" I wish," said Lady Harman when that storm had abated, " you'd come and look at the Hostel. Couldn't you come next Saturday afternoon. We could have a stand-up tea and you could see the place and then afterwards your committee and I—and my husband— could make out a real set of rules. . . ."

She went on for some little time longer, she appealed to them with all the strength of her honest purpose to help her to make this possible good thing a real good thing, not to suspect, not to be hard on her—" and my husband "—not to make a difficult thing impossible, it was so easy to do that, and when she finished she was in the happiest possession of her meeting. They came thronging round her with flushed faces and bright eyes, they wanted to come near her, wanted to touch her, wanted to assure her that for her they were quite prepared to live in any kind of place. For her. "You come and talk to us, Lady Harman," said one ; "*we'll* show you."

"Nobody hasn't told us, Lady Harman, how these Hostels were *yours*."

"You come and talk to us again, Lady Harman." . . .

They didn't wait for the following Saturday. On Monday morning Mrs. Pembrose received thirty-seven applications to take up rooms.

§ 13

For the next few years it was to be a matter of recurrent heart-searching for Lady Harman whether she had been profoundly wise or extremely foolish in tearing up that card of projected rules. At the time it seemed the most natural and obvious little action imaginable ; it was long before she realized just how symbolical and determining a few movements of the hand and wrist can be. It fixed her line not so much for herself as for others. It put her definitely, much more definitely than her convictions warranted, on the side of freedom against discipline. For indeed her convictions like most of our convictions kept along a tortuous watershed between these two. It is only a few rare extravagant spirits who are wholly for the warp or wholly for the woof of human affairs.

The girls applauded and loved her. At one stroke she had acquired the terrible liability of partisans. They made her their champion and sanction ; she was responsible for an endless succession of difficulties that

flowered out of their interpretations of her act. These
Hostels that had seemed passing out of her control,
suddenly turned back upon her and took possession of
her.

And they were never simple difficulties. Right and
wrong refused to unravel for her; each side of every
issue seemed to be so often in suicidal competition with
its antagonist for the inferior case. If the forces of
order and discipline showed themselves perennially harsh
and narrow, it did not blind her perplexed eyes to the
fact that the girls were frequently extremely naughty.
She wished very often, she did so wish—they wouldn't
be. They set out with a kind of eagerness for conflict.

Their very loyalty to her expressed itself not so
much in any sustained attempt to make the hostels
successful as in cheering inconveniently, in embarrassing
declarations of a preference, in an ingenious and
systematic rudeness to anyone suspected of imperfect
devotion to her. The first comers into the Hostels
were much more like the swelling inrush of a tide
than, as Mrs. Pembrose would have preferred, like
something laid on through a pipe, and when this lady
wanted to go on with the old rules until Sir Isaac had
approved of the new, the new arrivals went into the
cutting-out room and manifested. Lady Harman had
to be telephoned for to allay the manifestation.

And then arose questions of deportment, trivial in
themselves, but of the gravest moment for the welfare
of the hostels. There was a phrase about "noisy or
improper conduct" in the revised rules. Few people
would suspect a corridor, ten feet wide and two hundred
feet long as a temptation to impropriety, but Mrs.
Pembrose found it was so. The effect of the corridors
upon undisciplined girls quite unaccustomed to corridors

was for a time most undesirable. For example they were moved to *run* along them violently. They ran races along them, when they overtook they jostled, when they were overtaken they squealed. The average velocity in the corridors of the lady occupants of the Bloomsbury Hostel during the first fortnight of its existence was seven miles an hour. Was that violence? Was that impropriety? The building was all steel construction, but one *heard* even in the Head Matron's room. And then there was the effect of the rows and rows of windows opening out upon the square. The square had some pleasant old trees and it was attractive to look down into their upper branches, where the sparrows mobbed and chattered perpetually, and over them at the chimneys and turrets and sky signs of the London world. The girls looked. So far they were certainly within their rights. But they did not look modestly, they did not look discreetly. They looked out of wide-open windows, they even sat perilously and protrudingly on the window sills conversing across the façade from window to window, attracting attention, and once to Mrs. Pembrose's certain knowledge a man in the street joined in. It was on a Sunday morning, too, a Bloomsbury Sunday morning!

But graver things were to rouse the preventive prohibitionist in the soul of Mrs. Pembrose. There was the visiting of one another's rooms and cubicles. Most of these young people had never possessed or dreamt of possessing a pretty and presentable apartment to themselves, and the first effect of this was to produce a decorative outbreak, a vigorous framing of photographs and hammering of nails (" dust-gathering litter "—*Mrs. Pembrose*) and then—visiting. They visited at all hours and in all costumes; they sat in groups of three or four, one on the chair and the rest on the bed conversing into late hours,—entirely uncensored conversations too often accompanied by laughter. When Mrs. Pembrose took this to Lady Harman she found her extraordinarily blind to the conceivable evils of this free intercourse. " But, Lady Harman ! " said Mrs. Pembrose, with a note of horror, " some of them—kiss each other ! "

" But if they're fond of each other," said Lady Harman. " I'm sure I don't see—— "

And when the floor matrons were instructed to make little surprise visits up and down the corridors the girls who occupied rooms took to locking their doors—and Lady Harman seemed inclined to sustain their right to do that. The floor matrons did what they could to exercise authority, one or two were former department manageresses, two were ex-elementary teachers, crowded out by younger and more certificated rivals, one, and the most trustworthy one, Mrs. Pembrose found, was an ex-wardress from Holloway. The natural result of these secret talkings and conferrings in the rooms became apparent presently in some mild ragging and in the concoction of petty campaigns of annoyance designed to soften the manners of the more authoritative floor matrons. Here again were perplexing difficulties. If a particular floor matron has a clear commanding note in her voice, is it or is it not " violent and improper " to say "Haw !" in clear commanding tones whenever you suppose her to be within earshot ? As for the door-locking, Mrs. Pembrose settled that by carrying off all the keys.

Complaints and incidents drifted towards definite scenes and " situations." Both sides in this continuing

conflict of dispositions were so definite, so intolerant, to
the mind of the lady with the perplexed dark eyes who
mediated. Her reason was so much with the matrons ;
her sympathies so much with the girls. She did not
like the assured brevity of Mrs. Pembrose's judgments
and decisions ; she had an instinctive perception of the
truth that all compact judgments upon human beings
are unjust judgments. The human spirit is but poorly
adapted either to rule or to be ruled, and the honesty
of all the efforts of Mrs. Pembrose and her staffs—for
soon the hostels at Sydenham and West Kensington
were open—were marred not merely by arrogance but
by an irritability, a real hostility to complexities and
difficulties and resisters and troublesome characters.
And it did not help the staff to a triumphant achievement of its duties that the girls had an exaggerated
perception that Lady Harman's heart was on their
side.

And presently the phrase " weeding out " crept
into the talk of Mrs. Pembrose. Some of the girls
were being marked as ringleaders, foci of mischief,
characters it was desirable to " get rid of." Confronted
with it Lady Harman perceived she was absolutely
opposed to this idea of getting rid of anyone—unless
it was Mrs. Pembrose. She liked her various people ;
she had no desire for a whittled success with a picked
remnant of subdued and deferential employees. She
put that to Mr. Brumley and Mr. Brumley was
indignant and eloquent in his concurrence. A certain
Mary Trunk, a dark young woman with a belief that it
became her to have a sweet disorder in her hair, and a
large blonde girl named Lucy Baxandall seemed to be
the chief among the bad influences of the Bloomsbury
hostel, and they took it upon themselves to appeal to

Lady Harman against Mrs. Pembrose. They couldn't they complained, " do a Thing right for her. . . ."

So the tangle grew.

Presently Lady Harman had to go to the Riviera with Sir Isaac and when she came back Mary Trunk and Lucy Baxandall had vanished from both the International Hostel and the International Stores. She tried to find out why, and she was confronted by inadequate replies and enigmatical silences. " They decided to go," said Mrs. Pembrose, and dropped " fortunately " after that statement. She disavowed any exact knowledge of their motives. But she feared the worst. Susan Burnet was uninforming. Whatever had happened had failed to reach Alice Burnet's ears. Lady Harman could not very well hold a commission of enquiry into the matter, but she had an uneasy sense of a hidden campaign of dislodgment. And about the corridors and cubicles and club rooms there was she thought a difference, a discretion, a flavour of subjugation. . . .

CHAPTER THE ELEVENTH

The Last Crisis

§ 1

It would be quite easy for anyone with the knack of reserve to go on from this point with a history of Lady Harman that would present her as practically a pure philanthropist. For from these beginnings she was destined to proceed to more and more knowledge and understanding and clear purpose and capable work in this interesting process of collective regrouping, this process which may even at last justify Mr. Brumley's courageous interpretations and prove to be an early experiment in the beginning of a new social order. Perhaps some day there will be an official biography, another addition to the inscrutable records of British public lives, in which all these things will be set out with tact and dignity. Horatio Blenker or Adolphus Blenker may survive to be entrusted with this congenial task. She will be represented as a tall inanimate person pursuing one clear benevolent purpose in life from her very beginning, and Sir Isaac and her relations with Sir Isaac will be rescued from reality. The book will be illustrated by a number of carefully posed photographer's photographs of her, studies of the Putney house and perhaps an unappetizing woodcut of her early home at Penge. The aim of all British

378

biography is to conceal. A great deal of what we have already told will certainly not figure in any such biography, and still more certainly will the things we have yet to tell be missing.

Lady Harman was indeed only by the force of circumstances and intermittently a pure philanthropist, and it is with the intercalary passages of less exalted humanity that we are here chiefly concerned. At times no doubt she did really come near to filling and fitting and becoming identical with that figure of the pure philanthropist which was her world-ward face, but for the most part that earnest and dignified figure concealed more or less extensive spaces of nothingness, while the errant soul of the woman within strayed into less exalted ways of thinking.

There were times when she was almost sure of herself—Mrs. Hubert Plessington could scarcely have been surer of herself, and times when the whole magnificent project of constructing a new urban social life out of those difficult hostels, a collective urban life that should be liberal and free, broke into grimacing pieces and was the most foolish of experiments. Her struggles with Mrs. Pembrose thereupon assumed a quality of mere bickering and she could even doubt whether Mrs. Pembrose wasn't justified in her attitude and wiser by her very want of generosity. She felt then something childish in the whole undertaking that otherwise escaped her, she was convicted of an absurd self-importance, she discovered herself an ignorant woman availing herself of her husband's power and wealth to attempt presumptuous experiments. In these moods of disillusionment, her mind went adrift and was driven to and fro from discontent to discontent; she would find herself taking soundings and seeking an anchorage upon the

strangest most unfamiliar shoals. And in her relations
and conflicts with her husband there was a smouldering
shame for her submissions to him that needed only a
phase of fatigue to become acute. So long as she
believed in her hostels and her mission that might be
endured, but forced back upon her more personal life
its hideousness stood unclothed. Mr. Brumley could
sometimes reassure her by a rhetorical effort upon the
score of her hostels, but most of her more intimate and
inner life was not, for very plain reasons, to be shown
to him. He was full of the intention of generous self-
denials, but she had long since come to measure the
limits of his self-denial. . . .

Mr. Brumley was a friend in whom smouldered a
love, capable she knew quite clearly of tormented and
tormenting jealousies. It would be difficult to tell, and
she certainly could never have told how far she knew
of this by instinct, how far it came out of rapid intuitions from things seen and heard. But she understood
that she dared not let a single breath of encouragement,
a hint of physical confidence, reach that banked-up
glow. A sentinel discretion in her brain was always
on the watch for that danger, and that restraint, that
added deliberate inexpressiveness, kept them most apart,
when most her spirit cried out for companionship.

The common quality of all these moods of lassitude
was a desolating loneliness. She had at times a need
that almost overwhelmed her to be intimate, to be
comforted and taken up out of the bleak harsh disappointments and stresses of her customary life. At
times after Sir Isaac had either been too unloving or
too loving, or when the girls or the matrons had
achieved some new tangle of mutual unreasonableness,
or when her faith failed, she would lie in the darkness

of her own room with her soul crying out for—how can one put it?—the touch of other soul-stuff. And perhaps it was the constant drift of Mr. Brumley's talk, the little suggestions that fell drop by drop into her mind from his, that disposed her to believe that this aching sense of solitude in the void was to be assuaged by love, by some marvel of close exaltation that one might reach through a lover. She had told Mr. Brumley long ago that she would never let herself think of love, she still maintained to him that attitude of resolute aloofness, but almost without noting what she did, she was tampering now in her solitude with the seals of that locked chamber. She became secretly curious about love. Perhaps there was something in it of which she knew nothing. She found herself drawn towards poetry, found a new attraction in romance ; more and more did she dally with the idea that there was some unknown beauty in the world, something to which her eyes might presently open, something deeper and sweeter than anything she had ever known, close at hand, something to put all the world into proportion for her.

In a little while she no longer merely tampered with these seals, for quite silently the door had opened and she was craning in. This love it seemed to her might after all be so strange a thing that it goes unsuspected and yet fills the whole world of a human soul. An odd grotesque passage in a novel by Wilkins gave her that idea. He compared love to electricity, of all things in the world ; that throbbing life amidst the atoms that we now draw upon for light, warmth, connexion, the satisfaction of a thousand wants and the cure of a thousand ills. There it is and always has been in the life of man, and yet until a century ago it worked unsuspected, was known only for a disregarded oddity of amber, a crackling in frost-dry hair and thunder. . . .

And then she remembered how Mr. Brumley had once broken into a panegyric of love. " It makes life a different thing. It is like the home-coming of something lost. All this dispersed perplexing world *centres*. Think what true love means ; to live always in the mind of another and to have that other living always in your mind. . . . Only there can be no restraints, no reserves, no admission of prior rights. One must feel *safe* of one's welcome and freedoms. . . ."

Wasn't it worth the risk of almost any breach of boundaries to get to such a light as that ? . . .

She hid these musings from every human being, she was so shy with them, she hid them almost from herself. Rarely did they have their way with her and when they did, presently she would accuse herself of slackness and dismiss them and urge herself to fresh practicalities in her work. But her work was not always at hand, Sir Isaac's frequent relapses took her abroad to places where she found herself in the midst of beautiful scenery with little to do and little to distract her from these questionings. Then such thoughts would inundate her.

This feeling of the unsatisfactoriness of life, of incompleteness and solitariness, was not of that fixed sort that definitely indicates its demand. Under its oppression she tried the idea of love, but she also tried certain other ideas. Very often this vague appeal had the quality of a person, sometimes a person shrouded in night, a soundless whisper, the unseen lover who came to Psyche in the darkness. And sometimes that person became more distinct, less mystic and more companionable. Perhaps because imaginations have a way of

following the line of least resistance, it took upon itself
something of the form, something of the voice and
bearing of Mr. Brumley. She recoiled from her own
thoughts when she discovered herself wondering what
manner of lover Mr. Brumley might make—if suddenly
she lowered her defences, freed his suffocating pleading,
took him to herself.

In my anxiety to draw Mr. Brumley as he was, I
have perhaps a little neglected to show him as Lady
Harman saw him. We have employed the inconsiderate
verisimilitude of a novelist repudiating romance in his
portrayal ; towards her he kept a better face. He was
at least a very honest lover and there was little
disingenuousness in the flow of fine mental attitudes that
met her ; the thought and presence of her made him
fine ; as soon could he have turned his shady side
towards the sun. And she was very ready and eager to
credit him with generous qualities. We of his club
and circle, a little assisted perhaps by Max Beerbohm's
diabolical index finger, may have found and been not
unwilling to find his face chiefly expressive of a kind of
empty alertness ; but when it was turned to her its
quite pleasantly modelled features glowed and it was
transfigured. So far as she was concerned, with Sir
Isaac as foil, he was real enough and good enough
for her. And by the virtue of that unlovely contrast even a certain ineffectiveness—became infinite
delicacy. . . .

The thought of Mr. Brumley in that relation and
to that extent of clearness came but rarely into her
consciousness, and when it did it was almost immediately
dismissed again. It was the most fugitive of proffered
consolations. And it is to be remarked that it made
its most successful apparitions when Mr. Brumley was

far away, and by some weeks or months of separation a little blurred and forgotten. . . .

And sometimes this unrest of her spirit, this unhappiness turned her in quite another direction as it seemed and she had thoughts of religion. With a deepened shame she would go seeking into that other, that greater indelicacy, from which her upbringing had divorced her mind. She would even secretly pray. Greatly daring she fled on several occasions from her visitation of the hostels or slipped out of her home, and evading Mr. Brumley, went once to the Brompton Oratory, once or twice to the Westminster Cathedral and then having discovered Saint Paul's to Saint Paul's in search of this nameless need. It was a need that no plain and ugly little place of worship would satisfy. It was a need that demanded choir and organ. She went to Saint Paul's haphazard when her mood and opportunity chanced together and there in the afternoons she found a wonder of great music and chanting voices, and she would kneel looking up into those divine shadows and perfect archings and feel for a time assuaged, wonderfully assuaged. Sometimes, there, she seemed to be upon the very verge of grasping that hidden reality which makes all things plain. Sometimes it seemed to her that this very indulgence was the hidden reality.

She could never be sure in her mind whether these secret worshippings helped or hampered her in her daily living. They helped her to a certain disregard of annoyances and indignities and so far they were good, but they also helped towards a more general indifference. She might have told these last experiences to Mr. Brumley if she had not felt them to be indescribable. They could not be half told. They had to be told completely or they were altogether untellable. So she hid them and at once accepted and distrusted the consolation they brought her, and went on with the duties and philanthropies that she had chosen as her task in the world.

§ 2

One day in Lent—it was nearly three years after the opening of the first hostel—she went to Saint Paul's.

She was in a mood of great discouragement ; the struggle between Mrs. Pembrose and the Bloomsbury girls had suddenly reopened in an acute form and Sir Isaac, who was sickening again after a period of better health, had become strangely restless and irritable and hostile to her. He had thwarted her unusually and taken the side of the matrons in a conflict in which Susan Burnet's sister Alice was now distinguished as the chief of the malcontents. The new trouble seemed to Lady Harman to be traceable in one direction to that ardent Unionist, Miss Babs Wheeler, under the spell of whose round-faced, blue-eyed, distraught personality Alice had altogether fallen. Miss Babs Wheeler was fighting for the Union ; she herself lived at Highbury with her mother, and Alice was her chosen instrument in the hostels. The Union had always been a little against the ladylike instincts of many of the waitresses ; they felt strikes were vulgar and impaired their social standing, and this feeling had been greatly strengthened by irruptions of large contingents of shop assistants from various department stores. The Bloomsbury Hostel in particular now accommodated a hundred refined and elegant hands— they ought rather to have been called figures—from the

great Oxford Street costume house of Eustace and
Mills, young people with a tall sweeping movement
and an elevation of chin that had become nearly
instinctive, and a silent yet evident intention to find
the International girls " low " at the slightest provocation. It is only too easy for poor humanity under the
irritation of that tacit superiority to respond with just
the provocation anticipated. What one must re-
gretfully speak of as the vulgar section of the International girls had already put itself in the wrong
by a number of aggressive acts before the case came
to Lady Harman's attention. Mrs. Pembrose seized
the occasion for weeding on a courageous scale, and
Miss Alice Burnet and three of her dearest friends
were invited to vacate their rooms " pending re-
decoration."

With only too much plausibility the threatened
young women interpreted this as an expulsion, and
declined to remove their boxes and personal belongings.
Miss Babs Wheeler thereupon entered the Bloomsbury
Hostel, and in the teeth of three express prohibitions
from Mrs. Pembrose, went a little up the staircase and
addressed a confused meeting in the central hall.
There was loud and continuous cheering for Lady
Harman at intervals during this incident. Thereupon
Mrs. Pembrose demanded sweeping dismissals, not only
from the Hostels but the shops as an alternative to
her resignation, and Lady Harman found herself more
perplexed than ever. . . .

Georgina Sawbridge had contrived to mingle herself
in an entirely characteristic way in these troubles by
listening for a brief period to an abstract of her sister's
perplexities, then demanding to be made Director-
General of the whole affair, refusing to believe this

simple step impossible and retiring in great dudgeon
to begin a series of letters of even more than sisterly
bitterness. And Mr. Brumley when consulted had
become dangerously sentimental. Under these circumstances Lady Harman's visit to Saint Paul's had
much of the quality of a flight.

It was with an unwonted sense of refuge that she
came from the sombre stress and roar of London
without into the large hushed spaces of the cathedral.
The door closed behind her—and all things changed.
Here was meaning, coherence, unity. Here instead of
a pelting confusion of movements and motives was a
quiet concentration upon the little focus of light about
the choir, the gentle complete dominance of a voice
intoning. She slipped along the aisle and into the
nave and made her way to a seat. How good this
was! Outside she had felt large, awkwardly responsible,
accessible to missiles, a distressed conspicuous thing;
within this living peace she suddenly became no more
than one of a tranquil hushed community of small
black-clad Lenten people; she found a chair and
knelt and felt she vanished even from her own
consciousness. . . .

How beautiful was this place! She looked up
presently at the great shadowy arcs far above her, so
easy, so gracious that it seemed they had not so much
been built by men as shaped by circling flights of
angels. The service, a little clustering advance of
voices unsustained by any organ, mingled in her mind
with the many-pointed glow of candles. And then
into this great dome of worship and beauty, like a bed
of voices breaking into flower, like a springtime breeze
of sound, came Allegri's Miserere. . . .

Her spirit clung to this mood of refuge. It seemed

as though the disorderly, pugnacious, misunderstanding universe had opened and shown her luminous mysteries. She had a sense of penetration. All that conflict, that jar of purposes and motives, was merely superficial; she had left it behind her. For a time she had no sense of effort in keeping hold of this, only of attainment, she drifted happily upon the sweet sustaining sounds, and then—then the music ceased. She came back into herself. Close to her a seated man stirred and sighed. She tried to get back her hold upon that revelation but it had gone. Inexorably, opaque, impenetrable doors closed softly on her moment of vision. . . .

All about her was the stir of departure.

She walked out slowly into the cold March daylight, to the leaden greys, the hurrying black shapes, the chaotic afternoon traffic of London. She paused on the steps, still but half reawakened. A passing omnibus obtruded the familiar inscription, " International Stores for Staminal Bread."

She turned like one who remembers, to where her chauffeur stood waiting.

§ 3

As her motor car, with a swift smoothness, carried her along the Embankment towards the lattice bar of Charing Cross bridge and the remoter towers of the Houses of Parliament, grey now and unsubstantial against the bright western sky, her mind came back slowly to her particular issues in life. But they were no longer the big exasperatingly important things that had seemed to hold her life by a hundred painful hooks before she went into the cathedral. They were small still under this dome of evening, small even by the measure of the grey buildings to the right of her and the warm lit river to her left, by the measure of the clustering dark barges, the teeming trams, the streaming crowds of people, the note of the human process that sounds so loud there. She felt small even to herself, for the touch of beauty saves us from our own personalities, makes Gods of us to our own littleness. She passed under the railway bridge at Charing Cross, watched the square cluster of Westminster's pinnacles rise above her until they were out of sight overhead, ran up the little incline and round into Parliament Square, and was presently out on the riverside embankment again with the great chimneys of Chelsea smoking athwart the evening gold. And thence with a sudden effect of skies shut and curtains drawn she came by devious ways to the Fulham Road and the crowding traffic of Putney Bridge and Putney High Street and so home.

Snagsby, assisted by a new under-butler, a lean white-faced young man with red hair, received her ceremoniously and hovered serviceably about her. On the hall table lay three or four visiting cards of no importance, some circulars and two letters. She threw the circulars into the basket placed for them and opened her first letter. It was from Georgina; it was on several sheets and it began, "I still cannot believe that you refuse to give me the opportunity the director-general-ship of your hostels means to me. It is not as if you yourself had either the time or the abilities necessary for them yourself; you haven't, and there is something almost dog-in-the-manger-ish to my mind in the way in which you will not give me my chance, the chance I have always been longing for——"

At this point Lady Harman put down this letter for subsequent perusal and took its companion, which was addressed in an unfamiliar hand. It was from Alice Burnet and it was written in that sprawling hand and diffused style natural to a not very well educated person with a complicated story to tell in a state of unusual emotion. But the gist was in the first few sentences which announced that Alice had been evicted from the hostel. " I found my things on the pavement," wrote Alice.

Lady Harman became aware of Snagsby still hovering at hand.

" Mrs. Pembrose, my lady, came here this afternoon," he said, when he had secured her attention.

" Came here."

" She asked for you, my lady, and when I told her you were not at 'ome, she asked if she might see Sir Isaac."

" And did she ? "

" Sir Isaac saw her, my lady. They 'ad tea in the study."

" I wish I had been at home to see her," said Lady Harman, after a brief interval of reflection.

She took her two letters and turned to the staircase. They were still in her hand when presently she came into her husband's study. " I don't want a light," he said, as she put out her hand to the electric switch. His voice had a note of discontent but he was sitting in the armchair against the window so that she could not see his features.

" How are you feeling this afternoon ? " she asked.

" I'm feeling all right," he answered testily. He seemed to dislike inquiries after his health almost as much as he disliked neglect.

She came and stood by him and looked out from the dusk of the room into the garden darkening under a red-barred sky. "There is fresh trouble between Mrs. Pembrose and the girls," she said.

"She's been telling me about it."

"She's been here?"

"Pretty nearly an hour," said Sir Isaac.

Lady Harman tried to imagine that hour's interview on the spur of the moment and failed. She came to her immediate business. "I think," she said, "that she has been--high-handed. . . ."

"You would," said Sir Isaac after an interval.

His tone was hostile, so hostile that it startled her.

"Don't you?"

He shook his head. "My idees and your idees—or anyhow the idees you've got hold of—somewhere—somehow—— I don't know where you *get* your idees. We haven't got the same idees, anyhow. You got to keep order in these places—anyhow. . . ."

She perceived that she was in face of a prepared position. "I don't think," she threw out, "that she does keep order. She represses—and irritates. She gets an idea that certain girls are against her. . . ."

"And you get an idea she's against certain girls. . . ."

"Practically she expels them. She has in fact just turned one out into the street."

"You got to expel 'em. You got to. You can't run these places on sugar and water. There's a sort of girl, a sort of man, who makes trouble. There's a sort makes strikes, makes mischief, gets up grievances. You got to get rid of 'em somehow. You got to be practical somewhere. You can't go running these places on a lot of littry idees and all that. It's no good."

The phrase "littry idees" held Lady Harman's attention for a moment. But she could not follow it up to its implications, because she wanted to get on with the issue she had in hand.

"I want to be consulted about these expulsions. Girl after girl has been sent away——"

Sir Isaac's silhouette was obstinate.

"She knows her business," he said.

He seemed to feel the need of a justification. "They shouldn't make trouble."

On that they rested for a little while in silence. She began to realize with a gathering emotion that this matter was far more crucial than she had supposed. She had been thinking only of the reinstatement of Alice Burnet, she hadn't yet estimated just what that overriding of Mrs. Pembrose might involve.

"I don't want to have any girl go until I have looked into her case. It's—— It's vital."

"She says she can't run the show unless she has some power."

Neither spoke for some seconds. She had the feeling of hopeless vexation that might come to a child that has wandered into a trap. "I thought," she began. "These hostels——"

She stopped short.

Sir Isaac's hand tightened on the arm of his chair. "I started 'em to please you," he said. "I didn't start 'em to please your friends."

She turned her eyes quickly to his grey up-looking face.

"I didn't start them for you and that chap Brumley to play about with," he amplified. "And now you know about it, Elly."

The thing had found her unprepared. " As if—— "
she said at last.

" As if ! " he mocked.

She stood quite still staring blankly at this un-
manageable situation. He was the first to break
silence. He lifted one hand and dropped it again with
a dead impact on the arm of his chair. " I got the
things," he said, " and there they are. Anyhow,—they
got to be run in a proper way."

She made no immediate answer. She was seeking
desperately for phrases that escaped her. " Do you
think," she began at last. " Do you really think—— ? "

He stared out of the window. He answered in tones
of excessive reasonableness : " I didn't start these hostels
to be run by you and your—friend." He gave the
sentence the quality of an ultimatum, an irreducible
minimum.

" He's my friend," she explained, " only—because
he does work—for the hostels."

Sir Isaac seemed for a moment to attempt to consider that. Then he relapsed upon his predetermined
attitude. " God ! " he exclaimed, " but I been a
fool ! "

She decided that that must be ignored.

" I care more for those hostels than I care for anything—anything else in the world," she told him. " I
want them to work—I want them to succeed. . . . And
then——"

He listened in sceptical silence.

" Mr. Brumley is nothing to me but a helper.
He—— How can you imagine, Isaac——? *I !* How
can you dare ? To suggest——! "

" Very well," said Sir Isaac and reflected and made
his old familiar sound with his teeth. " Run the

hostels without him, Elly," he propounded. "Then I'll believe."

She perceived that suddenly she was faced by a test or a bargain. In the background of her mind the figure of Mr. Brumley, as she had seen him last, in brown and with a tie rather to one side, protested vainly. She did what she could for him on the spur of the moment. "But," she said, "he's so helpful. He's so—harmless."

"That's as may be," said Sir Isaac and breathed heavily.

"How can one suddenly turn on a friend?"

"I don't see that you ever wanted a friend," said Sir Isaac.

"He's been so good. It isn't reasonable, Isaac. When anyone has—*slaved*."

"I don't say he isn't a good sort of chap," said Sir Isaac, with that same note of almost superhuman rationality, "only—he isn't going to run my hostels."

"But what do you mean, Isaac?"

"I mean you got to choose."

He waited as if he expected her to speak and then went on.

"What it comes to is this, Elly, I'm about sick of that chap. I'm sick of him." He paused for a moment because his breath was short. "If you go on with the hostels he's—Phew—got to mizzle. *Then*—I don't mind—if you want that girl Burnet brought back in triumph . . . It'll make Mrs. Pembrose chuck the whole blessed show, you know, but I say—I don't mind. . . . Only in that case, I don't want to see or hear—or hear about—Phew—or hear about your Mr. Brumley again. And I don't want you to, either. . . . I'm being pretty reasonable and pretty patient over this, with people—people—talking right and left. Still, —there's a limit. . . . You've been going on—if I didn't know you were an innocent—in a way . . . I don't want to talk about that. There you are, Elly."

It seemed to her that she had always expected this to happen. But however much she had expected it to happen she was still quite unprepared with any course of action. She wanted with an equal want of limitation to keep both Mr. Brumley and her hostels.

"But Isaac," she said. "What do you suspect? What do you think? This friendship has been going on—— How can I end it suddenly?"

"Don't you be too innocent, Elly. You know and I know perfectly well what there is between men and women. I don't make out I know—anything I don't know. I don't pretend you are anything but straight. Only——"

He suddenly gave way to his irritation. His self-control vanished. "Damn it!" he cried, and his panting breath quickened; "the thing's got to end. As if I didn't understand! As if I didn't understand!"

She would have protested again but his voice held her. "It's got to end. It's got to end. Of course you haven't done anything, of course you don't know anything or think of anything. . . . Only here I am ill. . . . *You* wouldn't be sorry if I got worse. . . . *You* can wait; you can. . . . All right! All right! And there you stand, irritating me—arguing. You know—it chokes me. . . . Got to end, I tell you. . . . Got to end. . . ."

He beat at the arms of his chair and then put a hand to his throat.

"Go away," he cried to her. "Go to hell!"

§ 4

I cannot tell whether the reader is a person of swift decisions or one of the newer race of doubters; if he be the latter he will the better understand how Lady Harman did in the next two days make up her mind definitely and conclusively to two entirely opposed lines of action. She decided that her relations with Mr. Brumley, innocent as they were, must cease in the interests of the hostels and her struggle with Mrs. Pembrose, and she decided with quite equal certainty that her husband's sudden veto upon these relations was an intolerable tyranny that must be resisted with passionate indignation. Also she was surprised to find how difficult it was now to think of parting from Mr. Brumley. She made her way to these precarious conclusions and on from whichever it was to the other through a jungle of conflicting considerations and feelings. When she thought of Mrs. Pembrose and more particularly of the probable share of Mrs. Pembrose in her husband's objection to Mr. Brumley her indignation kindled. She perceived Mrs. Pembrose as a purely evil personality, as a spirit of espionage, distrust, calculated treachery and malignant intervention, as all that is evil in rule and officialism, and a vast wave of responsibility for all those difficult and feeble and likeable young women who elbowed and giggled and misunderstood and blundered and tried to live happily under the commanding stresses of Mrs. Pembrose's austerity carried her away. She had her duty to do to them and it overrode · every other duty. If a certain separation from Mr. Brumley's assiduous aid was demanded, was it too great a sacrifice? And no sooner was that settled than the whole question reopened with her indignant demand why anyone at any price had the right to prohibit a friendship that she had so conscientiously kept innocent. If she gave way to this outrageous restriction to-day, what fresh limitations might not Sir Isaac impose to-morrow? And now, she was so embarrassed in her struggle by his health. She could not go to him and have things out with him, she could not directly defy him, because that might mean a suffocating seizure for him. . . .

It was entirely illogical, no doubt, but extremely natural for Lady Harman to decide that she must communicate her decision, whichever one it was, to Mr. Brumley in a personal interview. She wrote to him and arranged to meet and talk to him in Kew Gardens, and with a feeling of discretion went thither not in the automobile but in a taxi-cab. And so delicately now were her two irrevocable decisions balanced in her mind that twice on her way to Kew she swayed over from one to the other.

Arrived at the gardens she found herself quite disinclined to begin the announcement of either decision. She was quite exceptionally glad to see Mr. Brumley; he was dressed in a new suit of lighter brown that became him very well indeed, the day was warm and bright, a day of scyllas and daffodils and snow-upon-the-mountains and green-powdered trees and frank sunshine,—and the warmth of her feelings for her friend merged indistinguishably with the springtime stir and glow. They walked across the bright turf together in a state of unjustifiable happiness, purring little admirations at the ingenious elegance of creation at its best as gardeners set it out for our edification, and the whole tenor of Lady Harman's mind was to make this occasion an escape from the particular business that had brought her thither.

"We'll look for daffodils away there towards the river under the trees," said Mr. Brumley, and it seemed preposterous not to enjoy those daffodils at least before she broached the great issue between an irresistible force and an immoveable post, that occupied her mental background.

Mr. Brumley was quite at his best that afternoon. He was happy, gay and deferential; he made her realize by his every tone and movement that if he had his choice of the whole world that afternoon and all its inhabitants and everything, there was no other place in which he would be, no other companion, no other occupation than this he had. He talked of spring and flowers, quoted poets and added the treasures of a well-stored mind to the amenities of the day. "It's good to take a holiday at times," he said, and after that it was more difficult than ever to talk about the trouble of the hostels.

She was able to do this at last while they were having tea in the little pavilion near the pagoda. It was the old pavilion, the one that Miss Alimony's suffragettes were afterwards to burn down in order to demonstrate the relentless logic of women. They did it in the same eventful week when Miss Alimony was, she declared, so nearly carried off by White Slave Traders (disguised as nurses but, fortunately for her, smelling of brandy) from the Brixton Temperance Bazaar. But in those simpler days the pavilion still existed; it was tended by agreeable waiters whose evening dress was mitigated by cheerful little straw hats, and an enormous multitude of valiant and smutty Cockney sparrows chirped and squeaked and begged and fluttered and fought, venturing to the very tables and feet of the visitors. And here, a little sobered from their first elation by much walking about and the presence of jam and watercress, Mr. Brumley and Lady Harman could think again of the work they were doing for the reconstitution of society upon collective lines.

She began to tell him of the conflict between Mrs. Pembrose and Alice Burnet that threatened the latter with extinction. She found it more convenient to talk at first as though the strands of decision were still all in her hands; afterwards she could go on to the peculiar complication of the situation through the unexpected weakening of her position in relation to Mrs. Pembrose. She described the particular of the new trouble, the perplexing issue between the "ladylike," for which as a feminine ideal there was so much to be said on the one hand and the "genial," which was also an admirable quality, on the other. "You see," she said, "it's very rude to cough at people and make noises, but then it's so difficult to explain to the others that it's equally rude to go past people and pretend not to see or hear them. Girls of that sort always seem so much more underbred when they are trying to be superior than when they are not; they get so stiff and—exasperating. And this keeping out of the Union because it isn't genteel, it's the very essence of the trouble with all these employees. We've discussed that so often. Those drapers' girls seem full of such cold, selfish, base, pretentious notions; much more full even than our refreshment girls. And then as if it wasn't all difficult enough comes Mrs. Pembrose and her wardresses doing all sorts of hard, clumsy things, and one can't tell them just how little they are qualified to judge good behaviour. Their one idea of discipline is to speak to people as if they were servants and to be distant and crushing. And long before one can do anything come trouble and tart replies and reports of " gross impertinence " and expulsion. We keep on expelling girls. This is the fourth time girls have had to go. What is to become of them ? I know this Burnet girl quite well as you know. She's just a human, kindly little woman. . . . She'll feel disgraced. . . . How can I let a thing like that occur ? "

She spread her hands apart over the tea things.

Mr. Brumley held his chin in his hand and said " Um " and looked judicial, and admired Lady Harman very much, and tried to grasp the whole trouble and wring out a solution. He made some admirable generalizations about the development of a new social feeling in response to changed conditions, but apart from a remark that Mrs. Pembrose was all organization and no psychology, and quite the wrong person for her position, he said nothing in the slightest degree contributory to the particular drama under consideration. From that utterance, however, Lady Harman would no doubt have gone on to the slow, tentative but finally conclusive statement of the new difficulty that had arisen out of her husband's jealousy and to the discussion of the more fundamental decisions it forced upon her, if a peculiar blight had not fallen upon their conversation and robbed it at last of even an appearance of ease.

This blight crept upon their minds. . . . It began first with Mr. Brumley.

Mr. Brumley was rarely free from self-consciousness. Whenever he was in a restaurant or any such place of assembly, then whatever he did or whatever he said he had a kind of surplus attention, a quickening of the ears, a wandering of the eyes, to the groups and individuals round about him. And while he had seemed entirely occupied with Lady Harman, he had nevertheless been aware from the outset that a dingy and inappropriate-looking man in a bowler hat and a ready-made suit of grey, was listening to their conversation from an adjacent table.

This man had entered the pavilion oddly. He had seemed to dodge in and hesitate. Then he had chosen his table rather deliberately—and he kept looking, and trying not to seem to look.

That was not all. Mr. Brumley's expression was overcast by the effort to recall something. He sat elbows on table and leant forward towards Lady Harman and at the blossom-laden trees outside the pavilion and trifled with two fingers on his lips and spoke between them in a voice that was speculative and confidential and muffled and mysterious. " Where have I seen our friend to the left before ? "

She had been aware of his distraction for some time. She glanced at the man and found nothing remarkable in him. She tried to go on with her explanations.

Mr. Brumley appeared attentive and then he said again : " But where have I seen him ? "

And from that point their talk was blighted ; the heart seemed to go out of her. Mr. Brumley she felt was no longer taking in what she was saying. At the time she couldn't in any way share his preoccupation. But what had been difficult before became hopeless and she could no longer feel that even presently she would be able to make him understand the peculiar alternatives before her. They drifted back by the great conservatory and the ornamental water, aripple with ducks and swans, to the gates where his taxi waited.

Even then it occurred to her that she ought to tell him something of the new situation. But now their time was running out, she would have to be concise, and what wife could ever say abruptly and offhand that frequent fact, " Oh, by the by, my husband is jealous of you ? " Then she had an impulse to tell him simply, without any explanation at all, that for a time he must not meet her. And while she gathered herself together for that, his preoccupations intervened again.

He stood up in the open taxi-cab and looked back. "That chap," he said, " is following us."

§ 5

The effect of this futile interview upon Lady Harman was remarkable. She took to herself an absurd conviction that this inconclusiveness had been an achievement. Confronted by a dilemma, she had chosen neither horn and assumed an attitude of inoffensive defiance. Springs in England vary greatly in their character ; some are easterly and quarrelsome, some are north-westerly and wetly disastrous, a bleak invasion from the ocean ; some are but the broken beginnings of what are not so much years as stretches of meteorological indecision, This particular spring was essentially a south-westerly spring, good and friendly, showery but in the lightest way and so softly reassuring as to be gently hilarious. It was a spring to get into the blood of anyone ; it gave Lady Harman the feeling that Mrs. Pembrose would certainly be dealt with properly and without unreasonable delay by Heaven, and that meanwhile it was well to take the good things of existence as cheerfully as possible. The good things she took were very innocent things. Feeling unusually well and enjoying great draughts of spring air and sunshine were the chief. And she took them only for three brief days. She carried the children down to Black Strand to see her daffodils, and her daffodils surpassed expectation. There was a delirium of blackthorn in the new wild garden she had annexed from the woods and a close carpet of encouraged wild primroses. Even the Putney garden was full of happy surprises. The afternoon following her visit to Black Strand was so warm that she had tea with her family in great gaiety on the lawn under the cedar. Her offspring were unusually sweet that day, they had new blue cotton sunbonnets, and Baby and Annette at least succeeded in being pretty. And Millicent, under the new Swiss governess, had acquired, it seemed quite suddenly, a glib colloquial French that somehow reconciled one to the extreme thinness and shapelessness of her legs.

Then an amazing new fact broke into this gleam of irrational contentment, a shattering new fact. She found she was being watched. She discovered that dingy man in the grey suit following her.

The thing came upon her one afternoon. She was starting out for a talk with Georgina. She felt so well, so confident of the world that it was intolerable to think of Georgina harbouring resentment; she resolved she would go and have things out with her and make it clear just how impossible it was to impose a Director-General upon her husband. She became aware of the man in grey as she walked down Putney Hill.

She recognized him at once. He was at the corner of Redfern Road and still unaware of her existence. He was leaning against the wall with the habituated pose of one who is frequently obliged to lean against walls for long periods of time, and he was conversing in an elucidatory manner with the elderly crossing-sweeper who still braves the motor-cars at that point. He became aware of her emergence with a start, he ceased to lean and became observant.

He was one of those men whose face suggests the word "muzzle," with an erect combative nose and a forward slant of the body from the rather inturned feet. He wore an observant bowler hat a little too small for him, and there is something about the tail of his jacket—as though he had been docked.

She passed at a stride to the acceptance of Mr. Brumley's hitherto incredible suspicion. Her pulses quickened. It came into her head to see how far this man would go in following her. She went on demurely down the hill leaving him quite unaware that she had seen him.

She was amazed, and after her first belief incredulous again. Could Isaac be going mad? At the corner she satisfied herself of the grey man's proximity and hailed a taxi-cab. The man in grey came nosing across to listen to her directions and hear where she was going.

"Please drive up the hill until I tell you," she said, " slowly "—and had the satisfaction, if one may call it a satisfaction, of seeing the grey man dive towards the taxi-cab rank. Then she gave herself up to hasty scheming.

She turned her taxi-cab abruptly when she was certain of being followed, went back into London, turned again and made for Westridge's great stores in Oxford Street. The grey man ticked up twopences in pursuit. All along the Brompton Road he pursued her with his nose like the jib of a ship.

She was excited and interested, and not nearly so shocked as she ought to have been. It didn't somehow jar as it ought to have jarred with her idea of Sir Isaac. Watched by a detective! This then was the completion of the conditional freedom she had won by smashing that window. She might have known. . . .

She was astonished and indignant but not nearly so entirely indignant as a noble heroine should have been. She was certainly not nearly so queenly as Mrs. Sawbridge would have shown herself under such circumstances. It may have been due to some plebeian strain in her father's blood that over and above her proper indignation she was extremely interested. She wanted to know what manner of man it was whose nose was just appearing above the window edge of the taxicab behind. In her inexperienced inattention she had never yet thought it was possible that men could be hired to follow women.

She sat a little forward, thinking.

How far would he follow her and was it possible to shake him off? Or are such followers so expert that once upon a scent, they are like the Indian hunting dog, inevitable. She must see.

She paid off her taxi at Westridge's and, with the skill of her sex observed him by the window reflection, counting the many doors of the establishment. Would he try to watch them all? There were also some round the corner. No, he was going to follow her in. She had a sudden desire, an unreasonable desire, perhaps an instinctive desire to see that man among baby-linen. It was in her power for a time to wreathe him with incongruous objects. This was the sort of fancy a woman must control. . . .

He stalked her with an unreal sang-froid. He ambushed behind a display of infants' socks. Driven to buy by a saleswoman he appeared to be demanding improbable varieties of infants' socks.

Are these watchers and trackers sometimes driven to buying things in shops ? If so, strange items must figure in accounts of expenses. If he bought those socks, would they appear in Sir Isaac's bill ? She felt a sudden craving for the sight of Sir Isaac's Private Detective Account. And as for the articles themselves, what became of them ? She knew her husband well enough to feel sure that if he paid for anything he would insist upon having it. But where—where did he keep them ? . . .

But now the man's back was turned ; he was no doubt improvising paternity and an extreme fastidiousness in baby's footwear—— Now for it !—through departments of deepening indelicacy to the lift !

But he had considered that possibility of embarassment ; he got round by some other way, he was just in time to hear the lift gate clash upon a calmly preoccupied lady, who still seemed as unaware of his existence as the sky.

He was running upstairs, when she descended again, without getting out ; he stopped at the sight of her shooting past him, their eyes met and there was something appealing in his. He was very moist and his bowler was flagging. He had evidently started out in the morning with misconceptions about the weather. And it was clear he felt he had blundered in coming into Westridge's. Before she could get a taxi he was on the pavement behind her, hot but pursuing.

She sought in her mind for corner shops, with doors on this street and that. She exercised him upon Peter Robinson's and Debenham and Freebody's and then started for the monument. But on her way to the monument she thought of the moving staircase at Harrod's. If she went up and down on this, she wanted to know what he would do, would he run up and down the fixed flight? He did. Several times. And then she bethought herself of the Piccadilly tube ; he got in at Brompton Road and got out at Down Street and then got in again and went to South Kensington and he darted in and out of adjacent carriages and got into lifts by curious retrograde movements, being apparently under the erroneous impression that his back was less characteristic than his face.

By this time he was evidently no longer unaware of her intelligent interest in his movements. It was clear too that he had received a false impression that she wanted to shake him off and that all the sleuth in him was aroused. He was dishevelled and breathing hard and getting a little close and coarse in his pursuit, but he was sticking to it with a puckered intensified resolution. He came up into the South Kensington air open-mouthed and sniffing curiously, but invincible.

She discovered suddenly that she did not like him at all, and that she wanted to go home.

She took a taxi, and then away in the wilds of the Fulham Road she had her crowning idea. She stopped the cab at a dingy little furniture shop, paid the driver exorbitantly and instructed him to go right back to South Kensington station, buy her an evening paper and return for her. The pursuer drew up thirty yards away, fell into her trap, paid off his cab and feigned to be interested by a small window full of penny toys, cheap chocolate and cocoanut ice. She bought herself a brass door weight, paid for it hastily and posted herself just within the furniture-shop door.

Then you see her cab returned suddenly and she got in at once and left him stranded.

He made a desperate effort to get a motor omnibus. She saw him rushing across the traffic gesticulating. Then he collided with a boy with a basket on a bicycle —not so far as she could see injuriously, they seemed to leap at once into a crowd and an argument, and then he was hidden from her by a bend in the road.

§ 6

For a little while her mind was full of fragments of speculation about this man. Was he a married man ? Was he very much away from home ? What did he earn ? Were there ever disputes about his expenses ? . . .

She must ask Isaac. For she was determined to go home and challenge her husband. She felt buoyed up by indignation and the consciousness of innocence. . . .

And then she felt an odd little doubt whether her innocence was quite so manifest as she supposed ?

That doubt grew to uncomfortable proportions.

For two years she had been meeting Mr. Brumley as confidently as though they had been invisible beings, and now she had to rack her brains for just what might be mistaken, what might be misconstrued. There was nothing, she told herself, nothing, it was all as open as the day, and still her mind groped about for some forgotten circumstance, something gone almost out of memory that would bear misinterpretation. . . . How should she begin ? " Isaac." she would say, " I am being followed about London." Suppose he denied his complicity ! How could he deny his complicity ?

The cab ran in through the gates of her home and stopped at the door. Snagsby came hurrying down the steps with a face of consternation. "Sir Isaac, my lady, has come home in a very sad state indeed."

Beyond Snagsby in the hall she came upon a lost-looking round-eyed Florence.

"Daddy's ill again," said Florence.

"You run to the nursery," said Lady Harman.

"I thought I might help," said Florence. "I don't want to play with the others."

"No, run away to the nursery."

"I want to see the ossygen let out," said Florence petulantly to her mother's unsympathetic back. "I *never* see the ossygen let out. Mum—my! . . ."

Lady Harman found her husband on the couch in his bedroom. He was propped up in a sitting position with every available cushion and pillow. His coat and waistcoat and collar had been taken off and his shirt and vest torn open. The nearest doctor, Almsworth, was in attendance, but oxygen had not arrived, and Sir Isaac with an expression of bitter malignity upon his face was fighting desperately for breath. If anything his malignity deepened at the sight of his wife. "Damned climate," he gasped. "Wouldn't have come back—except for *your* foolery."

It seemed to help him to say that. He took a deep inhalation, pressed his lips tightly together, and nodded at her to confirm his words.

"If he's fanciful," said Almsworth. "If in any way your presence irritates him—— "

"Let her stay," said Sir Isaac. "It—pleases her. . . ."

Almsworth's colleague entered with the long-desired oxygen cylinder.

§ 7

And now every other interest in life was dominated, and every other issue postponed by the immense urgencies of Sir Isaac's illness. It had entered upon a new phase. It was manifest that he could no longer live in England, that he must go to some warm and kindly climate. There and with due precautions and observances Almsworth assured Lady Harman he might survive for many years—"an invalid, of course, but a capable one."

For some time the business of the International Stores had been preparing itself for this withdrawal. Sir Isaac had been entrusting his managers with increased responsibility and making things ready for the flotation of a company that would take the whole network of enterprises off his hands. Charterson was associated with him in this, and everything was sufficiently definite to be managed from any continental resort to which his doctors chose to send him. They chose to send him to Santa Margherita on the Ligurian coast near Rapallo and Porto Fino.

It was old Bergener of Marienbad who chose this place. Sir Isaac had wanted to go to Marienbad, his first resort abroad ; he had a lively and indeed an exaggerated memory of his Kur there; his growing disposition to distrust had turned him against his London specialist, and he had caused Lady Harman to send gigantic telegrams of inquiry to old Bergener before he would be content. But Bergener would not have him at Marienbad ; it wasn't the place, it was the wrong time of year, there was the very thing for them at the Regency Hotel at Santa Margherita, an entire dépendance in a beautiful garden right on the sea, admirably furnished and adapted in every way to Sir Isaac's peculiar needs. There, declared Doctor Bergener, with a proper attendant, due precaution, occasional oxygen and no excitement he would live indefinitely, that is to say eight or ten years. And attracted by the eight or ten years, which was three more than the London specialist offered, Sir Isaac finally gave in and consented to be taken to Santa Margherita.

He was to go as soon as possible, and he went in a special train and with an immense elaboration of attendance and comforts. They took with them a young doctor their specialist at Marienbad had recommended, a bright young Bavarian with a perfectly square blonde head, an incurable frock coat, the manners of the less kindly type of hotel-porter and luggage which apparently consisted entirely of apparatus, an arsenal of strange-shaped shining black cases. He joined them in London and went right through with them. From Genoa at his request they obtained the services of a trained nurse, an amiable fluent-shaped woman who knew only Italian and German. For reasons that he declined to give, but which apparently had something to do with the suffrage agitation, he would have nothing to do with an English trained nurse. They had also a stenographer and typist for Sir Isaac's correspondence, and Lady Harman had a secretary, a young lady with glasses named Summersly Satchell who obviously reserved opinions of a harshly intellectual kind and had previously been in the service of the late Lady Mary Justin. She established unfriendly relations with the young doctor at an early date by attempting, he said, to learn German from him. Then there was a maid for Lady Harman, an assistant maid, and a valet-attendant for Sir Isaac.

The rest of the service in the dépendance was supplied by the hotel management.

It took some weeks to assemble this expedition and transport it to its place of exile. Arrangements had to be made for closing the Putney house and establishing the children with Mrs. Harman at Black Strand. There was an exceptional amount of packing up to do, for this time Lady Harman felt she was not coming back— it might be for years. They were going out to warmth and sunlight for the rest of Sir Isaac's life.

He was entering upon the last phase in the slow disorganization of his secretions and the progressive hardening of his arterial tissues that had become his essential history. His appearance had altered much in the last few months; he had become visibly smaller, his face in particular had become sharp and little-featured. It was more and more necessary for him to sit up in order to breathe with comfort, he slept sitting up; and his senses were affected, he complained of strange tastes in his food, quarrelled with the cook and had fits of sickness. Sometimes, latterly, he had complained of strange sounds, like air whistling in water-pipes, he said, that had no existence outside his ears. Moreover, he was steadily more irritable and more suspicious and less able to control himself when angry. A long-hidden vein of vile and abusive language, hidden, perhaps, since the days of Mr. Gambard's college at Ealing, came to the surface. . . .

For some days after his seizure Lady Harman was glad to find in the stress of his necessities an excuse for disregarding altogether the crisis in the hostels and the perplexing problem of her relations to Mr. Brumley. She wrote two brief notes to the latter gentleman breaking appointments and pleading pressure of business.

Then, at first during intervals of sleeplessness at night, and presently during the day, the danger and ugliness of her outlook began to trouble her. She was still, she perceived, being watched, but whether that was because her husband had failed to change whatever orders he had given, or because he was still keeping himself minutely informed of her movements, she could not tell. She was now constantly with him, and except for small spiteful outbreaks and occasional intervals of still and silent malignity, he tolerated and utilized her attentions. It was clear his jealousy of her rankled, a jealousy that made him even resentful at her health and ready to complain of any brightness of eye or vigour of movement. They had drifted far apart from the possibility of any real discussion of the hostels since that talk in the twilit study. To re-open that now or to complain of the shadowing pursuer who dogged her steps abroad would have been to precipitate Mr. Brumley's dismissal.

Even at the cost of letting things drift at the hostels for a time she wished to avoid that question. She would not see him, but she would not shut the door upon him. So far as the detective was concerned she could avoid discussion by pretending to be unaware of his existence, and as for the hostels—the hostels each day were left until the morrow.

She had learnt many things since the days of her first rebellion, and she knew now that this matter of the man friend and nothing else in the world is the central issue in the emancipation of women. The difficulty of him is latent in every other restriction of which women complain. The complete emancipation of women will come with the complete emancipation of humanity from jealousy—and no sooner. All other emancipations are shams until a woman may go about as freely with this man as with that, and nothing remains for emancipation when she can. In the innocence of her first revolt this question of friendship had seemed to Lady Harman the simplest, most reasonable of minor concessions, but that was simply because Mr. Brumley hadn't in those days been talking of love to her, nor she been peeping through that once locked door. Now she perceived how entirely Sir Isaac was by his standards justified.

And after all that was recognized she remained indisposed to give up Mr. Brumley.

Yet her sense of evil things happening in the hostels was a deepening distress. It troubled her so much that she took the disagreeable step of asking Mrs. Pembrose to meet her at the Bloomsbury Hostel and talk out the expulsions. She found that lady alertly defensive, entrenched behind expert knowledge and pretension generally. Her little blue eyes seemed harder than ever, the metallic resonance in her voice more marked, the lisp stronger. "Of course, Lady Harman, if you were to have some practical experience of control—— " and "Three times I have given these girls every opportunity—*every* opportunity."

"It seems so hard to drive these girls out," repeated Lady Harman. "They're such human creatures."

"You have to think of the ones who remain. You must—think of the Institution as a Whole."

"I wonder," said Lady Harman, peering down into profundities for a moment. Below the great truth glimmered and vanished that Institutions were made for man and not man for Institutions.

"You see," she went on, rather to herself than to Mrs. Pembrose, "we shall be away now for a long time."

Mrs. Pembrose betrayed no excesses of grief.

"It's no good for me to interfere and then leave everything. . . ."

"That way spells utter disorganization," said Mrs. Pembrose.

" But I wish something could be done to lessen the harshness—to save the pride—of such a girl as Alice Burnet. Practically you tell her she isn't fit to associate with—the other girls."

"She's had her choice and warning after warning."

" I daresay she's—stiff. Oh !—she's difficult. But—being expelled is bitter."

" I've not *expelled* her—technically."

" She thinks she's expelled. . . ."

" You'd rather perhaps, Lady Harman, that *I* was expelled."

The dark lady lifted her eyes to the little bridling figure in front of her for a moment and dropped them again. She had had an unspeakable thought, that Mrs. Pembrose wasn't a gentlewoman, and that this sort of thing was a business for the gentle and for nobody else in the world. " I'm only anxious not to hurt anyone if I can help it," said Lady Harman.

She went on with her attempt to find some way of compromise with Mrs. Pembrose that should save the spirit of the new malcontents. She was much too concerned on account of the things that lay ahead of them to care for her own pride with Mrs. Pembrose. But that good lady had all the meagre inflexibilities of her class and at last Lady Harman ceased.

She came out into the great hall of the handsome staircase, ushered by Mrs. Pembrose as a guest is ushered by a host. She looked at the spacious proportion of the architecture and thought of the hopes and imaginations she had allowed to centre upon this place. It was to have been a glowing home of happy people, and over it all brooded the chill stillness of rules and regulations and methodical suppressions and tactful discouragement. It was an Institution, it had the empty orderliness of an Institution, Mrs. Pembrose had just called it an Institution, and so Susan Burnet had prophesied it would become five years or more ago. It was a dream subjugated to reality.

So it seemed to Lady Harman must all dreams be subjugated to reality, and the tossing spring greenery of the square, the sunshine, the tumult of sparrows and the confused sound of distant traffic, framed as it was in the hard dark outline of the entrance door, was as near as the promise of joy could ever come to her. " Caught and spoilt," that seemed to be the very essential of her life ; just as it was of these Hostels, all the hopes, the imaginings, the sweet large anticipations, the generosities, and stirring warm desires. . . .

Perhaps Lady Harman had been a little overworking with her preparations for exile. Because as these unhappy thoughts passed through her mind she realized that she was likely to weep. It was extremely undesirable that Mrs. Pembrose should see her weeping.

But Mrs. Pembrose did see her weeping, saw her dark eyes swimming with uncontrollable tears, watched her walk past her and out, without a word or a gesture of farewell.

A kind of perplexity came upon the soul of Mrs. Pembrose. She watched the tall figure descend to her car and enter it and dispose itself gracefully and depart. . . .

" Hysterical," whispered Mrs. Pembrose at last and was greatly comforted.

"Childish," said Mrs. Pembrose sipping further consolation for an unwonted spiritual discomfort.

"Besides," said Mrs. Pembrose, "what else can one do?"

§ 8

Sir Isaac was greatly fatigued by his long journey to Santa Margherita in spite of every expensive precaution to relieve him; but as soon as the effect of that wore off, his recovery under the system Bergener had prescribed, was for a time remarkable. In a little while he was out of bed again and in an armchair. Then the young doctor began to talk of drives. They had no car with them, so he went into Genoa and spent an energetic day securing the sweetest-running automobile he could find and having it refitted for Sir Isaac's peculiar needs. In this they made a number of excursions through the hot beauty of the Italian afternoons, eastward to Genoa, westward to Sestri and northward towards Montallegro. Then they went up to the summit of the Monte de Porto Fino and Sir Isaac descended and walked about and looked at the view and praised Bergener. After that he was encouraged to visit the gracious old monastery that overhangs the road to Porto Fino

At first Lady Harman did her duty of control and association with an apathetic resignation. This had to go on—for eight or ten years. Then her imagination began to stir again. There came a friendly letter from Mr. Brumley and she answered with a description of the colour of the sea and the charm and wonder of its tideless shore. The three elder children wrote queer little letters and she answered them. She went into Rapallo and got herself a carriageful of Tauchnitz books. . . .

That visit to the monastery on the Porto Fino road was like a pleasant little glimpse into the brighter realities of the Middle Ages. The place, which is used as a home of rest for convalescent Carthusians, chanced to be quite empty and deserted; the Bavarian rang a jangling bell again and again and at last gained the attention of an old gardener working in the vineyard above, an unkempt, unshaven, ungainly creature dressed in scarce decent rags of brown, who was yet courteous-minded and, albeit crack-voiced, with his yellow-fanged mouth full of gracious polysyllables. He hobbled off to get a key and returned through the still heat of the cobbled yard outside the monastery gates, and took them into cool airy rooms and showed them clean and simple cells in shady corridors, and a delightful orangery, and led them to a beautiful terrace that looked out upon the glowing quivering sea. And he became very anxious to tell them something about " Francesco "; they could not understand him until the doctor caught " Battaglia " and " Pavia " and had an inspiration. Francis the First, he explained in clumsy but understandable English, slept here, when he was a prisoner of the Emperor and all was lost but honour. They looked at the slender pillars and graceful archings about them.

" Chust as it was now," the young doctor said, his imagination touched for a moment by mere unscientific things. . . .

They returned to their dépendance in a state of mutual contentment, Sir Isaac scarcely tired, and Lady Harman ran upstairs to change her dusty dress for a fresher muslin, while he went upon the doctor's

arm to the balcony where tea was to be served to
them.

She came down to find her world revolutionized.

On the table in the balcony the letters had been
lying convenient to his chair and he—it may be without troubling to read the address, had seized the
uppermost and torn it open.

He was holding that letter now a little crumpled in
his hand.

She had walked close up to the table before she
realized the change. The little eyes that met hers
were afire with hatred, his lips were white and pressed
together tightly, his nostrils were dilated in his
struggle for breath. " I knew it," he gasped.

She clung to her dignity though she felt suddenly
weak within. " That letter," she said, " was addressed
to me."

There was a gleam of derision in his eyes.

" Look at it !" he said, and flung it towards her.

" My private letter ! "

" Look at it !" he repeated.

" What right have you to open my letter ? "

" Friendship !" he said. " Harmless friendship !
Look what your—friend says !"

" Whatever there was in my letter—— "

" Oh !" cried Sir Isaac. " Don't come *that* over
me ! Don't you try it ! Oooh ! phew !" He
struggled for breath for a time. " He's so harmless.
He's so helpful. He— Read it, you—— "

He hesitated and then hurled a strange word
at her.

She glanced at the letter on the table, but made
no movement to touch it. Then she saw that her
husband's face was reddening and that his arm waved

helplessly. His eyes, deprived abruptly of all the fury of conflict, implored assistance.

She darted to the French window that opened into the dining-room from the balcony. " Doctor Greve ! " she cried. " Doctor Greve ! "

Behind her the patient was making distressful sounds. " Doctor Greve," she screamed, and from above she heard the Bavarian shouting and then the noise of his coming down the stairs.

He shouted some direction in German as he ran past her. By an inspiration she guessed he wanted the nurse.

Miss Summersley Satchell appeared in the doorway and became helpful.

Then everyone in the house seemed to be converging upon the balcony.

It was an hour before Sir Isaac was in bed and sufficiently allayed for her to go to her own room. Then she thought of Mr. Brumley's letter, and recovered it from the table on the balcony where it had been left in the tumult of her husband's seizure.

It was twilight and the lights were on. She stood under one of them and read with two moths circling about her. . . .

Mr. Brumley had had a mood of impassioned declaration. He had alluded to his " last moments of happiness at Kew." He said he would rather kiss the hem of her garment than be the " lord of any other woman's life."

It was all so understandable—looked at in the proper light. It was all so impossible to explain. And why had she let it happen ? Why had she let it happen ?

§ 9

The young doctor was a little puzzled and rather
offended by Sir Isaac's relapse. He seemed to consider
it incorrect and was on the whole disposed to blame
Lady Harman. He might have had such a seizure, the
young doctor said, later, but not now. He would be
thrown back for some weeks, then he would begin to
mend again, and then whatever he said, whatever he did,
Lady Harman must do nothing to contradict him. For
a whole day Sir Isaac lay inert, in a cold sweat. He
consented once to attempt eating, but sickness overcame
him. He seemed so ill that all the young doctor's reas-
surances could not convince Lady Harman that he would
recover. Then suddenly towards evening his arrested
vitality was flowing again, the young doctor ceased to
be anxious for his own assertions, the patient could sit
up against a pile of pillows and breathe and attend to
affairs. There was only one affair he really seemed
anxious to attend to. His first thought when he
realized his returning strength was of his wife. But the
young doctor would not let him talk that night.

Next morning he seemed still stronger. He was
restless and at last demanded Lady Harman again.

This time the young doctor transmitted the message.

She came to him forthwith and found him, white-
faced and unfamiliar-looking, his hands gripping the
quilt and his eyes burning with hatred.

" You thought I'd forgotten," was his greeting.

" Don't argue," signalled the doctor from the end
of Sir Isaac's bed.

" I've been thinking it out," said Sir Isaac. " When
you were thinking I was too ill to think. . . . I know
better now."

He sucked in his lips and then went on. " You've got to send for old Crappen," he said. " I'm going to alter things. I had a plan. But that would have been letting you off too easy. See? So—you send for old Crappen."

" What do you mean to do? "

" Never you mind, my lady, never you mind. You send for old Crappen."

She waited for a moment. " Is that all you want me to do? "

" I'm going to make it all right about those Hostels. Don't you fear. You and your Hostels! You shan't *touch* those hostels ever again. Ever. Mrs. Pembrose go! Why! You ain't worthy to touch the heel of her shoe! Mrs. Pembrose! "

He gathered together all his forces and suddenly expelled with rousing force the word he had already applied to her on the day of the intercepted letter.

He found it seemed great satisfaction in the sound and taste of it. He repeated it thrice. " Zut," cried the doctor, " Sssh! "

Then Sir Isaac intimated his sense that calm was imperative. " You send for Crappen," he said with a quiet earnestness.

She had become now so used to terms of infamy during the last year or so, so accustomed to forgive them as part of his suffering, that she seemed not to hear the insult.

" Do you want him at once? " she asked. " Shall I telegraph? "

" Want him at once! " He dropped his voice to a whisper. " Yes, you fool—yes. Telegraph. (Phew.) Telegraph. . . I mustn't get angry, you know. You —telegraph."

He became suddenly still.   But his eyes were active with hate.

She glanced at the doctor, then moved to the door.

" I will send a telegram," she said, and left him still malignant.

She closed the door softly and walked down the long cool passage towards her own room. . . .

§ 10

She had to be patient.   She had to be patient. This sort of thing had to go on from crisis to crisis. It might go on for years.   She could see no remedy and no escape.

What else was there to do but be patient ?   It was all amazing unjust, but to be a married women she was beginning to understand is to be outside justice. It is autocracy.   She had once imagined otherwise, and most of her life had been the slow unlearning of that initial error.   She had imagined that the hostels were hers simply because he had put it in that way. They had never been anything but his, and now it was manifest he would do what he liked with his own.   The law takes no cognizance of the unwritten terms of a domestic reconciliation.

She sat down at the writing-table the hotel management had improvised for her.

She rested her chin on her hand and tried to think out her position.   But what was there to think out, seeing that nature and law and custom have conspired together to put women altogether under the power of jealous and acquisitive men ?

She drew the telegram form towards her.

She was going to write a telegram that she knew would bring Crappen headlong—to disinherit her absolutely. And—it suddenly struck her—her husband had trusted her to write it. She was going to do what he had trusted her to do. . . . But it was absurd.

She sat making patterns of little dots with her pencil point upon the telegram form, and there was a faint smile of amusement upon her lips.

It was absurd—and everything was absurd. What more was to be said or thought about it? This was the lot of woman. She had made her struggle, rebelled her little bit of rebellion. Most other women no doubt had done as much. It made no difference in the long run.

But it was hard to give up the hostels. She had been foolish of course, but she had not let them make her feel *real*. And she wasn't real. She was a wife— just *this*. . . .

She sighed and bestirred herself and began to write.

Then abruptly she stopped writing.

For three years her excuse for standing—everything, had been these hostels. If now the hostels were to be wrenched out of her hands, if at her husband's death she was to be stripped of every possession and left a helpless dependant on her own children, if for all her good behaviour she was to be insulted by his frantic suspicions so long as he lived and then disgraced by his posthumous mistrust; was there any reason why she should go on standing anything any more? Away there in England was Mr. Brumley, *her* man, ready with service and devotion. . . .

It was a profoundly comforting thing to think of him there as hers. He was hers. He'd given so much

and on the whole so well.   If at last she were to go to
him. . . .

Yet when she came to imagine the reality of the
step that was in her mind, it took upon itself a chill
and forbidding strangeness.   It was like stepping out
of a familiar house into empty space.   What could it
be like ?   To take some odd trunks with her, meet him
somewhere, travel, travel through the evening, travel
past nightfall ?   The bleak strangeness of that going
out never to return !

Her imagination could give her no figure of Mr.
Brumley as intimate, as habitual.   She could as easily
imagine his skeleton.   He remained in all this queer
speculation something friendly, something incidental,
more than a trifle disembodied, entirely devoted of
course in that hovering way—but hovering. . . .

And she wanted to be free.   It wasn't Mr. Brumley
she wanted ; he was but a means—if indeed he was a
means—to an end.   The person she wanted, the person
she had always wanted—was *herself*.   Could Mr.
Brumley give her that ?   Would Mr. Brumley give her
that ?   Was it conceivable he would carry sacrifice to
such a pitch as that ? . . .

And what nonsense was this dream !   Here was
her husband needing her.   And the children, whose
inherent ungainliness, whose ungracious spirits demanded a perpetual palliation of culture and instilled
deportment.   What honest over-nurse was there for
him or helper and guide and friend for them, if she
withdrew ?   There was something undignified in a
flight for mere happiness.   There was something
vindictive in flight from mere insult.   To go, because
she was disinherited, because her hostels were shattered.
—No !   And in short—she couldn't do it. . . .

If Sir Isaac wanted to disinherit her he must disinherit her. If he wanted to go on seizing and reading
her letters, then he could. There was nothing in the
whole scheme of things to stop him if he did not want
to stop himself, nothing at all. She was caught. This
was the lot of women. She was a *wife*. What else in
honour was there but to be a wife up to the hilt ? . . .

She finished writing her telegram.

§ 11

Suddenly came a running in the passage outside, a
rap at the door and the nurse entered, scared, voluble
in Italian, but with gestures that translated her.

Lady Harman rose, realized the gravity and
urgency of the moment and hurried with her along the
passage. " Est-il mauvais ? " the poor lady attempted,
" Est-il—— "

Oh ! what words are there for " taken worse " ?

The woman attempted English and failed. She
resorted to her native Italian and exclaimed about the
" povero signore." She conveyed a sense of pitiful
extremities. Could it be he was in pain again ?
What was it ? What was it ? Ten minutes ago he
had been so grimly angry.

At the door of the sick-room the nurse laid a
warning hand on the arm of Lady Harman and made
an apprehensive gesture. They entered almost
noiselessly.

The Bavarian doctor turned his face from the bed
at their entrance. He was bending over Sir Isaac. He
held up one hand as if to arrest them ; his other was
engaged with his patient. " No," he said. His
attention went back to the sick man, and he remained

very still in that position, leaving Lady Harman to note for the first time how broad and flat he was both between his shoulders and between his ears. Then his face came round slowly, he relinquished something heavy, stood up, held up a hand. "Zu spät," he whispered, as though he too was surprised. He sought in his mind for English and then found his phrase: "He has gone!"

"Gone?"

"In one instant."

"Dead?"

"So. In one instant."

On the bed lay Sir Isaac. His hand was thrust out as though he grasped at some invisible thing. His open eyes stared hard at his wife, and as she met his eyes he snored noisily in his nose and throat.

She looked from the doctor to the nurse. It seemed to her that both these people must be mad. Never had she seen anything less like death. "But he's not dead!" she protested, still standing in the middle of the room.

"It iss chust the air in his throat," the doctor said. "He went—so! In one instant as I was helping him."

He waited to see some symptom of feminine weakness. There was a quality in his bearing—as though this event did him credit.

"But—Isaac!"

It was astounding. The noise in his throat ceased. But he still stared at her. And then the nurse made a kind of assault upon Lady Harman, caught her—even if she didn't fall. It was no doubt the proper formula to collapse. Or to fling oneself upon the deceased. Lady Harman resisted this assistance, disentangled herself and remained amazed; the nurse a little disconcerted but still ready behind her.

"But," said Lady Harman slowly, not advancing and pointing incredulously at the unwinking stare that met her own, "is he dead? Is he really dead? Like that?"

The doctor's gesture to the nurse betrayed his sense of the fine quick scene this want of confidence had ruined. Under no circumstances in life did English people really seem to know how to behave or what was expected of them. He answered with something bordering upon irony. "Madam," he said, with a slight bow, "he is *really* det."

"But—like *that* !" cried Lady Harman.

"Like that," repeated the doctor.

She went three steps nearer and stopped, open-eyed, wonder-struck, her lips compressed.

§ 12

For a time astonishment overwhelmed her mind. She did not think of Sir Isaac, she did not think of herself, her whole being was filled by this marvel of death and cessation. Like *that* !

Death!

Never before had she seen it. She had expected an extreme dignity, an almost ceremonial sinking back, a slow ebbing, but this was like a shot from a bow. It stunned her. And for some time she remained stunned, while the doctor and her secretary and the hotel people did all that they deemed seemly on this great occasion. She let them send her into another room; she watched with detached indifference a post-mortem consultation in whispers with a doctor from Rapallo. Then came a great closing of shutters. The nurse and her maid hovered about her, ready to assist her when the sorrowing began. But she had no sorrow. The long moments lengthened out, and he was still dead and she was still only amazement. It seemed part of the extra-ordinary, the perennial surprisingness of Sir Isaac that he should end in this way. Dead! She didn't feel for some hours that he had in any way ended. He had died with such emphasis that she felt now that he was capable of anything. What mightn't he do next? When she heard movements in the chamber of death it seemed to her that of all the people there, most pro-bably it was he who made them. She would not have been amazed if he had suddenly appeared in the door-way of her room, anger-white and his hand quiveringly extended, spluttering some complaint.

He might have cried: "Here I am dead! And it's *you*, damn you—it's *you!*"

It was after distinct efforts, after repeated visits to the room in which he lay, that she began to realize that death was death, that death goes on, that there was no more any Sir Isaac, but only a still body he had left behind, that was being moulded now into a stiff image of peace.

Then for a time she roused herself to some control of their proceedings. The doctor came to Lady Harman to ask her about the meals for the day, the hotel manager was in entanglements of tactful consider-ation, and then the nurse came for instructions upon some trivial matter. They had done what usage prescribes and now, in the absence of other direction, they appealed to her wishes. She remarked that everyone was going on tiptoe and speaking in undertones. . . .

She realized duties.   What does one have to do
when one's husband is dead ?   People would have to be
told.   She would begin by sending off telegrams to
various people, to his mother, to her own, to his lawyer.
She remembered she had already written a telegram—
that very morning to Crappen.   Should she still let the
lawyer come out.   He was her lawyer now.   Perhaps he
had better come, but instead of that telegram, which
still lay upon the desk, she would wire the news of the
death to him. . . .

Does one send to the papers ?   How does one send
to the papers ?

She took Miss Summersley Satchell, who was
hovering outside in the sunshine on the balcony, into
her room, and sat pale and businesslike and very careful about details, while Miss Summersley Satchell
offered practical advice and took notes and wrote
telegrams and letters. . . .

There came a hush over everything as the day crept
towards noon, and the widowed woman sat in her own
room with an inactive mind, watching thin bars of
sunlight burn their slow way across the floor.   He was
dead.   It was going on now more steadfastly than ever.
He was keeping dead.   He was dead at last for good
and her married life was over, that life that had always
seemed the only possible life, and this stunning incident,
this thing that was like the blinding of eyes or the
bursting of eardrums, was to be the beginning of
strange new experiences.

She was afraid at first at their possible strangeness.
And then, you know, in spite of a weak protesting
compunction she began to feel glad. . . .

She would not admit to herself that she was glad,
that she was anything but a woman stunned, she

maintained her still despondent attitude as long as she could, but gladness broke upon her soul as the day breaks, and a sense of release swam up to the horizons of her mind and rose upon her, flooding every ripple of her being, as the sun rises over water in a clear sky. Presently she could sit there no longer, she had to stand up. She walked to the closed Venetians to look out upon the world and checked herself upon the very verge of flinging them open. He was dead and it was all over for ever. Of course !—it was all over ! Her marriage was finished and done. Miss Satchell came to summon her to lunch. Throughout that meal Lady Harman maintained a sombre bearing, and listened with attention to the young doctor's comments on the manner of Sir Isaac's going. And then,—it was impossible to go back to her room.

" My head aches," she said, " I must go down and sit by the sea ; " and her maid, a little shocked, brought her not only her sunshade, but needless wraps—as though a new-made widow must necessarily be very sensitive to the air. She would not let her maid come with her, she went down to the beach alone. She sat on some rocks near the very edge of the transparent water and fought her gladness for a time and presently yielded to it. He was dead. One thought filled her mind, for a while so filled her mind that no other thought it seemed could follow it, it had an effect of being final ; it so filled her mind that it filled the whole world ; the broad sapphire distances of the sea, the lapping waves amidst the rocks at her feet, the blazing sun, the dark headland of Porto Fino and a small sailing boat that hung beyond came all within it like things enclosed within a golden globe. She forgot all the days of nursing and discomfort and pity behind her, all the duties and ceremonies before her, forgot all the details and circumstances of life in this one luminous realization. She was free at last. She was a free woman.

Never more would he make a sound or lift a finger against her life, never more would he contradict her or flout her; never more would he come peeping through that papered panel between his room and hers, never more could hateful and humiliating demands be made upon her as his right; no more strange distresses of the body nor raw discomfort of the nerves could trouble her— for ever. And no more detectives, no more suspicions, no more accusations. That last blow he had meant to aim was frozen before it could strike her. And she would have the Hostels in her hands, secure and undisputed, she could deal as she liked with Mrs. Pembrose, take such advisers as she pleased. . . . She was free.

She found herself planning the regeneration of those difficult and disputed hostels, plans that were all coloured by the sun and sky of Italy. The manacles had gone; her hands were free. She would make this her supreme occupation. She had learnt her lesson now, she felt, she knew something of the mingling of control and affectionate regard that was needed to weld the warring uneasy units of her new community. And she could do it, now as she was and unencumbered, she knew this power was in her. When everything seemed lost to her, suddenly it was all back in her hands. . . .

She discovered the golden serenity of her mind with a sudden astonishment and horror. She was amazed and shocked that she should be glad. She struggled against it and sought to subdue her spirit to a becoming grief. One should be sorrowful at death in any case, one should be grieved. She tried to think of Sir Isaac with affection, to recall touching generosities, to remember kind things and tender and sweet things, and she could not do so. Nothing would come back but the white intensities of his face, nothing but his hatred, his suspicion and his pitiless mean mastery. From which she was freed.

She could not feel sorry. She did her utmost to feel sorry; presently when she went back into the dépendance, she had to check her feet to a regretful pace; she dreaded the eyes of the hotel visitors she passed in the garden lest they should detect the liberation of her soul. But the hotel visitors being English were for the most part too preoccupied with manifestations of a sympathy that should be at once heart-felt and quite unobtrusive and altogether in the best possible taste, to have any attention free for the soul of Lady Harman.

The sense of her freedom came and went like the sunlight of a day in spring, though she attempted her utmost to remain overcast. After dinner that night she was invaded by a vision of the great open years before her, at first hopeful but growing at last to fear and a wild restlessness, so that in defiance of possible hotel opinion, she wandered out into the moonlight and remained for a long time standing by the boat landing, dreaming, recovering, drinking in the white serenities of sea and sky. There was no hurry now. She might stay there as long as she chose. She need account for herself to no one ; she was free. She might go where she pleased, do what she pleased, there was no urgency any more. . . .

There was Mr. Brumley. Mr. Brumley made a very little figure at first in the great prospect before her. . . . Then he grew larger in her thoughts. She recalled his devotions, his services, his self-control. It was good to have one understanding friend in this great limitless world. . . .

She would have to keep that friendship. . . .

But the glorious thing was freedom, to live untrammelled. . . .

Through the stillness a little breeze came stirring, and she awoke out of her dream and turned and faced the shuttered dépendance. A solitary dim light was showing on the verandah. All the rest of the building was a shapeless mass of grey. The long pale front of the hotel seen through a grove of orange trees was lit now at every other window with people going to bed. Beyond, a black hillside clambered up to the edge of the sky.

Far away out of the darknesses a man with a clear strong voice was singing to a tinkling accompaniment.

In the black orange trees swam and drifted a score of fireflies, and there was a distant clamour of nightingales when presently the unseen voice had done.

§ 13

When she was in her room again she began to think of Sir Isaac and more particularly of that last fixed stare of his. . . .

She was impelled to go and see him, to see for herself that he was peaceful and no longer a figure of astonishment. She went slowly along the corridor and very softly into his room—it remained, she felt, his room. They had put candles about him, and the outline of his face, showing dimly through the linen that veiled it, was like the face of one who sleeps very peacefully. Very gently she uncovered it.

He was not simply still, he was immensely still. He was more still and white than the moonlight outside, remoter than moon or stars. . . . She stood surveying him.

He looked small and pinched and as though he had been very tired. Life was over for him, altogether over. Never had she seen anything that seemed so finished. Once, when she was a girl she had thought that death might be but the opening of a door upon a more generous feast of living than this cramped world could give, but now she knew, she saw, that death can be death.

Life was over. She felt she had never before realized the meaning of death. That beautiful night outside, and all the beautiful nights and days that were still to come and all the sweet and wonderful things of God's world could be nothing to him now for ever. There was no dream in him that could ever live again, there was no desire, no hope in him.

And had he ever had his desire or his hope, or felt the intensities of life?

There was this beauty she had been discovering in the last few years, this mystery of love,—all that had been hidden from him.

She began to realize something sorrowful and pitiful in his quality, in his hardness, his narrowness, his bickering suspicions, his malignant refusals of all things generous and beautiful. He made her feel, as sometimes the children made her feel, the infinite pity of perversity and resistance to the bounties and kindliness of life.

The shadow of sorrow for him came to her at last.

Yet how obstinate he looked, the little frozen white thing that had been Sir Isaac Harman! And satisfied, wilfully satisfied; his lips were compressed and his mouth a little drawn in at the corners as if he would not betray any other feeling than content with the bargain he had made with life. She did not touch him; not for the world would she ever touch that cold waxen thing that had so lately clasped her life, but she stood for a long time by the side of his quiet, immersed in the wonder of death. . . .

He had been such a hard little man, such a pursuing little man, so unreasonable and difficult a master, and now—he was such a poor shrunken little man for all his obstinacy ! She had never realized before that he was pitiful. . . . Had she perhaps feared him too much, disliked him too much to deal fairly with him ? Could she have helped him ? Was there anything she could have done that she had not done ? Might she not at least have saved him his suspicion ? Behind his rages, perhaps he had been wretched.

Could anyone else have helped him ? If perhaps someone had loved him more than she had ever pretended to do——

How strange that she should be so intimately in this room—and still so alien—so alien that she could feel nothing but detached wonder at his infinite loss ! . . . *Alien*,—that was what she had always been, a captured alien in this man's household,—a girl he had taken. Had he ever suspected how alien ? The true mourner, poor woman ! was even now, in charge of Cook's couriers and interpreters, coming by express from London, to see with her own eyes this last still phase of the son she had borne into the world and watched and sought to serve. She was his nearest ; she indeed was the only near thing there had ever been in his life. Once at least he must have loved her? And even she had not been very near. No one had

ever been very near his calculating suspicious heart.
Had he ever said or thought any really sweet or tender
thing—even about her? He had been generous to
her in money matters, of course,—but out of a vast
abundance. . . .

How good it was to have a friend! How good it
was to have even one single friend! . . .

At the thought of his mother Lady Harman's mind
began to drift slowly from this stiff culmination of life
before her. Presently she replaced the white cloth
upon his face and turned slowly away. Her imagination had taken up the question of how that poor old
lady was to be met, how she was to be consoled, what
was to be said to her. . . .

She began to plan arrangements. The room ought
to be filled with flowers; Mrs. Harman would expect
flowers, large heavy white flowers in great abundance.
That would have to be seen to soon. One might get
them in Rapallo. And afterwards,—they would have to
take him to England, and have a fine great funeral, with
every black circumstance his wealth and his position
demanded. Mrs. Harman would need that, and so it
must be done. Cabinet Ministers must follow him,
members of Parliament, all Blenkerdom feeling self-
consciously and, as far as possible, deeply, the Chartersons by way of friends, unfamiliar blood relations, a
vast retinue of employees. . . .

How could one take him? Would he have to be
embalmed? Embalming!—what a strange complement
of death! She averted herself a little more from the
quiet figure on the bed, and could not turn to it again.
They might come here and do all sorts of things
to it, mysterious, evil-seeming things with knives and
drugs. . . .

She must not think of that. She must learn exactly what Mrs. Harman thought and desired. Her own apathy with regard to her husband had given way completely now to a desire to anticipate and meet Mrs. Harman's every conceivable wish.

CHAPTER THE TWELFTH

Love and a Serious Lady

§ 1

The news of Sir Isaac's death came quite unexpectedly to Mr. Brumley. He was at the Climax Club, and rather bored; he had had some tea and dry toast in the magazine room, and had been through the weeklies, and it was a particularly uninteresting week. Then he came down into the hall, looked idly at the latest bulletins upon the board, and read that "Sir Isaac Harman died suddenly this morning at Sta. Margherita, in Ligure, whither he had gone for rest and change."

He went on mechanically reading down the bulletin, leaving something of himself behind him that did not read on. Then he returned to that remarkable item and re-read it, and picked up that lost element of his being again.

He had awaited this event for so long, thought of it so often in such a great variety of relationships, dreamt of it, hoped for it, prayed for it, and tried not to think of it, that now it came to him in reality it seemed to have no substance or significance whatever. He had exhausted the fact before it happened. Since first he had thought of it there had passed four long years, and in that time he had seen it from every aspect, exhausted every possibility. It had become a theoretical possibility, the basis of continually less confident, continually more unsubstantial day dreams. Constantly he had tried not to think of it, tried to assure himself of Sir Isaac's invalid immortality. And here it was!

The line above it concerned an overdue ship, the line below resumed a speech by Mr. Lloyd George. "He would challenge the honourable member to repeat his accusations——"

Mr. Brumley stood quite still before the mauve-coloured print letters for some time, then went slowly across the hall into the breakfast-room, sat down in a chair by the fireplace, and fell into a kind of featureless thinking. Sir Isaac was dead, his wife was free, and the long waiting that had become a habit was at an end.

He had anticipated a wild elation, and for a while he was only sensible of change, a profound change. . . .

He began to feel glad that he had waited, that she had insisted upon patience, that there had been no disaster, no scandal between them. Now everything was clear for them. He had served his apprenticeship. They would be able to marry, and have no quarrel with the world.

He sat with his mind forming images of the prospect before him, images that were at first feeble and vague, and then, though still in a silly way, more concrete and definite. At first they were quite petty anticipations, of how he would have to tell people of his approaching marriage, of how he would break it to George Edmund that a new mother impended. He mused for some time upon the details of that. Should

he take her down to George Edmund's school, and let
the boy fall in love with her—he would certainly fall
in love with her—before anything definite was said,
or should he first go down alone and break the news?
Each method had its own attractive possibilities of
drama.

Then Mr. Brumley began to think of the letter he
must write Lady Harman—a difficult letter. One does
not rejoice at death. Already Mr. Brumley was
beginning to feel a generous pity for the man he had
done his utmost not to detest for so long. Poor Sir
Isaac had lived like a blind thing in the sunlight,
gathering and gathering, when the pride and pleasure
of life is to administer and spend. . . . Mr. Brumley
fell wondering just how she could be feeling now about
her dead husband. She might be in a phase of quite
real sorrow. Probably the last illness had tired and
strained her. So that his letter would have to be very
fine and tender and soothing, free from all harshness,
free from any gladness—yet it would be hard not to
let a little of his vast relief peep out. Always hitherto,
except for one or two such passionate lapses as that
which had precipitated the situation at Santa
Margharita, his epistolary manner had been formal,
his matter intellectual and philanthropic, for he had
always known that no letter was absolutely safe from
Sir Isaac's insatiable research. Should he still be
formal, still write to "Dear Lady Harman," or
suddenly break into a new warmth? Half an hour
later he was sitting in the writing-room with some few
flakes of torn paper on the carpet between his feet and
the partially filled wastepaper basket, still meditating
upon this difficult issue of the address.

The letter he achieved at last began, " My dear

Lady," and went on to, " I do not know how to begin this letter—perhaps you will find it almost as difficult to receive. . . ."

In the small hours he woke to one of his habitual revulsions. Was that, he asked himself, the sort of letter a lover should write to the beloved on her release, on the sudden long prayed-for opening of a way to her, on the end of her shameful servitude and his humiliations? He began to recall the cold and stilted sentences of that difficult composition. The gentility of it! All his life he had been a prey to gentility, had cast himself free from it, only to relapse again in such fashion as this. Would he never be human and passionate and sincere? Of course he was glad, and she ought to be glad, that Sir Isaac, their enemy and their prison, was dead; it was for them to rejoice together. He turned out of bed at last, when he could lie still under these self-accusations no longer, and wrapped himself in his warm dressing-gown and began to write. He wrote in pencil. His fountain-pen was as usual on his night table, but pencil seemed the better medium, and he wrote a warm and glowing love-letter that was brought to an end at last by an almost passionate fit of sneezing. He could find no envelopes in his bedroom Davenport, and so he left that honest scrawl under a paper-weight, and went back to bed greatly comforted. He re-read it in the morning with emotion, and some slight misgivings that grew after he had despatched it. He went to lunch at his club contemplating a third letter that should be sane and fine and sweet, and that should rectify the confusing effect of those two previous efforts. He wrote this letter later in the afternoon.

The days seemed very long before the answer to his

first letter came to him, and in that interval two more
—aspects went to her. Her reply was very brief, and
written in the large, firm, still girlishly clear hand that
distinguished her.

> "*I was so glad of your letter. My life is so strange
> here, a kind of hushed life. The nights are extraordin-
> arily beautiful, the moon very large and the little leaves
> on the trees sharp and black. We are coming back to
> England and the funeral will be from our Putney house.*"

That was all, but it gave Mr. Brumley an impression
of her that was exceedingly vivid and close. He
thought of her, shadowy and dusky in the moonlight
until his soul swam with love for her ; he had to get up
and walk about; he whispered her name very softly to
himself several times ; he groaned gently, and at last he
went to his little desk and wrote to her his sixth letter
—quite a beautiful letter. He told her that he loved
her, that he had always loved her since their first
moment of meeting, and he tried to express just the wave
of tenderness that inundated him at the thought of her
away there in Italy. Once, he said, he had dreamt that
he would be the first to take her to Italy. Perhaps
some day they would yet be in Italy together.

§ 2

It was only by insensible degrees that doubt crept
into Mr. Brumley's assurances. He did not observe at
once that none of the brief letters she wrote him
responded to his second, the impassioned outbreak in
pencil. And it seemed only in keeping with the

modest reserves of womanhood that she should be restrained—she always had been restrained.

She asked him not to see her at once when she returned to England; she wanted, she said, "to see how things are," and that fell in very well with a certain delicacy in himself. The unburied body of Sir Isaac—it was now provisionally embalmed—was, through some inexplicable subtlety in his mind, a far greater barrier than the living man had ever been, and he wanted it out of the way. And everything settled. Then, indeed, they might meet.

Meanwhile he had a curious little private conflict of his own. He was trying not to think, day and night he was trying not to think, that Lady Harman was now a very rich woman. Yet some portions of his brain, and he had never suspected himself of such lawless regions, persisted in the most vulgar and outrageous suggestions, suggestions that made his soul blush; schemes, for example, of splendid foreign travel, of hotel staffs bowing, of a yacht in the Mediterranean, of motor cars, of a palatial flat in London, of a box at the opera, of artists patronized, of—most horrible!—a baronetcy. . . . The more authentic parts of Mr. Brumley cowered from and sought to escape these squalid dreams of magnificences. It shocked and terrified him to find such things could come out in him. He was like some pest-stricken patient, amazedly contemplating his first symptom. His better part denied, repudiated. Of course he would never touch, never even propose—or hint. . . . It was an aspect he had never once contemplated before Sir Isaac died. He could on his honour, and after searching his heart, say that. Yet in Pall Mall one afternoon, suddenly, he caught himself with a thought in his head

so gross, so smug, that he uttered a faint cry and
quickened his steps. . . . Benevolent stepfather!

These distresses begot a hope. Perhaps, after all,
probably, there would be some settlement. . . . She
might not be rich, not so very rich. . . . She might
be tied up. . . .

He perceived in that lay his hope of salvation.
Otherwise—oh, pitiful soul!—things were possible in
him; he saw only too clearly what dreadful things
were possible.

If only she were disinherited, if only he might take
her, stripped of all these possessions that even in such
glancing anticipations begot —— this horrid indiges-
tion of the imagination!

But then, —— the Hostels? . . .

There he stumbled against an invincible riddle!

There was something dreadful about the way in
which these considerations blotted out the essential
fact of separations abolished, barriers lowered, the way
to an honourable love made plain and open. . . .

The day of the funeral came at last, and Mr.
Brumley tried not to think of it, paternally, at
Margate. He fled from Sir Isaac's ultimate withdrawal. Blenker's obituary notice in the *Old Country
Gazette* was a masterpiece of tactful eulogy, ostentatiously loyal, yet extremely not unmindful of the
widowed proprietor, and of all the possible changes
of ownership looming ahead. Mr. Brumley, reading
it in the Londonward train, was greatly reminded
of the Hostels. That was a riddle he didn't begin
to solve. Of course, it was imperative the Hostels
should continue—imperative. Now they might run
them together, openly, side by side. But then, with
such temptations to hitherto inconceivable vulgarities.

And again, insidiously, those visions returned of two figures, manifestly opulent, grouped about a big motor car or standing together under a large subservient archway. . . .

There was a long letter from her at his flat, a long and amazing letter. It was so folded that his eye first caught the writing on the third page; "*never marry again. It is so clear that our work needs all my time and all my means.*" His eyebrows rose, his expression became consternation; his hands trembled a little as he turned the letter over to read it through. It was a deliberate letter. It began—

"*Dear Mr. Brumley, I could never have imagined how much there is to do after we are dead, and before we can be buried.*"

"Yes," said Mr. Brumley; "but what does this mean?"

"*There are so many surprises ——*"

"It isn't clear."

"*In ourselves and the things about us.*"

"Of course, he would have made some complicated settlement. I might have known."

"*It is the strangest thing in the world to be a widow, much stranger than anyone could ever have supposed, to have no one to control one, no one to think of as coming before one, no one to answer to, to be free to plan one's life for oneself ——*"

He stood with the letter in his hand after he had read it through, perplexed.

"I can't stand this," he said. "I want to know."

He went to his desk and wrote :—

"*My Dear, I want you to marry me.*"

What more was to be said? He hesitated with this brief challenge in his hand, was minded to telegraph it and thought of James's novel, *In the Cage.* Telegraph operators are only human after all. He determined upon a special messenger and rang up his quarter valet — he shared service in his flat — to despatch it.

The messenger boy got back from Putney that evening about half-past eight. He brought a reply in pencil.

" My dear Friend," she wrote. *" You have been so good to me, so helpful. But I do not think that is possible. Forgive me. I want so badly to think and here I cannot think. I have never been able to think here. I am going down to Black Strand, and in a day or so I will write and we will talk. Be patient with me."*

She signed her name " *Ellen* "; always before she had been " E. H."

"Yes," cried Mr. Brumley, "but I want to know!"

He fretted for an hour and went to the telephone.

Something was wrong with the telephone, it buzzed and went faint, and it would seem that at her end she was embarrassed. "I want to come to you now," he said. "Impossible," was the clearest word in her reply. Should he go in a state of virile resolution, force her hesitation as a man should? She might be involved there with Mrs. Harman, with all sorts of relatives and strange people. . . .

In the end he did not go.

§ 3

He sat at his lunch alone next day at one of the little tables men choose when they shun company. But to the right of him was the table of the politicians, Adolphus Blenker and Pope of the East Purblow Experiment, and Sir Piper Nicolls, and Munk, the editor of the *Daily Rectification*, sage men all and deep in those mysterious manipulations and wire-pullings by which the liberal party organization was even then preparing for itself unusual distrust and dislike, and Horatio Blenker was tenoring away after his manner about a case of right and conscience, "Blenking like Winking" was how a silent member had put it once to Brumley in a gust of hostile criticism. "Practically if she marries again, she is a pauper," struck on Brumley's ears.

"Of course," said Mr. Brumley, and stopped eating.

"I don't know if you remember the particulars of the Astor case," began Munk. . . .

Never had Mr. Brumley come so frankly to eavesdropping. But he heard no more of Lady Harman. Munk had to quote the rights and wrongs of various American wills, and then Mr. Pope seized his opportunity. "At East Purblow," he went on, "in quite a number of instances we had to envisage this problem of the widow—— "

Mr. Brumley pushed back his plate and strolled towards the desk.

It was exactly what he might have expected, what indeed had been at the back of his mind all along, and on the whole he was glad. Naturally she hesitated; naturally she wanted time to think, and as naturally it was impossible for her to tell him what it was she was thinking about.

They would marry. They must marry. Love has claims supreme over all other claims and he felt no doubt that for her his comparative poverty of two thousand a year would mean infinitely more happiness than she had ever known or could know with Sir Isaac's wealth. She was reluctant, of course, to become dependent upon him until he made it clear to her what infinite pleasure it would be for him to supply her needs. Should he write to her forthwith? He outlined a letter in his mind, a very fine and generous letter, good phrases came, and then he reflected that it would be difficult to explain to her just how he had learnt of her peculiar situation. It would be far more seemly to wait either for a public announcement or for some intimation from her.

And then he began to realize that this meant the end of all their work at the Hostels. In his first satisfaction at escaping that possible great motor-car and all the superfluities of Sir Isaac's accumulation, he had forgotten that side of the business. . . .

When one came to think it over, the Hostels did complicate the problem. It was ingenious of Sir Isaac. . . .

It was infernally ingenious of Sir Isaac. . . .

He could not remain in the club for fear that somebody might presently come talking to him and interrupt his train of thought. He went out into the streets.

These Hostels upset everything.

What he had supposed to be a way of escape was really the mouth of a net.

Whichever way they turned Sir Isaac crippled them. . . .

§ 4

Mr. Brumley grew so angry that presently even the strangers in the street annoyed him. He turned his face homeward. He hated dilemmas; he wanted always to deny them, to thrust them aside, to take impossible third courses.

"For three years," shouted Mr. Brumley, free at last in his study to give way to his rage, "for three years I've been making her care for these things. And then—and then—they turn against me!"

A violent, incredibly undignified wrath against the dead man seized him. He threw books about the room. He cried out vile insults and mingled words of an unfortunate commonness with others of extreme rarity. He wanted to go off to Kensal Green and hammer at the grave there and tell the departed knight exactly what he thought of him. Then presently he became calmer, he lit a pipe, picked up the books from the floor, and meditated revenges upon Sir Isaac's memory. I deplore my task of recording these ungracious moments in Mr. Brumley's love history. I deplore the ease with which men pass from loving and serving women to an almost canine fight for them. It is the ugliest essential of romance. There is indeed much in the human heart that I deplore. But Mr. Brumley was exasperated by disappointment. He was sore, he was raw. Driven by an intolerable desire to explore every possibility of the situation, full indeed of an unholy vindictiveness, he went off next morning with strange questions to Maxwell Hartington.

He put the case as a general case.

"Lady Harman?" said Maxwell Hartington.

"No, not particularly Lady Harman. A general principle. What are people—what are women tied up in such a way to do?"

Precedents were quoted and possibilities weighed. Mr. Brumley was flushed, vague but persistent.

"Suppose," he said, "that they love each other passionately—and their work, whatever it may be, almost as passionately. Is there no way ——?"

"He'll have a *dum casta* clause right enough," said Maxwell Hartington.

"*Dum* ——? *Dum casta!* But, oh! anyhow *that's* out of the question — absolutely," said Mr. Brumley.

"Of course," said Maxwell Hartington, leaning back in his chair and rubbing the ball of his thumb into one eye. "Of course—nobody ever enforces these *dum casta* clauses. There isn't anyone to enforce them. Ever."—He paused and then went on, speaking apparently to the array of black tin boxes in the dingy fixtures before him. "Who's going to watch you? That's what I always ask in these cases. Unless the lady goes and does things right under the noses of these trustees they aren't going to bother. Even Sir Isaac I suppose hasn't provided funds for a private detective. Eh? You said something?"

"Nothing," said Mr. Brumley.

"Well, why should they start a perfectly rotten action like that," continued Maxwell Hartington, now addressing himself very earnestly to his client, "when they've only got to keep quiet and do their job and be comfortable. In these matters, Brumley, as in most matters affecting the relations of men and women, people can do absolutely what they like nowadays, absolutely, unless there's someone about ready to make a row. Then they can't do anything. It hardly matters if they don't do anything. A row's a row and damned disgraceful. If there isn't a row, nothing's disgraceful. Of course all these laws and regulations and institutions and arrangements are just ways of putting people at the mercy of blackmailers and jealous and violent persons. One's only got to be a lawyer for a bit to realize that. Still that's not *our* business. That's psychology. If there aren't any jealous and violent persons about, well, then no ordinary decent person is going to worry what you do. No decent person ever does. So far as I can gather the only barbarian in this case is the testator —now in Kensal Green. With additional precautions I suppose in the way of an artistic but thoroughly massive monument presently to be added—— "

" He'd—turn in his grave."

" Let him. No trustees are obliged to take action on *that*. I don't suppose they'd know if he did. I've never known a trustee bother yet about post-mortem movements of any sort. If they did, we'd all be having Prayers for the Dead. Fancy having to consider the subsequent reflections of the testator ! "

" Well anyhow," said Mr. Brumley, after a little pause, " such a breach, such a proceeding is out of the question—absolutely out of the question. It's unthinkable."

" Then why did you come here to ask me about it ? " demanded Maxwell Hartington, beginning to rub the other eye in an audible and unpleasant manner.

§ 5

When at last Mr. Brumley was face to face with
Lady Harman again, a vast mephitic disorderly creation of anticipations, intentions, resolves, suspicions,
provisional hypotheses, urgencies, vindications, and wild
and whirling stuff generally vanished out of his mind.
There beside the raised seat in the midst of the little
rock garden where they had talked together five years
before, she stood waiting for him, this tall simple
woman he had always adored since their first encounter,
a little strange and shy now in her dead black uniform
of widowhood, but with her honest eyes greeting him,
her friendly hands held out to him. He would have
kissed them but for the restraining presence of Snagsby
who had brought him to her; as it was it seemed to
him that the phantom of a kiss passed like a breath
between them. He held her hands for a moment and
relinquished them.

"It is so good to see you," he said, and they sat
down side by side. "I am very glad to see you again."

Then for a little while they sat in silence.

Mr. Brumley had imagined and rehearsed this meeting in many different moods. Now, he found none of
his premeditated phrases served him, and it was the
lady who undertook the difficult opening.

"I could not see you before," she began. "I did
not want to see anyone." She sought to explain. "I
was strange. Even to myself. Suddenly——" She
came to the point. "To find oneself free. . . . Mr.
Brumley,—*it was wonderful!*"

He did not interrupt her, and presently she went on
again.

"You see," she said, "I have become a human being——owning myself. I had never thought what this change would be to me. . . . It has been——. It has been—like being born, when one hadn't realized before that one wasn't born. . . . Now—now I can act. I can do this and that. I used to feel as though I was on strings—with somebody able to pull. . . . There is no one now able to pull at me, no one able to thwart me. . . ."

Her dark eyes looked among the trees and Mr. Brumley watched her profile.

"It has been like falling out of a prison from which one never hoped to escape. I feel like a moth that has just come out of its case,—you know how they come out, wet and weak but—released. For a time I feel I can do nothing but sit in the sun."

"It's queer," she repeated, "how one tries to feel differently from what one really feels, how one tries to feel as one supposes people expect one to feel. At first I hardly dared look at myself. . . . I thought I ought to be sorrowful and helpless. . . . I am not in the least sorrowful or helpless. . . ."

"But," said Mr. Brumley, "are you so free?"

"Yes."

"Altogether?"

"As free now——as a man."

"But——people are saying in London——. Something about a will——."

Her lips closed. Her brows and eyes became troubled. She seemed to gather herself together for an effort and spoke at length, without looking at him. "Mr. Brumley," she said, "before I knew anything of the will——. On the very evening when Isaac died——. I knew——I would never marry again. Never."

Mr. Brumley did not stir. He remained regarding her with a mournful expression.

"I was sure of it then," she said, "I knew nothing about the will. I want you to understand that—clearly."

She said no more. The still pause lengthened. She forced herself to meet his eyes.

"I thought," he said after a silent scrutiny, and left her to imagine what he had thought. . . .

"But," he urged to her protracted silence, "you *care* ?"

She turned her face away. She looked at the hand lying idle upon her crape-covered knee. "You are my dearest friend," she said very softly. "You are almost my only friend. But——. I can never go into marriage any more. . . ."

"My dear," he said, "the marriage you have known——."

"No," she said. "No sort of marriage."

Mr. Brumley heaved a profound sigh.

"Before I had been a widow twenty-four hours, I began to realize that I was an escaped woman. It wasn't the particular marriage. . . . It was any marriage. . . . All we women are tied. Most of us are willing to be tied perhaps, but only as people are willing to be tied to life-belts in a wreck—from fear from drowning. And now, I am just one of the free women, like the women who can earn large incomes, or the women who happen to own property. I've paid my penalties and my service is over. . . . I knew, of course, that you would ask me this. It isn't that I don't care for you, that I don't love your company and your help—and the love and the kindness. . . ."

"Only," he said, "although it is the one thing I

desire, although it is the one return you can make
me——. But whatever I have done—I have done
willingly. . . ."

"My dear!" cried Mr. Brumley, breaking out
abruptly at a fresh point, "I want you to marry me.
I want you to be mine, to be my dear close companion,
the care of my life, the beauty in my life. . . . I can't
frame sentences, my dear. You know, you know. . . .
Since first I saw you, talked to you in this very
garden. . . ."

"I don't forget a thing," she answered. "It has
been my life as well as yours. Only——"

The grip of her hand tightened on the back of their
seat. She seemed to be examining her thumb intently.
Her voice sank to a whisper. "I won't marry you," she
said.

§ 6

Mr. Brumley leant back, then he bent forward in a
desperate attitude with his hands and arms thrust
between his knees, then suddenly he recovered, stood up
and then knelt with one knee upon the seat. "What
are you going to do with me then?" he asked.

"I want you to go on being my friend."

"I can't."

"You can't?"

"No,—I've *hoped*."

And then with something almost querulous in his
voice, he repeated, "My dear, I want you to marry me
and I want now nothing else in the world."

She was silent for a moment. "Mr. Brumley," she
said, looking up at him, "have you no thought for
our Hostels?"

Mr. Brumley as I have said hated dilemmas. He started to his feet, a man stung. He stood in front of her and quivered extended hands at her. "What do such things matter," he cried, "when a man is in love?"

She shrank a little from him. "But," she asked, "haven't they always mattered?"

"Yes," he expostulated; "but these Hostels, these Hostels. . . . We've started them—isn't that good enough? We've set them going . . ."

"Do you know," she asked, "what would happen to the hostels if I were to marry?"

"They would go on," he said.

"They would go to a committee. Named. It would include Mrs. Pembrose. . . . Don't you see what would happen? He understood the case so well. . . ."

Mr. Brumley seemed suddenly shrunken. "He understood too well," he said.

He looked down at her soft eyes, at her drooping gracious form, and it seemed to him that indeed she was made for love and that it was unendurable that she should be content to think of friendship and freedom as the ultimate purposes of her life. . . .

§ 7

Presently these two were walking in the pine-woods beyond the garden and Mr. Brumley was discoursing lamentably of love, this great glory that was denied them.

The shade of perplexity deepened in her dark eyes as she listened. Ever and again she seemed about to speak and then checked herself and let him talk on.

He spoke of the closeness of love and the deep

excitement of love and how it filled the soul with pride and the world with wonder, and of the universal right of men and women to love. He told of his dreams and his patience, and of the stormy hopes that would not be suppressed when he heard that Sir Isaac was dead. And as he pictured to himself the lost delights at which he hinted, as he called back those covert expectations, he forgot that she had declared herself resolved upon freedom at any cost, and his rage against Sir Isaac, who had possessed and wasted all that he would have cherished so tenderly, grew to nearly uncontrollable proportions. "Here was your life," he said, "your beautiful life opening and full—full of such dear seeds of delight and wonder, calling for love, ready for love, and there came this *Clutch*, this Clutch that embodied all the narrow meanness of existence, and gripped and crumpled you and spoilt you. . . . For I tell you, my dear, you don't know; you don't begin to know. . . ."

He disregarded her shy eyes, giving way to his gathered wrath.

"And he conquers! This little monster of meanness, he conquers to the end—his dead hand, his dead desires, out of the grave they hold you! Always, always, it is Clutch that conquers; the master of life! I was a fool to dream, a fool to hope. I forgot. I thought only of you and I—that perhaps you and I—— "

He did not heed her little sound of protest. He went on to a bitter denunciation of the rule of jealousy in the world, forgetting that the sufferer under that rule in this case was his own consuming jealousy. That was life. Life was jealousy. It was all made up of fierce graspings, fierce suspicions, fierce resentments; men preyed upon one another even as the beasts they came from; reason made its crushed way through their conflict, crippled and wounded by their blows at one another. The best men, the wisest, the best of mankind, the stars of human wisdom, were but half ineffectual angels carried on the shoulders and guided by the steps of beasts. One might dream of a better world of men, of civilizations and wisdom latent in our passion-strained minds, of calms and courage and great heroical conquests that might come, but they lay tens of thousands of years away and we had to live, we had to die, no more than a herd of beasts tormented by gleams of knowledge we could never possess, of happiness for which we had no soul. He grew more and more eloquent as these thoughts sprang and grew in his mind.

"Of course I am absurd," he cried. "All men are absurd. Man is the absurd animal. We have parted from primordial motives—lust and hate and hunger and fear, and from all the tragic greatness of uncontrollable fate and we, we've got nothing to replace them. We are comic — comic! Ours is the stage of comedy in life's history, half lit and blinded,— and we fumble. As absurd as a kitten with its poor little head in a bag. There's your soul of man ! Mewing. We're all at it, the poets, the teachers. How can anyone hope to escape? Why should I escape? What am I that I should expect to be anything but a thwarted lover, a man mocked by his own attempts at service? Why should I expect to discover beauty and think that it won't be snatched away from me? All my life is comic—the story of this—this last absurdity could it make anything but a comic history? and yet within me my heart is weeping tears. The further one has gone, the deeper one wallows in the comic marsh. I am one of the newer kind of men, one of those men who cannot sit and hug their credit and their honour and their possessions and be content. I have seen the light of better things than that, and because of my vision, because of my vision and for no other reason I am the most ridiculous of men. Always I have tried to go out from myself to the world and give. Those early books of mine, those meretricious books in which I pretended all was so well with the world,—I did them because I wanted to give happiness and contentment and to be happy in the giving. And all the watchers and the grippers, the strong silent men and the calculating possessors of things, the masters of the world, they grinned at me. How I lied to please ! But I tell you for all their grinning, in my very prostitution there was a better spirit than theirs in their successes. If I had to live over again—— "

He left that hypothesis uncompleted.

" And now," he said, with a curious contrast between his voice and the exaltation of his sentiments, " now that I am to be your tormented, your emasculated lover to the very end of things, emasculated by laws I hate and customs I hate and vile foresights that I despise—— "

He paused, his thread lost for a moment.

" Because," he said, " I'm going to do it. I'm going to do what I can. I'm going to be as you wish me to be, to help you, to serve you. . . . If you can't come to meet me, I'll meet you. I can't help but love you, I can't do without you. Never in my life have I subscribed willingly to the idea of renunciation. I've hated renunciation. But if there is no other course but renunciation, renunciation let it be. I'm bitter about this, bitter to the bottom of my soul, but at least I'll have you know I love you. Anyhow. . . ."

His voice broke. There were tears in his eyes.

And on the very crest of these magnificent capitulations his soul rebelled. He turned about so swiftly that for a sentence or so she did not realize the nature of his change. Her mind remained glowing with her distressed acceptance of his magnificent nobility.

" I can't," he said.

He flung off his surrenders as a savage might fling off a garment.

" When I think of his children," he said.

" When I think of the world filled by his children, the children you have borne him—and I—forbidden almost to touch your hand ! "

And flying into a passion Mr. Brumley shouted, " No ! "

" Not even to touch your hand ! "

" I won't do it," he assured her. " I won't do it. If I cannot be your lover—I will go away. I will never see you again. I will do anything—anything, rather than suffer this degradation. I will go abroad. I will go to strange places. I will aviate. I will kill myself—or anything, but I won't endure this. I won't. You see, you ask too much, you demand more than flesh and blood can stand. I've done my best to bring myself to it and I can't. I won't have that—that—— "

He waved his trembling fingers in the air. He was absolutely unable to find an epithet pointed enough and bitter enough to stab into the memory of the departed knight. He thought of him as marble, enthroned at Kensal Green, with a false dignity, a false serenity, and intolerable triumph. He wanted something, some monosyllable to expound and strip all that, some lung-filling sky-splitting monosyllable that one could shout. His failure increased his exasperation.

"I won't have him grinning, at me," he said at last. "And so, it's one thing or the other. There's no other choice. But I know your choice. I see your choice. It's good-bye—and why—why shouldn't I go now?"

He waved his arms about. He was pitifully ridiculous. His face puckered as an ill-treated little boy's might do. This time it wasn't just the pathetic twinge that had broken his voice before; he found himself to his own amazement on the verge of loud, undignified, childish weeping. He was weeping passionately and noisily; he was over the edge of it, and it was too late to snatch himself back. The shame which could not constrain him, overcame him. A preposterous upward gesture of the hands expressed his despair. And abruptly this unhappy man of letters turned from her and fled, the most grief-routed of creatures, whooping and sobbing along a narrow pathway through the trees.

§ 8

He left behind him an exceedingly distressed and astonished lady. She had stood with her eyes opening wider and wider at this culminating exhibition.

"But, Mr. Brumley!" she had cried at last. "Mr. Brumley!"

He did not seem to hear her. And now he was running and stumbling along very fast through the trees, so that in a few minutes he would be out of sight. Dismay came with the thought that he might presently go out of sight altogether.

For a moment she seemed to hesitate. Then with a swift decision and a firm large grasp of the hand, she gathered up her black skirts and set off after him along the narrow path. She ran. She ran lightly, with a soft rhythmic fluttering of white and black. The long crêpe bands she wore in Sir Isaac's honour streamed out behind her.

" But, Mr. Brumley," she panted unheard. " Mis-ter Brumley ! "

He went from her fast, faster than she could follow, amidst the sun-dappled pine stems, and as he went he made noises between bellowing and soliloquy, heedless of any pursuit. All she could hear was a heart-wringing but inexpressive " Wa, wa, wooh, wa, woo," that burst from him ever and again. Through a more open space among the trees she fancied she was gaining upon him, and then as the pines came together again and were mingled with young spruces, she perceived that he drew away from her more and more. And he went round a curve and was hidden, and then visible again much further off, and then hidden ——.

She attempted one last cry to him, but her breath failed her, and she dropped her pace to a panting walk.

Surely he would not go thus into the high-road ! It was unendurable to think of him rushing out into the high-road—blind with sorrow—it might be into the very bonnet of a passing automobile.

She passed beyond the pines and scanned the path ahead as far as the stile. Then she saw him, lying where he had flung himself, face downward among the bluebells.

" Oh ! " she whispered to herself, and put one hand to her heart and drew nearer.

She was flooded now with that passion of responsibility, with that wild irrational charity which pours out of the secret depths of a woman's stirred being.

She came up to him so lightly as to be noiseless. He did not move, and for a moment she remained looking at him.

Then she said once more, and very gently—

"Mr. Brumley."

He started, listened for a second, turned over, sat up and stared at her. His face was flushed and his hair extremely ruffled. And a slight moisture recalled his weeping.

"Mr. Brumley," she repeated, and suddenly there were tears of honest vexation in her voice and eyes. "You *know* I cannot do without you."

He rose to his knees, and never, it seemed to him, had she looked so beautiful. She was a little out of breath, her dusky hair was disordered, and there was an unwonted expression in her eyes, a strange mingling of indignation and tenderness. For a moment they stared unaffectedly at each other, each making discoveries.

"Oh!" he sighed at last; "whatever you please, my dear. Whatever you please. I'm going to do as you wish, if you wish it, and be your friend and forget all this"—he waved an arm—"loving."

There were signs of a recrudescence of grief, and, inarticulate as ever, she sank to her knees close beside him.

"Let us sit quietly among these hyacinths," said Mr. Brumley. "And then afterwards we will go back to the house and talk . . . talk about our Hostels."

He sat back and she remained kneeling.

"Of course," he said, "I'm yours—to do just as you will with. And we'll work ——. I've been a bit of a stupid brute. We'll work. For all those people. It will be—oh! a big work, quite a big work. Big enough for us to thank God for. Only ——."

The sight of her panting lips had filled him with a wild desire, that set every nerve a quivering, and yet for all that had a kind of moderation, a reasonableness. It was a sisterly thing he had in mind. He felt that if this one desire could be satisfied, then honour would be satisfied, that he would cease grudging Sir Isaac—anything. . . .

But for some moments he could not force himself to speak of this desire, so great was his fear of a refusal.

"There's one thing," he said, and all his being seemed aquiver.

He looked hard at the trampled bluebells about their feet. "Never once," he went on, "never once. In all these years—have we two even—once—kissed. . . . It is such a little thing. . . . So much. . . ."

He stopped, breathless. He could say no more because of the beating of his heart. And he dared not look at her face. . . .

There was a swift, soft rustling as she moved. . . .

She crouched down upon him and taking his shoulder in her hand, upset him neatly backwards, and, doing nothing by halves, had kissed the astonished Mr. Brumley full upon his mouth.

THE END.

THE HOGARTH PRESS

This is a paperback list for today's readers – but it holds to a tradition of adventurous and original publishing set by Leonard and Virginia Woolf when they founded The Hogarth Press in 1917 and started their first paperback series in 1924.

Some of the books are light-hearted, some serious, and include Fiction, Lives and Letters, Travel, Critics, Poetry, History and Hogarth Crime and Gaslight Crime.

A list of our books already published, together with some of our forthcoming titles, follows. If you would like more information about Hogarth Press books, write to us for a catalogue:

40 William IV Street, London WC2N 4DF

Please send a large stamped addressed envelope

HOGARTH FICTION

Behind A Mask: The Unknown Thrillers of Louisa May Alcott
Edited and Introduced by Madeleine Stern

Death of a Hero by Richard Aldington
New Introduction by Christopher Ridgway

The Amazing Test Match Crime by Adrian Alington
New Introduction by Brian Johnston

Epitaph of a Small Winner by Machado de Assis
Translated and Introduced by William L. Grossman

Mrs Ames by E.F. Benson
Paying Guests by E.F. Benson
Secret Lives by E.F. Benson
New Introductions by Stephen Pile

Ballantyne's Folly by Claud Cockburn
New Introduction by Andrew Cockburn
Beat the Devil by Claud Cockburn
New Introduction by Alexander Cockburn

Chance by Joseph Conrad
New Introduction by Jane Miller

Lady Into Fox & A Man in the Zoo by David Garnett
New Introduction by Neil Jordan

The Whirlpool by George Gissing
New Introduction by Gillian Tindall

Morte D'Urban by J.F. Powers
Prince of Darkness and other stories by J.F. Powers
New Introductions by Mary Gordon

Mr Weston's Good Wine by T.F. Powys
New Introduction by Ronald Blythe

H.G. Wells
Christina Alberta's Father
New Introduction by Christopher Priest

The war is over: it is 1920, the threshold of a new age.
Christina Alberta – one of Wells's most endearing
heroines with her bobbed hair and short skirts – is ready
to plunge into the heady freedom of bohemian Chelsea.
But her father too desires liberty after a lifetime at the
Limpid Stream Laundry; and when a séance at the
Petunia Boarding House, Tunbridge Wells, entrusts him
with a message for the modern world from the lords of
Atlantis, Christina's plans are dramatically affected. First
published in 1926, *Christina Alberta's Father* is a novel
about idealists at odds with a conventional society, a tale
of change and growth – absurd, funny, sad, and totally
absorbing.

H. G. Wells

Mr Britling Sees it Through

New Introduction by Christopher Priest

In the idyllic summer of 1914 a bouncy, eccentric writer spends the long hot days uproariously entertaining his house-party guests and dashing across the county to the arms of his mistress. But across the Channel, Germany is marching into Belgium; and as the shadow of the trenches moves nearer those he loves, Mr Britling's life is thrown into darkness and confusion.

One of Wells's finest works, this intensely moving novel was written at the height of the First World War, with a sympathy and forgiveness exceptional for its time — it is one of the most touching accounts we have of the conflict, of the families at home, seeing it through.

H.G. Wells
Marriage

New Introduction by Victoria Glendinning

A plane crashes into a peaceful rectory garden: its dashing aviator hurtles into the life of the rector's daughter – educated, socialist, a thoroughly modern miss. While marriage may be the end of the comedy it turns out to be only the beginning of the drama. Here Wells attacks a perennial problem – how can marriage survive when convention stifles passion, domesticity dulls ambition? The couple set off to find the answer on a bizarre adventure which takes them halfway across the world.

One of Wells's engrossing novels about the interplay between sex and society, *Marriage* drew an enraged review from the young feminist Rebecca West, thus starting a new chapter in the saga of his own life.

H.G. Wells

The Passionate Friends

New Introduction by Victoria Glendinning

Stephen Stratton is cut off by gulfs of money and class from the aristocratic Lady Mary, the passionate friend of his childhood and great love of his youth. Determined to have independence and power, she turns from him to ally herself with the glittering world of wealth and high politics. But time passes and Mary and Stephen meet again . . .

Their love, a tale splendidly told, moves through English meadows to African veldts and Alpine glaciers, against a backdrop of the Boer War, fierce debates about Empire, labour and international harmony. A typically irreverent novel, *The Passionate Friends* is also one of Wells's finest love stories.

H.G. Wells
In the Days of the Comet

New Introduction by Brian Aldiss

A new comet moves into earth's skies, filling the world with fear. In the midst of the rising panic, among the allotments and furnaces of a grim Black Country town, young Leadford sets out with murder in his heart to find the unfaithful Nettie and her wealthy lover. But then the comet strikes, the Great Change occurs, and anything, or almost anything, seems possible. A grand sweep of comic realism mixed with a fantasy of equality, pacifism and, of course, free love, *In the Days of the Comet* is a utopia such as only H.G. Wells could have imagined.